Sun

The
Little
French
Guesthouse

Summer at The Little French Guesthouse

helen pollard

bookouture

Published by Bookouture
An imprint of StoryFire Ltd.
23 Sussex Road, Ickenham, UB10 8PN
United Kingdom
www.bookouture.com

ISBN: 978-1-78681-230-8
eBook ISBN: 978-1-78681-229-2

This book is a work of fiction. Names, characters, businesses,
organizations, places and events other than those clearly in the
public domain, are either the product of the author's imagination
or are used fictitiously. Any resemblance to actual persons, living or
dead, events or locales is entirely coincidental.

For Andrew and David

The best big brothers a girl could wish for

ONE

The pounding on the guesthouse door sounded like a battering ram.

Throwing myself out of bed with much toe-stubbing and cursing, I glanced at the clock on the dresser. Five thirty a.m. What the …?

I scrabbled in my cluttered top drawer for the key of the door that linked my quarters to Rupert's – only to be used in emergency – but when the next onslaught began, I gave up, grabbed a hoodie and staggered out through my private entrance and around the outside of the building. Believe me, gravel is *not* an ideal surface for bare feet. I would have gone back for flip-flops, but I was desperate to stop the violence on the door.

My heart stuttered in my chest as I rounded the corner to see that the racket was being perpetrated by a *gendarme*.

What was wrong? Who had been hurt? Had I only imagined hearing Rupert's return from the UK late last night? Had something happened with that wretched ex-wife of his? Had he been in an accident?

I looked across the courtyard and whooshed out a sigh of relief when I saw his estate car, although I wasn't sure why it had a tarp thrown over it.

The *gendarme*'s fists were raised, ready to knock again.

'*Arrêtez, s'il vous plaît!*' I waved madly at him as I painfully ooched and ouched my way towards him, eventually stepping blissfully onto the smooth doorstep.

'Can I help you?' I asked in my best French. Despite living in France for almost a year now, I'd had little experience with *gendarmes* – but I presumed it was best not to mess with them.

He was middle-aged and portly, with a poker face that fell by degrees as he took in my shorty-pyjamas, bed hair and bare feet, then glanced at the corner I'd appeared from. No doubt he was wondering why I hadn't opened the door like a normal person and saved my feet from laceration.

At that time in the morning and that stage of caffeine intake (nil), my French wouldn't stretch to explaining.

In rapid French, he began to interrogate me. Who was I, why I was there, did I know Monsieur Rupert Hunter and, if so, where was he?

Alarmed, I tried to formulate a coherent response, but I was mercifully saved when the door opened and Rupert stuck his head out.

He looked dishevelled – unshaven, his wavy silver hair uncombed, a bathrobe half-thrown on over boxers.

'Emmy. What's going on?'

The *gendarme* didn't wait for me to reply but repeated his interrogation, and when Rupert confirmed that he was indeed the hunted party, the diatribe lengthened.

Rupert looked shell-shocked, but I watched as enlightenment dawned. Thank God he knew what this was about. All I could gather was that something or someone had been *abandonné*.

Rupert invited our visitor in, took him into the kitchen and got to work at his state-of-the-art coffee machine to placate him with a strong espresso.

It did the trick. The law-upholder thawed with each sip as Rupert launched into a lengthy explanation, something to do with the car and tyres. I didn't tax my brain by trying to follow, since I intended to get the English version shortly. Rupert propped his broad frame – leaner nowadays – against the counter as he spoke, occasionally scrubbing at his close-cropped grey beard as he sought an explanation that would soothe, rather than inflame.

Seemingly satisfied, our uniformed friend departed with stern words.

I rounded on Rupert. 'What was that all about? Why did you get home so late last night? Why are we being visited by a *gendarme*?'

Ignoring me, Rupert set to again at the coffee machine, delivering the goods into my shaking hands and slurping his own as though his life depended on it. We sat at the large pine table and I gave him a questioning look.

'We had an incident on the way home,' he declared.

'What kind of incident? Did you crash the car? Why is it covered up?'

He glared balefully at me. 'Are you going to continue firing questions at me, or are you going to listen?'

'Sorry.'

'The trailer had a tyre blow-out. We had to limp it along to a layby.'

'I *told* you that trailer's too old.'

'And I told *you* that Bob and I thoroughly checked it over. Just because something's getting on a bit doesn't mean it's no use to anybody, Emmy. We overloaded it, that's all.'

'Didn't you have a spare?'

'We did. We changed it, but it must have had a leak we hadn't noticed.'

'What about breakdown cover?'

'It turns out I'm not covered for towing. Only for the car.'

I closed my eyes. 'You didn't think to check before you set off?'

'Checked the insurance. Didn't think to check the breakdown cover.'

'So where's the trailer now?'

'That was what our friend came about. We had to leave it where it was.'

'You abandoned a trailer in a layby halfway between here and Calais?'

'Didn't have any choice. Couldn't have got a tyre at that time of night for love nor money. The car was already stuffed full, so we loaded what we could onto the roof rack and tied it down. The least valuable items are still in the trailer, trusting to luck and the honesty of our fellow man. The idea was to get a tyre this morning, drive back and change it. But it's already been reported and traced to me. Hence our visit from the *gendarme*.' He sighed. 'I need to get it sorted by midday, or I'm getting fined or arrested or something. Will you be okay on your own? I know it's not convenient.'

You're telling me!

Saturday was *gîte* changeover day, and since it was the height of summer, that meant all three to clean out and get ready for arrivals. *And* a departure and a set of new arrivals for the guesthouse. *And* a guest meal to cook.

'I'll be fine,' I lied, taking in the bags under his eyes. 'You look tired, Rupert. All that driving and hoicking furniture about. Argy-bargying with Gloria – which I shall enquire about later.'

'Can't be helped. I'd better phone Bob, poor bugger, and tell him we need to get off. By the time we've found the right size tyre and driven back to the trailer, we might be pushing the *gendarme*'s deadline. Leave the welcome baskets for the *gîtes* till last, Emmy. I might be back in time to do those, at least.'

'Have you had your meds? Will you eat something before you go?'

'No, but I will. Yes, if you throw something together while I have a quick shower.'

He staggered off, and I sorted out fruit and yogurt and toast for him.

I couldn't help but feel sorry for Bob, our local hippie biker and soon to be my wedding photographer. The poor sod had already given up his time to drive and lift and carry and referee between Rupert and his very-nearly-ex-wife. That bloke deserved a good friend award.

The dog had begun to whine in Rupert's lounge. Since neither of us had time to walk her, I let her out into the small orchard at the side of the house to do whatever a dog needs to do, grimacing as I watched her crouch, then sighing as I grabbed a plastic bag and trudged out to pick up after her. I wasn't sure *that* was on my official job description. Not that I had an official job description.

The daft black Labrador was off, slaloming around the trees, the morning sun slanting through the leaves, the grass beneath her paws green and lush and dew-speckled, and I whistled for her to come back in. I refused to call her name as a matter of principle. I honestly believed that Rupert's decision to call her Gloria in a moment of irony was the worst idea he'd ever had. Nowadays, the dog seemed able to distinguish between when Rupert used the name Gloria to refer to her and when he was referring to the human Gloria, perhaps due to the differing intonation – joyous enthusiasm for his pet and weary resignation for his ex-wife. But as far as I was concerned, she was 'sweetie' or 'the dog', and, fairly frequently, 'that bloody dog of yours'… Although one look from those woeful eyes always made me melt, and I couldn't resist burying my face in her soft fur when we were lounging together.

When I saw her emerge from a tall hedge and streak towards the house, safe in the knowledge that she would settle in her basket in the hall, I went into the kitchen to lay out breakfast. Heroically forcing my hand away from the *pains aux raisins*, I grabbed a banana and gulped it down as the first guests appeared.

They seated themselves at the scrubbed pine table under the sloping roof of the kitchen extension, away from the business end of the kitchen, to enjoy the late July sunshine pouring through the large window and patio doors, and to peruse the breakfast goodies.

When I asked if they would like eggs (laid by Rupert's own chickens) and how they would like them cooked, I carefully omitted the fact that, with Rupert absent, they would get a much-inferior version. Despite his careful tutelage, eggs and I still did not get on from a culinary point of view.

Hopefully, any disappointment in the egg department would be offset by the array of fresh *pains aux raisins*, croissants, *pains au chocolat*, chopped fruit, yogurt and local-made preserves, to which our guests helped themselves as I brought coffee and tea to the table.

Breakfast was a busy time of day and meant a very early start, but I could hardly complain with the sun shining, the view of the garden through the patio doors so appealing, the table laden with goodies, the guests in a good mood and ready to start their day, happily chatting with each other and swapping sightseeing tips. With Rupert not available this morning, they turned to me for advice and I readily supplied answers to their questions, pleased that my knowledge of the area had improved so much over the past year.

For the zillionth time, I thanked my lucky stars that I'd found this place – and that I'd found the courage to take up Rupert's offer to live and work here. I didn't regret it for a single moment. I may not have thought it at the time, but my now-ex-boyfriend Nathan had done me a substantial favour by sleeping with Rupert's wife while we were on holiday at *La Cour des Roses* last year. If he hadn't, I never would have stayed behind to help Rupert through his illness, fallen in love with his home and business, made such a good job of looking after him and *La Cour des Roses* that he offered me a permanent position here, made a new life for myself away from the rat race, and made a bunch of fantastic new friends while I was at it. And, of course, met the man I was due to marry soon.

My morning idyll was shattered by an ear-splitting shriek.

When I'd recovered my wits, I streaked into the hall to find Abigail Harris clutching her chest in a dramatic manner, her husband Brian patting her arm.

'What's the matter?' I asked, thinking my heart might need massaging, too.

Abigail pointed shakily at the dog, who was curled up peaceably in her basket, cuddling her blanket and … something else.

I peered closer. Her velvety head lay next to what at first glance looked like a well-chewed soft toy but upon closer inspection was a rabbit carcass. An ancient rabbit carcass – nothing more than a frame of bones, with mangled fur dangling off it here and there.

Ugh.

'Gloria, you bad girl!' I wagged a finger at her, forgetting my aversion to her given name.

She gazed back at me with those adorable big eyes of hers, but I wasn't in the mood.

'Out!'

She stared back defiantly.

I tugged at her collar. 'Out, you naughty mutt!'

She settled further into her basket, lovingly nuzzling her prize. It turned my stomach, to the point where the banana threatened a comeback.

I turned to Abigail and Brian. 'I'm so sorry. I didn't see her bring it in. I'll deal with it immediately. Please go through to breakfast. I'll only be a minute.'

As they left the scene of the crime, I gave the dog a stern glare, but she wasn't budging. With a frustrated sigh, I opened the door to Rupert's quarters and resorted to lifting the basket with dog, rabbit carcass and all. She weighed a ton, but I carried her through to Rupert's lounge where we could fight over possession in peace.

The dog won.

I figured all I could do was wait for her to go to sleep and then sneak the offending – and offensive – item away from her.

Just another day at *La Cour des Roses*.

TWO

Madame Dupont usually walked home after her cleaning stints at *La Cour des Roses* – she claimed she'd walked all her life and wasn't going to stop now. The woman must be in her seventies, but I'd swear she was fitter than I was. The only time she allowed me to give her a lift was on a Saturday – after a longer, more tiring session.

'I have something for you, Emie,' she said as we got into the car. 'Can you come inside for a moment?'

On the short drive, my mind worried over what that 'something' might be. I hoped it wasn't another dead chicken. Madame Dupont kept a large flock of ugly black birds to dole out as eating chickens to her extensive family. She didn't gift them to non-family lightly, but I'd been on the receiving end a couple of times – and although I appreciated the sentiment, I wasn't too keen on the actuality.

I followed her up her path, peering over the fence into her yard where the noisy birds scurried about, scrapping with each other. In the kitchen, she invited me to sit at the scrubbed wooden table while she stowed her bag and cardigan and gave a brief tug at her support stockings, which had sagged during the course of the day. How she could bear to wear them in this heat, I would never know.

I'd been in here before, and it was like stepping back in time. No fitted units, but free-standing painted wooden cupboards, an old stove, a noisy fridge. Her appliances could have been used in a vintage TV programme, and the ancient wallpaper in a violent pattern of browns and yellows made me nauseous. But it was all, as you'd expect, spotlessly clean.

Madame Dupont bustled over to a huge pan on the stove. 'I made chicken stew yesterday. My niece and her family were coming to dinner, but the baby was poorly. Now I am left with all this. I will give you some, so you and that handsome fiancé of yours can have it one evening when you are too tired to cook.'

Her French was rapid, her accent strong, but nowadays I understood most of what she said, and she corrected my own French less and less.

'Couldn't you freeze it for yourself?' I asked her.

'There is plenty to spare.' She beckoned me over to peer into the pot. It was full to the brim and smelled delicious. 'Besides, I am not sure how much longer that freezer will last.' She pointed towards the ancient chest freezer in the corner of the room, its white enamel rusted around the bottom. 'Yet another thing that is past its best around here. It would be just my luck if it gave up when it was full of chicken casserole. You may as well take some.'

'Well, if you're sure …'

Smiling, she bent to open the door of a cupboard, the door dangling dangerously on its hinges, and I made a mental note to ask Rupert or Ryan to drop in and fix it. Taking a small brown casserole pot from the paper-lined shelf, she ladled a generous amount into it.

'Thank you.' I kissed her on the cheek. 'Alain and I will enjoy this. Do you need a lift into Pierre-la-Fontaine for the bus?'

Madame Dupont usually spent a night or two at her sick sister's each week. With no transport of her own, it was quite a trek for her, walking along the lane to the main road, waiting for a bus into town, then another bus on to her sister's.

'That is kind, Emie, but I have things to do. My neighbour, Monsieur Girard, will give me a lift into town later.'

Waving goodbye, I placed the pot carefully on the passenger seat and drove slowly back. The last thing I needed was gravy all over the upholstery – Jonathan would never forgive me, since it used to be his car. He'd sold it to me when he decided to give up driving.

I smiled with sweet anticipation at the thought of an evening with Alain, enjoying Madame Dupont's homely chicken stew – with the added advantage that I hadn't had to pluck and de-gut the chicken myself.

But that would have to wait until tomorrow. Tonight, I had to help Rupert cook for the guest meal and entertain.

Rupert got back from his jaunt with Bob to find me tired but chipper.

Overall, my day had been a success. My breakfast eggs had been palatable – or at least, nobody had left them; I'd plied Abigail Harris with cappuccinos until she didn't know whether she was jittery from the caffeine or her rabbit corpse encounter; I'd fitted in a quick morning phone call with my gorgeous half-French, half-English fiancé (best of both worlds, as Rupert once pointed out); I'd been on the receiving end of Madame Dupont's casserole, and I'd finally wrested the disintegrating rabbit from the dog without having my hand chewed off.

All in all, I figured I was on a roll.

I made Rupert a mug of tea while he filled the welcome baskets for the *gîtes* with homemade chutneys and jam, local bread and cheese. New arrivals were due any time now.

'Are you still a free man?' I enquired.

'Yes. Tired, but unarrested.'

I figured he was on a roll, too, then. 'Tell me what happened with Gloria in London.'

'You don't want to know.'

'But I do. That's why I asked. Of course, you're under no obligation to tell me.'

His lips twitched. 'No, but you'll nag me mercilessly until I do.'

'Well?'

He sighed. 'When we got there, I sent Bob for a coffee while I packed up my personal stuff. Gloria watched me like a hawk. We negotiated over furniture when Bob came back. He insisted he should be there in case my blood pressure got so high that I required an ambulance.'

Good old Bob. Rupert's angina attack last year had given his friends a scare, and we were all still mindful of it. I smiled at the extent of Bob's friendship. He knew what he was letting himself in for when he agreed to accompany Rupert – Rupert and Gloria had been at loggerheads for months over Rupert's assets – but it couldn't have been pleasant.

'Gloria's given notice to the tenants in her house, and she'll live in the Kensington flat until she can move back there. I've brought back a few smaller pieces of furniture, but there wasn't much I wanted. Gloria chose most of it, and it wasn't all to my taste.'

That, I could well imagine. Rupert had superb taste at the guesthouse – elegant but practical antiques, light walls, fabrics in naturals with splashes of colour in the rugs and cushions. Quality over quantity. Gloria, on the other hand, had not been able to deny the tackier side of her inner interior decorator, and when I'd first visited *La Cour des Roses*, it was an interesting clash. Slowly but surely, we'd consigned her influence to history.

'We signed a list of everything and what was to happen to it,' Rupert went on as he took milk and packets of butter from the fridge and added them to the baskets.

I raised an eyebrow. 'Sounds quite civilised, for you two.'

'Gloria's not stupid. She knows which battles to fight.'

'I'm amazed she hasn't fought to stay put in that flat.'

'The running costs are too high. Besides, it's worth a fortune. She'd rather have a stack of money in the bank so she won't have to work. It suits her fine.'

I shot him a sympathetic smile. 'You're holding up well, considering.'

'We all knew what it would be like, once the divorce got under way.'

'I know, but I'm sorry you have to go through it.'

'I'm not. It means there's a finite end to it. As long as I can keep *La Cour des Roses*, I'm happy to draw a line under the whole thing. Sending Gloria packing last year was the right thing to do.'

You're telling me. I opened my mouth to say it but closed it again, making Rupert laugh. Gloria waltzing off with my boyfriend, dumping him a few weeks later, then trying to inveigle her way back into Rupert's life had certainly been a trying phase in our lives.

'You will get to keep *La Cour des Roses*, won't you?' I asked him.

'Yes. Gloria's house is being taken into consideration, and since we're selling the London flat *and* the house in Mallorca, I can't see a problem. Although that sodding Mallorcan property's proving hard to shift. Ellie's been liaising on my behalf for months now, to no avail.'

'It's good of her to take some of the weight off your shoulders.'

As the town's estate agent, Ellie had homed in on the one thing she could do to help Rupert through his divorce, taking on the role of adviser and liaison with his estate agent in Mallorca.

'I can't believe Gloria's going for so much,' I said as I passed him bottles of local wine to finish off the baskets. 'You were only together for ten years, and most of your assets were yours already.'

'Gloria can argue – and does – that she gave up her job and friends to be with me. That she spent years in this place, hating every minute. That she added value to the business over those years.'

I snorted inelegantly, and Rupert put an end to the conversation by gathering up his baskets and dashing across the lavender-lined courtyard to the gîtes as the first car pulled up. Talk about cutting it fine.

'I wouldn't mind an early night tonight,' I told him as we started to cook.

No longer intimidated by his chefs' knives and fancy pans and super-duper gadgets in the huge wood and granite kitchen, I'd graduated from chopping vegetables and fruit, and was now allowed to do other things – although never pastry (mine ended up like grey putty, but less useful) and never sauces (gooey messes and burned pans).

'What makes you think you'll get that?'

'I live in hope. At least we have a fighting chance, now we hive the guests off outside or to the lounge after dinner.'

Our three guest meals a week were taken in the kitchen, and it used to be that people chattered and lingered after the meal, preventing us from clearing away and washing up. But over the winter, Rupert and I had decorated and refurnished the lounge until it was how I – er, I mean *we* – envisaged it, and now we had no qualms about shoving our guests in there for after-dinner coffee, or out to the patio with solar lanterns if the weather allowed, enabling us to get sorted in the kitchen.

'Anyway, they're hardly a lively bunch at the moment, are they?' I pointed out. 'We ran out of conversation by dessert last time. What are the newbies like?'

'Diane and John? They seem nice enough.'

But when we settled in the lounge after the meal, Diane spotted the pile of games on the bookshelf and squealed, 'Ooh, let's play something!'

Her husband was all for it, the other guests didn't want to be impolite, and Rupert and I felt obliged to join in to jolly things along, meaning that clearing up in the kitchen had to be done later – much later.

So much for an early night.

* * *

When I pulled up at Alain's neat suburban house the next morning, I walked straight into the comfort of his arms, my head against his chest – he was so tall, that was as far as I reached without standing on tiptoe. Sundays were my day to spend with him, and I looked forward to them immensely.

'Are you staying over tonight?' he murmured hopefully against my hair, leading me into the lounge, an airy space I loved with its cream walls and furnishings, wooden furniture and coffee-coloured cushions adding warmth.

'I can't see why not.'

We each had half our stuff at the other's, and I spent half my life wondering where I'd left my favourite T-shirt. I couldn't wait till I moved in with him properly, after our honeymoon, when *La Cour des Roses* was less busy and we could all settle into a new way of doing things.

'Good.' He fixed his cinnamon-brown eyes on mine. His gaze never ceased to make me feel warm and wanted. 'Want to get the bikes out?'

'Okay by me.'

The first time Alain put me on a bike, I was pretty dubious, but we cycled regularly at weekends now, and although I wasn't keen on busy roads, they were only a means to an end. Once we got onto a quiet country lane or track, I was happy to be out there. My leg muscles had improved and no longer felt like jelly. Unless we went too far. Or up any hills.

Alain's few attempts to get me into running hadn't met with the same success. I couldn't see the point of pounding the pavement – or grass or dirt track or any other surface, come to that. My knees ached and I would end up as red as a beetroot, not least because Alain was a good foot taller than me and I probably had to run twice as far to keep up. Eventually, he accepted that he was on a loser with that one. He continued to run early in the mornings before work, and I suspected he enjoyed the solitude. Each to his own.

As the main roads gave way to lanes, and the lanes to tracks, any tension in me gradually eased. How could it not? All I had to do was let my arms and legs worry about the bike while I greedily drank in the glory that was the French countryside. Farmers' fields, green and gold, crops in full swing. Hedgerows. Occasional fields of roses that the area was famed for, their vibrant colours stretching out and taking my breath away. Swathes of vines in straight rows, deep green in the afternoon sun, the soil beneath dry and dusty.

And then there were the sunflowers, a green carpet topped with bright yellow heads, their faces turned to the afternoon sun, a vast stretch of summer colour and, for me, the epitome of the season.

'I love those,' I said as we stopped by a field of them to drink from our water bottles.

'*Les tournesols?*'

'Yes. They're glorious. And so very French.'

Alain smiled. 'They're coming to an end now. It won't be long before they're dead and drooping and sad-looking.'

I pouted at the thought.

'Don't do that,' he murmured. 'It makes me want to kiss you.'

I stuck my bottom lip out further, and he obliged with a kiss that became heated in seconds, despite the months we'd been together. When he pulled back, those caramel eyes of his were intent on mine. 'Better get home.'

His words held wicked promise.

And that was another thing I liked about cycling on a Sunday – what happened afterwards. We would get back hot, sweaty and tired, necessitating showers followed by a … lie-down. No time limits. The rest of the afternoon stretched out in front of us as we stretched out on the bed, lazily kissing and stroking and making love, my body humming with pleasure as Alain worked magic with his hands until my limbs felt boneless, and stress and tension seemed a million miles away.

Best part of the week.

THREE

Alain was complimentary about the chicken stew – who wouldn't be? – and after dinner, we went for a stroll. This was another Sunday habit I enjoyed, at a time of day I loved, when the heat had subsided and the streets were quiet. We walked beyond the residential area where he lived, onto a short country lane and back – just far enough to work off a few calories.

Alain lapsed into French, something I was long used to. He knew I didn't get enough practice at *La Cour des Roses*, other than with Madame Dupont, and although my French had improved substantially over the past year, it was by no means perfect. Alain wanted me to be comfortable with the language of the country I now called home, and I'd learned to get over my embarrassment and accept this as an inevitable part of our dates. Besides, I still found it surprisingly sexy, hearing him speak it.

As we walked, he held my hand, absentmindedly stroking his thumb across my engagement ring. With all the chores I did around *La Cour des Roses*, I'd wanted something practical, so we'd chosen a simple white gold band inset with alternating blue topaz and diamonds, one diamond in the centre slightly larger and slightly raised. I loved the fact that it went with the necklace Rupert bought me last year as a thank-you present, a white gold pendant in the shape of the head of a rose with a small diamond in the centre. Both were symbols of my new life here in France.

Enjoying the evening breeze, I allowed contentment to permeate my senses, my stresses fading with each step and each stroke of Alain's long fingers … until my never-silent and ever-annoying brain reminded me that my parents were due next weekend.

I loved my parents, truly I did. My dad was ever patient and equable, with an enviable calming influence that went some small way to offset my mother's strident manner (and that was putting it kindly). My mother was best taken in small doses.

You'd have thought my moving to France was the perfect solution, and indeed it was – until I told them about Alain's proposal last September. My mother had been like an inexorable steamship of wedding organisation ever since. This had its upside – the more she did, the less Alain and I had to do – but at times it could try the patience. Even my dad's forbearance was wearing thin, and that was saying something.

Alain took it all in his stride. Perhaps he was still shell-shocked from getting to know her over the past few months.

I smiled as I remembered the first time they'd met, the weekend after I'd announced our sudden engagement, when my parents had stormed over to France.

I'd booked a restaurant as neutral territory. Alain had looked calm, but I knew his little quirks by then. He was petrified. You wouldn't think a businessman well in his thirties who'd been married before should be anxious about meeting his girlfriend's parents, but my mother's reputation preceded her.

He needn't have worried. I wasn't sure whether it was his handsome face or tall build or polite manner or that teensy hint of a French accent that did it, but my mother became quite coquettish and allowed herself to be easily won over. Her approval of my engagement ring sealed it.

After the meal, when Mum popped off to the loo, Dad let out a loud laugh. 'You got off lightly there, Alain. I wish I had your looks and charm.'

Alain grinned. 'You must have, otherwise she'd never have married you!'

On the drive home, Mum had given her verdict.

'Lovely man, Emmy. Don't let this one go running off with somebody else's wife, though, will you?' she said, making Nathan running off with Gloria sound like I'd carelessly misplaced my handbag. Just as Nathan carelessly misplaced Gloria a few weeks later. Shame.

'What are you smirking about?' Alain asked me now, squeezing my hand.

Risking raising his blood pressure, I casually said, 'Don't forget my parents are coming next weekend.'

'How could I forget?' He gave a mock shudder, but there was a twinkle in his eye.

I thumped him lightly on the arm. 'You know my dad loves you. You're kindred spirits.' I'd switched back to English, mainly because I didn't know how to say 'kindred spirits' in French.

'Hmmph. I think your mother still believes I'm defective because I'm divorced.'

'Not now she knows you better and knows why. Your wife running off with your brother was dramatic enough a story for her to sympathise. You charm her. In fact, I believe you put that French accent on stronger especially for her.'

'That's not charm tactics. It's nerves. She interrogates me about something every time we meet. I've told her things I wouldn't tell a psychiatrist!'

'She interrogates everybody. Don't take it personally. I warned you that she's an acquired taste.'

Alain laughed. 'That's one way of putting it.'

'It stems from good intentions. Mum only wants what's best for us. And of course, she always knows what that is.'

'Can I contract a tropical disease between now and Friday? Please?'

'No.'

'Will your mother want to talk about the wedding? *Again?*' His resigned expression made me smile.

'Very probably, but that's only to be expected, and I can't think of a way to deflect her. I can't see Nick tying the knot any time soon.'

'In that, at least, your brother shows a great deal of sense.'

That earned him another thump on the arm. '*You* were the one who proposed, Alain Granger. Didn't you think that might involve a wedding?'

He took my chin in his fingers, gazing deep into my eyes. Cue melting limbs and belly-flips.

'I thought it might involve getting married. I had no idea it would involve daily phone calls and e-mails from your mother about … I don't know what. I try to blank it all out in the spirit of self-preservation.'

'You're a wise man.' I sighed. 'She called me the other day. She'll be sending an updated spreadsheet of the guest list on a weekly basis.'

Alain shook his head. 'As an accountant, I love my spreadsheets, but that seems like a misuse of them, somehow.'

That guest list had been a bone of contention from the start. Mum wanted to invite everybody and his aunt and their dog, but Alain and I wanted a smaller affair. I'd rather spend my wedding day with people I know and care about, not some distant cousin I haven't seen since I was nine. We finally settled on around sixty, at which point my dad's bank balance let out a huge sigh of relief.

Rupert had initially offered to hold the reception at *La Cour des Roses*, but despite my secret hankering to go for it, we all agreed it wouldn't be practical. Rupert and I had hosted a large anniversary party there last year, but that was for thirty-odd people, not sixty-odd. And although my close family and Alain's

would stay at *La Cour des Roses*, we needed somewhere with rooms
for other guests travelling from the UK or elsewhere in France.

Cue several weekends inspecting some incredible venues until
we found a hotel that we all agreed we liked best. The pale stone
building was elegant, the entrance festooned with flowers, the
public rooms inside spacious and classy in creams and golds, the
staff attentive and polite in black and white uniforms. And the
grounds … How could I even begin to describe the neatly mown
lawns, the carefully tended flowerbeds, the shrubbery shaped to
within an inch of its life?

I sulked privately for a while over not holding it at *La Cour des
Roses*, because I hadn't wanted something so formal at first, but
Mum talked me round. The fact was, I couldn't ask for a lovelier
place to have my reception. And when people were travelling so
far for my wedding, staying somewhere so glorious offered some
compensation.

Of course, Mum had been telling everyone that her daughter
was getting married at a *château* ever since. It sounded so preten-
tious, but she'd done it for so long now, she'd got us all doing it.
To be fair to her, the hotel had been a small family *château* a long
time ago, and it did still have that air of grandeur in the building
and the grounds, but even so.

Alain must have read my mind. 'I bet you ten euros that your
mother never uses the word "hotel" all weekend.'

I laughed. 'Why on earth would I take a bet like that?'

'Okay. Ten euros that she doesn't slip even once between now
and the wedding day.'

I considered. Surely she'd slip just once? 'You're on. And while
she was on the phone …'

Alain groaned.

'She gave me an updated list of things that are all imperative,
apparently, so we can discuss it before she arrives – and preferably
action some of it.'

'Okay. We'll look at it when we get back to the house.'

'No need. I have it all up here.' I jabbed at the side of my head. 'We need to make an appointment at the *château* to confirm final numbers, menus, seating plan and all that. I need to confirm the cake with the *pâtisserie*.'

'I thought you and your mother sorted the cake out months ago?'

'We did. But Mum doesn't like things that have been sorted months ago being left to chance, and she wants them double-checking. I can kind of see her point.'

'Yeah. Me, too. Continue.'

'I have to confirm the flowers with the florist, but I can't do that till all the bridesmaids have dresses, and Kate hasn't found hers yet. The final fitting for mine's booked, so Mum can't have a go about that. We need to sort out the rings.'

'We already chose the rings.'

'Yes, but we're supposed to have a final fitting a few weeks before, remember? This *is* a few weeks before. Five weeks, to be precise.'

'Okay. Fair enough.'

'I need to check the status of the wedding gift list. You need to confirm the limo and the other cars. And you need to double-check that the jazz band still have us in the diary.'

'Just because they're musicians doesn't mean they're organisationally flaky, Emmy. Don't worry. They'll be there.'

I gave him a long look, inherited from my mother and designed to quell any disobedience.

'But of course, it would be sensible to make sure,' Alain hastily agreed.

'You should think about your speech. Maybe you could confer with Rupert, since he has to make his best man speech?'

Alain made a face. 'Why does your mother need to worry about that? Is she going to correct and grade the bloody thing?'

'I'm merely relaying her list.'

'How long *is* this list?'

'And Mum will want to discuss the seating chart at the weekend.'

His shoulders slumped. 'It's exhausting just thinking about it.'

I chuckled. 'Yes, it is, but Mum's point is that we should be *doing*, not just thinking.' I squeezed his hand tight. 'In a few weeks, we'll be on our honeymoon. A whole fortnight to ourselves.'

'Thank God.'

'And thank Rupert,' I reminded him.

When Rupert had offered us the use of his house on Mallorca, I hadn't thought twice. After a busy season and all the wedding preparations, the idea of two weeks alone with my new husband was nothing other than bliss.

'It'll be empty of tenants, waiting for a sale,' Rupert had told me. 'I'm selling it furnished, so it'll have everything you need.'

'What if it sells before then?'

'Not looking likely. And I can ensure it gets delayed, if necessary. Count it as my wedding present, if you like. If you'd rather choose somewhere yourselves, I understand. But this won't cost you anything, it has a pool, a view of the sea on one side and mountains on the other, and very few neighbours. Utter seclusion.'

As I thought about it now, I realised there was another incentive that Rupert hadn't pointed out – Alain and I were knackered. Sorting out a honeymoon on top of everything else could have been fun, but then again, it could have been a time-consuming pain. This had been handed to us on a plate, with nothing to do other than book flights and a hire car.

'Rupert does have his good points,' Alain agreed.

I snuggled against him. 'And then we can settle down a bit.'

'Promise?'

'Promise.'

His lips met mine in a long kiss.

'Mmm. Don't worry about the wedding,' I murmured. 'I know it seems like a palaver now, but it'll be a great day.'

Alain broke the kiss when he started laughing. 'I don't doubt it.'

I gave him a puzzled look. 'You don't?'

'Your mother will make sure of it.' He grinned. 'And she'll ruthlessly crush anything that gets in the way of it being perfect.'

When I laughed, he reapplied himself to the kiss we'd been in the middle of, his hands moving to my ribcage, his thumbs brushing my breasts. 'If we only have a few more weeks, we ought to get some practice in.'

I frowned. 'Practice for what?'

'Married life.'

'Ha! We've been practising for months already.'

'I know, but I don't think we've quite perfected it yet.'

'Oh, you don't?' I let out a long-suffering sigh. 'Well, if we *must* …'

Monday meant market day in Pierre-la-Fontaine, followed by coffee with Jonathan.

Town was summer-busy with tourists cluttering the square and taking forever to choose from the stalls, but I couldn't blame them for taking their time. Pierre-la-Fontaine was the perfect example of a small French town with its cream and white buildings, handsome town hall and cobbled streets leading off the main square, where the stone fountain stood festooned with flowers and cafés did a roaring trade in the summer sunshine.

Rupert's favourite haunt was more out of the way, beyond the top of the square near the food stalls, and frequented by locals.

My arm muscles were stronger nowadays, and I hefted the bags of fresh produce – cheeses, sausages, bright red tomatoes, juicy white nectarines, fragrant melons – without complaint as we staggered out of the sunshine and into the dark interior.

Jonathan was already leaning against the wood-panelled bar, his walking stick at his side. His tall frame was leaner since pneumonia nearly finished him off last year, something that worried me. He was chatting away to the bartender, who listened patiently with an occasional puzzled expression. Jonathan had lived in France for a quarter of a century and his French was good, but his pronunciation still left something to be desired.

'Emmy.' A hug for me. 'Rupert.' The same for Rupert.

We ordered coffee and chose a table away from the large television above the bar.

'Bob's not coming,' Jonathan said. 'I think his trip to London with you has driven him into hermit mode.'

'Not bloody surprised,' Rupert grumbled and proceeded to fill Jonathan in, while I sipped at the best coffee in the Loire valley.

'Sounds like it could have been worse,' Jonathan gave his verdict. His opinion of Gloria was as low as mine. 'Looking forward to the wedding, Emmy? Won't be long now.'

I thought about my conversation with Alain the previous evening and smiled. 'Well, there's still plenty to do, and Mum enjoys cracking the whip, but yes, we're both looking forward to it. Very much so.'

'Still up to the gills at *La Cour des Roses*?'

'We certainly are,' Rupert confirmed. 'Miss Marketing here has made sure of that. Never a minute's peace.'

'Isn't that why you hired her?'

Rupert only grunted.

'And how's your own business coming along, Emmy? Making a living yet?'

My online holiday agency for quality self-catering properties in the area was building steadily. It hadn't been easy, persuading property owners to sign up to a small company, but between the incentive of no upfront fees, the incredible job my brother Nick did on the website and Bob's fantastic photos, word was getting around. I might not have had a vast number of properties listed, but that was the idea – quality, not quantity.

'I'm pleased with it,' I told him. 'I don't know about making a living – I couldn't manage without my salary from Rupert – but I've had a good number of bookings, so an acceptable level of commission, and I'm hoping it'll grow.'

'That's good going for your first year,' Rupert said. 'I know it's been time-consuming setting it all up and visiting properties, but that should calm down once you have a solid base.'

I blew hair out of my eyes. 'Hope so. I've got an appointment tomorrow afternoon with someone who wants to list with me, but I have an iffy feeling about it.'

'What kind of iffy?'

'Not sure kind of iffy.'

'Ah. The Emmy kind of iffy.' Rupert turned to Jonathan. 'A woman's instinct is a worrying and puzzlesome thing.'

I glanced at my watch. 'Can I leave you here for half an hour or so, Rupert? I have to meet Alain at the jeweller's, then pop into *Cuisine et Décors*.'

'Of course. I'm happy to lurk, if it means avoiding wedding errands.'

I left the café and walked down a side street to the jeweller's, where Alain was already waiting for me. A quick kiss, and I would have entered the store – but Alain held me back.

'This is pretty momentous, finalising the rings, don't you think?' he said, gazing into my eyes, the soft brown of his making my heart melt.

With the list of things I had on my mind that all led up to our big day, I hadn't attached any particular importance to this one thing – but I was inordinately pleased that Alain had.

I leaned in for a much longer kiss. 'Mmm. Rings mean that in just over a month, you'll be mine for keeps.'

'Sounds good to me.'

We entered the store arm in arm, and the jeweller brought out our rings, mine a plain white gold band to nestle unostentatiously beside my engagement ring, and Alain's a wider platinum band. Both rings still fit us, so they were boxed and handed over to us with hearty congratulations by the elderly man behind the counter.

'One thing ticked off the list, two thousand to go,' Alain quipped as we left.

'And not at all painful.' I indicated the small bag in his hand. 'Don't lose them, whatever you do.'

We parted with a kiss, and I walked down to the bottom of the square to *Cuisine et Décors*, my favourite shop in town. I often perused the windows like a kid at a sweet shop, so when Mum had gone on about gift registration lists and the like – one for a store in the UK and one for a store in France, to suit all our guests – I hadn't hesitated.

I wasn't sure we needed a load of household stuff, but Alain wanted us to put our new, united mark on his house, and since I would practically kill for half the items in the store, I didn't take much persuading. I'd subsequently spent many a happy hour in there with Alain, picking out our list from the tasteful wares they displayed with such class.

Madame Bernard rushed to greet me, and despite my wondering why my mother actually needed an update as to which items had already been claimed – what was she going to do, call up and chastise the people who hadn't registered yet? – Madame Bernard was happy to oblige.

As I made my way back up to the café to fetch Rupert, I was more than satisfied with my morning. Two items ticked off Mum's list, rings that fitted, and the knowledge that we wouldn't be the unhappy recipients of three mismatching toasters and a set of mauve flannelette bedsheets seemed like a job well done to me.

FOUR

When we got back to *La Cour des Roses*, Ryan was in the garden.

Rupert took out cold drinks, and they began to discuss plans for the flowerbeds, Ryan's blond head bobbing while the dog fussed around him, nudging at his hands to be petted. She often accompanied him when he was working, and he enjoyed her company, unless she trampled delicate plants – and unless he was using any dangerous tools, when she was banished inside for safety.

I joined them, glancing at the nearest bed where nodding white daisies contrasted with bright orange nasturtiums.

'They're my favourite this year,' I told Ryan, pointing at them.

'I love them, too. Trouble is, they can take over. I think I'll get rid of them from here after this season.' He laughed when my face fell. 'But I'll put them in the borders instead, in front of the shrubs. Splashes of colour to break up the green. What do you reckon?'

'Sounds good to me.'

Rupert may have originally hired Ryan as a seasonal gardener, but nowadays, he was landscaper, occasional odd-job man, friend – and mug, when one was required for heavy-lifting. For the latter, I had no sympathy. He shouldn't flash all those muscles, if he didn't want to be asked to use them.

Bored with the horticultural technicalities, the dog wandered off to lie down in the middle of a clump of ornamental grasses warmed by the sun, making a bed for herself by flattening the lot.

Ryan sighed. 'I don't know why I bother, I really don't. So, Emmy, how's it going?'

'Depends what you mean by "it".'

'Work?'

'Busy but good.'

'Wedding?'

'Fine, as long as I'm not arrested for matricide before the day. Mum and Dad are due at the weekend.' I snatched his juice and drank the last dregs. 'Mmm. Did you know I'm at Sophie's tomorrow night?'

His face instantly lit up. Ryan had fallen for my hairdressing friend last autumn, and they'd had a few dates, but I'd worried – as had Sophie – that his annual return to the UK over the winter for work would scupper their growing romance. But when he came back in the spring, they took up right where they'd left off, and as far as I could see, they were as happy as pigs in … clover.

'Will there be *more* wedding talk?' Ryan enquired.

'Probably. It'll be the death of me.'

Rupert laughed. 'It'll be the death of Ellie, more like. Bridesmaids' dresses? Flowers? Shoes? It goes against the grain for her.'

'Shows what a good friend she is,' Ryan commented. 'I'd better get back to work. Enjoy tomorrow. You're having pizza.'

Rupert might mock a woman's instincts, but mine proved to be right on the button with regard to my appointment the following afternoon.

Mr Nightingale had e-mailed details and a couple of amateurish photos, but he was a bit shirty when I explained that I wouldn't list a property without seeing it and preferred to use my own photographer.

I drove past detached houses with well-tended gardens, taking in my surroundings with a professional eye. It was suburban, but I could tout it as suitable for a family.

Then I found the address.

The yellow exterior was peeling, but it was the garden that I was worried about. 'Garden' in the loosest sense of the word – a wilderness of bald patches interspersed with weeds and a few forlorn shrubs.

Mr Nightingale pulled up before I had time to take the disapproval off my face.

Shaking my hand a little too vigorously, he jerked a thumb at the lawn. 'Don't worry about that. I'll get it sorted. Won't take long.'

Any gardener worth his salt would beg to differ. How quickly did he think he could re-turf and get flowers and plants to grow?

But he was already ushering me inside.

The first thing that hit me was the smell. Old dogs. Possibly boiled cabbage. And fresh paint. Not an appealing combination.

I went further in with some trepidation. The décor wasn't as awful as I expected, but it certainly wasn't the tastefully decorated, pristine haven I was committed to providing for my customers. Everything was new – and cheap. Thin carpets, magnolia walls (an extra coat wouldn't go amiss), and furniture from a low-end range. Bland, with no character.

Mr Nightingale interrupted my thoughts. 'Great for a family holiday, isn't it?'

I wanted to ask him why he would even think that. Instead, I sought for something neutral to let him down gently. 'It's too far to walk to the local village.'

He shrugged. 'Whoever stays here will have a car.'

'The garden won't be useable this season.'

'Like I said, it won't take two minutes to neaten that up.'

Ostriches, heads and sand sprang to mind. 'Have you had the property long, Mr Nightingale?'

'Bought it a couple of months ago,' he admitted. 'Got it for a song.'

I bet you did.

He waved his hand at the newly painted walls. 'Thought we'd best do it up right away. Get it listed. Might catch a few weeks of rental before the end of the season, don't you think?'

No, I don't think. Not with my company, anyway. 'Have you listed with anybody else yet?' I asked him, curious.

'No. I did my homework, and you seemed the best bet. A lot of the others want a fee up front, don't they? You only charge commission. Much more sensible way of going about things, if you ask me.'

Hmmm.

'So, when can you get it onto your site?' he pushed on, oblivious to my lack of enthusiasm. The man was as thick-skinned as a rhinoceros.

I had no option but to be honest. 'I'm sorry, Mr Nightingale, but I can't take your property on. Its situation isn't appealing enough. I can't advertise the garden in its current state, and it'll take you longer to rectify than you think. As for the interior …' I sought desperately for tact. 'We advertise properties with character. Usually charming, well-converted older houses, but if they're new, with high-quality interiors and furnishings.'

His face was thunderous. 'You're telling me this is a load of old tat, are you?' He pointed at the flat-pack dining table as though it was antique solid oak. 'I spent weeks doing this place up!'

'I'm sure, but I'm afraid it's not …'

'Not up to your snobby standards? Pardon me for being an ordinary, hard-working bloke.'

'Mr Nightingale, what you've done here is fine, but I run a specialised business, and it wouldn't suit my clients.'

'Rich bastards, no doubt. Well, I won't take up any more of your time. There are plenty of other agencies around, Miss High-and-Mighty Jamieson.'

'I hope you find what you're looking for.' I nodded curtly and left.

As I drove away, my hands were shaking on the steering wheel from the confrontation, but I knew this would happen from time to time – people who hadn't read the company's ethos properly before contacting me or were deluded about what constituted a quality property with character and position. As an estate agent, Ellie Fielding dealt with people like that all the time – she'd regaled me with all sorts of tales. Maybe I should ask her for some pointers.

By the time I arrived back at *La Cour des Roses*, I was calm again. Climbing out of the car, I looked over at the guesthouse, green foliage clinging to its grey stone walls, jaunty blue-painted shutters, roses around the doorway, then swept my gaze across the lavender-lined courtyard to where the *gîte* building stood, long and low in cream stone, its three wooden doorways framed by climbing grapevines.

La Cour des Roses was, in my mind, perfect. And I could put up with the occasional awkward meeting in order to stick to my guns and advertise properties like *this*.

That evening, I collapsed with relief on Sophie's sofa in her tiny flat above her salon. It was a small but pretty space, with fairy lights and candles, and I immediately relaxed.

Pizza was in the oven, wine was chilled and Ellie was in the armchair, grumpy at Sophie for daring to comment on the parlous state of her love life – often non-existent, due to the fact that she was averse to romance in middle age, preferring companionship and sex without roses and candlelight.

I listened to them bicker with affection. When I'd walked into Sophie's salon for a haircut last year, I'd never have guessed that we'd become such firm friends. As for Ellie, she'd frightened the life out of me at first, but nowadays I loved her no-nonsense attitude and vicious sense of humour.

Both were my designated bridesmaids, along with Kate, my best friend back in the UK. Since we were just having a civil ceremony followed by a reception, I didn't officially need bridesmaids, only witnesses – but to pacify my mother (and probably, to be fair, our own subconscious desire to choose dresses we wouldn't normally get the chance to), we were going the whole hog.

'When did you last date someone properly?' Sophie asked Ellie, her English excellent (due to time in England in her misspent youth), her accent sexy.

Ellie squinted as she thought about it. 'Maybe five months ago? February time. Colin. Didn't last. Three weeks at most.'

'February?' I smirked. 'He didn't dare give you a Valentine's card, did he?'

Ellie curled her lip. 'Hardly. He knew the rules.'

'So what went wrong?' Sophie asked.

Ellie sighed. 'I think my age went wrong.'

Sophie and I greeted this with puzzled looks.

'I'm fifty-four,' Ellie told us. 'Let's face it, I'm unlikely to get together with anyone under fifty and probably wouldn't want to. But you know, somewhere deep inside, I *think* I'm only thirty, tops. It's not easy reconciling yourself to dating middle-aged, podgy blokes with a comb-over when what you really fancy is a slightly older version of Ryan.'

Sophie's eyes widened, and I burst out laughing.

'So it's not easy, finding someone I'm attracted to,' Ellie went on. 'Oh, I'm practical about it. I'm only asking for someone who's still reasonably fit. Someone with a sense of humour, who'll respect my boundaries. But men like that are few and far between, and I won't compromise. Why should I, at my age?'

Sophie nodded understanding. 'So what happened with Colin?'

'He was … okay. We slept together and it was okay. His conversation was okay. But I want something better. Or nothing at all. It's not as if I'm not content with my own company most of the time.'

'There is nobody at the moment?' Sophie asked.

Ellie sipped her wine, a hesitation that made me wonder if she was keeping something back, but then gave a definitive shake of her head. 'Nah. Not at the moment.'

'What about you and Ryan?' I asked Sophie, taking the opportunity to pry. 'How's that going?'

She smiled sweetly. 'It is going very well.'

'I *told* you he wouldn't lose interest over the winter,' Ellie reminded her. 'Anyone could see that he was as keen as mustard.'

Sophie frowned. 'What do you mean, mustard?'

I laughed. 'A very British expression you have no need for. How long have you been seeing each other now?'

'A few dates before he went back to the UK. And he came back to France in March, so … over four months now.'

Ellie raised a perfectly arched eyebrow. 'Sounds serious.'

Sophie's cheeks went a little pink. 'We like each other's company. But he will have to go back to England for the winter again, so I would be sensible not to get too settled.'

Ellie's lips twitched. 'You're already settled. Like the bride-to-be over here – disgustingly contented.'

'And what's wrong with that?' I asked.

'Nothing, if you like that kind of thing.' Ellie looked back at Sophie. 'You're not going to start flashing an engagement ring, too, are you?'

'It is far too soon for things like that,' Sophie chided. 'But …' She hesitated. 'He did buy me something.'

She disappeared into her bedroom, returning with a little jewellery box. Inside it lay a solid silver charm bracelet. She lifted it out and we peered closer.

'You see?' Sophie pointed to a couple of charms already attached. 'A pair of scissors for my hairdressing and a daisy head for his gardening, to start it off. He will buy something for each birthday and Christmas, he said.'

Ellie and I exchanged looks over the top of the bracelet.

'Sounds like he's thinking long term to me, Sophie,' Ellie said gently.

Sophie's eyes were shining. 'It sounded that way to me, too,' she admitted. 'Oh! The pizza!'

She rushed off to the tiny kitchenette, bringing back slightly burned pizza slices on plates.

We took hungry bites.

'Mum and Dad are coming again at the weekend,' I announced, now that I'd absorbed enough wine into my bloodstream to mention the unmentionable.

'Heaven preserve us.' Ellie rolled her eyes, but there was a smile at her lips. 'What's on the agenda this time? Surely everything's in place by now?'

When Ellie and my mother had first met, I'd thought it would be a Clash of the Redheads, but they got on surprisingly well. Ever since, Ellie *pretended* to complain about my mother, but it was really the wedding fuss she was complaining about, due to the fact that she didn't have a romantic bone in her body.

I wagged a finger at her. 'According to my mother, just because everything's in place doesn't mean it can't be checked, double-checked or tweaked more to one's liking.'

'She is not demanding to see us in our dresses again, is she?' Sophie asked.

'Like a general inspecting her troops,' Ellie grumbled.

'I think you're safe,' I reassured them. 'You two are teacher's pets at the moment, because you're all sorted. Kate's still in the doghouse.'

My choice of bridesmaids had been one of the heart and not of practicality.

Kate lived in the UK. Ellie and Sophie lived in France. Ellie was middle-aged, tall and thin, with short, bright red hair. Sophie was thirty, small and petite with a wavy blonde bob. Kate was a pretty blonde, too, but with impressive breasts that had most men struggling to concentrate on her face when they were talking to her.

When Kate came over in the spring to shop for dresses, we'd set off in high spirits, but it was soon apparent that my friends were so different in size and shape, no one style could do justice to them all.

After an exhausting day of trying every bridesmaid dress within a thirty-mile radius, we'd sat outside a café, pooped.

'I'm too short,' Sophie grumbled. 'Everything drapes a metre past my feet.'

'If it was big enough to fit my top half, the bottom half was the size of a tent,' Kate complained. 'Anything smaller was too clingy. That last one was ridiculous. The chances of these puppies staying in there were nil.' She cupped her breasts with her hands, to help Sophie with translation.

'At least you have something up top.' Ellie peered down her own T-shirt. 'I go straight up and down. That brown dress made me look like a twig. And there's a limit to how much skin I want to expose at my age.'

We fell quiet, but then Ellie slapped the table, making us all jump.

'We're coming at this from the wrong angle,' she said. 'Finding something we can *all* wear – same style, same colour – is impossible. We should *celebrate* the fact that we're different.'

Sophie looked at her hopefully. 'What do you mean?'

'We should pick a colour *range*. Emmy wants the flowers to include sprigs of lavender from *La Cour des Roses*, right? So we could agree, say, lilac through to purple, then each find something that suits us. If we're careful, it'll look great. Individual and unusual. We could send each other photos before we buy, to see what the others think. And Kate, you could take your time finding yours back in the UK.'

I planted a kiss on her cheek. 'You're a genius! If we get it right, you'll look beautiful *and* feel comfortable.'

Ellie grinned. 'And if we get it wrong, we'll look like an uncoordinated shambles.'

The rebel in me shrugged. 'I like a touch of individuality about a wedding.'

Since then, Ellie and Sophie had both found gorgeous dresses – Ellie's long and softly draping in a deep purple satin; Sophie's lilac in a 1950s-style, with a sweetheart neckline, cinched waste and flared taffeta skirt – and had moved on to a prolonged hunt for shoes and other accessories, Sophie loving every minute and Ellie grumbling in her wake.

I couldn't wait to see how they looked in everything at the wedding, and to see everyone's reactions.

But poor Kate was still at the starter's gate.

'She's scoured every shop in Birmingham,' I told them now. 'She even tried dieting.'

'That's ridiculous!' Ellie spluttered. 'Kate's not overweight.'

'That's what I told her. I had to point out that she can't expect to lose weight from only her boobs, so she'd still have the same proportions.'

They both laughed. And despite knowing that Kate was panicking, I joined in. I would be proud to have Kate by my side at my wedding, no matter what she wore.

I allowed my mind to drift to the idea of standing outside the town hall, married to my man and surrounded by friends and family, the fuss all worth it, and smiled.

'Oooh!' Sophie bounced up from her chair. 'I brought the colour charts up from the salon.' She placed them across our knees, her face suggesting she was hoping to experiment.

But Ellie jabbed at her regular colour on the chart with a midnight-blue nail. 'I'll have the usual, thank you.'

Sophie frowned. 'But you were worried it might clash with your dress.'

Ellie curled her lip. 'If you think I'm dying my hair *purple* for Emmy's wedding ...'

'It could look stunning,' Sophie mused. 'But no. I was only going to tone it down, so it's a little darker, a little less ...'

'Obtrusive?'

'I love your hair, you know I do. It would only be this once.'

Ellie smiled at Sophie fondly. 'I trust you.'

Satisfied, Sophie turned to me. 'Emmy?'

'I'll go with the usual, too.' My hair had been perfect ever since Sophie had got her hands on it – no longer mousy brown, but highlighted with blondes and golds.

Sophie tutted. 'You are both so unadventurous.' She fingered my hair. 'I think more gold and less blonde this time, or you will look pale in your dress.'

'Makes sense. Go for it.'

'I hate weddings,' Ellie muttered good-naturedly.

I laughed. 'Then why the hell did you agree to be my bridesmaid?'

'I was scared your mother might beat me up if I refused.'

'Emmy. Have you heard from Kate lately?'

My mother the next morning, on a mission. Was she psychic? Had she somehow sensed me talking to Ellie and Sophie about Kate last night? I wouldn't be at all surprised.

I suppressed a groan. 'I spoke to her a few days ago.'

'Has she found a dress yet?'

'No, but she spends every weekend looking. She's having trouble finding anything, Mum. I feel really sorry for her.' For good measure, I added, 'So do Ellie and Sophie,' in the hope my mother might take the hint and feel sorry for Kate, too.

She only harrumphed. 'It's all very well everybody sympathising with her, Emmy, but that isn't solving the problem, is it? It isn't just a question of the dress. I hope Kate hasn't underestimated the time it'll take to find shoes and other accessories.'

'I'm sure she hasn't.'

'Will you chase her?'

'If you like.' *As if we don't talk about it every time we chat.*

'Fine. Don't forget, mind. I'll see you on Friday, and you can give me a progress report.'

I ended the call with a sigh – and with no intention of nagging poor Kate to death.

My resolve wavered, however, when the florist phoned, asking when I could confirm the flowers.

'All I know is that you want lavender from *La Cour des Roses* and white roses,' Madame Pascal said gently. 'The other colours? You do not know yet? They must be ordered especially.'

'I know. I'm sorry I haven't been in touch.' I could sense my mother's *I told you so* from across the Channel. 'But only two of the three bridesmaids have their dresses.'

'Oh dear. With four weeks to go?'

'Yes. It's complicated.'

'Hmm. Could you bring the two dresses into the shop, at least? It will give me a starting point, and you said you want simple bouquets, so we do not want too many colours anyway.'

'Yes, I can do that.'

'And could you bring a sprig of lavender with you, so I can identify it? There are many different types, you know, all with a different shade.'

'No problem. Thank you for phoning. I appreciate it.'

Urgh. With a heavy heart, I texted Kate. *Any luck on the dress front yet?*

Her reply came back almost immediately. *No, but not through lack of trying. I'll keep at it.*

That was all I could ask.

The florist's call galvanised me into further action, and I brought up my to-do list on my laptop, cobbled together from Mum's frequent missives.

Hmm. The *pâtisserie* could wait till I was next in town. But I phoned the *château* to make an appointment for an evening the following week, texted Alain to let him know I expected him to accompany me, then texted Mum to let her know I'd done it.

Did I get any praise in return? No. What I got was, *Have you booked the final fitting for your dress yet?*

I texted back, *Yes. Next Wednesday.* And figured I still had a darned sight more to get through before I could expect a pat on the head for my efforts.

Our guest Diane's enthusiasm for board games knew no bounds. Even on non-meal nights, she collared people when they got in from a restaurant and only wanted to relax in a squishy armchair to allow their digestion to recover in peace.

'You and your ideas. Why you thought putting those games in the lounge was a good idea, I don't know,' Rupert grumbled as we cooked Thursday night's guest meal.

'I was only copying what you did in the *gîtes*.' I wafted my wooden spoon at him. 'They're a good idea for rainy and low-season days. It's a gesture.'

'I'll give you a gesture.' He did, and it wasn't polite. 'You watch the exodus tonight when we suggest coffee in the lounge.'

'Then we'll go outside, so she isn't reminded about the games.'

Reaching for my phone, I took photos of the baked brie that Rupert took out of the oven. I would do the same with each course. It was a habit that drove him mad.

'Do you *have* to do that?'

I checked the photo wasn't blurry before Rupert whisked the food to the table. 'I don't see you complaining about the result – people spotting all this fab grub on social media and booking for the food alone.'

'I hate social media.'

'I'm not a fan myself, but it does the trick.'

'I notice you don't take photos of any breakfast eggs *you've* cooked.'

'Duh. The idea is to tempt people, not put them off.'

When dinner was over, Rupert poked his head hopefully outside, but a light summer drizzle precluded coffee on the patio. Replete with baked brie, chicken in cider sauce and homemade meringues with summer berries, our guests didn't comment when we served coffee at the table instead of the lounge.

Except for Diane.

'Oh, what a good idea!' she exclaimed. 'There's *far* more room on here for that big war game.'

Abigail and Brian looked at the other guests in panic, and Abigail hastily piped up, 'How about good old-fashioned charades instead? Who's up for that?'

Sighs of relief, acceptance of brandy by a couple of the blokes to shore themselves up before making idiots of themselves, and we repaired to the lounge to scribble out movie titles on scraps of paper.

I hadn't played charades for years, but I'd imbibed enough wine to decide it was fun.

Not that I was any good at it. You try miming *Jean de Florette* at eleven at night after three glasses of wine, and see how well *you* do.

FIVE

Abigail and Brian Harris' departure the next morning paved the way for Mum and Dad's arrival later that afternoon.

My parents loved coming over to France for long weekends. I only wished my father could relax more when they were here, but there was always the wedding to discuss, a venue to see, a menu to peruse.

Rupert had taken it upon himself to rescue my dad at any opportunity, bless him, showing him around the garden (yet again) or taking him to the bar in town for a drink, under the guise of needing his advice on financial matters. Dad might have been an accounts manager for a large firm, but Rupert was savvy and didn't need advice. Perhaps they talked about cricket.

While we waited for them to arrive, I sat at the kitchen table with my laptop, looking ahead at the bookings.

'Urgh.'

Rupert came to my side to view the August spreadsheet. 'What's up?'

'The Hendersons are up. In just over a week's time.'

'Urgh,' he echoed.

I'd made the Hendersons' acquaintance last summer in the midst of Nathan's philandering and desertion with Gloria, and it wasn't something I had fond memories of. You could argue that I was bound to have an unfavourable opinion, considering the surrounding circumstances – that it coloured my opinion of them somewhat. I would argue back that you couldn't turn a stuck-up couple with as much empathy as a teabag into a delightful pair of guests overnight, and Rupert would agree with me.

It made no difference. They were Rupert's longest-standing customers, came each year, recommended *La Cour des Roses* to everyone they knew, and much buttering-up was required.

'And for almost a fortnight this time,' I lamented. 'A week was hard enough, last year.'

'Look at it this way, Emmy. It'll make you appreciate the other guests all the more, won't it?'

He was saved from an interesting reply by my parents' arrival.

When we'd greeted them, Mum and I settled on the patio while Dad took his usual garden tour, looking more enraptured by the minute as they wandered past roses and lilies, silvery weeping pears, delicate weeping willows. And since Ryan was working, that entailed even deeper discussions.

'Gorgeous,' Dad declared when he joined us, and Rupert went to make a pot of tea. 'Ryan knows his stuff. I don't know how you ever get anything done. I'd sit here all day!'

Dad needed a rest, not a weekend of wedding flurry.

Didn't look like he was going to get it.

'Now, Emmy, just four weeks to go,' Mum reminded me, as if I didn't already have the daily countdown built into my brain. 'While we're here, we need to—'

I placed a halting hand on her arm. 'Mum, I appreciate all you've done with the wedding. I couldn't have done it without you. But you are supposed to have a *bit* of a break while you're here.'

Overhearing as he came out with a tray of tea and homemade lemon drizzle cake, but pretending he hadn't, Rupert said, 'You won't believe what kind of a week I had going back to London to haggle with Gloria. Even the *gendarmes* got involved …'

And somehow, he managed to reroute the conversation by telling them all about his trip to London, his battles with Gloria and his subsequent brush with the law over his trailer.

I loved Rupert, I really did.

* * *

That evening, Alain joined us for a meal at a local restaurant.

Mum liked the place for its formal Frenchness, its white table linen and polite staff. Dad liked it for the superb food. Rupert liked it because it saved him from cooking, and Alain liked it because it saved him from my cooking.

As we sipped our wine, Rupert continued his mission to keep the conversation away from weddings by delving deep into his extensive library of anecdotes.

'This restaurant's a darned sight more civilised than the place Gloria and I once made the mistake of trying during a weekend in Carcassonne,' he announced.

'Why? Was the food awful?' Mum asked.

'Never got the chance to taste it. The service left something to be desired, though. There were three couples at the table next to us – French – getting a bit loud, a bit drunk. It all kicked off when the waiter reached across the table for a plate and knocked red wine over one of the women.'

Dad winced. 'Red wine?'

'Yup. Over white jeans and a pale top. One of the men jumped up and lambasted the waiter, whose apology, from what I could gather – bearing in mind this was all in rapid French and getting a bit heated – didn't hold much conviction. I'm not sure what the waiter said, but whatever it was, the women took offence. There was a lot of shouting, and they got up to leave.'

'Without paying?' I asked.

'Exactly. The waiter called across to a woman who must have been the owner, and they both followed the group outside, with everyone gesticulating and yelling insults at each other. Gloria and I felt more than uncomfortable by that stage, I can tell you.'

'I should imagine so.' Mum looked horrified. 'Did you leave?'

'We wanted to, but we didn't dare because we'd already ordered. But when the rest of the staff stormed outside, too, we decided to call it quits and sidle off.'

'Did you get caught?' Dad wanted to know.

'They didn't even see us go. The owner of the restaurant and the woman who'd had the wine spilled over her had got into a cat fight – hair-pulling, rolling around on the ground, the whole works. The blokes and the waiters were cheering them on and shoving each other around. Never seen anything like it! I half-expected the cook to come out brandishing a cleaver!'

'Tell me he didn't,' I begged.

Rupert shook his head sadly. 'No. It'd make a much better story if he had, don't you think?'

Our laughter was interrupted by the arrival of our starters. Bless Rupert for providing an opening for everyone to spend the rest of the meal exchanging tales of dubious restaurant experiences.

As we finished our main course, Alain's mobile rang.

'Excuse me.' He took the call in French, and I gathered it was his mother, Mireille, sounding flustered. He went outside so as not to disturb the other diners in the restaurant.

'Is everything okay?' I asked him when he came back.

'Yes and no. You know Mum and Dad are looking after Gabriel and Chloe for a week soon, while Adrien and Sabine go away together?'

I nodded. Alain's parents were usually more than happy to look after their grandchildren for Alain's brother and his wife. 'Is there a problem?'

'Yeah. Mum had it down as next week. She's positive that's what Sabine told her. But Adrien rang up to confirm, and it's this coming week. They arrive tomorrow.'

'Eek.'

'Double eek – Dad has old friends coming over from the UK, and they're all booked into a hotel in Honfleur for a mid-week break together. It can't be changed now.'

'Crap.'

'That about sums it up.'

My mind raced across the possibilities. 'So they can take the children for some of the time?' When Alain nodded, I said, 'Could you – we – take them for the rest of the time?'

He hesitated as the idea sank in. 'I guess so. They've never stayed down here with me, though – I always go up to Mum and Dad's when Adrien and Sabine come over from Kent.'

That was understandable. It was one thing playing happy families at his parents' place on the outskirts of Paris. Quite another to host his adulterous ex-wife, the brother she ran off with and their offspring in his own home – the home he bought with Sabine.

'What about your work?' I asked him. 'Would it be too difficult?'

He closed his eyes as he mentally went through his diary and workload, then opened them again. 'I'd have to rearrange a few things, then catch up next weekend. I don't want to get too behind before the wedding. But yes, it would be great to have them.' He reached out a hand. 'I could do with some help entertaining them whenever you're free, though.'

I smiled, perfectly happy with the idea of borrowing someone else's children, enjoying myself for a few days, then handing them back to their rightful owners.

'I'm sure we can carve Emmy some extra free time out next week,' Rupert said jovially.

'And it'll give you a chance to get to know them better before the wedding,' Mum chipped in.

Alain's four-year-old niece and almost-six-year-old nephew were to be our flower girl and page boy – something that had caused a great deal of excitement with Chloe. We'd asked them the one time I'd met them so far, at Christmas, when we'd stayed at Alain's parents with the whole family.

Mum frowned. 'Isn't your appointment at the *château* one evening next week?'

Damn. I was hoping she wouldn't remember that.

'Yes, but we won't be able to go if we have the children, Mum, will we?' *Shame.*

'Make sure you rearrange it,' Mum said firmly. 'And what about your dress fitting on Wednesday?' That woman had a memory like a computer chip. 'You can't miss that. If any alterations are needed, we'll run out of time. Only four weeks to go, remember.'

How could I forget?

'Okay,' I capitulated. *One out of two ain't bad.*

I turned to Alain. 'Call your mum back and tell her we can take them.'

I welcomed *gîte* changeover day when my parents were staying, because it meant a reprieve from wedding talk.

Mum understood that my Saturdays were spoken for and allowed Dad to take her out for the day, to explore local towns or *châteaux*, enjoy the scenery and lunch out. At the guest meal, she knew she was implicitly banned from wedding talk in front of the other guests, for fear of boring them to death. Dad would ply her with wine, and she would relax and enjoy the others' company – we hoped.

Since Rupert had managed to deflect her from her favourite subject yesterday, too, I knew we were in for it tomorrow, but that was fair enough. The wedding was one of the reasons for their visit, after all.

Game-mad Diane and John were leaving today, thank goodness. I hoped that their replacements, Kerry and Malcolm, would be a better bet.

'How are the wedding preparations?' Madame Dupont asked as we began to clean out the first vacated *gîte*, our routine like a well-oiled machine.

I would have said 'like a steamroller', but I didn't know the word in French. 'I'm sure we'll discuss it in great detail tomorrow when Alain comes round.'

Madame Dupont tutted. 'All this fuss nowadays. When I got married, we simply put on our best clothes and got married. Tea and cake afterwards, and that was that.'

'You didn't have a wedding dress?'

'We had no money for things like that. Some people did, but not us.' There was a trace of self-pity on her face, but it was quickly banished. Madame Dupont didn't believe in self-pity. 'I am sure *you* will look beautiful, Emie. Show me the photo of your dress again.'

I dug my phone out of my pocket, and when she squinted, her eyes not good enough to pick up the details, I did my best to find the vocabulary to describe the white satin dress with spaghetti straps and fitted bodice, the skirt flaring gently down to beyond my toes. The satin was overlaid with fine lace, and that lace outer layer went above the neckline – enough to hide any imperfections but still showing my suntanned skin – then stretched over my shoulders to form lacy capped sleeves over the thin ribbon straps.

Madame Dupont ran a bony finger across the screen. 'It is so pretty. And your mother approves?'

'Yes, thankfully.'

I smiled at the memory of the subterfuge employed to keep Mum happy. She'd wanted me to shop for my dress in England, but that was impractical. Instead, Sophie and Ellie and I had narrowed it down to three dresses, so Mum could come over and help me choose. The truth was, I'd known which one I wanted from the moment I'd tried it on, so we'd made sure the other two contenders weren't right – one too clingy, the other high-necked and trussed-up.

My mother had gasped the moment I came out of the changing room in my favourite one. 'Emmy, you look so beautiful.'

I'd gazed in the mirror, and for once I could believe it.

I made a hash of explaining all this to Madame Dupont now, but she got the gist.

'You are a good girl, Emie, doing all that to keep your mother happy.'

'I've learned that if my mother is happy, Madame Dupont, then so is everyone else.'

She cackled at the wisdom of that. 'As for your wedding favours, I have finished my part, and with time to spare. When you take me home, perhaps you should take photographs and send them to your mother for her approval?'

'I'd love to see them. You are so kind to do that for me.'

Discussions of wedding favours had not gone well at the start. I couldn't see the point of them, and in my effort to keep the wedding on this side of lavish, I'd told my mother I thought they were an unnecessary extra.

But she'd been reading too many magazines, had found out they were *de rigueur*, and she was insistent – although she did waver momentarily when her research led her to the likely cost, causing her to purse her lips and tighten her purse.

'Ridiculous. Have you seen the price of these? All for a little something that nobody wants!'

I should have known better than to think that would be an end to the matter.

'Although people sometimes make them themselves to keep costs down, apparently,' she went on. 'I bet something like this would be right up your Aunt Jeanie's street. She has a creative streak, doesn't she? Likes to think outside the box.'

That's the kindest term for it.

Sure enough, the minute Mum mentioned it to Jeanie, she was off and running. Knowing I wanted lavender from *La Cour des Roses* in my bouquet, she came up with the idea of pouches of dried lavender for the ladies, tied with ribbon and nestled in antique china cups and saucers sourced from jumble sales and flea markets, and pouches of sweets for the men.

When I'd told Madame Dupont many weeks ago, her eyes had lit up.

'I can save your aunt a little time and money,' she'd said. 'I have a few pieces of antique china at home that I never use, for your aunt to add to her collection. Those cupboards are far too cluttered. As for the lavender pouches, do you know what your aunt will make them from?'

I'd admitted I had no idea – crafts were not my forte – but she'd said, 'I have just the thing. I will show you when I come next time.'

The next day, she'd brought with her an example – a small, delicate, plain white handkerchief.

'Feel it. You see? It is so soft because it is silk. I have a whole drawer full at home.' When I'd raised an eyebrow, she'd explained, 'My grandparents ran a haberdashery store many decades ago, and these were left when they sold up. I have at least forty, and no use for them, so there would be enough for the ladies. I could embroider the corners with yours and Alain's initials, and you could use them to wrap the lavender. What do you think?'

I had hugged her tightly and said they would be admired and treasured, which made her beam with pleasure.

Now, she looked pleased that I was still enthusiastic. When we got to her cottage, she opened the glass door of her dresser to show me the dozen cups and saucers she'd promised, then pulled at a stiff drawer where the handkerchiefs were neatly laid flat, and lifted one out.

Taking it, I examined the neat purple embroidery in the corner – a cursive *E* and *A* intertwined.

I felt tears well, that she would do this for me, but held them back. Madame Dupont didn't approve of too much sentiment.

'Oh, Madame Dupont, they're perfect. They must have taken you *hours*!'

She shrugged. 'It gave me something to do, here on my own in the evenings.'

Her words gave me a jolt as I realised I'd never thought too much about how isolated Madame Dupont must feel out here.

I took the fact that I could drive and had a car for granted, zipping to Alain's or Ellie's or Sophie's whenever I wanted. I knew Madame Dupont's family visited when they could, that she spent a night at her sister's each week … She came across as so capable and self-sufficient, it hadn't occurred to me that perhaps she was also lonely.

As I took photographs to send to my mother, I resolved to bear Madame Dupont's situation in mind more in the future.

Sunday morning was laundry morning – shoving load after load of bedding from the gîtes into the washer, then pegging them out to dry at the bottom of the garden, as far from view of the guests as possible. The aesthetic downside of this was made up for by fresh-smelling linen that dried ridiculously quickly in the hot summer sunshine, and of course it was environmentally friendly. Madame Dupont would set to with Rupert's fancy pressing machine on Monday. It looked dangerous to me, so I never went near it – I had visions of pressing my arm flat by mistake.

With a couple of loads out and another in the machine, I sat out on the patio with Rupert, my parents and the dog. Gloria always gravitated towards my dad, and he was happy to indulge her, stroking her velvet ears as she rested her chin on his knees. Other guests had dotted themselves about the grounds on chairs and benches hidden away down little paths amongst the flowers and shrubs.

'Now, about the wedding,' Mum began, unable to delay her favourite subject any longer.

Rupert circumspectly offered to put some lunch together and scuttled off into the kitchen.

'First and foremost, you need to get Kate sorted with her dress, Emmy.'

I remembered the florist's phone call mid-week, and that I still hadn't taken her the dresses. I mentally moved it to the top of my list.

'I texted Kate. She's doing her best, Mum. It's not easy for her.'

'Easy or not, tell her to get a move on, otherwise I'll make her wear some tie-dye kaftan monstrosity of Aunt Jeanie's.'

I laughed. The epitome of the hippie who wouldn't let go, Aunt Jeanie was not famed for her conformity in fashion – or in any other area of her life, come to that – and my mother disapproved of the way her sister-in-law combined obscure items in her wardrobe and ever-changing hair colours with total abandon.

To change the subject, I updated Mum on the rings and gift list, and promised I'd double-check the cake soon.

'Alain's dealing with the cars and the band,' I told her confidently, with no idea whether he'd made any inroads or not, thereby throwing him to the wolves.

I could almost see her making a mental note to ask him when he got here. *Oops.*

She fished in her bag and handed me a printed spreadsheet of the guest list, showing where numbers stood.

I dutifully cast my eye down it. 'Not too many refusals.'

Mum smiled smugly. 'The temptation of a weekend at a *château* might have played a part in that, don't you think?'

I mentally rolled my eyes at her insistence on calling the hotel a *château*. I would owe Alain his ten euros, at this rate.

'And we made the right decision, choosing a Friday,' Mum went on. 'Quite a few people said they preferred it. Gives them a chance to recover on the Saturday before heading home on the Sunday.'

Talk about selective memory. That wasn't a decision; it was a necessity. I opened my mouth to remind her that the town hall was already booked up on the Saturday, as was the *château*, but I decided life was too short.

Rupert brought out a tray of white wine and glasses along with cheese, cold meats, bread and tomatoes for lunch – gently pushing the dog's hopeful nose away – and I grabbed a glass and filled it, earning a look of mild disapproval from my dad. I gave him a *Hey, don't deny me my anaesthetic* look back.

When Mum excused herself and went off to the loo, my audible sigh of relief made Dad and Rupert burst out laughing.

'If it's any consolation, Emmy, I get this all the time at home,' Dad said mildly.

'It's no consolation at all.'

Dad sipped his wine, allowing it to potter around his taste buds. 'Mmm. That's good.' Picking up the bottle, he studied the label. 'Might take some of that home. Where did you get it?'

'Supermarket,' Rupert told him. 'Nothing fancy, but nice and light for afternoon drinking.'

'Definitely.' Dad smiled across at me. 'You'll be pleased to hear that there is at least one thing regarding the wedding over which you will have no battles with your mother, Emmy.'

'Oh? What's that?'

'Your eschewing of stag and hen nights. Your mother can't bear them.' He turned to Rupert. 'Can you imagine Flo approving of strippers?'

Rupert snorted, sending wine down the wrong way and making him cough. 'As best man, I'm grateful not to get embroiled in any of that. Too old. Too worried about being un-PC. Too scared of what Flo would do to me if she found out.'

Dad laughed. 'Those hordes of young women who wander around Birmingham city centre on a Saturday afternoon in pink tutus and tiaras make Flo apoplectic. "Undignified" is the kindest word she comes up with. Good decision, Emmy, love.'

'It would be nice to be credited with the moral high ground and a sense of dignity and maturity, Dad, but I'm afraid our motives were more practical than anything else. It's hard enough getting everyone here for the wedding. Hen and stag nights would be impossible.'

'Has Alain's family confirmed when they'll come down to *La Cour des Roses* before the wedding yet?' Mum asked as she came back out.

I shrugged. 'They're taking the *gîtes*, so they can come any time from the Saturday before the wedding. Alain's mum's waiting for Adrien and Sabine to decide when they'll travel over from Kent.'

'Hmmph.' Mum didn't like such dilly-dallying. 'I must say, Sabine has some audacity, coming to her ex-husband's wedding – and with the man she left him for. It's all rather awkward, if you ask me.'

'Mum, we went through all this when we sent out the invitations. We could hardly invite Adrien and the children without Sabine, could we? I'm sure Sabine would have liked to skip it, but she could hardly do that, with Chloe and Gabriel's roles at the wedding. The children will already be staying somewhere new and meeting a bunch of people they don't know. Their mum should be here for them, and she will be. I admire her for not ducking out.'

Mum nodded, resigned. 'I do, too, Emmy. Putting your children above your own feelings is right and proper.'

Of course, Mum was right – a family situation like that *could* be awkward, but only for people on the outside. The principal players could deal with it. Alain had adjusted to his family situation as far as could be expected over the years, and although he and his brother were understandably less close than they once were, and relations with Sabine were on the strained side, the family dynamic was functioning at the best level anyone could realistically expect. Gabriel and Chloe had helped with that – they were so loveable, and it was important to the adults that they were kept oblivious of any undercurrents.

When I'd met them at Christmas, I'd found Adrien relaxed and easy-going, and despite feeling that I should dislike Sabine, she was friendly and made an effort to ask me about *La Cour des Roses*, my business and how I was finding my new life in France. If she hadn't been my fiancé's ex-wife who'd left him for his brother, perhaps we could have become good friends. As it was, I was happy to let bygones be bygones as far as possible. What was between her and Alain had taken place long before I was on the scene, and it wasn't in anyone's interests for us not to get along together.

My world brightened as Alain came around the side of the house.

'Sorry I'm late. Call from a client.'

I narrowed my eyes at him, although they were twinkling. *Call from a client, my arse.*

'Did I miss anything?' he asked innocently.

Rupert passed him a large glass of wine.

'We've covered Kate's dress and the guest list so far.' Mum kissed him and handed him the sheet of paper.

Alain reached into his shirt pocket, took out his reading glasses and slipped them on.

My stomach flipped. I had no idea why it still did that after all this time, but seeing him in his reading glasses never failed to turn me on. Don't get me wrong, I didn't *need* them, to be turned on – but they did add a certain something. Unfortunately, the ensuing tingles were hardly appropriate, with my parents breathing down our necks.

'You're sure there won't be any problems with Emmy's documents?' Mum asked him.

'Alain spends his working life buried in French red tape,' I chided gently. 'It's all been dealt with.' I shuddered as I remembered the to-ing and fro-ing of my documents to get this certified and that translated and the other legalised.

'I spoke to Patrice – the mayor – and he agreed everything's in order,' Alain reassured her patiently.

'Emmy said you're dealing with the cars and the band?'

Alain shot me a look, and I pasted an innocent expression on my face.

'I spoke to one of the guys in the band yesterday,' he told her. 'They're all set. I haven't talked to the car company yet, but I'll make it a priority this week.'

'What about Gabriel and Chloe? Has Sabine sorted their outfits out yet?'

'She had to leave it till the last minute, because they're growing so quickly.'

Mum backed off a little. 'Oh, yes, well, children do have a habit of doing that, don't they? As long as it's all in hand.'

Knowing she needed more to feed her endless appetite for wedding details, Alain kindly elaborated. 'Gabriel will be in trousers, shirt and tie. No jacket – he'll only get hot and take it off. They couldn't get Chloe's dress in the right colour range, so it'll be white, but Sabine's having a purple sash made, and a matching tie for Gabriel.'

Mum reached out to take his hand. 'I'm sorry I'm nagging. I know it's difficult for you, Alain, with the history between you all.'

'Don't worry, Flo. I know you need to know these things.'

'So. About the seating plan …'

Alain's smile was a tad forced as Mum went inside to retrieve it from her room.

Dad topped up Alain's wine. 'Don't worry, son, we'll get there in the end, and it'll all be worth it. You'll see.'

SIX

The next morning when the phone rang, I was harassed at breakfast and anxious to wave my parents off before going to the market – but I was happy to hear from Julia Cooper.

Julia had been my nemesis this time last year, when Rupert and I discovered she'd booked the entire place for her parents' golden wedding anniversary. It nearly killed us, initially because Gloria hadn't thought to tell him about it, and subsequently because Julia was demanding and overwrought – much like my mother with the wedding. Yet in the end, it was wonderful, and the fact that Julia single-handedly organised it filled me with admiration – and with hope that my wedding might turn out as well.

Julia ran specialist residential courses and had persuaded us to host some at *La Cour des Roses*. We'd held a couple in the spring and they were successful, although it was hard work providing meals every evening and feigning an interest in whatever the enthusiasts were there to learn. The photographers were fine, although I glazed over when they got technical. The aspiring thriller writers? Their topics of conversation weren't entirely suitable over dinner. There are only so many methods of murder you can stomach before it puts you off your rare steak in red wine sauce.

The photography course was a double triumph – not only good revenue for us, but I'd put Julia in touch with Bob, whose landscape photography was beautiful but who mainly subsisted by taking photos for the local estate agents and now for my company. He'd been nervous about running a course but was keen on the fee (it meant fresh tyres for his beloved motorbike) and the fact that he would be obliged to dine at *La Cour des Roses* (such a hardship).

'Julia! Lovely to hear from you. How are you?'

'I'm fine. Robert says our May break at *La Cour des Roses* wasn't enough. He wants to come back already.'

'That's nice. Let me know when you can get away.'

'Thanks, Emmy. I rang to update you on numbers for the courses at the end of September. Oil painting is three-quarters full. Landscape photography is booked up.'

I whooped. 'Bob will be thrilled.'

'We got great feedback from the one he did in Wales last month, and I have more weeks in the autumn if he can make it over here. Possibly Italy next year. I'll phone him this week.'

'Did you know he's doing my wedding photographs?'

'Really? Great! How's all that going?'

'My mother's driving me mad, but it wouldn't get done if it was left to me, so I can't complain.'

'How long now?'

'Just under four weeks.'

'Well, I hope it all goes to plan. Will that gorgeous fiancé of yours play the sax again?'

I laughed. Nobody was more surprised than me at how good Alain was when he'd had to stand in with the band at the anniversary party last year.

'No. You know how he feels about playing in front of people he knows, so it would hardly be fair at his own wedding! But we've hired the same band.'

'Good luck with it all. I'll speak to you soon.'

'Thanks, Julia.'

* * *

Mum was tearful when I saw them off. 'Just think, Emmy. The next time we're here, you'll be almost married.'

Yes, just think.

'Aunt Jeanie's travelling with you?' I asked her.

'Yes. It's easier than trying to get her here by herself. You know how scatty she is.'

That's one word for her.

'And …'

'Flo, we'll miss the plane. Get your backside in gear,' Dad growled, shooting a wink my way as he bundled her into the car.

Rupert tapped his watch. We were running late for the market and coffee with Jonathan and Bob.

By the time we got to the café, laden down with shopping, they were on to their second cup.

I relayed Julia's call to Bob. 'Better watch it, or you'll be ruining your laid-back image with all this proper work,' I teased.

Bob was the original hippie – faded denims, straggling grey beard and all.

'Talking of proper paid work, it seems Emmy will be doing very little of it this week,' Rupert told them. 'She's helping Alain babysit his niece and nephew for a few days.'

Bob smiled at me. 'Is that good or bad?'

'Good, I think. I met them over Christmas and they're sweet. Alain adores them. But they haven't stayed with him down here before, so it's new ground for us.'

'Any plans for how to occupy them?' Jonathan asked.

'We only found out we were having them a couple of days ago. But definitely the zoo. Maybe a walk – the scenery will be different enough to back home to keep them interested, I hope.'

'Throw the dog in as a sweetener, if you like,' Rupert offered. 'She'll liven a walk up.'

I thought about Gloria's wayward habits on a walk – pulling on her lead, running ahead when she was off it, burrowing around in heaven knows what – and made a face, making Bob roar with laughter.

But she would be a novelty for the children. I knew they didn't have a pet of their own. In fact, Gabriel had told me at Christmas that he was desperate for one – preferably a dog, if necessary a cat, but he would settle for a rabbit, if he had to.

'Good idea. Thanks.'

'You're welcome.'

'Any fun guests at the moment?' Jonathan asked. He loved hearing the gossip from *La Cour des Roses*, especially now he didn't get out and about as much.

'They were as dull as ditchwater last week,' Rupert pronounced glumly, and proceeded to explain about Diane. 'I'm bored just telling you about it. We could do with someone who'll liven things up this week, if you ask me.'

I put my head in my hands. 'Aargh! Don't *say* that, Rupert. You *know* you're only inviting trouble!'

By the time I'd caught up with my chores with Madame Dupont that afternoon, I'd have liked nothing better than a quiet evening at Alain's house – but he was devoting the evening to work, in readiness for devoting the next few days to his niece and nephew.

And since Ellie had come round to see Rupert – it wasn't unknown for them to closet themselves away in Rupert's quarters to thrash out international real estate – I figured I should catch up with e-mails and bookings for both *La Cour des Roses* and my own agency.

It gave me pleasure, seeing how well *La Cour des Roses* was doing and that my own business was coming along.

But it wasn't the same kind of pleasure I could have got from an evening with a handsome half-Frenchman.

* * *

The next day, I grabbed a quick coffee in Pierre-la-Fontaine with Ellie and Sophie at lunchtime before the children's arrival.

We settled ourselves outside the café nearest their businesses, overlooking the stone fountain with bright red and yellow flowers around its base, the trickle of water soothing my senses and Gloria at my feet, firmly tied around the chair leg for the safety of waiters and customers alike.

I explained her presence by telling Sophie and Ellie about the imminent arrival of Alain's niece and nephew.

'That will be nice for you, spending quality time with them,' Sophie said cheerily.

'Hmm. It won't do any harm to make sure your page boy and flower girl are on your side before the big day,' Ellie agreed cynically.

'How did it go at the weekend?' Sophie asked. 'Did your mother discuss the wedding?'

'Of course! Goodness knows what she'll find to talk about, once it's over and done with.'

'I gather it's common practice for the bride's mother to spend many months talking about the wedding afterwards as well as beforehand,' Ellie pointed out. 'There are speeches to dissect, photos to be pored over, anecdotes to be told, relatives to be gossiped about ... Plenty of fodder for quite some time.'

I groaned, and as though she was tuning in, the dog lifted her head, heaved a huge sigh and plunked her chin back down on the floor, making us all laugh.

'We should arrange an evening to practise make-up,' Sophie said. 'Although I cannot do anything about Kate, of course.'

Ellie shot her an expression of mock despair. 'So why put *us* through it?'

'We do not want any disasters on the day. I have to be sure I am doing the right thing for your skin tones. And ...' Her shoulders slumped. 'Flo texted me. She wants us to practise and send photos of the results. For her approval.'

I frowned. 'Why did she text you and not me?'

'Because she knows Sophie is less likely to answer back,' Ellie said wryly.

'*Because*,' Sophie corrected, 'she forgot to mention it to you at the weekend, and as I am the one doing the make-up, I am the one she needed to consult.'

Ellie and I exchanged a look. We both knew that Ellie's response was probably truer to the mark, but we dutifully took out our phones to arrange a date, while I quelled my irritation that Mum thought it was okay to bother my friends directly instead of going through me.

When I heard a car horn and glanced around, the florist shop's awning caught my eye, and I slapped my forehead with the flat of my hand.

'What?' Ellie asked, alarmed.

'I've got a mental block about that florist,' I complained. 'I need your bridesmaid dresses sometime soon, before either the florist or my mother lynches me.' I explained the phone call last week.

'Aren't you caught up with the kids and your own dress fitting this week?'

'Yeah. But Madame Pascal wants to discuss my needs and whatever.' My mind raced ahead. 'Is she open on a Monday, do you know?'

'It's her half day,' Sophie said. 'She's only open in the morning.'

'That'll do. Can I pop round to each of yours on Sunday morning to collect the dresses?'

'Do you want me to bring them over?' Ellie asked, concerned. 'You're tearing around like a …'

I held up a hand before she could elucidate. 'No, thanks, I can do it on the way to Alain's. Can you watch Gloria for a minute? I'll go over and let the florist know.'

That done, I drove the dog to Alain's, where we fed her the food Rupert had packed for her, then took her out to the back garden. This was a new space to her, and it was her doggy responsibility to explore it, christen it and whatever else.

When she'd finished, Alain tied her to a bench in the shade. 'She can have a nap before the walk. I thought it best not to have her inside when the kids land, so they can get used to the house and see Grandma off first. Then we'll let them get acquainted.'

The dog didn't seem to mind the arrangement. She flopped on the grass, closed her eyes and was off into doggy dreamland almost before we got back inside.

Mireille arrived with the children soon after, as neat and tidy as ever in navy cropped trousers and a smart striped top, a jaunty navy scarf around her neck, her grey hair in a short cut that I could never get away with.

I'd met Alain's parents several times over the past year and was grateful that we all got on well. Christopher – the English half of Alain's parentage – was quiet and personable. Mireille was a little mercurial, but I always appreciated the fact that in a house where conversations could be held in French or English, she kindly gave preference to English whenever I was around.

'Sorry we're late. Numerous toilet stops,' she said as she unbuckled the children from their car seats. 'Don't worry, they ate in the car.'

'I'd never have guessed,' Alain commented wryly as he helped Chloe out, glancing at the breadcrumbs scattered across the back seat and the chunk of raw carrot still clutched in Chloe's little fist. He tousled her mop of brown curls, and she reached her arms around him to hug him.

'Uncle Alain!' Gabriel had got himself out of the car and ran around to hug Alain tight. With Chloe still in his arms, Alain teetered with the force, making Mireille and me laugh.

Remembering his manners, Gabriel came over to hug me, too. Chloe wasn't relinquishing her hold on her uncle, but she reached out a hand to me, so I went over and kissed her rosy cheeks.

Mireille came inside with us for a cup of tea and to make sure they both settled, but it didn't take long to ascertain that, as the children had never been to Alain's house before, they would be content to explore and ask a million questions about his belongings for a while.

While Alain supervised them, Mireille and I settled on the sofa to enjoy our tea.

'Will you come with Alain when he brings the children back on Friday?' she asked.

'It depends on Rupert, and on how far behind I get at the guesthouse this week.' I leaned in conspiratorially. 'Not that I'm complaining about the distraction.'

She smiled. 'It would be nice if you could make it. Adrien and Sabine will be there, and we could all have a lovely family lunch. We haven't all been together like that since Christmas.'

My heart warmed to know that she so readily accepted me as part of the family. 'I'll do my best.'

Finishing her tea, she stood. 'Chloe, Gabriel, I'm going now. Be good, won't you?'

'I'm always good,' Gabriel declared as he ran back to her, a cheeky grin on his face that made his grandmother smile with affection.

She swooped him up and hugged him, and then did the same with Chloe. We followed her out to the car.

'Have fun,' she said as she climbed in. 'It will be good practice for when you have your own!'

The children waved until the car was out of sight, then shot back indoors to continue exploring.

'I like this photo,' Chloe said, dragging one of her and Gabriel from a wooden shelf.

Gabriel picked up one of his grandparents, then looked back at the shelves, his brown eyes serious. 'Why don't you have a picture of *Maman* and *Papa*?'

I winced, but Alain's hesitation was barely noticeable.

'I haven't got a good one of them yet,' he said smoothly. 'Maybe if we get some at the wedding, I can choose one and add it to the shelf.'

Gabriel nodded, satisfied, and picked up a little wooden box. 'What's this? Is it a treasure chest?'

'Only if you put treasure in it. Have you got any?' Gently steering them away from what could turn into twenty questions over every single object he possessed, Alain said, 'I have a treat for you outside, but it's only to borrow for this afternoon. Do you want to see?'

They followed him excitedly through the kitchen and out to the back garden, where Gloria lay sprawled where we'd left her.

'It's a dog! Is it your dog? What kind of a dog is it? What's it called? Can we play with it?'

Their clamour of questions made Alain smile, but he crouched down and patiently answered them all, showing them how to pet her without being *too* enthusiastic. Gloria took this sudden awakening from her afternoon nap in good part and washed the children's arms, much to their delight.

'Her owner, Rupert, asked us to take her for a walk,' Alain told them, and they cheered.

We set off along the streets, with Alain holding the dog tight at heel and me holding the children's hands.

'Are you glad you've broken up for the holidays?' I asked Gabriel.

'Yes, but I like school,' he said. 'We'll have a different teacher when I go back, though, and I don't know if I'll like her yet.'

'What do you like best about school?'

'Playtimes,' he answered immediately. 'And painting and drawing. Maths is okay. But I don't like reading. It's too hard. I don't know all the words.'

I squeezed his hand. 'Don't worry. It'll get easier as you get older, I promise.'

'I can't read yet,' Chloe chipped in. 'But I'm starting school soon, and then I'll be able to. I like stories. I like it when Mummy and Daddy read to me at bedtime.'

'What kind of stories do you like?'

She frowned in concentration. 'I like stories about animals best. Sometimes fairies and princesses.'

'Too girly,' Gabriel muttered.

'But I *am* a girl,' Chloe pointed out logically. 'And I like princess dresses. My dress for your wedding is like a princess dress.'

I smiled. 'Really?'

'Yes. All white and …' Her face screwed up as she sought the word she wanted. 'Fluffy.'

Alain and I exchanged a bemused look. Visions of a bunny rabbit costume sprung to mind.

'Do you mean lacy?' I suggested.

'Yes. And bouncy.'

Uh-huh. Well, Sabine was *Parisienne* by birth, so we could only trust to her taste.

'What will I have to do?' Chloe asked. 'On your wedding day?'

'All you have to do is carry a basket of flowers and look pretty. I'm *sure* you can manage that.' I turned to Gabriel. 'What's your outfit like?'

'Okay. Except I have to wear a tie.'

Alain tousled Gabriel's hair. 'Better get used to it, kiddo.'

'But Mum says it'll be *purple*.'

Alain cracked up laughing, but when Gabriel glared at him, he changed the subject back to safer ground. 'What kind of stories do *you* like, Gabriel?'

'I like it when people go on adventures.'

'Well then, here's an adventure for you,' Alain said as we reached a safe track. 'You two can take it in turns to hold Gloria's lead, if you like.'

'Yeah!'

The children loved it. It made them feel important, and they thought it was funny, being taken for a walk by the dog – because, as ever, Gloria set the pace.

Once we were on a path where she couldn't stray onto farmland, Alain let her off the lead so she could run ahead, the children displaying remarkable speed in their endeavours to keep up with her, but not quite managing it.

When Chloe lagged too far behind, Alain lifted her onto his tall shoulders, where she squealed happily, pointing out all the things she could see from her new vantage point.

'Don't go too far, Gabriel!' Alain shouted. 'If you turn round and can't see us, that means we can't see you.'

Gabriel half-turned his head, acknowledged the instruction … and promptly ignored it, racing around the next bend.

Alain shook his head. 'Boys.'

'Will he be okay?' I asked anxiously.

'He can only go straight on. Of course he will.'

He'd spoken too soon. We reached the bend in time to see Gabriel, well ahead and not watching his feet, go flying over a tree root and crash into a vegetation-filled ditch alongside the path. He let out a loud wail.

Since Alain was hampered by Chloe, I raced ahead.

Gabriel had landed in a huge clump of nettles, and by thrashing around, he was making it worse.

'Gabriel, lie still.'

He immediately did as he was told, looking up at me with tear-filled eyes, awaiting instruction.

Alain caught up with us, lowered Chloe to the ground and, without a thought, stepped into the nettles to gently lift the boy out and pass him to me.

I winced. They were both in shorts.

Gabriel hiccupped away his tears, and I realised it was only the shock that had caused them. Once those nettles did their work, there were going to be plenty more.

'We need to go back,' Alain told the children calmly, shooting me a worried look. 'Gloria's tired now.'

The dog pranced ahead of us, belying his words, as the consequences of Gabriel's choice of landing material made itself known.

'Ow! My arm stings. My legs hurt. Owwwww!'

His poor limbs were coming out in angry red and white blotches. Alain's legs were the same.

I hunted around for dock leaves, plucked a handful, handed some to Alain, then knelt in front of Gabriel to gently rub them over his rashes. Gloria had her own remedy in mind – slathering her tongue across his legs – but I pushed her away.

'It still hurts,' Gabriel mumbled, eyeing the dock leaves dubiously.

'Well, we have something at Uncle Alain's house that will make it better, but you have to be brave and walk back with us, okay?'

Alain lifted Chloe back onto his shoulders, while I held the dog's lead in one hand and Gabriel's hand in the other. As we marched back, we sang songs to take their minds off the nasty weals on Gabriel's legs, and the children gamely joined in.

Back at Alain's, as he opened his door he whispered, 'What remedy did you have in mind? I don't have any calamine lotion. I'll have to go into town to the *pharmacie*.'

'Do you have baking soda?'

'Maybe. Probably out of date, though.'

'That doesn't matter. We're applying it, not eating it. I'll wash him down while you look up the recipe on the internet.'

We tied the dog up in the back garden, then I took Gabriel upstairs and cooled his livid legs and arms with a cold flannel, while Alain mixed his potion downstairs. Gabriel wrinkled his nose up at the paste but didn't complain when Alain applied it, while Chloe watched proceedings.

They both found it hilarious when Alain pasted it over his own legs, too, where it got stuck in all the hairs and looked a complete mess. Alain smeared it around far more than necessary, purely for the kids' amusement, I was sure.

Back downstairs, we seated Gabriel on a large bath towel spread over the sofa – suddenly, cream upholstery didn't seem such a good idea – and distracted him with television and lemonade, Chloe at his side.

Catching Alain in the kitchen, I kissed him. 'I need to drive the dog back to Rupert. He'll be wondering where we are.'

By the time I got back to Alain's, Gabriel had cheered up considerably, so when I said I'd put together something to eat, Alain took them outside to play and work off any energy they might have left.

Treating myself to a sneaky glass of wine as I worked in the sage-green and blue tiled kitchen, I watched them through the kitchen window.

The kids' energy was boundless, but Alain kept up with them, giving piggy backs around the hydrangeas and kicking a ball around. All strategy, I was sure – to wear them out before bedtime, to take Gabriel's mind off his nettle rash, and to ensure that neither of them had any lingering fear of the outdoors. The children tumbled over the grass, laughing as Alain showed them how to roll down the gentle slope of the lawn, gathering momentum until they reached the bottom in a sprawl of arms and legs.

I wasn't sure who was having a better time, them or him.

SEVEN

When Alain brought the children back inside and poured us both a glass of wine, I didn't dare confess that I'd already helped myself.

'You're definitely tied up at *La Cour des Roses* tomorrow?' he asked.

'Yeah. We have guests leaving and new arrivals due, I need to catch up with my own business, I have my dress fitting, *and* we have a guest meal. Sorry.' I sipped my wine. 'What are you planning to do?'

He hesitated. 'I promised the kids I'd take them to the zoo.'

I stared at him. 'Without me?'

I loved that place, ever since he'd taken me there when I was first getting to know him. It was where we'd shared our first kiss, and I could still remember every detail.

He winced. 'Sorry, but it's the easiest thing for me to do on my own with them. We'll do it again all together some other time, I promise.'

Damping down disappointment, I said, 'I'll hold you to that, Alain Granger. Give my love to the gibbons.'

That extra glass of wine meant I spent the evening rather tipsy, and it was hard to say whether the warm glow I got from watching Alain engage with the children at supper and supervise their baths came from alcohol or emotion.

Alain was kind but firm; fun but drew a line when things got too giddy. When they were clean (unlike the sopping bathroom) and in nightclothes, they snuggled up to him on the sofa, Chloe insisting I sit beside her so she could hold my hand. Both heads flopped on Alain's chest, sleepy as they listened to the book he read in French, Chloe's little fingers pointing at her favourite pictures.

The idea that Alain would make a wonderful father entered my lightly intoxicated brain and wouldn't leave. We'd spoken about starting a family sometime, but in vague terms. With such a swift engagement, both of us had perhaps been tentative about making solid plans so soon.

But the feeling I got now, watching him with Gabriel and Chloe, was so strong, it took my breath away. Maybe it was time to discuss it more seriously.

Alain led the half-asleep children up to the twin beds in his spare room. By the time he came back down, I was half-asleep myself, lost in a dream world of maternal brooding.

'Move over, sleepyhead.' He lifted my feet, eased himself onto the sofa and put them back across his lap. 'What are you dreaming about?'

I gathered my courage. 'I was thinking what a great father you'll be.'

'You were?' A smile spread across his face. 'Really?'

'Really. You're great with those two.'

He gave a modest shrug. 'It's easy for a couple of days. What it'd be like twenty-four seven …'

I snuggled closer. 'Would you like to find out?'

'Are you propositioning me?' he joked, then gave me a long, considered look. 'Are you saying *you'd* like to find out?'

'Yes.' I took a deep breath. 'I know we haven't discussed it much, what with the wedding and everything, but maybe it's time we did.'

He bent his head to touch his lips to mine. 'I didn't want to pressure you into anything. I felt like I'd already rushed you into getting married.' His thumb played with my engagement ring. 'You're still building up your business. Busy at Rupert's.'

'That's all true. But?'

'You're only thirty-two, Emmy, but I'm thirty-seven now. Call it vanity, but I'd like to become a dad before I go grey.'

I gave him a wicked smile and stroked one of the *very* few silvering strands in his brown hair. 'Too late. And?'

He kissed me again. 'You and I are so right together. I can't think of anything I'd like more than to have children with you. So why wait?' When my eyes widened, he laughed. 'I don't mean now, this minute. We have a wedding and a honeymoon to get through. You need to move into this place. But I do mean in the near future.' He stroked my cheek. 'What do you think?'

With the serious turn the conversation had taken, suddenly I was stone-cold sober. And I was pleased to note that it didn't make a blind bit of difference to how I felt.

'I think we should get started soon,' I agreed.

His smile and the love in his eyes were the only reply I got, but they told me everything I needed to know.

After a few moments, I elbowed him in the ribs and eyed him quizzically.

'What was that for?'

'I've been waiting for some cheesy chat-up line about how we'd better start practising.'

His lips twitched. 'Do you *need* a chat-up line? I assumed that extra glass of wine you snuck before supper would do the trick.'

My mouth opened in a caught-out 'oh', making him laugh. And then his mouth was on mine, making it clear that no further verbal persuasion would be forthcoming.

'What about the children?' I gasped when I came up for air. 'Maybe we shouldn't.'

That made him pause. 'I'll check they're fast asleep. We'll have to stay under the sheets. We'll have to stop if we hear anything. And you can't make any noise whatsoever.'

My face must have been a picture.

'Emmy, if we do start a family, we can't not have sex for the next eighteen years. And you heard what Mum said – that it would be good practice for when we have our own.'

'Oh, well, if your *mother* gave us permission …'

The following day was a long one, made worse by the knowledge that Alain was taking Gabriel and Chloe to the zoo without me.

At least my dress fitting went well. No alterations would be needed, and the ladies were ecstatic as they put the whole ensemble together. As I gazed in the mirror, I was pretty ecstatic myself, and I texted my mother to tell her so.

Driving back to *La Cour des Roses*, I couldn't stop smiling. I had absolutely chosen the right dress. And the four-year-old little girl within me could connect with Chloe's sentiments – for one day, I would look and feel like a princess.

I worked like a whirlwind until, mid-afternoon, Rupert forcibly sat me down at the kitchen table and brought me a glass of iced tea.

'Emmy. Slow down. You're doing too much.'

'But we already lost some of the weekend to my parents, and I wasn't here yesterday afternoon, and tomorrow I want to …'

'I know. You want to spend time with the kids. I'd sympathise if you worked for some corporate dickhead who'd demote you with a single look. But you work for a kindly if occasionally grumpy boss who has more than a sneaking suspicion that you put in a darned sight more hours than he pays you for. As long as the paperwork's up-to-date and the guest rooms are ready for new arrivals, he'll be satisfied. Understood?'

I took a long drink to cool my parched throat and brushed stray hair from my eyes. 'Yeah. Understood.'

'Take a leaf out of Ryan's book.' He waved a hand towards the patio doors. Ryan was on his knees in the shade, tugging at weeds. 'He works hard, but he paces himself. He stops for regular refreshments. He plans his work, so he's in the shade when it's too hot. Why don't you do the same? Go to the den where it's cooler. Get some work done on your own business. I don't want you letting your own affairs get behind.'

I had to admit the idea appealed. With its leather-topped desk and captain's chair, the leather two-seater sofa and its bookshelves piled high, 'den' was an appropriate word. I liked working in my own room at the upholstered chaise longue by the window, too, but it would be too warm there right now.

Rupert's mobile rang and he glanced at the screen with a sigh. 'Back in a mo.'

He scuttled off to his rooms, while I allowed myself three minutes with my cool drink.

'Gloria,' he explained when he came back, kneading his temples. His ex-wife's verbal reaching out across the Channel always left him in need of headache medication.

I fetched him water and painkillers. 'What did she want this time?'

'More money, preferably. And less lawyer time, because it's racking up quite a bill and digging into her spoils.'

'What does she imagine you can do about that?'

'Duh, Emmy. Give her exactly what she wants without going through the solicitors, *obviously*.'

'Yeah, right.' I stared at him in panic. 'You won't, will you?'

'Not a matter of won't. More a matter of can't. My solicitor needs an extension on his mother-in-law's bungalow, and apparently my fees are paying for it.'

I *knew* I should have thumped Rupert for telling Jonathan that our guests needed livening up a bit.

New arrival Greg was certainly going to do that. An overly jovial sort, he laughed at … well, at everything. As I drove to

Alain's the next day for our afternoon outing with the children, I winced as I remembered the way Greg's raucous laughter had arrived in the kitchen for dinner before he did. And Greg didn't half pack it away. Last night was the first night in a long time that Rupert had had to raid his wine rack for an extra bottle. And the more Greg had, the more hilarious he found everything. We were going to have to keep an eye on him, that was for sure.

When I arrived at Alain's, Gabriel and Chloe had been wound into an excited frenzy, due to Alain keeping our destination a secret.

As he drove, the children clamoured to tell me about their day at the zoo.

'I liked the monkeys best,' Chloe announced decisively.

'I liked the lions best,' Gabriel said. 'The boy lion roared *really* loudly while we were watching.'

I could have told him that it was outside the lions' enclosure that his uncle had first kissed me, but I didn't think I should. *Oh, what the heck.*

'Shall I tell you a secret about the lions, Gabriel?'

'Yeah. What?'

'It was near there that Uncle Alain first kissed me.'

Alain snorted with surprised laughter, while I got a resounding 'Eeugh!' from Gabriel and an immediately copied one from Chloe.

'Good job we didn't take Aunt Emmy to the zoo with us yesterday, kids, eh?' Alain said. 'I might have had to do it all over again!'

With the children giggling, Alain parked up, and I recognised where we were. He'd brought me here a few months ago – a village of cave dwellings open to tourists.

'Good choice,' I murmured. 'It'll be quite a novelty for the children.'

That proved to be right on the button. Chloe and Gabriel gaped in awe as we began to explore, Alain explaining to them that the underground dwellings had been hewn from sandstone to shelter the people and their animals, while they farmed the land above.

As we walked around the place, brushing past ivy clambering down over the stone walls from above, rubbing our arms because of the chill away from the sun, Alain pitched his spiel just right, not complicating it with too many facts and figures. Simply to know that this place had been here for hundreds of years, that people had lived and worked here, some until just over a hundred years ago, was enough to get the children's imaginations going.

The tools, furniture and photos of the last inhabitants helped those imaginations along as we wandered through barns, wine cellars (it was France, after all), bedrooms and living rooms with their ovens and fireplaces.

'But what did they *do* here?' Gabriel asked as we looked into a sparsely furnished room.

'They had a hard working day,' Alain explained. 'At the end of it, they would be grateful to just eat and sleep.'

Gabriel nodded, but it was obvious that the concept of an evening without television and other distractions was quite beyond him.

'Do you do other things after school, like a sport?' I asked him.

'I play football on Saturdays. I got *really* muddy once.' He gestured from head to toe. 'Mum wouldn't let me in the house until Dad used the hose to get all the mud off me.'

Alain laughed. 'Was it a warm day, at least?'

'No, it was *freezing*!' Gabriel shivered with the memory.

'I do ballet,' Chloe piped up, performing a pirouette to illustrate. 'But when we do shows, we have to tie our hair in a bun, and mine won't.' She pulled at her corkscrew curls. 'Mummy says it's the knot fairy's fault.'

'The knot fairy?'

Chloe looked astonished at my ignorance. 'Of course! She comes in the night and puts knots in my hair and Mummy can't get them out in the morning and it hurts when she brushes it. Doesn't she come to you in the night?'

I tugged at my straight hair. 'Maybe she only comes to girls with curls.'

Chloe giggled at the accidental rhyme. 'Do you think they had knot fairies here, hundreds of tears ago?'

'I should imagine the knot fairies were much naughtier back then,' I assured her. *Along with the lice fairies and goodness knew what else, probably.*

After we'd inspected the village hall and the chapel with its arches, we called it a day and headed for home, the children chattering away in the car about what they'd seen and planning a game of pretending-to-live-in-caves for a rainy day.

Back at Alain's, I shoved pizza in the oven, then sat on the floor with Chloe to help with a wooden farm jigsaw she'd brought. Each animal had to be correctly named, and we had fun making all the different noises.

'Did you know there are chickens at *La Cour des Roses*, where I live?' I asked her when we'd finished clucking.

'How many?'

I held up the correct number of fingers. 'Six.'

'Can I see them?'

'You'll be staying at *La Cour des Roses* with your mum and dad for the wedding, so I'll show you them then. How's that?'

'Great! Do they lay eggs?'

'Yes. That's why my friend Rupert keeps them. He cooks the eggs for the guests who come to stay.' I leaned in close and whispered, 'But I'm not allowed to cook them, because I make a horrible mess and they taste like yellow rubber.'

Chloe wrinkled her nose, rolled over onto her back and giggled. It was too much of a temptation for Alain. From where he was sitting on the sofa, he reached out a foot and began to tickle her with his toes until she squealed and Gabriel threw himself on his back for the same treatment.

After pizza, I suggested hot chocolate in the animal mugs Alain had bought them at the zoo, and we curled up on the sofa while he read stories. They were soon sleepy little bunnies that made my heart melt.

It melted even more when Gabriel murmured, 'Thanks for the hot chocolate, Aunt Emmy. You make it yummier than Uncle Alain.'

'Yeah, thanks, Aunt Emmy,' Chloe echoed.

That was the first time they'd called me that. Perhaps the time I'd spent with them this past couple of days and the impending wedding meant they saw me as a permanent fixture now. That was a nice thought.

We carried them to bed and tucked them in.

'Can you tell us a story, Aunt Emmy?' Gabriel asked as he snuggled under his duvet.

'Yes, tell us a story, Aunt Emmy,' Chloe echoed.

Alain grinned. 'I'll leave you to it, Aunt Emmy.' He went downstairs.

'Er. What kind of story?' This wasn't something I'd done since I told my little brother stories when we were young.

'Something about animals,' Chloe suggested. 'Farm animals. Like in my jigsaw.'

I dredged my memory banks. 'How about a story about three little pigs? Will that do?'

'Yay!'

It was surprising how quickly it came back to me, although I sanitised it as best I could: none of the pigs got eaten like they had in the version I used to own, although there seemed no option but to give the wolf the sticky end he deserved.

They loved it, but by the time we'd done all the sound effects of the pigs building and the wolf huffing and puffing, it had made them more excitable than sleepy. Apparently, I still had a lot to learn about small children.

'How many sleeps till your wedding?' Gabriel asked as I tucked them in.

I had to think about that one. 'Er. Including tonight? Twenty-two.' *Crumbs.*

'Are you excited? Like waiting for Christmas?'

I smiled. 'Yes, I am.'

'Me too. 'Night.'

''Night.'

I kissed them both and went downstairs to curl up on the sofa with their uncle and listen to music.

'Only twenty-two sleeps till the wedding,' I informed him.

Alain rolled his eyes. 'Your mother's not started a countdown by the night, now, has she?'

'Not Mum. Gabriel.'

'Oh. That's sweet.'

'Yeah.' My eyes drooped as the slow jazz washed over me. Hmm. Maybe I should have tried the jazz on the kids.

'Do you think they're asleep yet?' Alain asked after a while.

'I'll go check.'

He chuckled. 'Any excuse to look in on them.'

'Yeah. But they're sweet kids.'

'That they are.'

I crept upstairs and peeped into their room. Chloe was curled up in a foetal position, her curls flopped across her face, fast asleep. Gabriel hadn't quite gone, but he was on the way.

'Aunt Emmy?'

My heart skipped a beat at my new moniker. 'Yes?'

But he was too sleepy to think of anything to say. ''Night.'

''Night, Gabriel.'

'Chloe's asleep. Gabriel almost,' I told Alain downstairs, leaning in for a kiss.

He pulled me across his lap to deepen it. We were getting into it, like a couple of teenagers necking on babysitting duty, but then he pulled back.

'Actually, can we do this in bed? I'm knackered.'

'Awww.' I laughed and led him upstairs. 'Does that mean that once we have our own kids, you're going to be tired all the time?'

'Not too tired for this.' He pulled me close. 'Never too tired for this.'

EIGHT

The drive to Alain's parents wasn't too onerous, although his little hatchback was more suited to zipping around town than travelling with a 'family' of four. But the kids happily squashed into the back, listening to the CDs that Mireille had lent us and laughing at my deliberately rubbish attempts to sing along to the French songs, allowing Alain to concentrate on the drive.

Alain's parents' house in the suburbs was large, surrounded by lawn and rockeries. Christopher had done well for himself in the engineering industry and was still adjusting to retirement. I wondered if they would think about downsizing soon, but I supposed they needed enough rooms to accommodate family coming to stay.

Adrien opened the door and the children threw themselves at him, jabbering about lions and caves and nettles.

'Sounds like you've had quite a time of it.' Adrien raised an eyebrow at Alain, his brown eyes matching the colour of his brother's. The main difference between them was height – Alain was a good six inches taller. 'Come on in.'

I'd thought maybe I imagined the reserve between the two brothers at Christmas – but if you looked for it hard enough, it was still there now, in the slight stiffness of their movements and speech. No doubt it had lessened over the years and would continue to do so.

We went into the lounge, where Chloe and Gabriel clamoured for their mother's attention. Sabine, tall and slim in skinny jeans and a cotton shirt, her short brunette hair the epitome of French chic, hugged them close.

'I got a nettle rash,' Gabriel told her proudly.

'Oh, my poor boy. Did it hurt?'

'It hurt *this* much!' Gabriel stretched her arms wide, making everyone laugh. 'But Uncle Alain put some white gooey stuff on and made it better.'

'Clever Uncle Alain.'

'And we walked a dog.' Chloe tugged at her mother's sleeve. 'A big, black dog. And we went in some caves where people used to *live.*'

Sabine raised an eyebrow at her ex-husband. 'You did have an exciting time!'

'We had a great time,' Alain said, smiling.

Christopher came through from the lounge, tall and trim like his sons, his grey hair thinning. He greeted the children with a broad smile and hugs. 'Mireille says lunch is ready, if you'd like to come through.'

The kids raced into the kitchen, leaving the adults to follow at a more sedate pace.

Mireille had set everything out on the large table on the patio, a selection of anything and everything for us to help ourselves – with a little guidance towards sensible choices for Gabriel and Chloe.

Christopher poured wine and we relaxed in the shade from the overhead pergola, twined with vines and honeysuckle. Mmmm. There was no doubt the French knew how to enjoy a leisurely lunch. Fresh air, a glorious garden, great food, a glass of wine, good company. Couldn't beat it.

While Gabriel and Chloe vied to tell everyone about their adventures, Sabine watched them indulgently, but she looked tired, the lines at her eyes noticeable against her tan, her mouth slightly downturned.

'Did you and Adrien have a good week away together?' I asked her.

'Er. Yes, thank you.'

'Whereabouts did you go?'

'We drove to the coast – St-Malo, Dinan, that area. A little sea air, a couple of nice hotels.'

'Must've been great to get away, just the two of you. Spend some proper time together.'

Another hesitation. 'Yes. We needed to. And it was good of you both to help with the children.'

'No problem. We had fun. It was a chance for me to get to know them better.' I turned to Mireille. 'How was your meet-up with your friends in Honfleur?'

Mireille beamed. 'Lovely. We haven't seen them for a few years, so it was nice to catch up. Have you ever been to Honfleur, Emmy?'

'No.'

'You must take her, Alain. Shops, galleries, cafés, seafood at the restaurants in the harbour. What's not to love?'

'Er. The prices?' Christopher muttered, making everyone laugh.

I absorbed the good-natured laughter and the children chattering with a happy smile. In-laws could be a nightmare, but I'd landed on my feet with this family.

As we drove home, I was tired, but in a good way. I'd had a lovely time with the children, enjoyed lunch with the family – and I'd thoroughly enjoyed the few days' respite from wedding arrangements. Apart from the brief mention of it by the children and my dress fitting, the subject hadn't come up. My mother had managed four whole days without an e-mail or text, and Alain's family had only brushed over the topic at lunch.

I wasn't complaining.

'So, Emie, how did it go with Alain's niece and nephew?' Madame Dupont asked the next day over our habitual *thé au citron* break in our favourite quiet spot at the back of the *gîtes*, next to floppy yellow roses climbing up the trellis and wafting their scent our way.

'It was tiring, but we had a good time.' I struggled to find the vocabulary I needed for nettles and rashes, but she got the gist.

'You loved being with them, didn't you?'

'Yes, I did. They're sweet children.'

'What about you and Alain?' She fixed me with a knowing look. 'Are you thinking about a family?'

'We've talked about it.'

Madame Dupont patted my hand. 'Then I hope it will happen for you.'

I changed the subject. 'How are the chickens? Any escaped lately?'

'No. But they are a pain.' When I gave her a quizzical look, she explained, 'I started with them when I was younger and not so tired. It seemed a good idea when the children were small. But they grew and we had grandchildren, so the number of chickens grew to feed everyone …'

I frowned. Madame Dupont rarely complained of tiredness. 'Couldn't you cut down the size of the flock?'

'Maybe.' She smiled at my worried expression. 'Do not worry about me, Emie. I am getting older, that is all. I am bound to be tired sometimes.' She sighed. 'That cottage seems so far from everything, nowadays. I am fine walking to *La Cour des Roses*, but it is difficult walking to the main road for the bus to town, and carrying my shopping back.'

'You should have said, Madame Dupont. I can help.'

'I don't like to ask for favours. I am only saying that you cannot expect not to be tired at my age. I am seventy-three, you know.'

I bet nobody knew that but me. Madame Dupont's age had always been a source of speculation – and admiration, due to her capacity for hard work.

'You're in good condition for seventy-three, Madame Dupont.'

'Yes, I am lucky.'

'Even so, you *must* tell me if you need a lift somewhere. Promise me?'

'I promise.'

But I knew she was too proud and stubborn to do it.

I was looking forward to the arrival of the Hendersons about as much as I would a visit to the dentist for root canal treatment.

They always insisted on the room with the best view over the garden, and I'd already checked it for wayward specks of dust, miniscule dead flies on the window sill and fingerprints on the mirrors. An antique glass vase of cut flowers on the polished dark wood dressing table, scented drawer liners, a bunch of fresh lavender hanging from the wardrobe rail – a trick I'd learned from Madame Dupont – and that was me done.

When their shiny black saloon rolled into the courtyard soon after I'd taken Madame Dupont home, Rupert and I plastered smiles on our faces and went out to receive them, like a royal visit.

Mr Henderson got out and stretched his arms, his blazer opening to reveal a slight paunch I didn't remember him having last year. As he crossed the gravel, I noticed a light stubble at his chin that he hadn't sported before, either.

'Hunter! Good to see you.' He shook hands with Rupert. 'And Emmy. I noticed on the website that you'd been promoted from guest lackey to manageress. Well done, you.'

He held his arms out wide, offering me no alternative but to go in for what I assumed would be a continental kiss-on-each-cheek thing but turned out to be more of an alarming hug. And I can tell you now, I didn't like his technique. Not only was his aftershave unpleasantly overpowering, but as his arms came around me, they lightly brushed the sides of my breasts before reaching around my back.

He pulled away as though nothing had happened, while I tried to work out whether it was my imagination, an unfortunate coincidence or a deliberate grope. Hmmm.

Rupert looked past him to the car. 'And Mrs Henderson?' he asked politely, although it was obvious by now that the passenger seat was devoid of a snobby woman in a linen trouser suit.

Mr Henderson followed his glance as though he, too, needed to check the car was empty. 'Not this year, Hunter. Came on my own.'

Rupert was quick to banish a puzzled frown. 'Oh? Well, how about a cup of tea? I'll fetch your bags.'

He went down to the car, leaving me to put the kettle on, and when he'd deposited our arrival's bags upstairs, he suggested tea be taken outside. Off they both went, leaving me to load up a tray with Rupert's heavenly crumbly shortbread and the brand of tea preferred by the Hendersons.

Carrying it out, I almost dropped the lot when I overheard the direction the conversation was taking.

'I must say, Hunter, you've done alright for yourself since that wife of yours ran off. As if Gloria wasn't young enough! But now you've gone and got yourself an even younger model, you old dog. Must tell me your secret. And the ring's a nice touch. Keep 'em sweet, eh?'

'I – er – hmmph.' Rupert struggled to compose himself, but when he saw me coming through the patio doors with a thunderous expression on my face, he straightened his shoulders pretty smart-ish. 'Oh no, Henderson, you're under a misapprehension. Emmy and I are not … I mean, she …'

I thumped the tray down on the table, rattling every piece of china on it. 'Rupert and I are not a couple.'

'Oh, I'm sorry,' Mr Henderson blustered. 'What with Gloria running off with your boyfriend, I assumed you two had got together.'

'Assumption can be a dangerous thing.' I shot him a brittle smile, but the calm on the surface did not match the livid panic underneath. There were nearly thirty years between Rupert and me. We'd worded the website very clearly. We referred to 'my room' and 'his quarters' in front of the guests. And yet how many of them jumped to the same conclusion as Mr Henderson? Don't get me wrong, it wasn't that this hadn't occurred to me before – but it *was* the first time someone had openly referred to it as a done deal, and I was *not* a happy bunny.

'My apologies, Emmy.'

'Apology accepted.' I poured him some tea.

'Any chance of a brandy to pep this up, Hunter?' he asked. 'Been a fraught drive.'

As 'Hunter' rose obediently to his feet, I wondered if we had any arsenic hidden away at the back of a cupboard to 'pep up' his tea instead.

Mr Henderson jolted me out of my fantasy. 'So, Emmy. That ring.' He gestured at my hand. 'Is that what I think it is?'

What? A pink hippo? A dead leaf? 'If what you think it is, is an engagement ring, Mr Henderson, you would be correct.'

'And may I ask who the lucky gentleman is?'

'You may. The local accountant.'

'Congratulations!' He rose to his feet to give me another hug – and used the same technique. No accident, then.

I quickly sat down, so there could be no more of it.

'Tell me all about your fiancé,' he said, as if nothing had happened.

I caught his eye and held it firm. I'd like to catch his balls and hold *them* firm – perhaps with a sharp twist.

'He's tall,' I told him. 'Maybe six-four. Very fit – he runs and cycles. He's not prone to violence, but he is loyal and defensive over his loved ones.'

Mr Henderson's Adam's apple bobbed in his throat. 'Sounds like a fine chap.'

'Indeed.'

Rupert rescued me from further desire to commit violence on his guest by appearing with the brandy. It was three in the afternoon, for God's sake. As Henderson sloshed some into his tea cup, I almost laughed at Rupert's expression. That was his best brandy.

I was concocting a decent excuse to take myself off – although it didn't have to be decent; any would do – but Rupert caught my eye, and the message was clear. *Desert me and you're fired.*

I looked pointedly at my watch. I would give him ten minutes.

'So, where is the lovely Mrs Henderson this year?' Rupert asked when the first cup of tea was downed and the next was being concocted. Since his guest had shown so little tact over our relationship, he'd obviously decided he didn't deserve any in return.

Mr Henderson sipped, shuddering as the brandy hit the spot. 'Gone, Hunter. Upped and left. Last week.'

We both did our best to hide our surprise, and our murmurs of sympathy were genuine. Having gone through the same thing last year, neither of us would wish it on anyone, not even Mr Henderson.

'I'm *so* sorry,' Rupert said kindly.

'So you bloody well should be, since it's your fault.'

Rupert balked. '*My* fault? In what way?'

'Not your fault directly, I suppose. More the fault of that flighty wife of yours.'

'*Gloria?*'

'It gave Anita ideas when Gloria shot off with Emmy's fella last year, if you ask me. Hasn't been the same since. Odd. Furtive. Awkward. The closer it got to coming away, the odder she got. She's usually so meticulous with holiday planning – new dresses for Paris, cancelling the papers, having the car valeted. This year? Nothing.'

He took another large gulp of 'tea' while Rupert and I sat frozen to our seats, agog.

'When I told her it was time to start packing, do you know what she said? She said, "It certainly is, Gavin," and proceeded to pack every last thing in the house. And off she flounced. See? Just like your Gloria.'

Rupert and I exchanged a look. It could only be like Gloria if she …

'Got herself another bloke,' Mr Henderson confirmed with a sniff. 'Builder chappie. I *thought* he made a meal out of that sodding extension. Turns out he was making a meal out of more than that! Ruddy disgrace. Tried to stop the cheque, but it'd already cleared. Bastard bank.'

I consciously closed my mouth before he could catch me gaping, and shot Rupert a look to do the same.

'I'm sorry to hear that, Henderson,' Rupert said politely.

'Oh, please. Call me Gavin. We're both in the same boat now, old chap, aren't we? Might as well be on first name terms, eh? Rupert, isn't it?'

I turned laughter at Rupert's expression into a cough, and when my phone beeped, I stood. 'If you two will excuse me …'

It was a text from Kate, asking for a quick online chat.

It would have to be quick – I had a guest meal to deal with – but I would always make time for the one friend whose common sense had anchored my ever-shifting world since we were at primary school.

'Hi, Kate. Do you have any sanity to spare?'

'Hardly. I've just got back from your mother's.'

'That's enough to unhinge anyone. Why did you go there?'

'She's been haranguing me on a daily basis about the dress. I decided it would be easier to go round there and show her what I got.'

'You *found* one?' I squealed, my relief just about outweighing annoyance at the idea that my mother had put my best friend under so much pressure.

Kate clapped her hands over her ears. 'Yes. There's no need to deafen me.'

'There's every need. Show me!'

She unzipped her baggy hoodie and stepped back from her laptop.

I clapped my hands in delight. 'Oh, Kate. It's beautiful. *You're* beautiful.'

The dress was the perfect shade, somewhere between Sophie's lilac and Ellie's midnight purple, and it was mid-length, with soft folds of fabric draping over Kate's bust and the rest clinging ever so slightly to her lovely waist and hips.

'I don't know about beautiful. But it fits, and I'm not going to fall out of it and give your relatives an eyeful.'

'Where did you find it?'

'I tried it on a while ago and liked it, but the size that fit my bust looked huge everywhere else. I was desperate, so I went back. The sales assistant said she had a friend who could alter it. She left the top half as it was and took in the rest, and *voilà*. Even your mother couldn't find fault with it.'

'Bonus points all round, then, I'd say. Can you send me a photo? I need it for the florist.'

After a quick catch-up, followed by a private sigh of relief – with three weeks to go, Kate *had* been cutting it fine – I went through to find Rupert.

He was mercifully free of Gavin, who must be unpacking, but our other new arrivals had just driven up.

Grace and Peter had told us they would be on their honeymoon, so we were fazed to see that they were perhaps in their early seventies. I'm not at all ageist, but if someone says they're on their honeymoon, you do tend to expect a younger couple.

They were a wonderful antidote to anything and everything. Charmed by their drive through the Loire countryside, they enthused about *La Cour des Roses*, their room (with extra flowers and champagne) and the garden, then gratefully accepted the tea and homemade almond cookies that Rupert proffered, settling on the patio, Grace's shiny new wedding ring glinting in the sunshine – although I noticed she had a duller gold band on a chain around her neck.

I glanced at my watch, but if Rupert felt we had time for a quick cup of tea with them, I would sit back and enjoy the unexpected break.

'So. You're on your honeymoon? Congratulations!'

Grace smiled. 'Thank you. We got married a couple of days ago. Registry office, nothing fancy. A few family and friends.'

'I hope you have a lovely honeymoon here,' Rupert said. 'We love to share in people's special occasions. Where did you two meet?'

'At school.' When Rupert looked puzzled, Grace explained, 'We dated for a year or so when we were fifteen. In those days, it was known as courting, I suppose. But then life got in the way. My family moved to the next town, the bus was a pain, and it fizzled out. I eventually married a boy from my new town. He died a couple of years ago.'

Peter took up the tale, 'And I gave up on Grace and got married, too. My wife died three years ago. Then, last year, I was with friends in a café and saw Grace. I knew her immediately. How could I not?' He took her hand. 'I went over to say hello, and it was like the years dropped away and we were fifteen again.'

'We've both had good lives, good marriages. I still miss Roland.' Grace fingered the ring at her neck. 'And Peter still misses Marjorie. But we have a good few years in us, we hope, so we decided to enjoy it while we could.'

'Quite right,' Rupert asserted, smiling. 'I hope you'll both be very happy.'

'Thank you.'

I followed Rupert into the kitchen to start on the guest meal.

'What a lovely couple,' he commented. 'We'd better live up to being the perfect idyll for them, hadn't we?'

'They like it here so far. If they enjoy the food and get on with the other guests, I reckon we'll have done the trick.'

We stared at each other in dismay as we thought about Gavin Henderson *and* remembered we still had our one-man laughter factory in the form of Greg to contend with.

'What are we going to do about Greg?' I hissed.

Rupert ignored me, opening a couple of bottles of red wine to breathe. To my amazement, he proceeded to pour a third of one of them into a carafe, which he set on one side, and top the bottle up with water.

'Rupert, what on earth are you doing?'

'Needs must, Emmy. That man's drinking is denting my brain as well as my wallet. I don't want him denting my honeymooners' brains, too.'

'But how will you make sure he gets that bottle? If the other guests do, they won't be happy.'

'I'll pour him his first glass from a normal bottle, then make sure this one is placed nearest to him. You've seen how he hogs a bottle.'

'You're a crafty old sod. But I'm not sure it's ethical.'

'It's the only time I've ever done it. I can live with myself, just this once.'

Rupert's ploy was successful. Greg didn't notice, and his manner was mildly tempered by the lower alcohol content in his glass. When another bottle was required, Rupert went off to the other side of the kitchen, and I kept Greg distracted while Rupert performed his little trick. Only this time, I noticed from the corner of my eye, it was nearer half and half.

There was a tense moment when Malcolm, sitting next to Greg, reached for the doctored bottle and poured himself some. Rupert's eyes went wide with panic. When Malcolm tasted it, his eyebrows shot up in surprise, then drew down in a frown. He looked at the bottle, worked out whose elbow it resided by, glanced across at Rupert – and grinned. Then he surreptitiously topped up his glass from a different bottle.

I went to bed that night tired but chipper. I'd got through all my chores; Peter and Grace were lovely; Greg's drinking had been successfully managed, and he and his wife were due to leave on Monday; we only had one half of the Hendersons to contend with … and Kate had finally found a bridesmaid dress, thus appeasing my mother.

All in all, it had been a good day.

NINE

The fire engine's siren cut through the night. At first, I thought I was dreaming, but when the dog howled in Rupert's quarters, I shot out of bed.

Deciding this was an emergency that warranted an invasion of privacy, I let myself through into Rupert's lounge, where he was already telling the dog to hush.

We listened intently as the noise faded a little.

'They've gone past the end of our lane,' Rupert muttered. Then the sirens stopped, and he paled. 'It's nearby, Emmy. Chuck some clothes on. We should go and see.'

I threw on jeans and a T-shirt and met him at his car. At the end of the lane leading away from *La Cour des Roses,* my heart stuttered as he turned left onto the lane that led to Madame Dupont's house.

Please, don't let it be hers.

My entreaty was in vain. A couple of bends on, the fire engine was stationary where black smoke reached into the airless summer night sky.

Thank God Madame Dupont was away at her sister's.

Rupert pulled over and we got out, standing well back so we weren't in the way of the fire team, watching flames lick at the kitchen end of the house. We were approached by Monsieur Girard, the farmer whose land bordered on Madame Dupont's cottage and the one entrusted with feeding her chickens when she was away.

'I called them as soon as I could,' he told us, agitated. 'But we were asleep. It was only when the smell crept through our bedroom window that we realised.'

I grabbed his arm. 'Are we *sure* she isn't in there?'

'I drove her into Pierre-la-Fontaine for the bus this afternoon. And when I shut the chickens away this evening, there was no sign of her. The firemen have checked. Don't worry.'

Above the noise of the hoses and the men calling to each other, the racket from the yard impinged. 'What about the chickens?'

'They're safe in their shed,' Monsieur Girard assured me. 'There's no wind, so the smoke's going straight up. I daren't let them out.'

'Emmy, take the car and go back to the guesthouse,' Rupert said. 'There's nothing you can do here. One of us should be there to reassure the guests.'

He was right. I smiled shakily at Monsieur Girard, turned Rupert's car around and drove back.

He'd made the right call. Kerry and Malcolm were in the kitchen, making a cup of tea.

'Want one?' Malcolm asked.

'Please. I'm so sorry we left you all. We needed to see what was happening.'

'Of course,' Kerry said kindly. 'Where's the fire?'

'Half a mile away. A friend's house.' My voice hitched. 'Our cleaner, Madame Dupont.'

'That old dear? How awful. Is she alright?'

'Yes. She's away tonight.'

'That's a mercy.'

'Yes.' I sipped gratefully at my tea and tried hard to remember my responsibilities. 'Are the other guests okay, do you know?'

'Don't worry, Emmy. We all heard the sirens and got out of bed to look, but they sounded far enough away, so everyone else went back to bed. The people in the middle gîte came out, but I told them we'd let them know if it was important.'

'Thank you for your help.'

'These things happen. I hope your friend will be alright. Such a shock to come back to.'

I allowed the full impact of that statement to sink in. Poor Madame Dupont, fast asleep in bed at her sister's, with no idea that the house she'd lived in all her married life had gone up in flames.

It was almost light when Rupert came back. I was in the kitchen with the laptop, trying to do something useful, a large mug of tea at my side.

'Emmy. You should have gone to bed.'

'You know I couldn't.'

He sat wearily. I pushed my tea towards him, and he took a grateful gulp.

'Throat's dry,' he said, running a hand over his beard. 'All that smoke. Is Gloria alright?'

'Yes. She heard me come back and started whining, but I shushed her back to sleep.'

'Thanks, love.'

'What about the cottage? Could they save it?'

Rupert closed his eyes for a moment. 'Depends what you mean by "save". It wasn't up to much before, was it? The kitchen's ruined. Otherwise, it's mainly smoke damage, but of course that permeates everything. And it's such an old property, there could be any number of unforeseen problems.'

'So it started in the kitchen? Did Madame Dupont leave something on the stove?'

'No. They think it was an electrical fire. The wiring was ancient.'

'She'll have insurance, won't she?'

'Yes. But her policy might be outdated or limited. Especially with the state of the electrics. They'll need to rewire, fit a new kitchen, make good the smoke damage. It'll take weeks, if not months, to make it liveable again.'

'So what happens next?'

'Monsieur Girard will phone her to tell her what's happened. I'll drive over to her sister's to fetch her. We can hardly expect her to get the bus back.'

'But where will she stay? We're full here.'

'Don't worry, Emmy. She has a large family. She'll be alright.'

As soon as it was a reasonable time, I phoned Alain. He was as saddened by the news of the fire as we were.

'Do you need me to do anything?'

I knew he had a ton of work to catch up on, after having the children last week. 'No, thanks. But I don't know what time I'll get to yours. I should be around for Madame Dupont when Rupert brings her from her sister's.'

'Do whatever you need to do, Emmy. And if you need me, let me know.'

Just a few of the reasons I loved him so much – immediate understanding, kindness and compassion.

Madame Dupont stared, disbelieving, at the blackened walls of her little cottage, the home in which she began her married life so long ago, the home in which she brought up her children. The home in which her husband died. Decades of memories.

I reached out to gently wipe away the tears that had begun to fall down her wrinkled cheeks, but they soon became a silent river, unstoppable, so I pulled her to me and hugged her tight, feeling her bony shoulders shake with grief.

Monsieur Girard's wife had walked across the fields and she took the other side, so we were like two columns holding her upright.

Rupert shuffled his feet, helpless. He'd tried to prepare her on the drive back, but the reality was so much worse.

'Where will you go?' I asked her. 'Do you need Rupert to drive you back to your sister's?'

She straightened her spine. 'No, Emie, it is too far away. I phoned one of my daughters. She can take me in for a few days. Then we will see.'

'My husband will gather some of your belongings if they tell him it's safe to go in,' Madame Girard said kindly. 'He will bring them to you.'

Madame Dupont lifted her chin. 'Thank you. That is very kind.'

I walked the lanes back to *La Cour des Roses* with a heavy heart. Not wanting to interrupt Alain from his work, I tried to distract myself by working too, but I didn't like missing Sunday with my man, even though I'd seen more of him during the week than usual.

When my phoned pinged with a text from Ellie, I jumped.

Everything okay or did you forget about the dress because you're having Sunday afternoon sex with the best-looking accountant in town?

I cursed. With everything that had happened, I'd forgotten all about picking up the bridesmaid dresses.

So sorry. Long story. On my way now.

Ellie was sympathetic and concerned when I got there and told her about the fire. 'No wonder you forgot about the dresses. Least of your worries! Poor Madame Dupont.'

Sophie was equally moved. 'Oh, Emmy, I am so sorry for that poor old woman,' she said as she handed over her dress. 'Go to Alain's. Do something that will take your mind off it for a little while.'

Damn right.

At Alain's, I lifted the dresses carefully out of the car, took them in and hung them over the lounge door.

He was in the dining area, his table scattered with papers, but he immediately came to me and held me while I recounted Madame Dupont's distress.

'That poor woman.' He pulled back. 'You must be exhausted.'

'Yes.'

Concern showed in his eyes. 'But if you flop here, you'll only brood.' He noticed the bridesmaids' dresses adorning the door, and shook his head. 'I won't ask. So, what would you like to do with what's left of the day?'

I tried to think of something that would be quick, fun and preferably not involve exerting ourselves too much.

'Crazy golf,' I told him decisively.

'Oh.' His shoulders sagged.

The first time Alain suggested crazy golf, he was under the illusion that he was bound to thrash me. He was sadly mistaken. I may not be a natural sportswoman, but it turned out that I was a natural at crazy golf. Alain assumed my first win was a fluke, but we'd played numerous times since, and I'd won maybe eighty per cent of the time. It had become an obsession with me. Whenever we were out and I saw a course, I insisted on playing. I absolutely loved it. While I was concentrating on that, I wasn't thinking about anything else, so I found it really relaxing.

Our nearest mini-golf course was a municipal one on the outskirts of town, where the holes were inventive and well-maintained, and trees around the edges provided a modicum of shade.

But today, my luck was out and Alain's was in. It was the final hole that did it – a stupid mound with the hole in the side, where the chances of getting your ball in were infinitesimal. It took Alain ten tries. Took me twenty and cost me the game.

'I *did* it. I won!' Alain leaped around like a power-mad six-year-old, jumping up and down and waving his club in the air, to the consternation of the actual six-year olds on the hole behind us.

'You did. Well done. Now calm down before you have a heart attack.' I grabbed his club and led him away.

'I want ice cream to celebrate.'

'Fine. You can have ice cream.'

We stood in the queue at the kiosk, and Alain laughed. 'You're sulking.'

'Am not.'

'Yes, you are.'

'Am not.' But I ruined the statement by stamping my foot.

Alain pulled me to him and kissed me long and hard, much to the disapproval of the family behind us and what looked like open jealousy on the part of the forty-something female ice cream vendor.

When he pulled away, he tipped my chin up with his finger. 'I *would* ask you not to pout, but you know it turns me on.'

Good job we were speaking English, or the French people behind us would have been livid by now.

'We need to get our ice creams and go, before we get lynched,' I hissed.

'Then stop sulking.'

Later – much later, after I'd pouted to my heart's content and Alain had made the best use of it – we settled in the garden with a glass of wine and a simple risotto which Alain had made. Give me rice to cook, and I'll give you a blackened, starch-ridden pan back.

For my contribution, I lit a couple of citronella candles to keep hungry insects at bay.

'How do you feel about this house?' Alain asked. 'Are you still okay about moving in after the wedding?'

'Of course. We agreed – it's sensible to live here for a while, settle into our new routine, *then* decide whether to move.'

'I know, but it's months since we discussed it. I thought you might have changed your mind.'

'Are *you* changing your mind?'

'No. I'm comfortable here. I have a lot of happy memories, especially since you've been around so much. It'll be convenient while you to get used to working at *La Cour des Roses* but not living there. But a lot's changed since we last spoke about it, and after we talked about a family the other day, it made me wonder whether this house will be suitable.'

'You're right. Things *have* changed since we last discussed it. Back then, I still had half the mortgage to pay on that flat of mine and Nathan's, and I was worried whether we could keep tenants in there long term. I was too scared to make expensive plans. And I had no idea whether my business would get off the ground. But it *has* – in a small way, but I can make it grow. I got those bits of freelance work in the winter. Nathan buying me out in Birmingham made a huge difference – not having that debt hanging around my neck.' I took his hand. 'As for starting a family? This place has room for a nursery. The garden's big enough for a toddler to toddle. Maybe when we get on to the second, we should look at somewhere bigger. But one step at a time for now.'

He squeezed my hand. 'As long as you're sure. I wouldn't want you to see it as me taking the easy option.'

'It *is* an easy option. But I'm all for easy options at the moment. Life's complicated enough. Let's get used to being married first. Start a family. Where we go from there will fall into place, you'll see.'

'Know-it-all.'

I gave him a supercilious smile. 'I am my mother's daughter, remember.'

A mock shudder. 'How could I forget?'

* * *

Rupert and I weren't sorry to see Greg and his wife go the next morning.

'Never thought I'd see the day that I'd deliberately diddle my guests,' Rupert commented as we waved them off.

'It was a one-off, and it was justified.'

Ryan pulled up for a gardening stint as we were about to set off for town.

'I heard about Madame Dupont's fire,' he said, his tone sober. 'I can't tell you how sorry I am. She's staying with relatives?'

Rupert nodded. 'Her daughter, for now.'

'If you need me to do anything, you'll let me know?'

'Yes. Thanks, Ryan.'

'He's a good lad,' Rupert commented as we drove towards Pierre-la-Fontaine.

'Yes. He is.'

'Ryan and Sophie. Do you think they'll …?'

'I quizzed her about it the other week. They've been pretty solid since he came back in the spring.'

'But?'

'He's younger than her, remember. I get the impression she's worried about making him feel tied down.'

'I can understand that. But if you've got a good thing going, you have.'

'True.' I cast him a sidelong glance. 'What about you?'

'What about me?'

'No entanglement in the offing?'

He negotiated a junction on the outskirts of town. 'You know full well that my entanglement with Gloria was enough to put me off for life, thank you.'

His face was poker-straight, making me laugh, despite wishing he would consider moving on eventually.

When we got to the café, Bob and Jonathan had also heard about the fire through the grapevine.

'How is Madame Dupont?' Bob asked.

'She was distraught yesterday, when she saw it,' Rupert told them. 'I spoke to her on the phone this morning, though, and she was calmer.'

'Where's she staying?' This from Jonathan.

'With her daughter, but they can't have her for long – only while the granddaughter's away on holiday.'

'She stays at her sister's sometimes, doesn't she?'

'Yes, but only for a night or two. It's too far away, and the flat's tiny.'

'There's nothing you can do?'

'We're full for a while yet,' Rupert explained. 'If it had happened in the winter, we'd gladly have taken her in for a good long while.' He manfully refrained from squawking as a woman pushed past him with several bags of shopping and spiked him with a fresh pineapple. 'Madame Dupont is the stoical kind. She's always taken whatever life throws at her and done her best. That will see her in good stead now.'

'Will you visit her?' Bob asked.

'Yes, but I'm going to leave it a couple of days,' I told him. 'She needs time to come to terms with it, and I don't want her to think we're trying to strong-arm her into coming back to work. Even if she felt up to it, she couldn't get to us unless one of us fetched her. It's not practical.'

'Will you get someone else in?'

'I'm not sure that's fair yet, even on a temporary basis,' Rupert said. 'Emmy and I will manage, for now. Let the dust settle a bit.'

I could have stayed with these kindly men for longer, but I had a florist to see, so I left them to it, retrieved the dresses and a sprig of lavender from the car and made my way across the square, pausing to admire the window display before going in.

No boring containers of flowers here. Madame Pascal had a stylish, imaginative streak, changing her displays with the seasons.

At the moment, giant tissue sunflowers filled the windows, interspersed with containers of the real thing at different heights, a fence painted along the entire length of the window, and a miniature metal tractor driven by a scarecrow at one end. Fabulous.

She greeted me when I entered and admired the dresses and the photo of Kate's, mused a while, then beckoned me over to her laptop. 'I have already chosen the white roses for you. Small, delicate. The lavender will be a little taller, poking out. We can match this pale lilac.' She pointed to Sophie's dress, and found a matching rose on her screen. 'But this one, I cannot match.' She indicated Kate's dress. 'Perhaps one dark purple rose in the centre of each bouquet, to match *this* dress' – she indicated Ellie's – 'and to contrast with the pastel colours.' She searched until she found what she was looking for. 'Like purple velvet, yes? And a little greenery. What do you think?'

'That sounds wonderful. Thank you.'

'You will get the lavender to me the day before?'

'Yes.' *Hmm. Still need to speak to Ryan about that.* 'I'm sorry we took so long with the dresses.'

'That does not matter. It is important to get everything right for your special day.'

Was she in league with my mother? Talking of whom …

Leaving the shop, I crossed to the fountain and sat on a bench to e-mail her with details of my latest wedding conquest.

That evening at the guest meal, Gavin drank more than he should, and it put him in a maudlin mood, harping on about unfaithful women and the difficulties of loneliness in your fifties. Since he'd only been single for a week, I wasn't sure he was fully qualified to pontificate on that subject yet. And it was hardly conducive to a jovial atmosphere, especially with a honeymooning couple in our midst.

To avoid inflicting him on our other guests for any longer than necessary, Rupert made coffee and settled everyone in the lounge, then diplomatically suggested to Gavin (I was still struggling to get to grips with this first-name business) that we three take ours out on the patio – something the other guests were grateful for, judging by their sighs of relief and a smile from Grace as we guided Gavin back through the kitchen.

We settled him in a sturdy chair, ignored his request for a brandy, and Rupert placed a stiff black coffee in front of him. And when I say stiff, put it this way: if he drank it, he would get no sleep tonight.

Gloria came out with us, but she kept a wary distance from our guest, slinking to Rupert's side and hiding under his chair. A dog of discernment.

'How did you do it, Rupert, old friend?' Gavin mumbled, glaring at his coffee in the hope it would change into something alcoholic.

Rupert winced at 'old friend'. 'Do what?'

'How did you cope, when Gloria left you?'

'Ah, well, I had an Emmy, didn't I?'

Gavin's glazed expression sidled my way. 'I wouldn't mind an Emmy. Do you have a spare?'

'Sorry, pal. There's only one. She's unique.'

'Can I borrow her?'

'She's needed here. And she's getting married soon, remember?'

'Ah. Yes.' He focused his gaze somewhere near my face. 'Waste of time, Emmy. They only up and leave you in the end.'

'I don't think mine will.'

'That's what *I* thought.' He sipped his coffee and made a face, but took a second sip anyway. 'I don't understand it. Anita had everything she wanted. Clothes, jewellery, four-bedroom detached in a neighbourhood with no riff-raff. What more could she want?'

A husband who isn't a complete arse, presumably.

'She must have felt she was lacking *something*, Gavin,' I ventured, curious despite myself. Besides, it would be good to let him get it all out of his system while it was just us three. 'You said she left you for the builder?'

'That's what I don't understand, Emmy. Why would she go off with a bit of rough like that when she had me?' He waved a hand at his expensive shirt, which had lost its appeal due to the red wine and coffee he'd dripped down it. 'I can't get visions of them out of my head.' His chin wobbled.

'Did you catch them together?' Rupert asked cautiously.

'No, thank God. First I knew about it was when she stormed out of the house with her cases. And there he was at the kerb, the blighter, waiting for her in his white van.'

'She didn't tell you why she was going?' I prodded.

'No. Only said she needed a change. That she didn't love me any more. That maybe she never had.'

'That's harsh.'

Gavin brushed away a tear. 'I can't stand the thought of them together. The idea of his grubby hands on her. Those callouses and dirty fingernails.' He held out his own hands to inspect his man manicure. 'It doesn't bear thinking about.'

'Then don't,' Rupert said sternly. 'Stop dwelling on it and move on.'

'How did *you* do that?'

'I had this place to distract me,' Rupert admitted. 'And the support of some very good friends.'

'Friends?' Gavin frowned, as though trying to remember the dictionary definition. 'Trouble is, most of ours were couples and whatnot. Anita dealt with that side of things. Can't imagine seeing them on my own. No doubt she'll hijack them, anyway.'

I felt genuinely sorry for him. I couldn't contemplate where I would have been without my friends through the years – and

I knew damned well that I would never have found the courage to start a new life in France without their support.

'Then you need to get out and make new ones,' I told him briskly.

'Too hard,' he murmured. 'Too old for that crap.'

To my alarm, his shoulders began to shake. I sent Rupert a despairing look, but he only gave me a *You're a woman, you deal with this* look back.

Patting Gavin's back in a *there there* shushing manner more suited to a toddler who'd hurt his knee, I remembered once telling Rupert that it was okay for men to cry – that it was an idiotic and outdated tradition that suggested they shouldn't – and I realised that my distaste in this case wasn't that a man was crying, but a man I didn't like.

'You came here on your own,' I reminded him. 'That's a start. You have to do the same when you get back home.'

He composed himself. 'You're right, Emmy. Need to pull myself together. I'm not too far on the wrong side of fifty. Got plenty of dosh, even if Anita nabs some of it. It won't be hard to get myself another woman, surely?'

'That wasn't quite what I had in mind.'

But he was nodding to himself, his mind made up. Good friends, as opposed to superficial acquaintances, were obviously unfamiliar to him – and you could, it seemed, simply swap one life partner for another as easily as buying a new sweater.

He stood shakily, draining his coffee. 'Right. Bed. Thank you both for listening. And to you, Emmy, for your advice. You've been a comfort.'

We stood, too. Before I could anticipate it, he'd leaned in for one of his hugs, and all I had time to do was close my nostrils to the aftershave assault.

That man was heading for a knee in the crotch.

TEN

'Any exciting plans for today?' I asked Grace and Peter the next morning, as they lingered over breakfast.

'Grace wants to visit a *château*, but I fancy touring a vineyard,' Peter said.

'Ah, decisions, decisions. The joys of married life.'

'Rupert told us you're getting married soon, Emmy. To a handsome accountant?'

'Guilty on all counts, only my wedding won't be a quiet affair like yours. My mother won't allow it.'

Grace patted my hand. 'It'll be wonderful, I'm sure.'

'Yeah, me too. Well, if the *château* wins between you two today, I can recommend Chenonceau – magnificent, but a long drive. Or Montreuil-Bellay – much nearer, in a picturesque little town, but smaller. Then there's Ussé, which inspired *Sleeping Beauty*. And then …'

Peter gave me a pleading look to stop.

I smiled. 'You did bring her to the Loire, Peter. What did you expect? As for vineyards, Rupert's your man for that kind of info.'

Rupert came into the kitchen. 'What kind of info?'

While Peter explained their dilemma, I left them to it to make a start on chores. I loved having guests like those two – sweet, lively, interested, interesting.

'That was quite a night,' Rupert commented as we grabbed a quick coffee mid-morning. 'Do you think Henderson's got it out of his system, or do you think we'll have to baby him all the way through his stay?'

'I'm hoping he's got it out of his system. I could do without any more hugs from him, for one thing.'

'He's only being smarmy, Emmy.'

I shook my head. 'Not smarmy. Letchy.'

Rupert immediately sat up straight. 'What do you mean?'

'Gavin's hugs. They're letchy.'

'In what way?'

'He slides his arms around you in a certain way.' I puffed out an embarrassed breath. 'He brushes my breasts on the way round.'

Rupert spluttered coffee. 'For God's sake! Why didn't you say anything?'

'The first time, I thought it was my imagination, or unfortunate. The next couple of times? It's a clever technique, Rupert. Subtle. Nothing you can put your finger on, if you'll pardon the pun. It's not an aimed grope. The grope comes across as an accidental casualty of the hug.'

'Accidental, my arse.'

'Yes, well, I know that *now.*'

Rupert's expression was livid, something I found touching. It was like having my very own knight in shining armour.

'Don't worry, Emmy. Gavin and I will be having words.'

I laid a hand on his arm. 'No, don't. Too heavy-handed. Now I know it's deliberate, I'll avoid any more hugs. And if I do land up in one, I'll say something.'

'I want to know if that doesn't work out. Promise?'

'I promise. So, do you reckon he's genuinely cut up about Anita leaving him because he loves and misses her?'

'Nah. I'd say she was a trophy wife – she has class, knows what to wear, what to say. I never got any real sense of affection between those two. Did you, last year?'

'No. He seems more upset that she's run off with someone socially beneath them. He spoke about that builder like he's a lesser life form!'

My mother rang when I had my head in the far corner of a king-sized duvet cover, battling to get the duvet in.

'Hi. Mum. What can I do for you?'

'I don't even get a "How are you"?'

'I only e-mailed you yesterday.'

'Anything could've happened since then. I could have broken my leg, your dad could have the flu …'

'Okay. How are you?'

'Fine, thank you.'

I couldn't help but smile. 'Now we've established that you're both fine, what's up?'

'There was something I forgot to talk to you about when we were over there.'

Really? I thought we'd covered all bases.

'We didn't discuss the photographer,' she said.

I pulled my head out of the duvet cover, frowning. 'No, but we spoke about him the previous time you were over, and nothing's changed.'

An audible sigh at her end. Clearly she was hoping something *had* changed. Like my mind.

'Emmy, I know this Bob person is a friend of yours, but are you sure he's up to the job? You said he takes pictures of houses for Ellie, for goodness' sake.'

I bit back a tart response. She'd picked on the least artistic aspect of Bob's work.

'Mum, I told you, he's a brilliant landscape photographer. *And* he runs residential photography courses. I'll e-mail you the link to his website, so you can see for yourself.'

'He won't be taking landscapes on your wedding day, though, will he?'

Still smarting over her haranguing Kate about the dress and texting Sophie about make-up trials, I had to make an effort to rein in my irritation.

'No, but he has a good eye, and neither Alain nor I want formal wedding photos. We want casual shots, and Bob's really good at those.' When there was silence at the other end of the phone, I sent a mental apology to Bob. 'I'll arrange for you to meet him before the wedding, if you like.'

I knew I should have done that sooner, but I'd worried Mum wouldn't approve of Bob's casual style and way of going about things. My mother wasn't narrow-minded – she was perfectly tolerant to alternative lifestyles – but someone who spent more money on his beloved motorbike than he did on himself wouldn't be the first person she'd trust with capturing those precious, once-in-a-lifetime moments of her daughter's wedding.

'That would be good, Emmy. Although it will be too late by then to find an alternative.'

Yep. That's the general idea.

'Did you rearrange the appointment at the *château*?'

'Yes. Tonight at eight o'clock.'

'Make sure you double-check the …'

But I tuned out. I had the list imprinted on my brain already. 'Okay, Mum. Anything else?'

'I'll let you know if I think of something.'

I'm sure you will.

Clicking off the phone, I flopped across the half-made bed. Heaven knew what my dad was going through, listening to this kind of thing, night after night. Good job he was still head over heels in love with her. It takes all sorts.

* * *

The conversation was still preying on my mind when I went round to Alain's that evening. Since he'd texted to say he was delayed at work, I made a start on supper so we wouldn't be late for our appointment.

'Sorry I'm late.' He came into the kitchen and nuzzled my neck, then peered dubiously into the pan I was stirring. 'What's that?'

'It's a noodle thing. It had to be something quick.'

Alain dipped a finger into the substance and tasted, screwing up his eyes and nose against possible disaster. 'It's okay, actually.'

'Good, 'cause it's all you're getting.'

As we drove to the *château* after dinner – if you could call it that – I told him about my mother's phone call.

'So now you're subjecting Bob to an interview with your mother?'

'I didn't have much choice. She disapproves of his lack of "qualifications" with regard to wedding photography.'

'Hmm. I'm not so sure that's all there is to it, you know.'

'What do you mean?'

'The photographs are practically the only thing your mother hasn't been in charge of, because you insisted from the start that we wanted Bob to do them.'

'You're saying she's sulking?'

'It's a possibility.'

'You may be right. But that won't improve when she meets him, will it? First impressions-wise, I mean.'

'Bob's an intelligent bloke and a damned good photographer. All you have to do is agree a strategy with him beforehand. He knows his stuff and he's personable. Between you, you'll win her over.' When I only chewed my lip, he said, 'Emmy, your mum's been brilliant organising this wedding. We could never have done it without her help – not with everything else that's going on. But it is your big day, and you have the right to *some* input. There'll be times when you need to stand up to her. This is one of them. By the sound of it, you did. Good for you.'

Our appointment at the hotel was as anticipated – a courtesy, to confirm everything, hand over the seating plan, thrash out any problems and ask any as-yet-unasked questions (basically none, with my mother at the helm).

But I was glad we went, all the same, because the visit reminded me why we'd chosen this place above all the others. The building was so handsome and photogenic, the grounds gorgeous. Bob would have no shortage of locations for his shots, that was for sure, and I reminded myself that *La Cour des Roses* simply wouldn't have worked.

Back at Alain's, I e-mailed my mother to update her.

Heaven forbid that something should be ticked off the list without tagging another one on.

She texted back, *Don't forget your make-up session with Sophie tomorrow night.*

I frowned, knowing I hadn't told her the specifics about that. Had she been in touch with Sophie yet again? It was bad enough that she was on *my* back, let alone harassing my friends night and day.

The following morning proved to be my chance to deal with Gavin as I'd promised Rupert I would.

I hadn't had the time or energy to come up with a strategy yet – but since I was still stewing over my mother doubting Bob and bothering Sophie, I was already up for a fight.

Rupert had gone to visit Jonathan, and the other guests had pottered off, so I was alone in the kitchen by the time Gavin came down late for breakfast.

'Emmy. I didn't manage to catch you on your own yesterday.'

I hid a grimace. I wasn't sure I liked the idea of him catching me on my own.

'I wanted to apologise for the other night,' he went on. 'I'd had too much to drink. Didn't mean to pour out all my troubles like that.'

'We all need to get things off our chest from time to time,' I said chirpily. 'Tea or coffee?'

'Tea, please. I only hope you can forgive me.'

'Of course.'

'You're a good egg, Emmy. Thank you.'

Before I could blink, he moved in for a thank-you hug. Clearly, the threat of a tall, fit accountant hadn't done the trick.

It occurred to me that if Rupert were here, after what I'd told him yesterday, he might have been inclined to swing a punch or two. Good job he was out.

I moved like lightning, gripping Gavin's wrists tight. 'I don't think so.'

He put on a startled expression. 'What?'

'You know what. I wasn't born yesterday – and you certainly weren't. Touch me again, and I'll pack your stuff and throw you out.'

He barked out a strangled laugh. 'You'll do *what*? You're only a manager here, Emmy. Rupert knows who his valued guests are.'

I stared him down. 'If you want to test where Rupert's loyalty lies, go right ahead. And if I can't break your arm, maybe Rupert or my fiancé can have a crack at it. What do you think?'

Shock warred with defiance. 'I don't …'

I folded my arms across my chest and softened my tone. 'Gavin, neither Rupert nor I want to lose your custom. We know you like it here, and we like having you here.' *Like hell.* 'You've been through a hard time. But that technique of yours has to go.'

He stood his ground for a moment, then gave a helpless shrug. 'Okay. I'm sorry.'

'Apology accepted. Milk in your tea?' *Along with a dose of political correctness, perhaps?*

'Please.'

And that, thank goodness, was an end to the matter.

Seeing Ryan out in the garden, I took him an espresso.

'Thanks.' He sipped appreciatively.

'It's a sweetener for a favour,' I admitted.

He laughed. 'What can I do for the best espresso-maker in France?'

I explained about the lavender for my bouquets. 'I wouldn't know where to start – which to cut, how to cut it. All that green-fingered stuff.'

'Don't worry, Emmy. I'll deal with it – cut it and deliver it to the florist the day before.'

'Thanks.'

'You're welcome.' His lips twitched as he stared at what I'd hoped to pass off as a messy up-do but was probably just a mess. 'You look hot and bothered. Still chocka with guests?'

'Yup. But that's not why I'm hot and bothered.'

'Oh?'

'The hateful Mr Henderson is here for his annual visit – on his own. His wife left him.'

'Is he better company solo?'

'No. He's turned into a letch, actually.'

He frowned. 'With you? I hope you put him straight.'

'I threatened him with a tall accountant and a loyal guesthouse owner.'

Ryan lifted his arm to show off his impressive biceps. 'You can add a muscled gardener to the gang if you need to.'

I laughed. 'Appreciated.'

That afternoon, I visited Madame Dupont at her daughter's in a village a couple of miles beyond town; a small house that opened onto the street and was a little run-down. Through our many conversations over the months, I knew that Madame Dupont's daughter's job wasn't well-paid and her son-in-law was often off work with a bad back.

'Emie, it is so kind of you to come.'

I held out a bunch of flowers I'd brought from the garden. 'For your room.'

'Thank you.' She kissed my cheek. 'It is nice to have something from *La Cour des Roses*. I will put them in water and make you tea. Come.'

I followed her into a small lounge-diner-kitchen, where her son-in-law was in an armchair, watching television.

'This is Jean-Claude, my son-in-law.'

He nodded politely. 'I'm sorry I can't get up. My back, you see.'

'Please don't worry.'

'I'm making tea,' she told him. 'Would you like some?'

'No, thank you, Renee.'

His use of her first name startled me. To me, she had always been Madame Dupont, and I was amazed to realise that I hadn't known her name until now.

She put the kettle on and reached for mugs from a cupboard. 'How are you?'

'I am well, Emie, thank you. Under the circumstances.'

I couldn't think of anything to say that wouldn't be a platitude of some kind. 'What's happening with your chickens?'

'Monsieur Girard will feed and check on them, for now.' While she waited for the kettle, she found a squat plastic vase for the flowers.

'That's good of him. And he brought you some things?'

'Yes. His wife picked out some clothes for me. Everything smelled of smoke, so she had to wash them several times.'

'That was good of her.' I glanced at her garish floral dress and wondered how many decades ago she'd bought it. It must be made of sturdy stuff, to last all this time.

'Yes. And they will fetch me tomorrow, so I can go through the rest, to see what can be salvaged. They will box up what I don't need for now and store it in their barn.'

I thought about how busy a farmer must be at this time of year, and how kind Madame Dupont's neighbours were.

'Come, Emie, we can go to my room. Let's leave Jean-Claude to his favourite programme.'

She handed me my tea, and with hers in one hand and the flowers in the other, she ushered me into the hall and up the stairs.

Her temporary accommodation was small and neat with a single bed, a chest of drawers and a rail for clothes. Madame Dupont's bag was on the floor in a corner.

She saw me glance at it and shrugged as she placed the flowers on the drawers.

'No point in unpacking. This is my granddaughter's room. She'll be back from her holiday tomorrow, so I will go to my niece's. Then to my sister's over the weekend. Then back to my niece, I hope.'

'Why don't you stay at your sister's for longer?'

'I need to be near my house to sort things out. My sister is too far away, and her flat is too small. It is okay for a night or two, but not longer.' She gave me a sly smile. 'And we would drive each other mad.'

'I'm so sorry we can't put you up at *La Cour des Roses*.'

'You are full, Emie. It is good that you are busy.' Her face fell. 'But I am sorry I cannot clean for you. I would like to, but I have no transport, you see.'

'You already have enough to worry about.'

'But how will you manage the *gîte* changeovers on Saturday?'

Good question. 'Maybe Rupert could get someone from town.'

She sipped her tea, her wrinkled brow furrowed, and then her eyes lit up. 'No, Emie. Perhaps you could come for me at my niece's and drive me to *La Cour des Roses* for our Saturday work?

And afterwards, you could drive me into Pierre-la-Fontaine for the bus to my sister's?'

'I could, but I'm not sure you should be working yet.'

'I would like to come,' she said decisively. 'I will enjoy your company. Please let me do it. Especially as I cannot help during the week.'

'If you're sure.'

She smiled, happy that I'd capitulated, but then a sad expression took its place. 'Emie, there is something I need to tell you about.'

'Oh?'

'The embroidered squares for your wedding favours.' She spread her hands out, palms up, in apology. 'They are all gone. They were in the kitchen, you see, and the fire … The crockery, too. I am so sorry.'

I hadn't even thought about that. My heart sank. 'I'm sorry, too, but only because you spent so much time embroidering them.' I took her wrinkled hand. 'All those evenings …'

She managed a stoical shrug. 'It kept me occupied. Will you apologise to your mother and aunt for me?'

'No.' When she looked startled, I explained, 'I'll tell them, but I won't apologise for something out of your control.' I kissed her cheek. 'Please don't worry. My aunt and mother are resourceful creatures.'

I phoned my mother as soon as I got home.

'Oh? But, Emmy! That means we'll need to find an alternative, and there's only just over two weeks to the wedding, well, only ten days till we come out there …'

'Mum! Madame Dupont spent evening after evening on those silk squares, and now they've gone up in flames. As has her *house*.'

That silenced her for a moment. 'Yes. Of course. I'm sorry, Emmy. That poor lady. Do tell her she mustn't worry about the wedding favours. Jeanie and I will come up with something else.

There's still time. Please pass on my sincere sympathies to Madame Dupont. Such a shame.'

Alain came to *La Cour des Roses* for supper that night, and Rupert left me in charge of it (only fresh vegetable soup – what harm could I do?) while they walked along the lane to see the damage to Madame Dupont's cottage.

A heavy rain began soon after they returned and looked like it had no intention of giving up till morning, forcing us to eat in the kitchen, so Rupert decided to liven up the atmosphere by regaling Alain with the tale of Gavin's wandering hands.

And liven things up, it did. Alain's expression went from livid at the idea of someone daring to touch me right through to a victory punch in the air as I described my solution.

'Good for you, Emmy. Although I'd have beaten him to a pulp, if necessary.'

'As would I,' Rupert chipped in.

I laughed. 'Lovely though it is to know that I have such valiant protectors, I was trying to make sure it *wasn't* necessary.'

A few minutes later, Gavin poked his head round the door. He'd kept a low profile all day, so I was amazed that he dared put in an appearance.

'Sorry to interrupt.' He shot me a sheepish look. 'My light bulb's given up the ghost. Any spares?'

'I'll sort it out.' Rupert stood. 'Gavin, this is Alain – Emmy's husband-to-be.'

'Oh. Er. Pleased to meet you.'

Alain stood, towering over him as Gavin reached out a hand which Alain politely shook, although I could tell he put more grip into it than was strictly necessary.

Gavin winced, and as Rupert followed him out into the hall, we heard him mutter, 'I say, that chap of Emmy's *is* tall, isn't he?'

I burst out laughing and Alain joined in, but when we'd subsided, he gave me a serious look.

'Emmy. Let me or Rupert know if he misbehaves again. I mean it.'

'Okay, but I don't think he will.'

'Any follow-up from your mother about the photographs?'

'No, thank goodness.'

He reached across to kiss me. 'See? All you have to do is stand up to her a bit more.'

'Not talking about Emmy's mother, are we?' Rupert commented as he came back in, defunct light bulb in hand. 'Standing up to Flo is like trying to stand up to that storm out there. The woman's an unstoppable force of nature!'

Alain shot him a look that said his comment was unhelpful, but it made me smile.

We relaxed over a glass of wine. Or the boys tried to, until I brought up the wedding speeches.

'Have you written them yet?' I asked, sounding too much like my mother for my liking.

'Written them?' Rupert looked bewildered. 'Why do we have to write them? Isn't the clue in the word "speech"?'

'According to my mother, you should write it out, rehearse it, then have crib cards in case you get flustered on the day.'

Alain and Rupert exchanged glances.

'I'll be keeping mine short,' Alain declared. 'There's nothing worse than speeches that go on forever, with somebody trying to be funny but it falls flat, and everyone shuffling in their chairs.'

'What he said,' Rupert hastily chipped in.

I smiled, but felt obliged to make one more attempt. 'But Mum …'

'Emmy.' Alain cut me off. 'I promise we'll think about what we want to say, go over it in our heads beforehand. But if the speeches are short, that should suffice. Writing it out, rehearsing it? It'll sound stilted, when what we want is for our words to come across as genuine and heartfelt.'

Well! Mum couldn't argue that my fiancé hadn't put any thought into his speech, even if it might not be the kind of thought she had in mind.

Rupert looked at me questioningly, awaiting my verdict.

I jerked my thumb at Alain. 'What he said.'

Rupert laughed. 'You know, Alain, they say you should take a long hard look at your prospective mother-in-law before you propose to her daughter.'

Alain blew out a breath. 'Hmm. I have a nasty feeling I might regret missing out that step.'

I slapped his arm, but I couldn't help laughing.

Depressed by the rain, we retired early to my room, where Alain suggested television in bed to take our mind off the storm and my mother. Apart from my habit of leaving it on in the background sometimes in order to absorb French by osmosis, I barely watched it – and I can't say I missed it. But this was cosy, snuggling up with my man under the covers.

Besides, I wanted to leave any bouncing around until Rupert might be asleep. Ridiculous, I knew, but somehow it still felt a little clandestine, having Alain stay overnight – like a naughty teenager defying her parents.

I flicked through the channels, ignoring news and sport and secretly hoping for a schmaltzy rom-com.

'How about this?' Alain asked as spooky music and opening credits filled the screen.

'A vampire movie? *Very* romantic.'

'It could be. It's an oldie, so it won't be too gory. And if you get scared, you can leap into my arms, and I can help calm you down.'

Hmmm. I could see the merits in that.

Cuddled together with the lights out and only the eerie glow from the telly, we got caught up in the movie. It ticked all the boxes – not too gruesome, amusing due to the dated special effects, but engrossing all the same. There were plenty of jump-out-of-your-skin moments (each leading to a reassuring hug from Alain), not least when we heard a tapping on the window.

And I don't mean the vampire in the film, who was at that very moment tapping and scratching on a window to be invited in by his next idiot victim, who should learn to close her curtains before she went to bed. I mean tapping on *our* window.

I nearly had a heart attack. Alain jumped, too – something that seriously unnerved me.

I swallowed. 'Was that on the telly, or was it …?'

'I think it was real life,' he asserted dubiously.

'The rain?'

He shook his head.

We both looked towards the window, the light cotton curtains allowing a glimpse of a shadowy form behind them. I wished I'd closed the shutters. And that I kept garlic in the room. And that I wasn't an atheist and therefore lacking a sizeable crucifix.

Clambering out of bed, we crept to the window. Taking a deep breath, I pulled the curtains aside. The form was gone.

'What the hell was that?' I whispered.

Alain looked a little pale. 'Kids?'

'All the way out here?'

'An animal?'

'How tall do you think the field mice are around here, Alain? I'd rather encounter a vampire!'

'I know it wasn't *that*.'

I looked doubtful.

'Come on, Emmy, it's only our imaginations.' He switched the telly off, then turned on the bedside lamp, flooding the room with a comforting glow. 'That's enough of *that* for one night.' He pulled me down onto the bed beside him. 'I've decided we need to switch roles.'

'What do you mean?'

'I'm a bit shaken up. I need comfort and reassurance.'

I hit him with a pillow. 'You big baby. It was you that chose the movie!'

The corners of his mouth twitched. 'Can we sleep with the light on?'

'I thought you needed comfort and reassurance. Who said anything about sleep?' My mouth came down to meet his as I rolled onto him, the solid wall of his chest a comforting presence beneath me as he wrapped his arms around my waist, then broke the kiss to nuzzle at my neck – and nip at it with his teeth.

'Not funny, Alain,' I warned.

He spun me so that I was pinned beneath him. 'I'm not aiming to make you laugh. You can moan a little, if you like, though.'

ELEVEN

Mornings were more leisurely for Rupert when Alain stayed over, since my fiancé was in the habit of taking the dog with him on his early morning run.

'Sleep alright, Emmy?' Rupert asked as we got breakfast organised, spooning locally made preserves into dishes and chopping fruit into a large glass bowl.

I narrowed my eyes, but he didn't appear to be referring to Alain's sleepover and the lack of sleep *that* might entail. 'More or less. Why?'

'Wondered if you'd been disturbed. Ruddy guests.'

'Which guests?'

'James and Caroline. Came back late last night and forgot their key. They didn't want to wake everyone up by knocking at the main door, so they went around the side of the house and rapped on my window till I got up to see who the hell it was. Had to go through and let them in. Said they'd knocked somewhere else first. They weren't sure if it was yours, but when you didn't answer, they moved on to mine. Were you asleep?'

'No. We were awake, but we didn't look straight away.'

'Why the hell not?'

'We thought it was a vampire.'

'You thought it was a *what*?'

I told him the tale, making him laugh loudly. And if his guffaws woke James and Caroline, it served them right.

'I trust you and Alain got over your fright in a satisfactory manner?' he asked when he'd stopped laughing.

'Very satisfactory, Rupert, thank you.'

'Glad to hear it. Also glad I *didn't* hear it.'

I threw a strawberry at him and began to hull the rest.

That evening was designated as the make-up trial that Mum had insisted on, over at Ellie's house. I'd hoped to get out of it, or delay it, at least, since it was a guest meal night. But Rupert said that as long as I helped him prep before and clear up after, he didn't mind entertaining the guests by himself while I disappeared for a couple of hours.

I suspected he was trying to keep me at arm's length from Gavin. If so, I wasn't complaining. I drove the country road to Ellie's house like a truanting schoolgirl.

Ellie and I goggled as Sophie laid out the make-up she'd brought with her, amazed at the number and variety of pots and palettes and brushes.

Ellie picked up the eyelash curler and looked at it as though it was an instrument of torture. 'You're not coming near *me* with this thing!'

It was another world to me, too. I was not famed for my cosmetics repertoire. A dash of mascara and a swish of lippy was the most I bothered with nowadays. Since I'd moved to France, my skin had a golden glow and I didn't feel the need to plaster it in anything artificial. But a wedding day was different.

'Be thankful that you live in sunny France,' Sophie echoed my thoughts. 'Or you would have to have spray-tanning sessions.' She looked over at Ellie. 'Although in your case …'

'It's not my fault I don't tan,' Ellie cut her off. 'And if you think my duty as a bridesmaid stretches as far as standing in a pair of paper knickers while a twenty-year-old sprays every inch of me with disgusting gloop, you can go and …'

'We all love your alabaster complexion, Ellie,' I said hastily. 'Don't we, Sophie?'

'We do if I can find a foundation paler than palest ivory,' Sophie grumbled, rummaging. 'Ah, here's one.' She pretended to peer at the label. '"Vampire white". That should do it.'

She ducked as a cushion flew her way like a heat-seeking missile.

When I looked in the mirror half an hour later, I gawped. Sophie had heeded my plea that I wanted to look natural and had enhanced everything, but no one would have had any idea how much work had gone into it. The same with Ellie, who was struggling to tear herself away from her reflection, muttering about looking five years younger.

We took photos to send to my mother for approval, and to Kate so that she knew she would be in good hands on the day, and considered it an evening well spent.

As did Mum. Her response to our photos?

Great. Aren't you glad you had this practice run, Emmy? Now you can relax about it!

Hmmm. Clearly, it hadn't occurred to her that we wouldn't *need* to relax about it if she hadn't stressed us out in the first place.

'Sorry, Emmy, but a client's asked me to go round to see him,' Alain told me on the phone the following evening. 'He's panicking over some missive from the tax authorities. I need to see what it's all about, or he'll worry the entire weekend. Will you still come round later?'

'Of course. Give me a ring when you know what's what.'

I went round to the kitchen to grab a glass of wine, but *that* was a mistake.

'Emmy. Why the long face?' Rupert asked, coming in from the garden.

'Alain's been detained on a matter of dire accounting urgency. He won't be free till later.'

'Why not join me for a drink on the patio till you hear from him?'

Since I could think of worse ways to spend my evening, I accepted his offer. As I settled myself outside, I noticed a third glass. 'Got someone else here?'

'Ah, yes, well ...'

Gavin came through the patio doors. 'Sorry about that, Rupert, the old bladder's not what it used to be. Emmy! Joining us? Lovely.'

I flashed him an insipid smile and narrowed my eyes at Rupert, but the string of expletives I would have directed his way had to remain unspoken.

'Emmy can't stay long.' Rupert did his best to get back into my good books. 'She's off to Alain's shortly.'

'Oh. Right. Hmm. Hmm. Nice chap,' Gavin mumbled.

I placed my phone on the table, so I couldn't miss my rescue call, and sipped my wine. Well, I took a large gulp first to get the effect going, *then* sipped. Since I would be driving to Alain's, I needed to take it easy.

'You've not found yourself another lady friend yet?' Gavin asked Rupert.

Rupert played for time, sipping his wine, presumably deciding how to handle the nosiness of his guest.

'No. Still dealing with the divorce, Gavin. Another relationship isn't high on my priority list. So, what do you reckon about England's chances in the next test match?'

We heard tyres on gravel, and a minute later, Ellie walked round the corner, smart in a pale green linen shift dress that fitted her slim figure perfectly and showed off her long legs.

Rupert stood. 'Hi. I wasn't expecting you.' He looked mightily pleased to see her, but that was hardly surprising if he'd thought he was going to have to entertain Gavin all evening by himself.

'I know. Sorry to turn up unannounced,' Ellie said. 'I spoke to Luiza today. She wants to try a different tack with the Mallorcan property, and I said I'd talk to you about it.'

'Great! Have a glass of wine out here first, then we'll go into the den for a chat.' No doubt a hint for Gavin to sling his hook shortly. 'This is Gavin Henderson, by the way. Gavin, this is Ellie, a good friend of mine.'

Gavin stood to greet her. 'Any friend of Rupert's is a friend of mine. Pleased to meet you.'

I left them to the pleasantries and followed Rupert into the kitchen. 'Don't you *dare* disappear with Ellie and leave me with him!'

'Don't worry, Emmy. We'll stay outside for a bit longer,' Rupert soothed.

When we went back out, Gavin had pulled up a chair for Ellie next to his and was busy smarming.

I smirked. He wouldn't get far with her.

We settled back down and the conversation got going again, after a fashion. When my phone rang, I snatched it up, but it was only my brother Nick, confirming his travel arrangements for the wedding. I went a little way down the garden to take the call, but a few minutes in, I heard a scrape of chairs on the patio and glanced sharply back.

Ellie was standing, her hands on her hips. As I watched, Gavin stood too, then Rupert. I didn't like the way they were looking at each other.

'Nick, I have to go.' I clicked off without even giving him a chance to reply, and shot back up the garden.

'… his hand on my knee!' Ellie was saying, apoplectic. 'Never mind that dodgy greeting earlier.'

'For God's sake!' Rupert moved in threateningly close to Gavin. 'First Emmy, and now this! You're heading for trouble, "old friend".'

I goggled. Ellie was quite capable of dealing with something like this herself. And sure enough …

'Rupert, there's no need,' Ellie tried to intervene. 'I can fight my own battles.'

'Not on my premises,' Rupert ground out. He and Gavin were almost nose to nose now, Gavin's face shocked, Rupert's red with anger. It would have been almost comical to an outsider.

But I wasn't an outsider. 'That's enough!'

Rupert finally took a couple of steps back, and Gavin recovered his poise with the safer distance between them – and the fact that Ellie practically had Rupert in an arm lock.

'How dare you speak to your guests like that?' Gavin braved.

Rupert glared at him. 'How dare you treat women like that? My friends? You've gone too far, Gavin. I want you to …'

I knew Rupert was going to ask him to leave. But *that* was a step too far, I felt.

'I'll deal with this,' I told Rupert firmly. 'Gavin. A word. Inside.'

As I propelled him through the patio doors, I heard Ellie saying, 'He was only trying it on, Rupert. Do you honestly think I've never had an unwanted hand on my knee before? No harm done. Calm down before you set your angina off.'

In the kitchen, I stared Gavin down. 'I've already told you, you can't do that kind of thing. Sympathy for your wife leaving you only stretches so far, and you've gone past the point of no return with Rupert. If you're going to finish your stay here, that has to be an end to it. I know you've been out of the loop for a long while, so I'll give you a handy tip. Nowadays, you need to be *absolutely* sure the attraction works both ways before you try anything on.'

'Hmmph.'

Leaving him to sulk, I went back outside. 'I'm sorry, Ellie.' I kissed her on the cheek.

'It's fine. I'm fine.' She rolled her eyes. 'Rupert said he tried something on with you, too.'

'Yeah. That man's judgement is seriously out of kilter at the moment. But his wife's just left him, and he was already an idiot before that.'

'I want him out,' Rupert declared.

'Rupert, I've spoken to him, and I think that'll be that. You can't throw someone out for making a pass at someone he thinks is attractive and available.'

'Yes, well, Ellie's not …'

'Not attractive?' Ellie cut him off, glaring at him.

'You know I didn't mean that.'

Thankfully, my phone rang at that point.

It was Alain. 'Hi. Accounting crisis averted. Can you come over and make wild, passionate, end-of-the-week love to me now?'

'With pleasure.' I clicked off. 'Gotta go.' I wagged my finger at Rupert. 'You? Behave. Ellie, keep an eye on him.'

'Won't let him out of my sight, I promise.'

When I got to Alain's, he was on the phone to his mother, frowning. He delivered a glass of wine into my waiting hands, and when he'd clicked off, he pulled me down on the sofa next to him and slung his arm across my shoulders.

'What's up?' I asked.

'Not sure. In theory, she was ringing to pass on a message from Sabine that the tie and sash for the kids' outfits are finished and looking good.'

'But?'

'She also mentioned that Adrien's away for the weekend.'

I looked at him blankly. 'And that's important because …?'

'Not important, but odd.'

I sipped my wine and tried to concentrate. 'Why? Is he joined to Sabine at the hip, or something?'

'Hardly. But he's visiting an old university mate he hasn't seen in years. And he never mentioned it to Mum last week. Spur of the moment, apparently.'

'So? He had a sudden whim.'

He prised my glass from my hands and took a large gulp of wine. 'Mum thinks he might be having a mid-life crisis.'

'*What?*' I laughed. 'You're older than he is. Doesn't that mean you should have had yours first?' I sobered up when I saw he was still worried. 'That's ridiculous. One weekend visiting an old friend doesn't mean Adrien's having a mid-life crisis. Let me know when he buys a red sports car and a leather jacket, and I'll rethink it.' I frowned. 'Are *you* worried about him?'

'No. I learned not to worry too much about Adrien or Sabine a long time ago.' He leaned in for a kiss. 'So. What's what at *La Cour des Roses*? No more unwanted advances from Handy Gavin, I hope?'

'Not for me. But …' I told him what had happened with Ellie.

'That guy needs rewiring,' Alain grumbled. He cocked his head to one side. 'Makes me wonder, though. Don't you think Rupert overreacted?'

'I would, if it hadn't been for the fact that he knew Gavin had already had a go at me. And you wanted to thump Gavin when you found out about that, remember?'

'That's different. You and I are together.' His eyes widened. 'Do you think there's something going on between those two?'

'Ellie and Rupert? No. Ellie doesn't want romance and Rupert doesn't want complications. Besides, I asked him about potential entanglements the other day.'

'You did? What did he say?'

'He said nothing doing.'

Alain wasn't convinced. 'Remember at Rupert's sixtieth birthday party last year, when we played kids' games? Ellie and Rupert passing that balloon between them with no hands was pretty interesting, if you ask me.'

'That was ages ago. I kept my eye on them after that, but nothing else happened. Tipsy fun at a party, that's all.'

'They see a lot more of each other nowadays.'

'True. But I think that's because their friendship became easier after Gloria left. They chat and laugh at each other's jokes. Ellie's been fantastic, keeping Rupert's head above water during his divorce and helping over the Mallorcan property. But there are no outward shows of close affection, really, other than friendly pecks on the cheek and the like.' I shook my head. 'I'm inclined to think it's just a case of him needing to spend time with someone nearer his own age.'

Alain's lips twitched. 'What about his other needs?'

I spluttered on my wine. 'I try not to delve too deeply into those, if you'll pardon the expression.'

He laughed. 'What about my needs, then?'

I placed my wine glass carefully on the coffee table. 'Those, I *am* prepared to think about.'

I kissed him long and deep, pushing him back into the corner of the sofa, pressing my breasts against his chest. His response was swift, but I didn't want to rush anything. I was feeling lazy tonight.

We necked on the sofa, only getting around to buttons and zips when urgency got the better off us.

Good job we'd closed the curtains earlier.

Saturday saw the departure of Grace and Peter. I was sad to say goodbye, but delighted they'd enjoyed their stay.

'Will you come back sometime?' I asked them as Rupert carried their bags to the car.

'You try to keep us away!' Grace's blue eyes twinkled. 'We love it here.'

'And you've done us a favour.' Peter reached down to pet Gloria, who had come out to say farewell. 'This four-legged character has, anyway.'

'Oh?'

'I was brought up with dogs. Always loved them. Haven't had one for a few years now. But Grace here has never had a dog, and she wasn't sure about my wanting one. Gloria's helped change her mind.'

I turned to Grace. 'Really?'

'Yes. Not something as big, of course. But I can see the appeal now.'

I crouched down, taking the dog's muzzle in my hands and gazing into her big, dopey eyes. 'See, Gloria? Somebody saw your appeal, at last. You must have some, after all.' I kissed her on the nose and had my face licked for the trouble.

Everyone laughed. As we hugged goodbye, I knew we would see Peter and Grace again, and I was more than glad about that.

'How is it at your niece's?' I asked Madame Dupont as I drove her to *La Cour des Roses* for our Saturday session. 'You look tired.'

'Ah, not too bad, Emie. But my niece has small children, and the baby cries in the night.'

'Is it stopping you sleeping?'

She cast me a resigned smile. 'Yes. But that is what babies do, after all – I remember it well. I will get used to it.'

What could I say? Madame Dupont had cared for her family her whole life, and they were trying to do their best for her. It wasn't their fault that nobody had the right set-up.

'So you'll stay with your sister this weekend, and next week with your niece again?'

'Yes. I will be okay.'

I marvelled at her stoicism. 'What's happening with your house?'

'The insurance company are busy with their assessments and calculations. They will make good the house, but my policy was basic, so it will be limited to making it habitable.'

I sensed a reticence. 'But?'

She sighed. 'But it will not be my house any more, Emie, will it? I know it wasn't much, and it was becoming difficult for me, but I was familiar with every last centimetre. And the work will take so long.'

'What about your chickens?'

'I offered to give them to Monsieur Girard, but he insisted on paying me something for them. We are both content with that.'

'I'm glad,' I said. 'One less worry off your mind.'

'Yes. It is a relief.'

We set to work, and Madame Dupont threw herself into it with gusto, chattering at me nineteen to the dozen, as though she'd missed my company terribly over the past few days.

I was secretly flattered, although it gave me a headache, trying to keep up with the speed of her enquiries about the guests (good apart from Gavin), the wedding preparations (getting there, slowly but surely) and Rupert's position with Gloria (going nowhere fast).

Later that afternoon, as I drove her into Pierre-la-Fontaine for the bus to her sister's, she fixed her steely eye on me.

'You must be worn out, doing all the cleaning yourself,' she said. 'I do not want you to get too tired before your wedding.'

'Rupert's helping.'

'You should get someone in. I would like to help on Saturdays if you will fetch me, but during the week, you should get someone else. Promise me.'

I glanced at her resolute expression. 'I promise.'

I relayed the conversation to Rupert as we cooked the guest meal.

'Now that Madame Dupont has given us permission, as it were, I'll make enquiries,' he said. 'Perhaps Juliette, who helped me last year after you went home, when I wasn't well?'

His voice lacked enthusiasm. Apparently, Juliette was efficient but stony-faced and had no sense of humour whatsoever. Still, we wanted a hard-working cleaner, not a comedian.

'Will you call her sometime?'

'I can't wait.'

My phone rang as I was making the filling for Rupert's marinara quiche. When I saw it was my mother, my blood pressure began to soar. She *knew* Saturdays were outrageously busy, she knew they involved a guest meal and that I helped Rupert to cook. Why did she have to pick now to phone?

'Hi, Mum. I'm sorry, but I can't talk right now.'

'It's only quick, Emmy. I need to speak to you about the cake.'

The cake. Damn. Haven't done anything about that, yet. 'And the wedding favours.'

Doesn't sound quick to me. 'Mum, I can't. I'm right in the middle of cooking the guest meal.'

'Oh,' she huffed. 'Will you call me back tomorrow? We only have two weeks left, and …'

'Okay. I'll call you tomorrow.'

Rupert gave me a sympathetic look as I tossed my phone onto the counter.

'She *knows* this is a bad time to ring,' I ranted. 'But she gets something in her head and she's off and running.'

'Put you in a bad mood, has it? Do you want to take a couple of minutes to cool off?'

'Why?'

He pointed to the bowl I was clutching to my chest. 'You're whisking those poor eggs into oblivion, Emmy. Show them some mercy, love.'

'Oops. Sorry.'

Our new arrivals, Kathleen and Deborah, were twin sisters in their late forties and an open-hearted pair, seemingly happy to tell everyone everything about themselves.

When Gavin mentioned his recent separation from his wife over the *moules marinières*, they were full of sympathy.

'I'm so sorry, Gavin,' Deborah said kindly. 'My husband ran off with his PA years ago, so I know exactly how you feel. Left me with three kids to bring up on my own. Had the cheek to try to come back a couple of years later, but I told him where to stick it.' She jabbed her fork in the air for emphasis.

'Quite right, quite right,' Gavin muttered, clearly taken aback by Deborah's vehemence and perhaps realising he'd opened a can of worms that might best have been left firmly shut.

Rupert hid a smile as he brought over the marinara quiche, garlic potatoes and salad, and I saw him glance at the band on Deborah's ring finger.

'But you found someone else?' he asked her, to bring the conversation back to happier times.

'Local butcher, would you believe?' She laughed, then made a face. 'The shop turns my stomach, to be honest, but he's good with the kids – well, teenagers now. Heart of gold. He's looking after them so I could come on holiday with Kathleen. Can't say I didn't go through the wringer before I found him, though. Still, they say you have to kiss a lot of frogs to find a prince, and we've all been there, done that, haven't we?'

Since our other guests were happily married couples, her only response was from her sister.

'Hmm,' Kathleen mused. 'I was more of the *once bitten, twice shy* persuasion after *my* divorce.' I thought I detected a hint of disapproval in her voice, suggesting her sister had not been very discerning, but then she patted her hand in solidarity. 'At least Toby left me well-provided-for.'

This was borne out by the classy jewellery she dripped with, wherever it was possible to hang jewellery. Indeed, as we sampled Rupert's excellent white chocolate *crème brûlée*, Gavin was unable to take his eyes off Kathleen's spray-tanned and gold-and-diamond-clad cleavage.

Letch.

On the bright side, he wasn't letching after me any more.

TWELVE

When I got to Alain's the next morning, he was on the phone to his mother. Again. I helped myself to coffee, only half-listening to his placatory tone.

Then that tone changed. 'Of course. Put them on.'

I could tell immediately that he was chatting to his niece and nephew, the smile at his mouth readily reaching his eyes as he asked them what they'd been up to. Eventually, he waved at me to get my attention.

'They want to speak to you, too.'

'They do?' Pleased, I took the phone from him. 'Hi.'

'Hi, Aunt Emmy.'

'Hi Chloe. I didn't know you were with Grandma and Grandpa this weekend.'

'We came to France yesterday. Daddy is away so Mummy decided to bring us to see our other Granny and Grandpa in Rouen, but we stopped off here first. Grandma and Grandpa took us to see the Eiffel Tower last night. It was all lit up with pretty lights. We were allowed to stay up *really* late.'

'Wow, Chloe, that sounds amazing. I've never seen that.'

'Maybe I could take you when I'm older?'

I smiled. 'That would be lovely. What else have you been doing?'

'We went to the park this morning, but we're going to Rouen soon.'

'I hope you have a lovely time there.' I heard a slight kerfuffle.

'Gabriel wants to speak to you.'

'Okay.' When he came on the line, I asked him about the Eiffel Tower.

'It was brilliant. We couldn't go up it, but Grandma says we can when Chloe's older. I'm old enough already.'

I chuckled. 'So you are. Are you looking forward to visiting your other granny and grandpa?'

'Yes. But …'

'But what?'

He lowered his voice. 'But Mum's grumpy and cross.'

'Oh.' I wasn't sure what to say that. I supposed occupying two small children for the whole summer holiday wasn't all a bed of roses. 'I'm sure she'll cheer up once she sees her parents.'

'Maybe.' Gabriel lowered his voice even further, until he was almost whispering. 'She was *really* mad with Dad for going away this weekend.'

Urgh. 'Perhaps it was only that she hadn't expected it. You know, because he decided last minute.'

'I don't understand grown-ups,' he declared.

I couldn't help but laugh at that. 'Neither do I, half the time, Gabriel. Don't worry about it. Have a good time in Rouen.'

'Okay.'

I heard Mireille call him in the background.

'I have to go now. See ya.' And he was off.

Handing Alain his phone back, I told him what Gabriel had said.

Alain frowned. 'He didn't say anything like that to me, although Mum's still harping on about Adrien. She says he's been acting strangely lately. Doesn't sound himself on the phone. Apparently, mothers know these things.'

I started to laugh, but stopped. Mothers *did* know these things. At any rate, mine always managed to guess exactly what was going on in my mind when I least wanted her to.

'Hmmm,' I said wisely.

Talk of the devil … My phone pinged, and I dug it out of my pocket.

'Who is it?' Alain asked.

'E-mail from Mum. She tried to call me last night, but I had to put her off. I haven't checked on the cake, and she's on about the table favours.' Realising I sounded a little hysterical, I stopped to take a breath.

'Right. That's it!' Alain's tone of voice was decisive with a hint of masterful as he took my phone and reached up to place it on top of the kitchen units – a place that involved him stretching his six-foot-plus a little further, but would involve me fetching a stepladder.

'What are you doing?'

'Is it a matter of life and death?'

'No, but …'

'Is it a matter of life and death in *our* eyes as opposed to your mother's eyes?'

'No.'

'Then she'll have to wait. For the rest of today, we are having a ban on all talk of your mother, your family, my family, the wedding.' He took my face in his hands. 'We spend half our time together on other people, Emmy. I want today to be about you and me, for a change.'

'I won't argue with that.'

'Good, because we're going on an adventure.' He ran his gaze over my T-shirt, cropped trousers and canvas pumps. 'You're fine dressed as you are.'

That meant he didn't have anything too weird planned, didn't it? Trustingly, I followed him to his car. We drove for twenty minutes, away from town and out into the countryside, past fields reflecting golden in the sun, the trees lining one side of the road a thick, summer green, until Alain parked by a riverside and we walked along a dirt path to a clearing at the water's edge, where there were a dozen overturned ... *Oh God* ... canoes.

'You want me to get in one of those?' I croaked.

'Yup. Do you want to go in a double or one of your own?'

'Er. Neither?'

'Not an option.' He gave me a quizzical look. 'You've never been canoeing?'

'No. Thank God.'

'Why "Thank God"?'

'Call me cautious, but I don't want to find myself upside down in the water, trapped in a plastic boat, with my head banging against large rocks.'

The man in charge saw us and began to approach.

'Emmy, I'm not taking you white-water rafting,' Alain said. 'This is a placid river. The boat is open, so you won't be trapped in it if you do overturn – which you won't. It'll take your mind off your mother and the wedding.' His last gambit? 'And it'll be cool on the water, with the trees shading it.'

That appealed. And we were here now. I nodded my head in mute agreement.

The attendant reached us. '*Monsieur?*'

Alain negotiated a canoe for two, and the man handed us life jackets. Perhaps he took one look at me and decided we needed them. Or maybe it was standard procedure. Either way, I was happy to put mine on.

He lugged a two-man canoe to the water's edge and helped me in. It wobbled alarmingly. Alain made it wobble more as he settled in behind me, then launched into a conversation with the man about which direction to go and which forks to avoid because they would end badly for us. (I didn't listen to the details. I was too busy panicking.)

Waving a cheery goodbye to the bemused bloke, Alain plunged his paddle into the water and pushed off.

'Right, Emmy. Grip the handle of your paddle in one hand and the shaft further down near the blade with the other.'

'Then hit you over the head with it?' But I did as I was told. The river *did* look temptingly pretty. And cool. I bet it was even cooler when you fell in.

'You are *such* a baby. Put the blade in the water ahead of you – keep it vertical – then pull it back towards you.'

I tried. The canoe moved. Yay! I did it again. And again. The canoe began to go in a circle.

'A straight line would be good, Emmy. I'll do one side and you do the other, and I'll steer.'

'Okay.' It wasn't easy at first, because Alain's strokes were more powerful than mine, but he compensated, and we got into a rhythm.

I immediately took to the magic of it. The river wasn't wide, and as promised, it was shaded by lush green trees along the riverbank. I loved the way the willows draped themselves over and into the water.

An old wooden footbridge spanned the river ahead, its structure weathered to grey, flowers draping over its sides from troughs. It was like going through a fairy tunnel as we drifted underneath it.

On the other side, my magical wonderland vanished. Two canoes were heading towards us, and I had no idea what to do next. I flailed around with my paddle.

'Pull your paddle out of the water, Emmy,' Alain warned as the canoe tipped about.

I didn't quibble. With no time to manoeuvre, Alain held our canoe steady, allowing the other, more adept river-users to go around us.

'Right, off we go again.'

'What if we meet someone else? You said you'd steer,' I accused.

He spluttered with indignation. 'I can't steer if you're thrashing about like a madwoman. You nearly knocked my teeth out!'

'Sorry.'

'Swap to the other side so you even out the tiredness in your arms, we'll get going again, then I'll show you how to brake.'

When I'd successfully learned how to slow the canoe by putting the flat of the paddle against the water, I felt a little better, and with no other canoes in sight, I allowed myself to relax again. As we moved smoothly along, I enjoyed the rhythm and gazed at the passing riverbanks, catching glimmers of birds flitting past and wildflowers poking their heads out. Blissful.

'What's that?' I asked Alain as we approached an open-sided structure – a tiled roof held up by sturdy wooden posts, with a floor of smooth stone slabs set right to the water's edge.

He slowed the canoe. 'That will be the old *lavoir* for the nearby village. It's where the women came to do their laundry. It would have acted as a kind of community centre, too, I expect.'

I imagined a group of women on their hands and knees scrubbing away on the stones, and made a disapproving noise.

Alain laughed. 'Makes you think of your automatic washing machine with more affection, doesn't it?'

By now, things were going so well that Alain decided I needed a lesson on how to handle one of these things on my own.

'Why?'

'Because we could go in separate canoes next time.'

'You don't want to be in a canoe with me?'

'You should know how to do it on your own, that's all. Right. I'm not going to do anything. You go ahead.'

I started to go in a circle. The panic was back.

'No, Emmy. Swap the paddle from side to side.'

'That's harder. Takes more work.'

'Yup.'

Ever hopeful, he taught me a couple of steering techniques. The bend ahead was hard enough, but the family of canoes heading towards me past the bend was worse.

'You have to steer!' I shrieked.

'No, Emmy. You can do it.'

I did it, alright. First, I steered us broadside to the river and the oncoming canoes. Then I made a diagonal beeline for the nearest bank. We didn't crash into it. Oh, no. That wasn't possible due to the overhanging trees into which we speedily sailed, ducking until we could duck no more and ending up tangled in the branches.

'Aaargh,' I managed.

Alain was too busy laughing to speak. I don't know why. Being so much taller, he'd got the brunt of it.

'It's not funny,' I snapped through a mouthful of leaves.

'Yes! Yes, it is! How did you *ever* pass your driving test?'

'A car's different,' I grumbled. 'Get us out of here. I don't want a bra full of caterpillars!'

When he'd pulled himself together, he manoeuvred us out with a lot of huffing and puffing and jabbing at tree trunks with his paddle. Back in the middle of the river, we plucked chunks of vegetation out of our hair.

'Enjoying yourself?' he asked serenely.

I would have slapped him, but I was too hampered by my life jacket to twist round far enough.

'Time to turn back anyway,' he said. 'I don't like the look of those clouds.'

I glanced up at the sky. What I'd taken for shade had become clouded over and threatening.

'Turn back? Doesn't that mean we'll be paddling against the current?'

'Yes, but this is a slow-flowing part of the river. In other places, they send a minibus to pick you up at the other end, but it's not necessary here.'

Hmm. It might not have been geographically necessary, but my arms begged to differ as we turned the canoe – with me showing a minimal amount of competence, for which I was praised – and headed back. The going wasn't much harder, as Alain had promised, but my arms were tired now. It seemed like ages until we reached the *lavoir* again, and we had quite a way to go beyond that.

Alain tapped my shoulder and pointed. A man in a wooden boat was rowing towards the opposite bank, his passenger standing at the back of the boat – a large, lanky black dog with ginger paws, muzzle and floppy ears that watched us warily. It made me smile.

A good ten minutes beyond the *lavoir* – too far to go back for shelter – the heavens opened and heavy rain began to patter all around us.

'You can steer us into the trees now, if you like, Emmy.'

We hurriedly made for a large overhanging tree, ducking until we were under its branches. My T-shirt was wet where it wasn't protected by the life jacket, but at least under here we wouldn't gather so much water in the canoe. I didn't fancy bailing out.

It was atmospheric, listening to the rain patter on the trees and watching it bounce on the river's surface, each drop rippling out. Occasionally, large drops would work their way through the tree and down the back of my neck, but it was better under here than out on the water.

'What if it doesn't stop?' I asked.

'We'll wait for it to die down a bit, then go. They only forecast infrequent showers today. I wouldn't call this a shower. More like a deluge.'

Alain reached forward and put his arms around me, pulling me back against his chest, his life jacket acting as a pillow. Cosy.

I realised that I hadn't thought about my mother or the wedding once since I'd wobbled my way into the canoe, and that my neck and shoulders were almost stress-free for a change.

Then I realised that realising I hadn't thought about it was a kind of thinking about it, so I blanked it out before it could take a hold. Sunday was my day with Alain, and he was right. We needed a day off from it all.

After a while, the rain calmed and we pushed out from under the tree. By the time we got back to our starting point, it had stopped and we were beginning to dry out.

'Did you find shelter?' the man asked as he helped me out, then helped Alain haul the canoe back up onto the bank.

Alain answered. 'Yes. It turns out that my wife-to-be is skilled at steering into trees.'

The man laughed, shouting 'Congratulations!' after us as we walked back to the car.

Back at Alain's house, we took turns with hot showers, then sat out on the patio with a glass of wine, hoping the neighbours didn't see us in our lazy robes at such an early hour of the evening.

I rolled my shoulders.

'Pulled something?' Alain asked.

'Yes. You, or so I was led to believe.' I waggled my engagement ring at him.

'Ha ha. I meant your neck.'

'No, it's just aching. Tops of my arms too.' I saw the concern on his face and smiled. 'But it was fun. I like it when you surprise me with things like that.'

'Good.' There was a glint in his eye. 'Because I still have a few surprises up my sleeve.'

I raised an eyebrow. 'Glad to hear it.'

He cupped my neck in his hand and pulled me to him, kissing me long and sweet. He tasted of wine. Mmmm.

'Want to find out what kind of surprises?' he murmured.

I laughed, although it came out a little croaky as his other hand slid to the knot on the belt of my robe.

'Alain, we've been together for a year now. I doubt you have *those* kinds of surprises up your sleeve.'

He gave me a long, disapproving look. 'That's exactly the kind of thinking that will turn us into an old married couple before we know it. Come inside, Emmy. Let's surprise each other.'

I was happy enough to go inside, so I allowed him to lead me in.

But he didn't aim for the stairs as I expected. Instead, he led me into the dining area, pulled the curtains closed and pushed all his accounting papers off the table with one sweep of his arm. Oh my …

The next morning, most of our guests decided over breakfast that they would go into town for the weekly market. It was something Rupert and I encouraged – we felt it showed small-town France at its best. Gavin was dubious but said he might take a look around.

Only Kathleen declined. 'I have a headache and I feel achy. You go without me, Deborah. You love mooching around.'

'You could have lunch with us afterwards, Deborah,' Barbara, one of the other guests, offered.

Deborah acquiesced with a look of concern for her sister, and we got on our way.

In town, I left Rupert to make a start on the shopping while I went to the *pâtisserie*. Conscious that I still owed my mother a phone call and she would soon be on the warpath, I figured I ought to have something concrete to report. But as I stepped into the cool shop and drooled over the fresh strawberry tarts and gooey meringues, not to mention my favourite *tartes au citron*, it occurred to me that I wasn't sure why the hell I was here.

The cake had been agreed upon weeks ago, when the manager-ess had spent a long session with my mother and me, showing us designs for traditional French wedding cakes – numerous variations on the theme of a *croquembouche*, traditionally a tall pyramid of cream-filled puff pastry balls or sometimes *macarons*, decorated with any combination of icing, chocolate, ribbons, even fireworks.

Mum had countered with images of traditional British wedding cakes on her tablet. She would have had it made in England, but even my mother knew that transporting a wedding cake to France was virtually impossible.

We reached an impasse. The manageress had looked at me and asked, 'What would you prefer? French or English?' and I'd looked thoroughly woebegone, until she'd said, 'Wait. How about this?'

She'd rushed off to fetch a pad and pencil and began sketching. When she showed it to us and explained, we knew it was the perfect compromise. A large circular sponge, covered in white fondant icing in British fashion, would act as a base layer to a French pyramid of macarons in white, lilac and a deeper purple, with thin strands of ribbon draping down the pyramid to the base cake.

When the manageress approached me now and politely asked what she could do for me, I had to stop myself from saying, 'I honestly have no idea.'

Instead, I tried to put myself in my mother's brain (heaven help me), imagining anything and everything from the cake being an ugly monstrosity to the woman getting the date wrong or her schedule being eaten by a werewolf, then babbled something about my mother being nervous about the cake and could I see the sketch again?

She kindly obliged, reassured me that it would be magnificent and confirmed that they would deliver it by van to the *château* on the morning of the wedding (and yes, she had the date right). I thanked her profusely and left.

Miffed about the awkward conversation I felt my mother had put me through for no good reason, I trailed grumpily up to the stalls at the top of the market, where Rupert was still battling holidaymakers to complete his shopping. How long could it take someone in shorts and a straw sunhat to choose which cheese to buy, for goodness' sake?

While Rupert queued, I texted Mum about my visit to the *pâtisserie*. She would have to make do with that for now. I was in no frame of mind to hold a civil conversation on the phone.

Ensconced in the café, the fragrant coffee soothed my senses enough for me to recount my first canoeing experience to Rupert and Jonathan, making them laugh – although I left out the sex-on-the-dining-table finale.

'How's Madame Dupont?' Jonathan asked with concern afterwards.

'She's staying with her niece this week.'

Jonathan sighed. 'I can't imagine something like that happening at that time of life. My house may be humble, but it's my home. It's easy to take it for granted.'

I sipped my coffee. 'That's true, Jonathan, but you know, I think that house was becoming more of a burden than a help to her.'

'How do you mean?'

'Before the fire, she said a few things that made me wonder. The whole place needed refitting, but of course she doesn't have the money to do anything major.'

Rupert tutted. 'I should have asked her if she needed anything doing over the winter, when I had time.'

I shook my head. 'You know as well as I do that she's too proud to accept that kind of help. Besides, creosoting her fence is one thing. Replacing her kitchen and bathroom and heating system and boiler and heaven knows what is another.'

'My DIY skills don't stretch that far,' Rupert admitted. 'And I suppose she has plenty of family to help.'

'She has, and they do, when they can. But they're busy working and bringing up children.'

'That cottage *is* isolated,' Jonathan mused. 'Especially with no transport.'

'Maybe she's better off with family for a while,' Rupert said. 'Give her a chance to regroup.'

Bob arrived late, and Rupert was set to order me a second coffee, but I declined.

'I need to get this stuff back before it wilts.' I pointed at all our bags. 'And with Madame Dupont missing in action, I have too much to do. Might be best to do the daily room clean while everyone's still in town.'

'I can give Rupert a lift home on the bike later, if you like,' Bob suggested.

The idea of Rupert riding pillion made me smirk. 'Okay. But I want him back in one piece, preferably.'

Back at *La Cour des Roses*, I stored the shopping away and went upstairs to make a start on my daily whizz around the guest rooms.

I heard giggling coming from Kathleen and Deborah's room. Good. Kathleen must be feeling better, if she was well enough to chat with a friend on the phone. Since I couldn't do her room, I decided to start on Gavin's – he was the least keen on the market and might be back soonest.

As I entered, I wrinkled my nose. That man could do with a lesson in *less is more* when it came to aftershave. I started on the bathroom, puzzled that it was still steamed up, wiping it down and chucking bleach down the loo.

I got to the doorway, ready to minister to the bedroom, just as Gavin came back into the room, wearing only a robe. It wasn't tied as tightly as I would have liked, allowing glimpses of pale chest and thighs not reached by the French August sun.

I jumped a mile. As did he.

'Gavin! I assumed you were out, or I never would have come in to clean,' I blustered, keeping my distance.

'Ah. Hmm. I *was* going out, but there was a change of plan. I mean, I didn't feel too good, so I came back to bed for a while.'

'Oh dear. Perhaps it's the same thing that Kathleen's got. I'll get out of your way.' I forced a smile, thinking none of this explained why he'd been outside his bedroom in his robe, unless …

'Gavin, how long can it take to get a condom from your wallet, for God's sake?'

Kathleen stopped short in the bedroom doorway, also in a robe, with nothing under it other than the usual gold glinting against tanned skin.

Gavin went the kind of colour that makes you want to reach for a blood pressure cuff. 'Oh. Er. Ah.'

Well, *this* was exciting for a Monday morning.

'I'll leave you to it,' I said clumsily. 'Excuse me.' With as much dignity as I could muster, I walked past Gavin to the doorway, where it took Kathleen a few stricken seconds to work out that she needed to move in order for me to exit.

'As you were,' I said as I rushed into the next room, knocking first to avert any further unwanted discoveries.

Collapsing in the tub chair in the corner, I closed my eyes, then grinned at the idea of Deborah lunching with Barbara and Keith, oblivious to the fact that Twin Sister Bling was pain-free and busily bonking Mr Aftershave. And I couldn't help wondering if Gavin would manage to recover his … poise.

When the two available rooms were done, as I went downstairs I heard a moan from behind Kathleen's closed door. Since I doubted it was down to the flu, I assumed Gavin must have got over his embarrassment satisfactorily, after all.

THIRTEEN

Rupert was childishly delighted by the Gavin and Kathleen story when he got back from town.

Neither of us was delighted when I answered the phone.

'Emmy? Gloria here.'

Oh, joy. 'Gloria!'

Rupert waved his hands madly, indicating he didn't want to speak to her, and shot off into the garden. Getting that dog had made him a darned sight fitter – he moved pretty fast for a sixty-year-old.

Gloria usually phoned Rupert on his mobile, so I hadn't spoken to her for nearly a year. Indeed, the last time we spoke, she tried to tell me that my boyfriend had slept with her. It wasn't true, but it caused an awful lot of trouble and almost ruined Rupert and Alain's friendship for good. I wasn't ready to forgive her for that.

Staring at the magnetic strip of chefs' knives across the kitchen – a subconscious choice? – I mustered up some courtesy, but I had to dig deep.

'How are you, Gloria?' *Not that I care.*

'Is Rupert around?' Polite chit-chat wasn't on Gloria's agenda either, then. 'I've been trying his mobile, but he's not answering.'

Then he probably doesn't want to talk to you, and who could blame him? 'He's round at Jonathan's' was what came out of my mouth, to buy him some time.

'That old coot's still going strong, is he?'

Bitch. 'Indeed he is, and we all love him dearly. I'll tell Rupert you phoned.'

'Do that, Emmy. It's important.'

'I'm sure it is.' *All your demands are important to you. The rest of us live a life that doesn't involve seeing how much we can squeeze out of others.*

I would have choked out a goodbye, but Gloria wasn't interested in pleasantries. She'd already gone.

Rupert was down at the chicken run, inspecting the fence. The dog was splayed out in the shade with one eye on what her master was doing, although it looked like sleep would get the better of her any minute now.

'Little buggers tried to escape this morning,' he explained. 'One of 'em was almost out.'

'Gloria says it's important. She's been trying your mobile.'

'Ah. Yes. I have had several missed calls. Couldn't face them today. Sorry you had to talk to her.'

'No problem,' I lied. 'I told her you were at Jonathan's, so you have time to steel yourself.'

'Thanks, Emmy. I'll fix this, then get it over with.'

Ten minutes later, I heard raised voices and went to the patio doors to see Rupert pacing the garden, throwing his arms about in agitation as he spoke.

When he came back in, I had a cup of tea waiting for him.

'Need something stronger than tea,' he grumbled.

'What does she want?'

'What *doesn't* she want?'

'Shouldn't the solicitors deal with that?'

'Hmm. That trip of mine to London couldn't be done by them, though, could it? That went okay. Lulled me into a false sense of security. But these phone calls? They tire me out.'

'There's no need for all this,' I said sternly. 'If there's nothing more to do in person, you should tell her you'll only negotiate via your solicitor.'

'I'm worried that'll make her sulk and lead to more demands.'

'Surely there's a limit to what else she can demand?' Although as far as I could see, there were few limits – or depths – to anything with Gloria. 'Why don't you e-mail her? Tell her you don't think personal contact is good for *either* of you, and you'd prefer to go through the proper channels?'

He puffed out a breath. 'I'll think about it. Oh, by the way, I phoned Juliette about cleaning for us.'

My eyes lit up – the extra cleaning was taking its toll. 'Can she help?'

'Yes. She can start tomorrow, but she wants a pay rise and she can only do two mornings a week to suit her.'

'Oh. Well. Better than nothing. Thanks.'

The next day was Juliette's first cleaning shift, and she was, as Rupert suggested, lacking in humour. A stout woman in her late thirties, she greeted me curtly, listened politely to what I wanted her to cover in her two shifts a week and got on with it.

'See what I mean, Emmy?' Rupert muttered out of earshot. 'That woman is hard work.'

'As long as she *does* some hard work. We'd be worse off with someone who spent the whole morning chattering.'

But when I took an espresso out to Ryan in the garden, he also had an unfavourable opinion.

'I see the crabby bag that Rupert had helping out last year is back. Went into the kitchen for a glass of water and she frightened me to death, demanding to know what I was doing in there. Didn't dare ask for a coffee.'

'She'll be here twice a week.'

'Hmmph. Might start bringing my own water bottle with me,' he muttered. 'Makes you appreciate Madame Dupont all the more, doesn't it?'

'It certainly does.'

When I got back to *La Cour des Roses* after running errands that afternoon, I found Jonathan ensconced in a chair in the garden, an iced tea at his elbow and the dog stretched across his feet. He bent to absentmindedly fondle her ears from time to time, and they both seemed content with the arrangement.

'Hi, Jonathan. A special occasion? Or are you just soaking up the grandeur of the garden?'

Rupert sometimes brought Jonathan over for that sole purpose, but usually when we weren't so busy.

'I asked Rupert to fetch me. I want to talk to you both.'

'Oh?'

He waited until Rupert came from the kitchen with iced tea for me, too.

'Now then,' Jonathan said, 'What about poor Madame Dupont? Is there anyone who can take her in long term yet?'

'Her niece says she's welcome, but she has small children, and the baby cries in the night. It can't be helped.'

'You're worried about her?'

'I'm worried that all this upheaval is a bit much at her age.'

He nodded. 'I've been thinking. She can come to me. I have a spare room. I'm in town, so she has access to anything she needs, and she can stay as long as it takes to get her house sorted.'

Rupert and I exchanged a surprised look.

'That's kind of you, Jonathan, but you don't know each other well,' Rupert said cautiously.

'I've had a few chats with her here at *La Cour des Roses* over the years. We're a similar age. It might be nice for me to have someone around, now I can't get about as much. And due to my sexual persuasion, she can rest assured that her virtue will remain safe.' He winked at me. 'What do you reckon?'

'It sounds like a great idea, but …'

'Will you speak to her about it?' Jonathan pushed.

'I could take you round to see her now, Jonathan, if you like,' Rupert offered.

I leaned over to kiss Jonathan's papery cheek. 'Thank you.'

Since we had a guest meal that night, I would have no opportunity to tell Alain about Jonathan's offer, so I phoned him when I could grab a break from the kitchen.

'I'd never have thought of it,' he admitted. 'But it's better than her being huddled with family when they haven't got room for her. Hope they get on alright. It's not like they know each other too well, is it?'

'No, but it's a mutual arrangement. Madame Dupont needs somewhere to stay, and Jonathan needs the company and some help.'

'I'm glad.' He hesitated. 'Mum phoned again.'

'Oh?' I wasn't sure which of us would win the competition for whose mother was bothering them most at the moment. 'Is everything okay?'

'Not sure. They've got the kids staying with them.'

'*Again?*'

'Yep. Last minute, too. Sabine brought them from Rouen yesterday, and she's gone back to her parents on her own. Mum thinks that's odd.'

'Your mother thinks everything's odd at the moment.'

'I know, but it is, isn't it?'

'Adrien had a weekend on his own, remember. Maybe Sabine feels she deserves a little me-time, too. It is strange, though. I mean, Sabine and Adrien already had a child-free week together, didn't they?' I shrugged. 'But your mother adores having them, so it's a bonus for her, isn't it?'

When my mother phoned the following afternoon, I was *so* not in the mood. I'd just had a text from Kate telling me she'd finally found all her accessories – a relief, after daily reminders from my mother, apparently. I was *not* happy that my mother had continued to harangue Kate even after she found her dress. That she'd gone through Sophie directly about the make-up trial. And I was still cross with her for phoning me on Saturday evening, when she *knew* I would be tired and busy. For making me have that awkward conversation over the wedding cake on Monday. More than once recently, I'd told myself I only had to get through the wedding, and then this would all be over. And then I'd realised what a sad state of affairs that was, to be thinking that way.

So no, I wasn't in the mood for more of the same.

The topic for discussion this time? The night before the wedding. It had already been decided upon, but my mother wasn't ready to let go. It felt like every conversation we had lately was about her having one last shot at something I'd already put my foot down over.

Well, she was messing with the wrong woman on the wrong day.

'I don't understand your thinking, Emmy.'

I looked through the kitchen window at the afternoon sun glinting off the gravel and took a deep breath to catch a waft of calming lavender.

'And I don't understand yours. Why do you want a big group of people going out for a restaurant meal the night before the wedding? It'll detract from the specialness of the reception if we've already seen practically everybody the night before.'

'I'm not talking about everybody, Emmy,' she snapped. 'Only close family – the people staying at *La Cour des Roses*. Rupert. Your bridesmaids.'

'That's over a dozen people! We'd never get anywhere booked now.'

'If you'd pulled your finger out …'

I remembered what Alain had said about putting my foot down.

'I don't *want* to pull my finger out. Rupert has kindly offered supper at *La Cour des Roses*, and that suits me.'

'But that leaves out anyone staying at the *château*.'

I took a deep breath. 'That's the whole point of the wedding, surely – to see everyone at the reception?'

Although pardon me for thinking that the whole point of the wedding is to get me and Alain hitched.

Mum huffed. 'If you're sure that's what you want.'

'I'm positive. It would be too late a night for Gabriel and Chloe, and I don't want a gutful of rich food before the wedding.'

'There's no need to be snippy, Emmy.'

There's every need.

'And another thing,' Mum went on. 'You never phoned me back about the wedding favours on Sunday.'

No, because my fiancé confiscated my phone so you couldn't drive me mad. And we had a fabulous day and made fabulous love on the dining table instead.

'I'm sorry. I was busy and I forgot.' When she tutted, I went a step further. 'I'm *really* busy, Mum. It's August. We're booked up here. My own business is busy, too. I'm up to my eyes.'

'Oh, and I'm not? Coordinating the guests and answering everyone's queries and giving out directions and heaven knows what?'

I took a deep breath and quelled the feeling that I was thirteen again, my mother and me in a battle of wills that neither of us was going to win.

'I appreciate that. And I'm sorry I didn't get back to you. What did you need to talk about?'

'It doesn't matter now. Aunt Jeanie and I dealt with it.'

Then why make such a fuss? 'Thank you.'

'You're welcome. But bear in mind that we only have just over a week to the wedding, Emmy, so a swifter response time on your part wouldn't go amiss. I'll see you on Sunday.'

She clicked off, leaving me with a bad taste in my mouth. Disagreements between my mother and me were certainly not unheard of, and it wasn't unknown for one or the other of us to take our bat and ball home occasionally – but I could do without it, the week before the wedding.

'Well, he did it, Emmy,' Rupert commented the next morning as we waved Gavin off for another year.

The dog sat calmly by Rupert's legs, watching as the car disappeared. I think she was glad to see Gavin go, too.

'Did what?'

'He said, "It won't be hard to get myself another woman." Remember? And he was right.'

'How do you know, though? Just because he and Kathleen slept together doesn't mean it's serious.'

'They were making plans to meet up once the ladies get back to England. Seems he's swapping one trophy wife for another. Or trophy girlfriend. Kathleen has class, independent means thanks to her loaded ex-husband, no kids and a decent figure. She only lives fifty miles away. And she's a few years younger than him. I imagine he'll be keen to show her off at the golf club. Deborah doesn't look too happy about it, mind you.'

'She's got a warm-hearted butcher and three teenagers to go back to. What's she got to complain about?'

I went back indoors to supervise Juliette for another shift, but she was as hard work as last time. She was a grafter – and I appreciated that – but not much of a social animal.

By the time we'd finished, I was relieved to get away for my afternoon appointment for highlights and a final cut at Sophie's salon. I never really enjoyed going to the hairdresser back in the UK, not quite knowing what they would do to me and always fearing the worst. But I'd struck gold with Sophie. I immediately relaxed, knowing she would do a perfect job.

'So, Emmy. Catch me up on the latest gossip,' she said as she arranged her dishes of highlighting goo and brushes and foil squares.

'*La Cour des Roses* is running smoothly,' I told her brightly. *Always start with a positive.*

'You have done a great job there, Emmy. Rupert must be very pleased.'

'Rupert is very busy. I don't know about pleased.'

Sophie laughed. 'And your business is doing well?'

'I've had problems to deal with, and there's no chance of becoming a millionaire, but by the end of this year I'll have paid myself back the money I borrowed from that inheritance from my grandmother, and a little more besides. I'm satisfied.'

'You should be. You have done so much in just one year!' She held my gaze in the mirror. 'And?'

I frowned. 'And what?'

'I get the feeling there is something that is not going quite so well, Emmy. What is it?'

I toyed with denial, but I knew Sophie would never allow me to get away with that. Shrugging, I admitted, 'Weddings. Mothers. Urgh.'

'Ha! That is expected.'

'Yeah, but it's getting worse, Sophie. I know we all laugh about it, but she's really starting to get my goat now.'

'What is this goat?'

'Er. She's getting on my tits,' I rephrased.

Her eyes lit up. 'Ah, yes, this I understand. In what way?'

'Pushing for things I don't want and never did. Not seeing my point of view.'

'You should stand up to her. This is your wedding, not hers.'

'That's what Alain says. I'm trying, but it's not easy when she's done the bulk of the hard work. She's put so much time and energy into this.' I sighed. 'But I could do without fighting these battles so close to the wedding. I'm worried we'll fall out properly, and it'll ruin the day.'

Sophie gave me a stern glare. 'You should not have to do something you do not want to, not at your age.'

'That's partly the trouble. On the phone yesterday, I felt like I was back in my teens.'

'But your mother has always been like this, *n'est-ce pas*? Surely you have found a way to handle her by now?'

'I wish I could say yes, but I can't. When I was little, I soon learned that fighting her was hard work – it was easier to do what I was told. And to be fair, Dad would always step in if he thought she was being unreasonable – beyond her usual unreasonableness, that is. In my teens, I rebelled, and it was exhausting for both of us. I suppose we've found a halfway house over the past few years, but we go through patches of good and bad. Right now, we're heading rapidly into a bad patch, and the timing isn't ideal.'

'It will be alright, Emmy.' Sophie shook her head. 'Poor you. Working so hard, arguing with your mother, worrying about Madame Dupont, running two businesses.'

'I know. How I'm still sane, I don't know.'

Sophie laughed. 'Who said you are sane?'

When she'd finished, I looked in the mirror. My hair was a fabulous golden blonde, and the soft waves I would have on my wedding day were a new look that I wanted to adopt for*ever* but I knew could never be practical. I didn't have that amount of time on a morning.

* * *

'It's good to have Marcus and James back, isn't it?' Rupert said that evening as he placed flatfish fillets on parchment, slathered them with his special seafood sauce, then loosely wrapped the paper into a parcel. It was one of my favourites, and my mouth watered with anticipation.

I smiled. Marcus and James had stayed last year and said they would be back. This year, they could only manage a long weekend, but I loved that aspect of *La Cour des Roses* – that magic that made people want to return. I could faff about on social media till I was blue in the face, advertise, send newsletters, update the website, all to attract new customers. It worked well and gave me satisfaction. But it was nothing like knowing you'd hooked someone in for ongoing visits.

When Marcus and James came down for dinner, I greeted them like old friends.

'See, Emmy? We told you that wild horses wouldn't keep us from coming back every year!' Marcus reminded me.

'Indeed, you did. It's lovely to see you both again.'

We exchanged kisses, and I got that lovely glow I always got at times like this, reminding me why I loved this place, and why Rupert had been determined to hang onto it when Gloria would have had him walk away from it. Rupert was a gregarious man who enjoyed others' company. This way, he got plenty. If he didn't like someone, it wasn't long before they left, but if he did, there was every chance he'd see them again in the future. Perfect.

The only exception to the rule was Gavin Henderson, whom nobody liked but who kept coming back year after year like a bad penny.

By Friday evening, Rupert was already on a high after getting Madame Dupont settled in with Jonathan, so when Ellie rolled up in her open-top saloon with possible good news about his

Mallorcan property, he thought all his Christmases had come at once.

'You may have a buyer, Rupert,' Ellie told him the minute she got out of the car. 'I spoke to Luiza at the end of play today. She wants to talk to you tomorrow, so I arranged to call her from my office. Can you be there at eleven?'

'Anything to offload that place.' Rupert pecked her on the cheek, then turned to me. 'Still time for you to enjoy your honeymoon there, though.' He fetched wine and three glasses. 'We'll wait for bubbly till it's signed and sealed, but I don't see why we shouldn't have something grape-based now, do you?'

I enjoyed a glass of wine with them, but since the conversation was bound to be dominated by details of the offer, I excused myself and went to my room.

Alain had an evening meeting with a client, so I worked late, too, catching up with e-mails, bookings, queries, a review trawl, and beginning to formulate plans for next year – possible changes to the website for Nick to sink his teeth into and publicity for next year's holiday season.

And for some of the time, I simply stared through the window at the dark orchard, moonlight casting a glow so the tree trunks stood dark against the rest, enjoying the peace.

I was closing down the laptop when I got an e-mail from Mum. I don't know why I panicked. Just because it was after eleven and she should be in bed and Dad might be seriously ill … I should know better by now. My mother liked to offload her thoughts as soon as they entered her head. That way, it made room for more thoughts. Heaven help us all.

Emmy

Jeanie came round today for our final session on the wedding favours.

They look lovely, and I have to admit, Jeanie's idea was brilliant. See photos attached.

And we've saved so much money. Although your father has been moaning about transporting them all.

Mum

I wondered if the fact that she'd signed off as *Mum* rather than her usual *Love, Mum* meant that she was still fed up that I hadn't phoned her back over this when I should have. But the tone of the rest of the e-mail was upbeat, so maybe she'd cooled off and I was in the clear.

I admired the photos of lilac netting bags of dried lavender for the ladies, tied with ribbon and nestled in antique china tea cups and saucers, and white sugared almonds in white netting for the gents. They looked lovely, even if my dad was having transport kittens because of the china.

Then I fired off an effusive thank you e-mail to Mum, the same to Aunt Jeanie, and breathed a sigh of relief. Another wedding item ticked off, and without much hassle on my part, although my heart sank when I thought of all Madame Dupont's hard work, gone up in flames.

Waving off Kathleen and Deborah the next morning, I wondered if Kathleen really would take up with Gavin Henderson once they got back home. What I did know was that the two sisters had not been getting on as well as when they first arrived. Since I doubted Deborah was jealous – Gavin was a cold fish in comparison with her kind butcher, by the sound of it – I could only presume she resented coming on holiday for quality sister-time, only for Kathleen's attention to be directed elsewhere.

When they'd gone, I drove off to fetch Madame Dupont from Jonathan's.

'How are you managing with Juliette?' she asked.

'She's competent, and I'm grateful for the help. But it's not like having you around.'

This pleased her enormously. As we got to work in the first *gîte*, I asked how she was finding her new temporary home.

'It is good, Emie, thank you. Monsieur Jonathan is a kind gentleman and my room is nice. He likes my cooking. He had not been eating properly before. And I made him tell that useless once-a-week-I-might-dust-if-I-can-be-bothered cleaner that she is no longer needed.'

Her nose went up in the air, making me smile. It seemed that both she and Jonathan were suited with the arrangement.

'Do you spend much time together?' I asked her curiously, unable to imagine how two old people, who had each spent years living on their own, would get along in a small house with an open-plan downstairs.

'I am content to read in my room and listen to the radio, to give Monsieur Jonathan his own space. I do not want to take over his house. Sometimes we watch television together, if there is a film. He often sits in his little yard, and I can go into town if I want a walk.'

'What will you do in the long term?'

'We will see. When you get to my age, Emie, the long term is quite short, *n'est-ce pas?*' She patted my arm. 'But I do not want to impose on Monsieur Jonathan for too long. I will stay a while, since he has been so kind, but then I will go back to staying with family.'

I frowned at that. 'I'm sure Jonathan is happy for you to stay for as long as your house takes, Madame Dupont.'

A shake of her head. 'I do not want to outstay my welcome. And I might be wise not to let myself get *too* comfortable. I am spoiled there. It is easy to walk into town to get what I need, any day of the week. The bus to my sister's. The market every Monday.' She sighed. 'The longer I spend away from my house, the more I realise it was becoming too hard for me. I loved my cottage, Emie. It was my home. But it is a chapter of my life – a long book, really – that feels closed now.'

'Once they've repaired it, could you sell it? Buy something in town?'

She cackled. 'That place will not be worth much, even when it is fixed. Who wants a small place like that in the middle of nowhere? Much of it will still need modernising. And places in town are expensive. It is unlikely I could afford it.'

I suspected she was right. 'Could you move nearer your sister?'

'I have lived in Pierre-la-Fontaine all my life, Emie. All my friends are here. My children, grandchildren, nieces and nephews. I do not want to live anywhere else now.'

'I still don't think you should move out of Jonathan's.'

'I won't for a while. But then we will see.' Her face was set.

FOURTEEN

After driving Madame Dupont back to Jonathan's, I joined Rupert in the kitchen for what would be our final 'official' guest meal for a while. The two sets we still had in were due to leave tomorrow, ready for Nick arriving on Monday and Kate on Tuesday.

Rupert pushed a fresh pineapple towards me. A year ago, I would have looked at it as if it were an alien from outer space, knowing what it was but having no idea what to do with it. Now, I didn't think twice.

While I set about coring and de-spiking it, I told him what Madame Dupont had said.

'Don't like the sound of that.' He wound string around the pork loin he'd stuffed and tied it off, while I watched in admiration. Rupert's deftness in the kitchen never ceased to amaze me. 'I can't say I like the idea of her going back to a nomadic existence amongst her family.'

'Me either. Jonathan has the space, and he seems happy to have her there.'

When the pork was nestled in its stoneware dish in the oven, Rupert poured us both a glass of wine.

'It's a generational thing, Emmy. She's a proud old woman, and she'll see it as one thing putting upon family, quite another relying on the kindness of acquaintances.' He sighed. 'We'll speak to Jonathan about it on Monday, shall we?'

As Rupert put the finishing touches on his starters, one couple came downstairs, but there was no sign of Marcus and James.

'They said they were tired when they came back mid-afternoon,' Rupert supplied helpfully. 'Maybe they fell asleep. Could you check?'

They'd fallen asleep, alright, but not in their rooms. I finally found them up on the roof terrace, stretched out on sunbeds, fast asleep and turning rather pink. It seemed a shame to wake them.

Then again, it would be a shame for them to miss out on Rupert's mushrooms Provençale, stuffed pork loin with fresh pineapple, and tarte tatin.

When Alain phoned the next morning, I'd had a restless night with a series of unsettling dreams centred on varying wedding disasters, and I felt disoriented.

'Any chance of you coming round this morning for a little … exercise?' he asked.

'Ha! Er. Mum and Dad and Jeanie arrive mid-afternoon, so I ought to …'

'You know, once family arrive, we'll barely be alone until we get on that plane?'

He was right. I said a fond goodbye to Marcus and James, got straight in the car and drove to Alain's.

He touched his lips to mine. 'Coffee or sex?'

'Hmm. That's a hard one.'

Alain's lips twitched. 'I could make a crass joke, but I'll refrain.' Instead, he cupped his hand around the back of my neck and dragged me closer, deepening the kiss.

I broke off. 'Okay. Sex wins.'

Alain laughed. 'I'm flattered. It takes quite something to waylay you from your caffeine.'

He led me upstairs and we made the most of our last quiet Sunday morning together before we would be married.

And I got my coffee afterwards.

Back at *La Cour des Roses*, there was no sign of Rupert. That wouldn't usually worry me, but with the impending family invasion, I wanted to make sure he wasn't feeling overwhelmed.

I found him in the den. It was Rupert's thinking room, and when I peeped in, that was what he was deeply involved in. There were papers scattered across the leather-topped desk, but he was staring at the teetering bookshelves, his fingers steepled at his chin.

His faithful canine companion was sprawled across the small leather sofa, from which she was strictly forbidden.

'Hi. Are you okay?'

He jolted. 'Hmmm?'

'I thought the prospect of my family and in-laws-to-be might be too much.'

'No. Everything's fine, Emmy. Bordering on hunky-dory. Possibly even peachy.'

'Really?' I perched on the arm of the sofa, earning myself a baleful glare from its main resident.

'Gloria's been in touch.'

'And that's good because …?'

'It's good, Emmy, because the woman has finally decided to see sense. She's accepting the offer our solicitors currently have on the table.'

'But she usually quibbles and throws a spanner in the works.'

'Not this time.'

'Why the sudden change of attitude?'

'Maybe she's as tired of the merry-go-round as I am.'

'And?' There was something else, I could tell.

'And I sent her a note last week,' he admitted.

'You mean an e-mail?'

'No, I mean a handwritten letter. People still do that occasionally, you know.'

'Not to their ex-wives, they don't. I thought you were leaving everything to the solicitors, so you couldn't argue.'

'I decided it was worth a try. She could read it or not. Chuck it or not. I figured I didn't have anything to lose.' He wafted at the papers in front of him detailing what he was *actually* going to lose. 'Not much more, anyway.'

I was intrigued. 'What did you say in this note?'

For a moment, I thought he wouldn't tell me, but he was in a sharing mood today.

'I said it was a shame that ten years together had to end like this. That I'm willing to give her her fair due and plenty more, but surely she must be as tired as I am with the process. Couldn't we let go now? I said I didn't regret marrying her, the years I spent with her, but I *do* regret how tainted it's all become. I regret that any good memories are being eroded by all these bad ones. That I'd like to be at peace, as I'm sure she must.'

I stared at him, open-mouthed. Even the dog gave him a look of disbelief.

'Before you say anything, Emmy, all that was genuine. I know Gloria behaved badly, but we did have some good times, and I was at fault, too.'

'She took it to heart, then?'

'Must've done. Her solicitor has instructed my solicitor to go ahead.'

'You haven't had a personal response from her?'

He smiled sadly. 'I got an e-mail. Three little words.'

'Oh? What three words?' Knowing Gloria, they could have been anything.

'"What you said".'

I smiled. 'Could've been worse.'

'It certainly could.'

'Are you okay, Rupert?'

'Yes. All this …' He waved at the papers on his desk. 'It was inevitable, but I need it to be over now. It's exhausting.'

'I know. I'm glad it worked out.'

He stood, indicating an end to the subject. 'Lunchtime. Tomato and basil soup?'

Since I knew it had been made with basil from the garden and fresh tomatoes – no tinned stuff here – I happily followed him to the kitchen.

While the soup heated, he took a bottle of chilled white from the fridge and waggled it at me.

'One glass to shore yourself up before your mother descends? 'Cause I know I need one.'

I took a gulp from the glass he handed me. 'Nope. It's going to take more than this.'

'I am *not* medicating you with hard liquor at lunchtime, Emmy.' Rupert poured the soup into bowls and carried them to the table. 'It's not like your parents haven't been here before. What's so different about this time?'

'My mother on turbo-charge is what's wrong this time,' I grumbled. 'I got through everything on the sodding list from the last time she came, but she's never satisfied.' I tasted the soup. It was, as tomato soup always is, immensely comforting.

'Your mum just wants you to have a great day.'

'I know. But the way she's going about everything, she'll have the opposite effect at this rate.'

He thought for a moment. 'Try to see it this way. You have the perfect wedding planned. Everything's done, whatever your mother says, from the florist to the cake to whatever. That hotel is fantastic, and I hear the food is superb there. You have the photographer you want. You kept the numbers down, so you'll spend the day with people you *want* to spend it with. Surely there's a limit to what your mother can come up with between now and Friday?' When I gave him a doubtful look, he said, 'And if not? Let it wash over you and remember the end result – being married to the love of your life.' He reached across and took my hand. 'With regard to your mother, Emmy, you only have to get through the wedding. Then you'll be off on your honeymoon, your parents will be back in the UK, and without the wedding to plan any more, your mother will calm down and you'll be back to a manageable number of visits a year.'

I tried to keep his wise words in mind when my parents arrived mid-afternoon, their car full of white and lilac wedding favours and boxes of newspaper-wrapped antique china crockery, Aunt Jeanie hidden somewhere amongst them.

'Emmy, how exciting!' Jeanie gave me a tight hug as soon as she fought her way out of the car, beating my mother to it, much to my mother's annoyance, while Dad looked on with his usual benign patience. It was this lifelong brotherly indulgence that had allowed his younger sister to be too much of a free spirit in my mother's eyes. Jeanie's brunette-heading-for-grey hair, flowing down her back, currently sported vibrant purple stripes, and her enviably slim figure was clad in dungarees to match. Hand-painted canvas pumps completed the ensemble.

Rupert came out to greet his guests, as did his canine companion.

Jeanie put the dog first, greeting her effusively, her natural rapport with animals shining through, before moving on to Rupert.

'So you're the infamous Rupert,' she exclaimed, taking the hand he offered. 'I've heard so much about you.'

'I'd say "All good, I hope", but I suspect that's not the case.'

'Oooh, no, not at all,' Jeanie said cryptically, while Rupert accustomed himself to her hair. She tugged at it. 'Do you like it? I thought I'd fit in with Emmy's colour scheme for the wedding.'

I glanced at Dad, and we both hid a smirk. There was not one item planned for the wedding that Aunt Jeanie's hair would match.

'It's … lovely,' Rupert said politely. 'Let me help with your bags and show you to your room. Flo, you and Dennis are in your usual. Like a second home to you now, eh?'

When they were sorted, we sat out on the patio.

'Oh, this is so *glorious*.' Aunt Jeanie drank in her surroundings. 'No wonder you wanted to live here, Emmy.' Her face fell. 'Won't you miss it when you move to Alain's?'

'She'll still be here all day every day, Jeanie,' Rupert pointed out. 'And I suspect Alain's holds its own attractions.'

Jeanie giggled. 'I can imagine! I couldn't *believe* it when Emmy brought him over for New Year. So *handsome*! If I were ten years younger …'

'Twenty. At least,' Mum corrected tersely, making everyone laugh. 'Now then, Emmy.'

I knew that tone. Getting down to business already. Rupert knew it, too, and hurriedly offered to make a pot of tea for everyone.

'When are Alain's family arriving?' Mum wafted a hand towards the *gîtes*. 'They must have formulated a plan by now, surely?'

Heaven forbid that anyone might not have their plan formulated.

'They arrive tomorrow afternoon,' I told her confidently.

'And the third *gîte*? A relative of Mireille's, is it?'

'Mireille's sister and brother-in-law. But he had a minor heart attack and needs a stent, so they've had to cancel.'

'Oh dear, what a shame.'

This last-minute dent in the guest list didn't seem to worry her as much as I thought it would, and I eyed her carefully. There was something skittish in her manner. Dad was distracted, too, fiddling with his shirt buttons.

'Oh, for goodness' sake, get the girl told, Dennis,' Aunt Jeanie said impatiently.

'Tell me what?' I asked Dad, but he batted the ball back to my mother.

'Tell me *what?*'

'Your dad's retiring, Emmy,' Mum announced.

My jaw dropped. 'When?'

'Next month.'

I gawped at Dad. 'I thought you were carrying on for another year or so?'

'I changed my mind,' he said mildly, closing his eyes and lifting his face to the sun.

'But what will you do with yourself?' I asked, surprised that he would drop from forty years of working to nothing quite so suddenly.

He opened his eyes again. 'If your mother has her way, I'll be swapping one form of slave labour for another. Apparently, the whole house needs decorating.'

Mum slapped him playfully on the arm. 'Your father's exaggerating. I don't want him to wear himself out, but he needs to keep active.'

I gave my father a sympathetic look. 'She'll have you on a regime of tai chi, Sudoku and ginkgo biloba by the end of the first week.'

'Don't I know it. Can't say I mind, though.' He took my mother's hand and stroked it affectionately. 'We deserve a bit more time together.'

The realisation crept upon me that we were about to enter a whole new phase of family dynamics. I wasn't sure how I felt about my father being old enough to retire.

'Anyway, the decorating would depend,' Mum went on. 'We need to get the house valued first.'

'You're selling the *house?*'

'Of course. We've been rattling around in there for far too long, since you and Nick left. It's a family house.'

My head reeled. They'd lived in that house all my life. It was my childhood home.

Mum read my mind. 'Don't be sad, Emmy. We want you to be pleased for us.'

'I am.' I pulled myself together. 'It's a surprise, that's all.'

'Oddly enough,' Dad said, 'It's you and Nathan we have to thank. And Rupert.'

'*Nathan?*

'If your ex-boyfriend hadn't run off with Rupert's wife,' Jeanie explained, 'you never would have ended up staying over here, and Dennis and Flo never would have seen *La Cour des Roses* and Pierre-la-Fontaine and realised what they were missing.'

'Huh?'

'Your dad likes it out here, Emmy,' Mum said.

The penny dropped. 'You're moving to France?'

'Not *moving* here,' Dad qualified. 'We'll buy a small flat in Birmingham and a small house here. If we like it here, hopefully we'll spend more time here than back home.'

I fought to keep the mixed emotions out of my expression. I didn't know whether to laugh or cry. I was pleased that Dad was going to retire. But the idea of them owning a holiday home nearby … I liked being with them, a week or so at a time. But if they took to France like ducks to water, would they be breathing down my neck all the time?

Jeanie shot me a sympathetic look. She knew exactly what was going through my mind.

I thought about the way Mum had been over the past few months, obsessed with the wedding, nattering about every last detail. The only thing that had kept me sane was the fact that it had been mostly from a distance, with the odd visit that I'd

just about coped with. The idea that soon she might be more …
available … really didn't appeal.

I remembered what Rupert had said this lunchtime, about
getting through the wedding and then everything settling back
down to the way it was. Looked like his crystal ball was on the
blink. And sure enough …

'Just think, Emmy,' Mum said. 'We'll be able to see each other
so much more often.'

Rupert came out with a tray of tea and homemade lemon drop
scones. 'Lovely to have you all here,' he said equably.

'You'll be seeing a great deal more of us soon, Rupert,' Mum
said. 'Dennis is retiring, and we're hoping to buy a little holiday
home out here.'

Rupert fought hard to keep his expression neutral. I might
have imagined it, but I would swear his hand shook lightly as he
poured the tea. In merriment at my impending doom? Or in fear?

'That's wonderful news,' he blustered. 'Have you spoken to
Ellie Fielding about it?'

'No point yet,' Dad said mildly. 'We need to get our house
valued. Until we've done that, we won't know how much we've
got left to spend over here.'

'It'd be nice if you could get sorted by early next year, though.
It'd be a shame to miss spring and summer out here.'

Dad sighed with contentment at the prospect, and my heart
did a see-saw action, my desire to see my parents happy in their
retirement warring with concern that they might crowd my
hard-won new life here in France.

What I wouldn't have given for a quiet evening at Alain's. But
no – we went out to a restaurant to celebrate my family's arrival.
It seemed that Alain might have been right about us not getting
a moment alone once my parents arrived. We probably wouldn't

until after the wedding, now. For a brief moment, it occurred to me that I couldn't wait till it was all over ... and then I felt terrible for even thinking that, with such a lovely day planned.

Rupert ducked out of the meal, playing the 'I'm not strictly family' card. Coward. He had plans with Ellie, to go over the paperwork for the Mallorcan property.

'What time will Nick arrive tomorrow?' Alain asked my parents.

'Late,' Mum said sniffily. 'He's working all day. 'I don't know why he couldn't have finished on Friday and travelled over with us.'

Because he didn't fancy spending hours in a car with his parents and aunt, surrounded by wrapped china and being asphyxiated by dried lavender?

Alain suppressed a smile. 'He wouldn't have fitted in your car with all those boxes,' he pointed out more tactfully than I would have.

'That's true,' Mum mused. 'I was hoping he'd bring someone with him, but he never sees one girl for more than a few weeks. He'll never settle down at this rate.' She tapped a finger against her wine glass. 'Although, when he sees how lovely your wedding is, Emmy, you never know. It might give him ideas of his own, mightn't it?'

Alain made the mistake of catching my dad's eye, and they both cracked up laughing.

'What's so funny?' Mum demanded.

But they were laughing too much to reply, exchanging glances to sober each other up but only ending up in further fits of merriment.

It was left to Aunt Jeanie to voice everybody's thoughts. 'The only ideas this wedding is likely to give Nick, Flo, is that living in sin or a swift elopement are both excellent options!'

The evening was pleasant enough. My mother managed not to discuss the wedding arrangements for the gazillionth time – Dad must have had a quiet word – and Alain managed not to choke when my parents told him their plans to buy a holiday house on his home turf. I hadn't had the chance to pre-warn him, but it was good fun, seeing his reaction.

I went home with Alain, and when he'd come up for air from a heartfelt kiss, I discovered that his feelings about my parents' latest news were much the same as mine. I *knew* we were soulmates.

'It'll be good for them, having a holiday home here,' he said diplomatically. 'And it means we won't have to travel to Birmingham to visit, if we don't want to. It'll be nice, seeing them more often.'

My lips twitched. 'But not *too* often?'

He gave me a sheepish smile. '*Exactement.*'

I blew out a sigh. 'I'm pretty worried about it, Alain. Mum doesn't have the same boundaries as me. Just because I'm living in France doesn't mean I'm not working hard. I don't want her coming round all the time, interfering, dominating our time.'

'Don't jump ahead too far, Emmy. They haven't done anything yet – they're only talking about it. Let's cross each bridge when we come to it.'

'Okay.' I puffed out a frustrated breath. 'I was telling Sophie the other day, I'm beginning to feel like a teenager again. All those times I dug my heels in, and Mum dug hers in …' I shuddered. 'We used to shout ourselves hoarse. I remember the first time I tried to go out with black eyeliner on. You'd think I'd had it tattooed on, the fuss she made!'

'How old were you?'

'Thirteen.'

He grinned. 'Did you give in?'

'Ha! Not on your life! We nearly blew the roof off, arguing! She made me clean it off, so I went out without it, then put it back on at Kate's.' My shoulders slumped. 'But I forgot to take it off again before I came home.'

Alain chuckled. 'She was furious?'

I shook my head. 'She just led me to the mirror in the bathroom, under the harshest light, and made me look at myself for five solid minutes.' I rolled my eyes at the memory. 'Of course, I'd put it on far too thick, just to spite her, and it had smudged while I was out. It looked pretty dire.'

'So she was kind of right?'

'Yeah. I *hated* that! Trouble is, I still feel exactly the same way, every time I argue with her about something, putting my foot down but knowing she *might* have a point.'

Alain nodded in sympathy. 'Tense?' He moved his hands to my neck and shoulders and kneaded with long fingers.

'Ow. That hurts.'

'That's because you have rocks in there,' he grumbled. 'Your muscles are so tight, they're hurting my hands.' He slapped my backside. 'Upstairs and find the massage oil, and I'll see what I can do.'

I knew what Alain could do already, and I was usually up for the experience. But tonight? Tonight, I realised, all I wanted was comfort and reassurance.

I caught his hands before they strayed. 'Would you mind if I said I'd rather just curl up for a cuddle and try to get a good night's sleep?'

For a brief moment, he looked disappointed, but he quickly hid it with an accommodating smile. 'Of course not. If that's what you need.'

I knew Aunt Jeanie would love Pierre-la-Fontaine, especially on market day, so I figured if I could get my parents to show her around, that would distract my mother long enough for Rupert and me to stock up on fresh stuff and have a quick chat with Jonathan. I was still worried about what Madame Dupont had said on Saturday, and I wanted to find out how the land lay from the other half of the arrangement.

My parents could then join us for coffee so Mum could interrog—, er, I mean, discuss the wedding photographs with Bob. I resented having to put him through this, but he'd said he was willing to speak to her for mine and Alain's sake.

At the café, Jonathan looked glum.

'Everything alright?' Rupert asked his old friend. 'You seem a little down.'

Jonathan mumbled into his coffee, 'It's that Dupont woman. She's driving me mad.'

Rupert cast a worried look at me. 'You'll have to do better than that, old chum. Emmy and I have enough on with the wedding. Bob here needs to save his patience for Emmy's mother, due any minute. We can't work out your cryptic comments. Spit it out, there's a good lad.'

Jonathan harrumphed. 'She's threatening to move out soon, even though it'll be months before that house of hers is sorted.'

'You didn't criticise her cooking, did you?'

'Hardly.' Jonathan smoothed a hand across his stomach. 'Haven't been as well fed since before Matthew got poorly. No, she says it isn't right to abuse my hospitality for too long, blah blah blah. I can't talk any sense into her.'

I sighed. 'I'd hoped she didn't mean it.'

Jonathan glared at me. 'You knew?'

'She mentioned it on Saturday.'

'I don't see why my hospitality's a *problem*,' Jonathan grumbled.

'It's made her realise how difficult her old house was and how convenient it would be to live in town – something she can't afford,' I explained. 'She wants to move out before she gets too settled.'

'That's daft,' Jonathan said. 'She's welcome *chez moi* for as long as it takes.' He held his hands out, palm up. 'I get fed properly, the house is the cleanest it's ever been, I have company when I want it, but she understands when I don't. I feel safer, knowing there's someone around if I'm not well.' He sighed. 'Fact is, I'd be sorry to see her go.'

Rupert, Bob and I exchanged glances, and I detected a slight shake of Rupert's head. *Don't push the old duffer. Let him come to his own conclusions.*

When my parents and Aunt Jeanie arrived, more coffees were ordered and introductions made.

Aunt Jeanie and Dad greeted Bob warmly – no doubt Jeanie saw in him a kindred spirit, a fellow ageing hippie – but Mum had that air of reserve she specialised in. I was well-versed in that slight flare of nostrils and downturn at the corners of her mouth, and they annoyed me. She knew Bob wasn't a professional wedding photographer, so she shouldn't expect him to look like one.

But Bob, comfortable in his own skin, remained unruffled.

'I've studied your website, Bob.' Mum adopted a strident tone. 'But as it's landscapes, I can't get a feel for the people pictures you take.'

Bob was prepared. 'Mrs Jamieson.'

'Please, call me Flo.'

'Flo, then. Emmy's given me a clear brief.' He emphasised *Emmy*, allowing the subtext, *I answer to her, not you.* Taking a tablet out of his backpack, he flicked across the screen. 'She wants casual shots – small groups and individuals. Some candid and unawares. I've put together a selection of the kind of thing she envisages.'

He handed the tablet to Mum, and Jeanie and I moved in closer, Aunt Jeanie's patchouli oil perfume wafting around us.

As Mum scrolled through, I smiled at photos of Jonathan, Rupert, Ellie and her business partner Philippe, taken in cafés or bars or at home. Many, Bob had caught off guard, and the picture captured the essence of that person. Where someone was conscious of his presence, they still smiled naturally, at ease with his unobtrusive manner. He had a photo of Ellie rolling her eyes at him in annoyance – and it was perfect.

'Oooh, these are *just* the kind of thing I want.'

Bob winked. He knew that. We were playing out this charade for my mother.

Mum pursed her lips. 'Surely we need formal shots, too? The bride and groom. Parents of the bride and groom. Bridesmaids and flower girl. Each side of the families. All the ladies, all the gents – the *traditional* shots.'

'If that's what Emmy wants, Flo.' Again, the emphasis on *Emmy*. 'But traditional group photos are time-consuming. You need numerous shots for one that works. Every single person must be smiling *and* not blinking *and* not moving. Then there are the little things, like making sure nobody has their hand in their pocket – it ruins the line of their suit – or stands with their feet unevenly planted, so their shoulder line is crooked.'

Mum stared at him. 'I had no idea.'

'The *château* and its gardens are a beautiful backdrop,' Bob went on. 'But consider how long you want people standing around in the heat. And children get bored quickly.'

At this, Dad piped up, 'That's a fair point, Flo.'

Bob pressed his advantage home. 'I bet if you ask any married couple to pick out their favourite wedding photos twenty years later, it won't be those large group ones. They're fraught with difficulty: so-and-so died; the Browns are divorced; we fell out with Kathy, I wish she wasn't on the photo. No. People inevitably pick a photo of the two of them that reminds them how much in love they were on the day. And then there'll be that unposed photo of Grandpa Joe, long gone, teaching coin tricks to little Emily, or the bridesmaids laughing as someone's headdress flies off in the wind.'

Oh, I could have hugged that man right now. My mother wavered … and crumbled. *Yessss.*

'You're right, Bob,' she said thoughtfully. 'Having people stand around when the sun's beating down, making everyone sweat and wilt? No. We'll have a quick bash but not spend too long on it.'

Aunt Jeanie had kept out of it, but now she delivered the *coup de grâce*. 'What's *your* favourite wedding photo, Flo?'

Mum's face softened. 'That one of me, Dennis and Great-Aunt Ivy.' She turned to Bob. 'It was only a quick snap taken by my uncle outside the church. We didn't even know he was taking it. It captures my great-aunt's gentle face in the soft afternoon light, and she was beaming at me, so proud. Gosh, I treasure that one.'

Bob looked over at me and grinned. We'd done it.

And yet as we drove back to *La Cour des Roses*, the victory felt hollow, somehow, and it dawned on me that I shouldn't have to feel victorious – I shouldn't even have had to fight the battle. All I'd done was choose my own bloody wedding photographer, then stick by my choice. Hardly a major achievement. It was only the thousand-and-one 'discussions' with my mother that made it feel like a hard-won cause. And so many discussions shouldn't have been necessary, let alone that practised performance with Bob back there at the café.

But over lunch, Mum's brain had already moved on to other aspects of the wedding she still wasn't satisfied with.

'You know, it might not be too late to arrange some sort of blessing at the *château*.'

'Mum, we've been through this. Neither Alain nor I are religious. And it's awkward, with Alain being divorced.'

'I know you didn't want a church ceremony, but surely, a little blessing at the reception?'

'A blessing would be performed by a person of the church. We don't attend church.'

'What about reading vows to each other, at least? We could make a little ceremony out of *that*.'

The tension in my shoulders tightened. Ever since Alain had explained to my mother many months ago (or possibly many lifetimes ago – it felt like it, anyway) that the only ceremony legally recognised in France was performed at the *mairie* – town hall to you and me – she'd sulked big-time, more so after she read on the internet (thank you, technology) about how perfunctory it was, and that people often had a church ceremony afterwards.

'Mum, neither of us wants to announce our innermost feelings for each other in front of all our friends and relatives.'

She harrumphed. 'It could be a damp squib, if you ask me. A quick whizz-through at the town hall, then straight to the reception.'

'It won't be,' I reassured her. 'The mayor is a friend of Alain's and Rupert's, so it won't be too impersonal. It'll be in French, so that's a novelty for the British guests. Then our lovely reception at the *château*. It'll be fabulous.'

But at this point, I wasn't sure whether I was trying to convince my mother or myself of that.

FIFTEEN

Alain's family arrived mid-afternoon, Mireille and Christopher in one car, Adrien and the kids in the other.

The children got out a little grouchy from being cooped up, but that soon turned to excitement and curiosity about their new surroundings.

'No Sabine?' I asked Adrien.

'She'll be here later this afternoon,' he said. 'She's driving down separately, from her parents at Rouen.'

'Oh. Right.'

Mireille smiled. 'So I got extra time with my gorgeous grandchildren.'

'I had to work,' Adrien explained.

I refrained from asking the obvious question: *Why didn't Sabine keep the kids with her in Rouen?*

Instead, I showed them all into their *gîtes*. Gabriel and Chloe made a tour of theirs in all of three minutes.

'We want to see outside,' Gabriel informed Adrien while he was still bringing in luggage.

'Don't you want to unpack your things first?' he asked hopefully.

'Later!' Chloe rebelled.

I stepped in. 'Right, you two, if you take your bags to your room and show me your clothes for the wedding, I'll show you every last corner of the garden. But after that, you have to unpack.'

'Yay!' They grabbed their bags, shot off, and were back in less than a minute.

We went into Mireille and Christopher's *gîte*, where Mireille had the wedding outfits in clear plastic wrappers. She took them out carefully, sternly forbidding sticky little fingers from touching, and held them against each child in turn.

'What do you think, Aunt Emmy?' Gabriel asked.

'I think you'll look smart and handsome.'

'As handsome as my dad?'

'Handsomer.' I put a finger across my lips. 'But don't tell him I said that.'

Gabriel thought that was hilarious, running around the room chortling as Mireille held Chloe's dress against her.

'And you, young lady, will be so pretty that everyone will want to dance with you,' I told her.

Chloe's apple cheeks blushed a delightful pink. 'As pretty as *Maman*?' she copied her brother as she always did.

'Of course.' I turned to Mireille. 'Sabine did a good job with the tie and sash.'

Chloe started chasing her brother around the room, and Mireille shot them a pained look.

'I'd love you to meet Rupert,' I told her. 'Why don't you come over to the house? Have some tea with my parents while I show the kids around.'

Adrien appeared at the doorway. 'Sounds like a plan.'

I led them over to the guesthouse, where Rupert was taking fresh cookies out of the oven.

'Nice to meet you all. Welcome to *La Cour des Roses*.' He came over to shake hands, even with Gabriel and Chloe.

Chloe giggled, and Rupert couldn't help himself – he popped a kiss on top of her curls.

Hearing new voices, the dog came to investigate. The children were thrilled to see her again, and it seemed mutual, Gloria taking their effusive patting in her stride.

'Tea?' Rupert asked.

Christopher smiled. 'Please.'

'Why don't you sit on the patio, and I'll bring it out? Mireille, do you take yours black or with lemon?'

'Milk, please. That is one of my husband's English customs that has rubbed off on me.'

I went upstairs to tell my parents that their company was required. Back in the kitchen, Gabriel and Chloe were edging closer to the cookie tray, the sugary smell tantalising their little taste buds.

Rupert smiled at them. 'They're too hot. I don't want you to burn your mouths. You can have one when they've cooled.'

Foiled for now, Gabriel asked, 'Will you show us round like you said, Aunt Emmy?'

'We'll take the dog with us, shall we? That tail of hers is too dangerous near delicate tea cups and hot liquid. And I don't trust her with those cookies.'

I watched as my parents settled themselves outside with the others, then took my posse around the side of the house.

'This is the orchard. Look, those are apple trees. This area used to be bigger, but Rupert had that extension built on the side of the house.'

'Why?' The inevitable question from Gabriel.

'Rupert needs his own rooms, away from the guests, for privacy.'

'What's privacy?'

'Yes, what's p- pivacy?' Chloe echoed.

'Er.' *Why do children ask so many questions?* 'Privacy is when you'd like to be on your own for a while, away from other people – if you need to think, or sometimes if you're upset.'

Gabriel frowned. 'Is Rupert upset? Because he wants privacy?'

'No. Not at all.' I revised my explanation. 'Grown-ups who don't know each other prefer their own space. So Rupert chats to his guests and cooks for them, but then everyone has their own room to go to. Like you two have your own bedrooms at home.'

Gabriel moved on to something less abstract. 'Why do dogs wee everywhere?' He pointed at Gloria, who was busy sniffing and peeing and sniffing again. *Delightful.*

'Well, I ...'

'Where's your room?' Chloe asked. 'For your p- pivacy?'

I crooked my finger and she trotted after me to my outside entrance. 'In here.'

'Can we see?'

The next ten minutes were a frenzy of picking things up and asking questions and moving on to the next thing, while I panicked about what I might have left lying around that I didn't fancy explaining. When Chloe made a beeline for the bathroom, I decided a distraction was in order.

'Would you like to see Rupert's chickens?' I asked in a tone of voice that suggested seeing some chickens was the most exciting thing in the world.

'Yes! Chickens!' Chloe clapped her hands.

Out we went, past the patio with a quick wave at gathered family, and on down the garden – a process that took forever as the children spied little nooks and crannies, hopping from flagstone to flagstone to find a bench amongst the flowerbeds or following a gravel path to a secluded sitting corner.

I'd forgotten how simple a child's world can be, away from television and computer games. It was heart-warming to know that pleasure could still be derived from a spot of nosy exploring. Chloe pointed at the blooms, Gabriel measured himself against tall sunflowers, Chloe watched for butterflies, delighted if they settled, and ran away from bees until I explained to her that bees were our friends, although it was best not to get *too* near.

When we reached the chickens, Chloe clambered onto the fence that surrounded their run, pointing as the half-dozen birds fussed around and poking her fingers through the chicken wire.

I gently pulled her hand away. 'In case they peck at you.'

'What's that?' Gabriel indicated the small shed at the bottom of the run.

'That's where they sleep at night. Do you want to see?'

Nodding, he pulled at the gate.

I reached over to unlatch it. 'Mind where you walk. Chickens can be messy.' I shut the gate carefully behind us and pointed down at an example of chicken poop.

Chloe wrinkled her nose and took my hand so I could guide her, while Gabriel made a production of hopping about, trying not to tread in anything and startling the feathered ladies, who scurried off in all directions.

When we reached our destination, Gabriel admired the structure. 'Not bad.'

During the quiet winter months when he dealt with jobs and repairs, Rupert had re-stained the walls their usual honey colour but changed the roof to sage green, so it looked like a proper little house now.

Gabriel crouched down with his hands on the ramp up to the doorway and peered inside at the straw and the roosting ledge that ran around the walls.

'Let me see! Let me see!' Chloe tugged at his T-shirt.

'It's small,' Gabriel said as he moved back to let her look.

'There are only six chickens. It only needs to be big enough for them to sleep and lay their eggs and be safe.'

'Safe?'

'We lock them in at night.' I lifted Chloe out of the way so I could show them how the ramp became a door.

'Why?'

'So nothing can hurt them. Dogs, foxes, that kind of thing.'

'But they have a fence,' Gabriel pointed out.

'Yes, but we can't guarantee that something won't get through.'

'Doesn't it annoy them? Being locked away?'

'No. Their little house makes them feel cosy and safe from anything bad that could happen to them.'

'Can't they have a bigger house?'

'They don't need one,' I repeated. 'You should see my friend Madame Dupont's chicken house. She had *loads* of chickens, so their coop was *much* bigger.'

'How many chickens? Can we see them?'

'Too many to count. They're staying with a farmer now, because my friend's house was damaged in a fire.'

'I got poo on my sandal,' Chloe declared pragmatically.

As we walked back up the garden, I congratulated myself on occupying forty-five minutes of the children's time with an orchard, my bedroom and a chicken hutch. Who said the age of making your own entertainment was dead?

'Did you enjoy seeing your granny and grandpa in Rouen?' I asked.

'Yeah.' Gabriel scuffed his feet along the grass, stopping to pull a handful of leaves off a nearby willow tree. 'But *you* said Mum might cheer up when she got to Rouen, and she didn't. We weren't there long, then Mum drove us back to Paris because she said she wanted to spend time with Granny and Grandpa in Rouen on her own.'

I glanced at his expression, but he was concentrating on shredding the leaves in his hands and sprinkling them onto the grass.

'Well. Maybe she'll have enjoyed that and be more cheery when she gets here, eh?' I said brightly, sincerely hoping so.

While I ran Chloe's footwear under a hosepipe round the side of the house, in a circumspect change of subject I asked her if she was looking forward to starting school soon.

She nodded, although she seemed a little worried about it.

'Will all your friends from nursery be in your class?' I asked.

'Some. But not everybody.'

'I'm sure you'll make new friends quickly. Have you met your teacher yet?'

'Yes. She's nice. She has *really* long hair.'

I smiled. I wasn't sure that hair length was the most important criteria for primary school teaching, but children had their own priorities.

'How about you, Gabriel? Are you looking forward to going back to school?'

'S'pose.'

I laid a sympathetic hand on his shoulder. 'It's always hard, going back after the summer. But you'd get bored if the holidays were any longer. Honest.'

We joined the grown-ups on the patio, where Mum and Mireille were chatting about the reception and who the various relative and friends on each side were, and Dad and Christopher were avoiding weddings altogether and discussing cars.

Sabine arrived at that point and was greeted with a rush of affection by Gabriel and Chloe.

'Did you have a good week in Rouen?' I asked her as Rupert went to make fresh tea.

'Er. Yes. Thank you. I … needed a break.' She ruffled the children's hair. 'Even from these two. But I am here now.'

'Adrien and Sabine seem nice,' Mum pronounced later that evening as she and Dad got ready to go out to eat.

I'd pleaded tiredness, so they were allowing me to stay home. What they didn't know was that Alain was coming round after he'd taken *his* family out for an early meal.

'Although I can't imagine having a week away from your own children like that,' Mum went on, judgement creeping into every syllable and making my nerves jangle. 'I suppose people do that, nowadays, don't they? We never did.'

'Yup. Twenty-odd solid years of you and Nick,' Dad agreed dubiously, making me laugh.

'Gabriel and Chloe are delightful,' Mum continued her verdict on the Granger family. 'I still find Mireille a little uptight, mind you.'

It wouldn't occur to my mother that might be anything to do with her harping on about the wedding arrangements, would it?

'Christopher's a decent chap,' Dad said brightly, to deflect. 'A bit quiet, though.'

'I'm not surprised,' Mum said. 'It's obvious who rules the roost in *that* marriage!'

By the time Alain arrived, I could have headed straight for bed. The long, deep kiss he'd saved up for me cemented the feeling. But since Mum and Dad weren't back yet, we settled for tea in the kitchen so we would be around to greet Nick.

Alain studied my face. 'Come outside for a minute.'

I looked at him, startled. 'Why?'

'Out of earshot.'

Frowning, I followed him halfway down the garden to a bench, tea in hand. 'Why out of earshot?'

'Because I'm going to ask you what's up, and I want you to give me an honest answer. What's up, Emmy?'

'I'm tired.' Knowing I wouldn't get away with that, I added, 'My mother's driving me mad.'

He chuckled. 'What's new about that?' Then sobered up. 'Sorry. Why?'

'She really put Bob through the wringer this morning, Alain. He was brilliant, and Dad and Aunt Jeanie helped, and Mum was persuaded.'

'But?'

'But I don't see why he had to go through the whole rigmarole. We asked him to do it. It is our wedding, after all.'

'Yeah. The problem is, it's not our wedding entirely, though, is it?'

'What do you mean?'

'We relinquished control to a greater extent right from the start, didn't we? And we had good reason at the time. When I proposed, you had far too much going on. A new life in a new country, a new job, setting up your business, learning the language. You couldn't possibly have coped with the wedding as well.'

'I know. But so many things have been a battle with her. And Mum keeps coming up with new problems, even this late in the game, and I'm fighting the same *old* battles over stuff I thought was already sorted. Like when she rang last week about going out to a restaurant the night before the wedding. And today, would you believe, she was *still* harping on about a blessing or vows.'

Alain made a face. 'I hope you put her straight.'

'I did, but it's exhausting.'

He stood and began to pace in front of the bench. 'You need to stand up to her more, Emmy.'

'I do! Didn't you hear what I said?'

He gave me a long look. 'But do you, really?'

'You know I do. I've spent months doing just that.'

He took a deep breath. 'I admit you've done well over the wedding. God knows, if your mother had her way, we'd be getting married in Notre Dame with five hundred guests and a reception at Versailles. But those are surface issues. There's a deeper problem here.'

My brows drew together. 'What are you saying?'

He placed his mug carefully on the arm of the bench. 'I'm saying that you only stand up to her over a few things that really matter.'

I looked at him, askance. 'Of course I do. If I didn't pick and choose my battles, we'd spend half our lives at loggerheads!'

'I know *why* you do it. I just don't think that's the way it should have to be.'

My temper rose. I wanted sympathy, not a lecture. 'Oh? And how *do* you think it should be, in this ideal world of yours?'

Alain ignored my sarcasm and sat beside me, taking my hand. 'Your mother's always been a forceful woman. It's in her nature. I *would* say she doesn't know how to be any other way, but I'm not sure that's true. Nobody tells her she needs to moderate that side of her personality. It's like water off a duck's back with your dad. Nick's fairly oblivious. But you …'

I glowered. 'What about me?'

'Emmy, you're thirty-two years old. Don't you think it's time to tell her how much it wears you down?'

I couldn't believe what he was suggesting. 'Oh, and you want me to have a conversation like that, just before the wedding?'

He shook his head, exasperated. 'Not necessarily, but I *am* saying it's a conversation that needs to be had. Your relationship with your mother … You lock horns over something, one of you wins, you move on … That will never change unless you put your foot down over the *basis* of your relationship. She needs to know you've had enough – that you're an adult, meeting her on the same level.'

'You're saying she still treats me like a child?' I jumped up, disentangling my fingers from his, my eyes flashing fire. 'Or that I'm *acting* like one?'

Memories flashed across my mind, a rapid succession of fights over everything from owning a hamster to homework, from burning incense to short skirts, from whether I deserved that maths detention to why I shouldn't be best friends with Kelly down the street because she was a bad influence, from why I smelled of cigarettes to a definitive no, Zak was a totally unsuitable boyfriend and what on earth did I see in him?

Alain chose his words carefully. 'Emmy, parenting is a never-ending condition whereby a parent always thinks they know what's best for their child, even when they've long flown the nest. It's instinct on your mother's part. But for your part? You've left home, developed a successful career, started a new life in a foreign country, you're running your own business, getting married – and yet you still deal with your mother the same way you always have. I'm saying it's time to move on from that now.'

I curled my lip. 'You're saying I should grow up.'

'You're putting words in my mouth, Emmy. That's not fair.'

'What's not fair, Alain, is that you're bringing this up four days before the wedding!'

He tried to take my hands, but I pulled away. He raised an eyebrow but let the gesture pass and began to pace again, catching his head on the branch of a weeping pear and slapping it out of the way.

'Emmy, we'll be married soon. Starting a family. Your parents might be living half the year here. And, much as I love them, I think that sometime in the near future would be a good time to make it clear that this is no way to move forwards.'

'That's easy for you to say.'

He wheeled on me. 'It is *not* easy for me to say!' He didn't shout, but he was raising his voice – something I'd rarely heard him do. 'Do you think it's easy for me to want you to have the best day of your life, the wedding of your dreams, but to have to watch you battle for every last sodding detail? Do you think it's easy for me to know you'll spend our married life in ongoing battles with your mother about everything from where we should live to how we should raise our children to what colour we should paint the lounge?'

'I didn't know you felt that way about my mother.'

Alain ran a hand through his hair. 'I don't. That was over the top. But I'm like you at the moment – most of the time I can

live with it, but sometimes it builds up into something more.'
He paused. 'Your dad's not going to do this thing, Emmy. Nick
won't. It's down to you.'

He came closer, and this time I didn't pull away when he took
my hands. Even though I was angry with him for his timing, the
sensible part of my brain told me he was right. But I didn't have
the heart to continue this now.

I squeezed his hands. 'What would you say if I asked you to
shut up because I don't want to have this conversation any more?'

Alain let out a surprised laugh. 'I'd say you're a wise woman
who knows how to nip a growing domestic in the bud.'

SIXTEEN

Nick looked knackered when he arrived. Blond, handsome in a rakish way, he wore cotton slacks and a short-sleeved shirt that needed ironing.

I hugged him tight, and he and Alain shook hands.

'Do you want anything?' I asked him.

'All I want is a bed,' Nick said apologetically. 'I was working all weekend as well as today. Needed to finish something for a client. Do you mind? I haven't got it in me to be sociable tonight.'

'No problem.'

While Alain put the kettle on, I led him upstairs, and Nick complimented the room as he hoisted his bags onto the bed.

'You'll be pleased to know that Mum and Dad are next door,' I told him.

'Great. Thanks for that, Emmy.'

'Ha! Tea or a nightcap?'

'I'd kill for a tea.'

'Chamomile?'

He shuddered. 'No, thanks. Tastes like gnats' piss.'

Smiling, I went downstairs to deliver his order to Alain.

Rupert came into the kitchen. 'Nick arrived? Sorry I wasn't here to say hi.'

'Don't worry. He looks tired out. Better to save the pleasantries till the morning. Are Mum and Dad back yet?'

'No. The food might be fantastic at that place, but it's notoriously slow service.'

I took Nick's tea up, placed it on a crocheted mat on the antique satin walnut dressing table, and closed the door.

'Nick, did you know about Mum and Dad retiring and selling the house and possibly moving to France?'

'Yes.'

'Why didn't you *tell* me?'

'I was under pain of death not to. Mum didn't want you distracted from getting your arse in gear with the wedding.' A pause. 'You sound upset about it.'

'Not upset, as such. But don't you think it's a bit drastic?'

'Emmy, you've said yourself that you wished he'd retire.'

'I don't mean that. I mean about buying a house over here.'

'It's your fault they're tempted by the paradise that is France.' He gave me a knowing look. 'Worried they're going to cramp your style?'

'No. Yes.' I sighed. 'A bit. But I don't want them to rush into anything.'

He ruffled my hair. 'Don't worry. Dad's level-headed. They're only talking about spending a few weeks or months a year over here. It's not like they're emigrating to Australia. It's what they want. Let them have their adventure.'

I heard the front door open and Mum, Dad and Jeanie pile in. Nick heard, too, judging by his expression.

I left him to crash out – if Mum and Dad would let him. But as I went back downstairs, I felt both childish and churlish. Mum and Dad *did* have the right to do whatever they wanted. They'd put in their time.

Saying hi to them but leaving them to bother Nick, I snuck off to my room to make up and make love with Alain. But when I got there and sank into the mattress with Alain by my side, my eyes were closing before either of us could make a move, and I soon drifted into a much-needed deep sleep.

* * *

'Emmy, I'm sorry I upset you last night,' Alain said the next morning when we woke, the early sunlight reaching across the bed. 'I only want you to have the best day on Friday. I want it to be special for you.'

'It will be, because I'm marrying you. But *you're* supposed to enjoy it, too, you know?' I kissed his shoulder. 'Perhaps we could lock Mum up for the day?'

He chuckled. 'Chance would be a fine thing. And I know your mum means well.'

I glanced at the bedside clock. 'I should shower and get going.'

Letting the warm spray slide over my skin, I thought that despite our words this morning, we were both still a little bruised by our frankness the night before, and as I towelled myself dry, I vowed that I would at least be resolute with my mother this week.

God give me strength.

Alain threw on shorts and a T-shirt and we went round to the kitchen for him to retrieve the dog and go for his morning run before work, and me to get an early caffeine fix.

Looking through the patio doors, I saw Nick wandering aimlessly in the garden. Since he wasn't remotely enthusiastic about horticulture, I assumed he couldn't sleep or was worrying about something, or both.

Kissing Alain goodbye, I made a couple of coffees and took them down the garden, the dew-damp grass tickling my feet, the morning still fresh before the heat began to build.

I loved this time of day. It was even nicer to have the time to enjoy it without worrying about getting a perfect breakfast ready for guests and pandering to their whims and requests. It was more relaxed when it was family.

Nick took the coffee gratefully, sipped and smiled. 'How come coffee tastes so much better over here?'

'It's psychological,' I assured him. 'It's bound to taste better in a glorious French garden in the morning sunshine than in your poky flat in drizzly London.'

'Then why did I spend two hundred and fifty quid on a fancy espresso machine?'

I laughed. 'Because you hate instant coffee and like gadgets?'

'Hmmph.'

I steered him to a bench and we sat, Nick distractedly sipping at his coffee. He'd always been monosyllabic of a morning, but even so.

'Is everything alright?' I ventured.

He scratched the back of his head. 'Yeah. It's kinda weird, you getting married.'

'You've known that for months.'

'But it's imminent now, isn't it? Don't you think it's a bit scary?'

'Nick, I'm the bride. I'm not supposed to find it scary.' I studied his face. 'Why do *you* think it's scary?'

He stared out across the lawn, but he wasn't focusing. 'This being in love lark. I don't get it.'

'That's because you've never tried it.'

'But even if I did – even if I wanted to – how do you know if it's the real thing?'

'I thought I was in love with Nathan, remember? We were together five years! It wasn't till after he left that I realised I'd only *assumed* I was in love with him. And once Alain and I got together, I knew that what I'd had with Nathan was nothing like what I have with Alain.'

Nick smiled warmly. 'I can see that for you. The difference.'

'What's all this about? Have you found someone?'

'Nah. But I've got to the point where I've had enough of casual relationships. I'm thirty, you and Alain are getting married, and … I think I want something more for myself now.'

'You're quite a catch. Handsome, high earner, flat of your own in London – teensy though it may be.'

Nick grinned. 'Thanks, Emmy. You're the best.'

He wrapped his arms around me, his affection for me so clear that it warmed me from my head to my toes. I loved my little brother.

The first test of my resolve regarding my mother came over breakfast.

Fired up by her conversation with Bob, she wanted – no, *needed* – to go back to the *château* to refamiliarise herself with the grounds and plan some of those group photos she still hoped for. Oh, and to deliver the wedding favours.

I couldn't think of anything I wanted to do less, for so many reasons. Kate was arriving later, and I wanted to spend the evening with her. Before then, I needed to catch up with e-mails and bookings for *La Cour des Roses* and my own business, and I needed a handover meeting with Rupert.

I explained all this to Mum, but she was having none of it.

'You work all hours here, Emmy. I'm sure Rupert won't mind if you slack off a bit to come to the hotel with me. You are getting married on Friday, after all. It's only three days away, now.'

Ha! She was finally cracking under pressure – she'd called it the hotel and not the *château*! Alain owed me ten euros.

'Rupert's been extremely kind about my workload lately, Mum, but I am deserting him for a fortnight soon. We both need to be up-to-date. And it's not only *La Cour des Roses*. There's my own business, too.'

Aunt Jeanie turned to her sister-in-law. 'Flo, you don't want Emmy stressed for the wedding, do you?'

Dad placed a hand decisively over my mother's. 'Jeanie and I will go with you to the hotel. There's no need for Emmy to come.'

'I suppose.' Mum's tone was decidedly disgruntled, but I took it as a victory, kissed her cheek, shot a grateful smile at Dad and Aunt Jeanie, and legged it to the den.

With everyone out of my hair, I got a ton of work done and felt pretty good about it.

I wasn't sure Rupert felt the same way.

'I'd forgotten how much crap you deal with,' he admitted. 'A fortnight on my own will remind me why I employed you in the first place. Make me appreciate you more.'

'Always good to hear. But you'll be fine. And at least I'll be back in time for the residential courses.'

'I'll be busy enough, thanks to you touting us as the ideal place to stay for the jazz festival.'

I smiled. Custom for that through Julia Cooper's family gathering was accidental last year, but I hadn't left it to chance this year. 'I got us bookings, didn't I?'

'And you're buggering off to sunny Spain and leaving me to it.'

'You didn't make all this fuss when I left you over Christmas and New Year.'

He grunted. 'Far fewer guests then.'

'*And* you ran this place perfectly well before I came on the scene – and that was with your ex-wife gumming up the works.'

At least I could leave *La Cour des Roses* in Rupert's hands. As for my own business, I'd have to check e-mails while I was away, although I promised myself I'd keep it to a minimum. And I was leaving spare keys to all the properties with Rupert in case of emergency.

As though thinking about it had conjured up trouble, my mobile rang.

'Ms Jamieson? This is Margaret Saunders.'

The name rang a bell, but between my own business and *La Cour des Roses*, I dealt with an awful lot of names.

'Hello, Mrs Saunders. Can I help?'

'I sincerely hope so. This property isn't up to scratch, and I'd like to know what you intend to do about it.'

'I – er – I'm sorry to hear that. Which property?'

She huffed, as though I should be expected to have a mental list of every single occupant of every single property at any given moment, but told me.

'Really?' That property was beautiful, one of a group of buildings developed by Jerry Barnes, one of the first clients to list with me. 'What's the problem?'

'The staircase is unmanageable, the kitchen's smaller than advertised, the bathroom hasn't been properly cleaned, and the gardens are bare.'

What?

'Under the circumstances, I believe we're entitled to compensation, don't you?'

No, I bloody well don't. 'Mrs Saunders, I can't see how—'

'Are you saying you won't take my word?'

That made my mind up. I glanced at my watch, trying to calculate how much I still had to do and guess when my parents would be back.

'Mrs Saunders, I'm afraid I can't speak to you right now. Could I phone you back in, say, half an hour?'

'If that's the best you can do. I'll be waiting.' She clicked off.

Honestly, some people.

'Sorry, Rupert, but I have to go out.'

'Problem?'

I filled him in. 'I want to go round there in person. I can't imagine what she's complaining about.'

'Be careful, Emmy. I know how fastidious you are with the properties you list, so if she's got bugger all to complain about, don't let her bully you. Some people don't half try it on. I've had it here, over the years – people finding spurious things to complain about and demanding I knock something off the bill.'

'And did you?'

'If I thought their complaint had grounds and they might be a returning customer if I played ball, then occasionally, yes. If I thought they were trying it on to get a cheaper holiday, then definitely not.'

'Wasn't that awkward?'

'Yes. But since they probably had no intention of coming back, and I didn't want them back, I stood my ground. It's up to you to judge.'

'Urgh.' I grabbed my laptop and hurried to the car.

As I drove to Margaret Saunders' holiday accommodation, I cursed the time this was costing me. Rupert and I had more or less finished up, but there were plenty of other things I'd have liked to complete so I could relax on the final run-up to the wedding.

At that thought, I rolled my eyes at myself in the driver's mirror. Relax? With my mother breathing down my neck about blessings and vows? With the possibility of her living nearby for several months a year? With Alain and his grand ideas of solving our thirty-two-year mother–daughter relationship just before the big day? Hardly!

As I took the turning to the complex, I looked around. Jerry Barnes had known what he was doing when he bought this run-down piece of land. He'd tastefully converted the old barns and outbuildings, and landscaped the grounds so each property had its own little garden and patio with hedges for privacy – although those were still a work in progress. You couldn't hurry nature.

Margaret Saunders was unnerved when I introduced myself, and her husband looked equally uncomfortable. Both were perhaps in their late fifties, grey-haired and steely-eyed, and their wary expressions suggested that Rupert's instinct was right on the button.

We shook hands briefly as I stepped inside and looked around the lovely space with original beams, plenty of glass to let the light in, pale wood furniture.

'I didn't expect you to come all the way out here.' Margaret Saunders glanced at her husband. 'A phone call would have sufficed.'

'I want my customers to be happy, Mrs Saunders, so I thought I'd better come right over. Shall we go through the issues?'

'Well … It isn't what we expected from your website.'

'I take care to ensure all details and photographs are accurate.'

She walked me over to the spiral staircase at the far end of the spacious lounge. 'This is totally unsuitable.'

'The website states that there's a spiral staircase.'

'But it's tighter than we expected, and steeper.'

'There is a photo of it. And we do suggest it's unsuitable for the infirm.'

Her eyes flashed fire. 'I wouldn't consider us infirm. Merely cautious.'

I pretended to muse. 'If I was cautious, I wouldn't like it, either. But then, I wouldn't book somewhere with a spiral staircase.' I moved swiftly on. 'The kitchen?'

'You can't swing a cat in there.' She led me to the long, narrow room.

'It's described as a galley kitchen, Mrs Saunders.'

'It looks bigger on your photo.'

I feigned concern. 'Really?' I opened my laptop to show her. Bob knew I preferred accurate photos, and he hadn't used any clever angle techniques.

Mr Saunders shuffled.

'The bathroom isn't clean, you said? I'd better go and see.'

At this, Margaret Saunders looked stricken. Rupert was *so* right in his evaluation of these two. If I'd warned her I was coming, no doubt she would have deliberately covered the bathroom in spit toothpaste or dirty soap.

As I expected, the bathroom was relatively pristine, allowing for a couple of days' use, but I made a show of inspecting every last corner. 'It looks more than good enough to me.'

Mrs Saunders stood with her arms folded. 'It's not up to my standards.'

'Gosh, your own home must be *amazing*, Mrs Saunders. Anything else before we go outside?'

She opened her mouth, but her husband shot her a glare, and she closed it again. Outside, she swept a hand at the small lawn, the patio with its shiny barbeque and table and chairs, and the flowerbeds with young but growing shrubs. 'It's too bare.'

'It states on the website that these are newly converted properties. You can't expect lush gardens at somewhere less than a year old. The photographs reflect that.' I showed her my screen. 'In fact, it looks much better than when these photos were taken.'

'So you're not prepared to do anything for us?'

I arranged a puzzled expression on my face. 'What did you have in mind?'

'We're not satisfied. I think a substantial discount is in order.'

I couldn't believe she wasn't backing down. Time to call her bluff.

'As far as I'm concerned, you have everything as described, but since you're unhappy, I *could* move you to another property.'

'We've unpacked and settled in. We have no intention of moving.'

'Then I take it you're fine here, after all. I'm so glad we've settled the matter.'

She wagged a finger at me. 'Your company's new, isn't it? You have a lot to learn. I've been in business all my life, and we were taught that the customer is always right.'

'And I've been in business all *my* career, Mrs Saunders. It may not be as long-spanning as yours, but I was taught to look at things fairly. You don't have any complaints that justify a discount.'

She fixed me with a steely look. 'When we've had occasion to complain in the past, we've usually received satisfaction.'

And *that* confirmed exactly who I was dealing with. No doubt they did this wherever they went – a phone call (which was all she'd originally intended, until I turned up) and a little unpleasantness were worth the trouble if they received their 'substantial discount'.

'Do you regularly complain about your accommodation?'

She hesitated, realising she'd said too much. 'If a place isn't up to scratch, yes.' One last gambit. 'We're prepared to take this further, Miss Jamieson.'

Unbelievable. 'If you mean legally, you don't have a leg to stand on.'

'And what's to stop us posting poor reviews?'

'Er – common decency?'

'I *beg* your pardon?'

'If you leave a poor review, it will be a drop in the ocean. Every other holidaymaker who stayed here loved it. I'll leave that to your conscience.'

Leaving her gaping at my effrontery, I stalked out to my car, climbed in and drove out of the grounds onto the main road, where there was a wide verge for me to pull over and wait till the adrenaline dropped away and I stopped shaking.

As I put the car back into gear and pulled back onto the road, I was proud of myself for standing up to such a formidable character. Alain's words from yesterday evening came to mind. If I could stand up to someone like Margaret Saunders, why couldn't I stand up to my mother? Not the usual skirting-round-the-houses, but a straight-shooting session, once and for all, to get off this ... this merry-go-round?

Maybe. But this week was not the time.

SEVENTEEN

On the drive back to *La Cour des Roses*, I sighed heavily at the thought of Mum coming back from the *château* and regaling me with the many things she thought needed to be discussed. If she mentioned exchanging vows one more time, I wouldn't be responsible for my actions.

As I skirted the edge of town, it occurred to me that I could drop in at Jonathan's to see how he and Madame Dupont were getting on. I was still worried about what she'd said at the weekend about not staying for too long, and Jonathan's confirmation of that yesterday. The fact that such a visit delayed me getting back to my mother never crossed my mind, of course.

It was Madame Dupont who opened the door of Jonathan's little blue terraced house. Glancing around his open-plan lounge and kitchen as I stepped in, the transformation took me aback. Jonathan had previously got by with the ministrations of his rather limited cleaner and occasional spring-cleaning offers from friends. But in the short time she'd been here, Madame Dupont had made huge inroads. Everything was neat and sparkling, even if it was old and in need of renovation, and fresh flowers on the mantelpiece gave the place a real feeling of home.

'You two sit in the yard. I will bring *thé au citron*,' Madame Dupont declared.

Jonathan and I did as we were told, settling ourselves in his little back yard full of ceramic pots riotous with colour. His patio furniture had been scrubbed, I noticed, and the crazy paving swept. We could hear the perpetrator of those deeds filling the kettle and slicing lemon.

'Wow, this place has had quite a face lift!' I commented.

Jonathan grinned. 'Great, isn't it? I keep telling her not to do so much, but she seems determined to repay me. I think she misses coming to *La Cour des Roses* as often, and this has given her a project to sink her teeth into.'

'Has she said any more about when she might leave?'

'No, thank God, but …'

'What are you two whispering about?' Madame Dupont asked cheerfully as she came out and placed the tray on the little table, then sat down with us.

Switching back to French, I quickly said, 'I was admiring the house. You've done an amazing job, Madame Dupont.'

She beamed, pleased at the compliment. 'I have only done the downstairs so far. There is still the upstairs to tackle.'

I glanced at Jonathan with a look that said, 'That means she'll stay at least another week or so'.

'So, why this lovely surprise visit?' Madame Dupont asked as she poured the tea.

Urgh. I could hardly say I was checking up on them. 'I had an unpleasant encounter with a client, and I felt like being with friends.' I told them all about Margaret Saunders.

Madame Dupont nodded wisely. 'These holidaymakers can be a pain.'

I laughed. 'They keep us employed, though.'

'Your parents arrived safely?' Jonathan asked with a mischievous twinkle in his eye.

I let out an exaggerated sigh. 'Indeed. My mother went to inspect the *château* today. Again.'

Jonathan chuckled. 'Your visit to us wouldn't have anything to do with avoiding her, would it?'

I laughed. 'You caught me.'

Madame Dupont tutted. 'You are welcome here, whatever the reason.' She studied me shrewdly, making me squirm in my seat. 'If your mother is making you unhappy, you should stand up to her, Emie. It is *your* wedding day.'

I rolled my eyes. 'Don't *you* start. Alain gave me a lecture on that very subject last night!'

At that, she frowned. 'I hope your mother is not causing you two to fall out?'

'No. What Alain said made sense, but I don't think this week is the time to do it. There'll be plenty of time and reason to do it soon, though.' With a sigh, I told them about my parents' retirement plans, at which Madame Dupont cackled loudly.

'Ah, Emie, you are not sure you like this idea, eh?'

'Hmmph. I'll get used to it, I suppose.'

The doorbell sounded, and Madame Dupont stood. 'I'll go.' When she came back, she was huffing and puffing. 'These people who bother you on your doorstep about things you don't want and can't afford. Disgraceful! I told him not to call again, Jonathan.'

Jonathan winked at me. 'Seems I have my own personal guard dog, now, too.'

Seating herself again, Madame Dupont reached into the pocket of her apron and placed a tiny, tattered leather box in front of me, then took my hand.

'Emie. I am still so sad about the favours for your wedding. I have tried to think of something else I could do for you, but with the fire and moving around so much …' She shrugged off any self-pity. 'These earrings were my grandmother's. I thought they would go with the lace on your dress. I know you will already have something, but you are welcome to wear these if you would like to, and you can keep them anyway. I want you to have them.'

Swallowing back tears, I prised open the little box. Nestled in ancient red silk was the perfect pair of antique earrings – delicate, silver filigree teardrops, embedded with tiny marcasites.

I thought about the simple dangling pearls I'd planned to wear and immediately dismissed them. 'Oh, Madame Dupont, these are perfect! Thank you so much!' I reached over and hugged her tightly.

She accepted the hug, then pulled away and patted my hand. 'I am glad you like them. Now, isn't it time you were getting back to your mother?'

Feeling over-emotional, I said my goodbyes and drove back to the guesthouse with my glorious gift stowed carefully in the glove compartment.

Mum, Dad and Jeanie were piling into the kitchen as I pulled up in the courtyard.

Rupert filled the kettle for them. 'Good day?'

Mum opened her mouth to expound when we heard an angry shout and looked out of the window.

Gabriel had opened the *gîte* door and was thinking about escaping, but he hadn't got ten yards before Adrien caught him by the collar. Sabine came out to give him a stern reprimand in French.

Both parents looked fraught, Adrien's face taut, his mouth a thin line, and Sabine's cheeks flushed with anger. They'd looked fraught since they arrived, come to think of it. I knew Gabriel and Chloe could be a handful sometimes, as all small children could be, but even so, it seemed the effect of their child-free week away (two, in Sabine's case) had already worn off. They were great kids, and Adrien and Sabine were usually so busy at work, I'd have thought they would want to make the most of this family time together.

I weighed up offering to take the kids off their hands for half an hour to give them a chance to regroup, versus a cup of tea with my parents, listening to Mum spout about the *château* and the reception.

The kids won, hands down.

'I'll take the children for a walk,' I suggested. 'Give their parents a break.'

When my mother looked mutinous, Rupert jumped in. 'Gloria's due for a walk anyway, Emmy, if you're willing.'

Across the courtyard, when I knocked on their door and explained the scheme, Sabine grabbed at it like a drowning woman after a life raft.

'What a good idea, Emmy. Thank you.'

The kids pulled on their sandals and bounced out.

The lane was safe enough to walk along with them and the dog. Finishing in a dead end at *La Cour des Roses*, the only traffic that used it was us, our guests and local farmers. When we reached the end, I avoided turning right – which would eventually lead to the busy main road – and instead went left onto the lane leading to Madame Dupont's house.

The children were happy enough, pointing out tractors in the fields when they spied them through the hedges (or if I lifted them to look) and seeing who could spot the most rabbits darting about in the verges and ditches. Half a mile along, Chloe was tiring, but as we neared Madame Dupont's cottage, the sight of the blackened walls made her forget all about her worn-out little legs.

'What's that?'

'That's my friend's cottage. Madame Dupont. I told you she had a fire, remember?'

Chloe peered through the gate and wrinkled her nose at the boarded-up mess. 'Does she live in there?'

'No. The house needs to be mended, so she's staying with a friend. Luckily, she wasn't there when the fire happened.'

Chloe, who couldn't take her eyes off it, nodded her agreement that this was a good thing.

'Is Madame Dupont the lady with all the chickens?' Gabriel piped up.

'Yes. You've got a good memory, Gabriel. She kept them in her yard.'

I opened the gate and led them onto the path to the cottage, then through the side gate, into the yard. Gloria went mad sniffing, her tail twitching, the smell of the chickens still tangible to her doggy nose. I let her off the lead to explore.

Gabriel looked around. 'Wow. This is big.'

'There were a lot of chickens.'

'But they're with a farmer now?'

'Yes, with Madame Dupont's neighbour. They're fine.' *Well, most of them. Several may have seen the inside of a cooking pot by now.*

'Did they have a house, like Rupert's chickens?' Gabriel wanted to know. 'Where is it? Can we look?'

Talk about filling in time.

I led them around the bend in the L-shaped yard, round the back of the house to the large, ramshackle wooden structure almost hidden away by trees encroaching from the neighbouring land.

'Be careful,' I warned as Gabriel raced ahead.

The chicken house was in need of external TLC, but when we peered inside, there was no straw or mess. Monsieur Girard must have cleaned it out and hosed down the inside, and even the yard. He was a good neighbour.

I pushed the dog out of the way as Gabriel clambered onto one of the little ledges and lay down. Good job Monsieur Girard *had* cleaned up.

'It's like a bunk bed,' he said with satisfaction.

'I want to! I want to!' Chloe bounced up and down until I helped her up.

The things you have to do to keep small children occupied.

'Two minutes,' I told them. 'I doubt it's designed to take your weight. Chickens are *much* lighter than you two are.'

They giggled and snuggled onto their perches, making clucking noises, until I called it a day and got them back down.

Chloe wrinkled her nose. 'It's smelly.'

I laughed. 'Imagine what it smelled like with all those chickens in here!'

Gabriel made a gagging noise and they ran out into the sunshine, giggling. As I rounded up the dog and we closed the gate behind us, I glanced back at the house and felt so sad.

'Are you scared?' Chloe asked me as we retraced our steps.

'Scared? What about?'

'The wedding.'

'Weddings are a happy occasion, Chloe.'

'But *are* you scared?' Chloe repeated her question.

Wondering what she was thinking, I answered carefully. 'No, but I am a bit nervous. It'll be a busy day with a lot of people.'

Her eyebrows drew together and her breath caught.

Ah. So that was it. 'Are *you* scared about the wedding, Chloe?'

She looked down at her feet.

'Why are you scared?' I stopped and lifted her chin so she was looking at me.

'Because everybody says it's a big day. That we have to be good *all day!*' Her voice hitched. 'I might do something wrong. I might get my dress messy.'

That wasn't like Chloe. She was normally so bubbly and confident, and she didn't usually worry about being told off.

'Chloe, you won't do anything wrong. My bridesmaids, Ellie and Sophie and Kate, will help you, but you don't have to do anything special, just wear your dress and carry your flower basket – and it won't be for long. Only at the *mairie* and for a few photos at the hotel. And in years' and years' time, when you're as old as me, you'll have those photos to remind you what you looked like when you were a flower girl.'

'I s'pose.'

'It would be nice if you *try* to be good, but not everybody can be good for a *whole* day, not even me. If you get your dress messy, it's not the end of the world. I want you to enjoy yourselves. Can you do that?'

Chloe's face lit up. 'Really?'

'That's all I can ask.'

As we walked the dog back to *La Cour des Roses*, I glanced at Gabriel from the corner of my eye. He was suddenly very quiet.

'Are *you* okay about the wedding, Gabriel?' I asked him cautiously. 'You're not nervous?'

'Nu-uh. Course not!' He shook his head but kept his eyes firmly on his feet as he scuffed his way along the lane.

Hmm. I stopped and crouched down to his level. 'Well, I'm sure you're not, but in case you *start* to feel that way later, I can tell you there's nothing to be nervous about. We're going to have a great day with lovely food and a band and dancing. And you can even take your tie off later, if you like.'

He lifted his gaze to me, opened his mouth to say something, then seemed to think better of it. Instead, he reached his arms round me and hugged me tight. 'Thanks, Aunt Emmy.' A hesitation. 'But I'm not nervous or scared at *all*.'

Kate's arrival was greeted with delight on all sides.

Rupert was delighted because they'd got on like a house on fire when she came over in the spring.

Alain was delighted to meet her again because he knew how much she meant to me.

My parents were *always* delighted to see Kate – my mother thought she was the only one who could keep me on the straight and narrow and talk any sense into me.

But Nick was the most delighted of all. 'Kate! I haven't seen you for ages. It must be, what, six or seven years now?'

He folded her in his arms, and I was touched by his affection for my oldest friend.

Kate smiled as she pulled away. 'Nearer nine, I reckon. I came to your twenty-first party, remember? You moved to London soon after that.'

'Doesn't time fly?'

They stepped apart, eyeing each other to identify the changes those years had wrought.

'You look fantastic,' Nick conceded. 'Not a day over thirty-two.'

'Ha! And you've become quite handsome in your old age. Not so geeky any more. Where are your glasses?'

'Contact lenses.'

Rupert broke the suddenly interesting atmosphere. 'I think pre-dinner drinks outside are in order.' Rupert saw alcohol as the panacea for any situation.

Alain declined, as his mother had insisted he join them for dinner, and while everyone else settled outside, Kate and I took our wine for a stroll around the grounds, grabbing a few minutes to ourselves.

'I love this garden,' Kate declared. 'You're so lucky.'

'I know. Trouble is, I'm lucky if I get more than half an hour out here at a time. It's funny, really. Until I moved here, I wasn't remotely interested in gardens. When we were kids, they were just somewhere to run around and chuck a ball – preferably not into Dad's beloved begonias.'

Kate chuckled. 'That's the only time I've ever seen your dad lose his temper.'

'Yeah. I never understood why he wanted to spend his weekends gardening.'

'Probably trying to avoid your mother.'

I laughed. 'I wouldn't be surprised.'

'We've never had a garden of our own, though, have we? And, let's face it, any plant unfortunate enough to be gifted to you always wilts and dies.'

'True. But I'm beginning to see the appeal nowadays.'

'Ryan certainly knows what he's doing with this place,' Kate agreed. 'Are he and Sophie still together?'

'Very much so.' I told her about the charm bracelet.

'Oh, that's so romantic.' There was a wistful note to her voice.

I shot a sharp glance her way. 'There was nobody you could have brought as a plus one for the wedding?'

'Nah. I'm taking a break from men. Things never work out. I'm tired of it.'

I studied her face and could, indeed, see an element of emotional fatigue. 'You never have any shortage of admirers,' I reminded her.

She rested her head on my shoulder and sighed. 'I know, but I've finally admitted to myself that it's the tits that are the problem. They're the first thing men see. All they want to do is stare at them – and preferably get their hands on them. When the novelty wears off, there's no foundation for anything else.'

'Then you need to find a bloke who sees past them and enjoys your fabulous personality and sharp mind,' I told her firmly.

Kate pushed her boobs out. 'How am I supposed to do that? These things are always miles out in front of the rest!'

The next morning, my mother was going through what she saw as necessary wedding details with me when there was a knock on the door. Grateful for whatever distraction it might offer, even if it involved buying double-glazing, I went into the hall to find Gabriel standing there.

'*Maman* is making Chloe have a nap because she's being annoying. She said I could come over to see Gloria, if it's okay with you.' His face was comically hopeful.

Glancing across the courtyard, I spotted Sabine watching anxiously from a corner of her *gîte* window. Obviously she was trying to allow him a little freedom but couldn't quite trust him yet.

I gave her a surreptitious wave to show it was fine. Any escape from my mother's agenda was welcome.

'Gloria's in Rupert's lounge,' I told him. 'I'll go and get her. Do you want to play ball in the garden?'

'Yeah. Great!'

He wasn't the only one who was enthusiastic. I'd been speaking as I opened the door to Rupert's rooms, so the dog heard the word 'ball'. She was on her feet and through the door before we could blink.

With an apologetic shrug to my mother that said *Is it my fault that small children need me to occupy them?*, I grabbed some toys and led my charges to the open lawn area near the *gîtes*, where there was plenty of space to run around.

I taught Gabriel how to use Rupert's arm-saving ball launcher, then how to take the ball gently from the dog's mouth, until he exclaimed in a mock-repulsed manner about the amount of slimy drool that coated it after a few throws. Then they played tug with her rope toy.

After twenty minutes, Gabriel was dripping with sweat and the dog was panting. Boy and dog exchanged a look, and as if they could read each other's thoughts, they flopped down in the shade of the tall hedge that separated the lawn from the courtyard.

'I'll get you both something to drink.'

I was back a few minutes later with a bowl of water for the dog and tall glasses of iced grenadine for Gabriel and me.

Gabriel was enthusiastic about his drink, then lay down, his head resting on Gloria's belly, his face comically studious.

'What are you thinking so hard about?' I asked him.

He squinted up at me through hooded eyes. 'Do you and Uncle Alain shout at each other?'

Well. *There* was a question out of the blue.

'No.' I remembered our heated discussion about my mother the other night. 'Sometimes we disagree and get a bit cross. Maybe say things we shouldn't.'

'Will you shout at each other when you're married?'

Crumbs. 'I hope not. Why do you ask?'

A long minute of silence. 'Mum and Dad shout at each other a lot.'

Urgh. 'Do they?'

'They used to only shout after we went to bed. But sometimes they shout when we're there, too.'

What on earth was I supposed to say to that? 'Maybe they're tired at the moment. Sometimes people lose their temper when they're tired.'

'They must be *very* tired, then,' he commented, lapsing into a doze while I wondered what – if anything – to do about his little revelation.

I worried about what Gabriel had said all through lunch, but figured the best I could do was speak to Alain that evening.

'Glass of wine, Emmy?' Rupert asked, dragging me out of my thoughts.

I eyed the bottle he was proffering and was about to say no, then thought, *What the heck?*

'Only one glass,' Mum warned as he began to pour. 'Ellie and Sophie are coming for a final dress thing this afternoon, now that Kate's here.' She glanced at her watch. 'They'll be here in half an hour.'

Nick, Dad and Rupert looked suitably bewildered as to why a 'final dress thing' was required.

Kate looked like her afternoon had suddenly altered course in a way she didn't fancy.

Jeanie looked uncomfortably at her sister-in-law.

I just looked at her askance, bordering on angry. 'Since when?'

'I texted them this morning. I know Wednesdays are Sophie's mid-week closing, and Ellie's agreed to take an hour out from work. We haven't had a chance to see all three together, and it needs to be done.'

High-handed was the kindest word that sprang to mind, but I could go a long way downhill from there. Bossy, annoying, inconsiderate ... How *dare* she snatch my afternoon from me in a manner I wouldn't have chosen in a month of Sundays? I was fairly sure that Kate, Sophie and Ellie could find better ways to spend their afternoon, too.

I found my voice. 'Couldn't it be this evening? It's hardly fair, dragging Ellie away from the office.'

'Dad and I are out to dinner with Mireille and Christopher this evening, remember? And we're running out of time to get anything sorted if there's a problem.'

There was a problem alright, and it wasn't the damned dresses. But when Jeanie caught my eye, all I managed was a tight-lipped smile and a shrug. It was a done deal.

That didn't mean I had to like it. When Ellie and Sophie arrived, and Mum got up to usher us inside, I stopped her in her tracks.

'No point in you coming with us, Mum. There's hardly enough room for all four of us to move about in there. I'll fetch you when the three of them are ready.'

Mum opened her mouth to protest, but I stared her down, hoping I wouldn't have to resort to pointing out in front of everybody that, although my friends had responded to being summoned, they might want to draw the line at undressing in front of my mother.

But Dad tugged at her wrist until she huffed and sat back down, accepting the top-up of wine that Rupert circumspectly poured for her.

'I'm *so* sorry my mother called you over like that,' I said to Ellie and Sophie as they fetched their things from Ellie's car and trudged with laden arms round the back of the house to my room, while Kate went upstairs to get hers. 'She had no right. I would have stopped her, if she'd bothered to tell me.'

Ellie shrugged. 'If it makes her happy.'

'We tried our dresses on at the shop *and* for your mother weeks ago,' Sophie complained. 'How many more times must they be tried on?'

I raised an eyebrow. That kind of reluctance was more Ellie's trademark.

Kate stumbled through the door with her stuff. 'She hasn't seen them with all the shoes and accessories, and now I'm here, she wants to see all three of us together.'

'Might as well get on with it.' Ellie pulled her top over her head, then smirked mischievously. 'Are you looking forward to your parents owning a holiday home in the vicinity, Emmy?'

'How did you hear about that?'

'Rupert told me.'

'Hmmph. It'll be great for them, I'm sure.'

Sophie and Kate burst out laughing.

'But not for you?' Kate prodded.

My shoulders sagged. 'I can't stop them, can I?'

Kate wriggled into her dress. 'What if they like France too much and start spending a *lot* of time out here?'

'Then I'll have to find myself a nerve specialist and a pharmacist willing to dole out large quantities of something calming and possibly illegal.' I sighed. 'Seriously? I'm fine with it. It's fine.'

Ellie's eyes twinkled. 'That's good, because I have a few suitable properties they might like.'

'Ah. Hmm. They said they won't look properly until they get the UK end sorted,' I said, a tinge of desperation in my voice.

'There is not enough room in here,' Sophie grumbled. 'I will change in the bathroom.' Plucking up her dress, off she went, although she left the door open so she could join in the conversation.

Ellie frowned after her, then continued to torture me for sport as she slithered into her slender dress, Kate lending her a hand. 'I could e-mail them details. It'll give them an idea of what they can get for the money. That might help them make decisions.'

I closed my eyes in resignation, then opened them again. 'E-mail them with as many details as you like. It'll keep Mum occupied and out of my hair.' I jabbed a finger at her. 'But it would be preferable if you could ensure that these "suitable properties"' – I made quotation marks in the air with my fingers – 'are a minimum of, say, ten kilometres from *La Cour des Roses*.'

Ellie's lips twitched. 'Ten kilometres? Will that be enough?'

'I won't get away with suggesting anywhere else. This is the area they know and love. All I'm asking is that they're far enough away that Mum won't feel free to drop in any time she pleases. When I'm at *La Cour des Roses*, I'm working. I can't take an hour out to have coffee with my mother several times a week. If she has to climb into her car and drive a while, she might check whether I'm available first.'

'I'll see what I can do.'

'Ryan thinks your mother wants to be near you and Alain so she can see her grandchildren as often as possible,' Sophie called from the bathroom.

'She doesn't have any grandchildren!' I spluttered.

'Yet,' Sophie called back.

'And how does Ryan know about all this?'

Sophie's head appeared around the doorframe. 'Rupert told Ellie, she told me, and I told Ryan. It is not moon science.'

Wretched local grapevines.

'That's *rocket* science, Sophie.' Ellie performed a twirl. 'What do you think?'

She looked a knock-out, the deep purple, satiny fabric skimming her tall frame without clinging, her creamy cleavage on show for a change.

She caught the direction of my gaze. 'I need to find a large necklace. Too much skin on show.'

'I disagree. With that bra, you have cleavage – you might as well show it off. I hereby ban you from middle-aged beads or pearls on my wedding day.'

Kate laughed and shoved her shoes on. 'Will I do, too?'

'You'll more than do.' I manoeuvred them till they were side by side. 'I was worried you might not be in the same colour range, but you are.'

'Sophie? What are you playing at in there?' Ellie called over her shoulder. 'Let's get this over with. I need to get back to work.'

Sophie came out of the bathroom in her dress.

'Talking of cleavage,' Ellie said, 'I don't remember that dress making you look so busty when you got it.'

'I'm wearing a different bra today,' Sophie said hurriedly, giving us a quick twirl. 'Do you want to fetch your mother, so I can get changed again?'

'You've only been in it two minutes.' I lined them up. 'You all look so lovely. Shoes on, and then I'll call Mum in.'

Sophie turned, and a button pinged off the back of her dress.

Kate stooped to pick it up. 'Let me see where this came from.'

'Oh, no, thanks.' Sophie snatched the button from her. 'Vintage-style dress – must have vintage fastenings. I'll sew it back on later.'

Ellie shot me a look. That dress was tight. Tighter than when Sophie chose it. How did you tell one of your best friends that she'd put on weight at a rather inconvenient time?

I shook my head to warn Ellie against saying anything. She gave a nod, took her low kitten heels from their box and slipped them on. I smiled at her choice. In higher heels, she would have been taller than every man at the wedding.

Kate put her shoes on, then slid Sophie's shoe box across the room. Sophie bent to retrieve it. We got an eyeful of cleavage – and a ripping sound.

'*Merde!*'

'Let me see.' Kate rushed across, inspecting the seams of the dress. 'It's next to the side zip at your waist.'

To our alarm, Sophie began to cry.

'Don't worry, Sophie,' Ellie said. 'It can be fixed.'

'But it *can't* be fixed,' Sophie wailed, pulling at the zip so hard that Kate had to grab her hands and hold them still while Ellie and I undid it and helped to get the dress over her head without doing any more damage.

'I'm sure it can,' Ellie soothed, dismayed when Sophie plopped down on the bed in her underwear, her head in her hands. 'It'll only take a needle and thread.'

'It will take more than that,' Sophie mumbled through her fingers.

'What do you mean?'

'I'm *pregnant!*'

EIGHTEEN

Shocked silence filled the room.

Ellie was the first to recover. 'Are you sure?'

'Of course I am sure,' Sophie snapped, standing to face us in her underwear. She cupped her boobs. 'Do you think I grew these overnight through wishful thinking?' She tugged at her waist. 'Do you think I have been eating croissants night and day?'

Ellie reached for a robe, gently easing Sophie's arms into it, tying it around her waist and sitting her back on the bed. 'But that's wonderful news. Isn't it?'

'Maybe,' Sophie mumbled.

'Maybe?' I frowned. 'What does Ryan say?'

'Ryan does not say anything, because he does not know.'

'You haven't told him yet?' Kate asked gently.

She shook her head.

'You two are pretty solid, Sophie,' I said softly. 'I'm sure when he knows …'

'It is a question of timing.' She sighed. 'I know he is pleased for you and Alain, Emmy, but I also know he is not affected by all these wedding preparations. That kind of thing is not for him. If I tell him about the baby in the middle of it all, it might look like I caught the wedding bug and I am trying to trap him.'

I dropped to my knees on the floor and took her hands. 'Sophie, Ryan is one of the most understanding men I've ever met. I can't *begin* to imagine he would think that way. And I can only assume it's hormones making *you* think that way. Ryan's so easy-going.'

'But that's the problem!'

Ellie looked at her, bewildered. 'Ryan being easy-going is a problem in a situation like this? Why?'

'Ryan is a free spirit. He does his own thing. What we have together fits with that. I don't see how a baby could. He is only in France for eight months a year. He goes back to the UK in the winter for work. My flat is tiny. And now that Ryan's parents' *gîtes* are finished and in use, he is back to staying in a room in their house. None of it is suitable, is it?'

Ellie patted her knee. 'All those things can be dealt with. The main thing is this: are you happy that you're having Ryan's baby?'

Sophie's eyes immediately filled with fresh tears, but they were joyful ones, judging by the broad smile that accompanied them. 'Yes.'

'And if you ignore all those practicalities, do you think Ryan will be happy?'

Her smile faltered. 'I do not know.'

'Well, Emmy and I think we do know.' Ellie glanced at me. 'We think Ryan will be thrilled. Maybe he can find work here in the winter. You'll get a place to live that's big enough for the two … for the three of you.'

'If you leave it too long, Sophie, Ryan may guess,' Kate said. 'Then he *will* be upset. And he'd have less time to set something up for the winter months.'

I nodded my agreement. 'You should tell him.'

'Oh … I suppose.'

'And how are you?' I asked her. 'Have you had any sickness?'

'Sometimes I feel queasy. I have to eat small amounts regularly. But it is not too bad.' She glanced at the bed behind her. 'What about the dress?'

'Maybe they can take it out or add an extra seam or something, so you can breathe,' Ellie said.

'But there is no time.'

'There's tomorrow. We'll drive over there this afternoon. I'm sure they'll want to help.'

I hid a smile. With Ellie in charge, they would probably realise they had no choice.

'Don't you have to go back to work?' Sophie asked worriedly.

'That's the beauty of running your own business, isn't it? You can prioritise. And I'm prioritising *this*.'

'But if they can't …'

'If they can't, we'll sort something else out,' Ellie said firmly. 'And you'll look beautiful, like you always do. Unlike some of us, who'll look like a shiny barber's pole, no matter what.'

Sophie laughed, her fingers feathering across her stomach.

Kate turned to me. 'What are you going to tell your mother?'

I made a face. 'You want me to tell her that one of my brides-maids is unexpectedly pregnant and her dress no longer fits?' I tried to lighten the atmosphere. 'That she could throw up on the day? Mum might spontaneously combust!'

Kate let out an uneasy laugh.

'She'd be better not knowing, if we can get away with it,' Ellie decided. 'Especially since Ryan doesn't even know yet. Sophie, when will you speak to him?'

'Maybe I should do it soon. While I still have the courage you have all given me. But I am so nervous.'

'The sooner the better, then,' Ellie said. 'Do you know where he is at the moment?'

'He's working at his parents' this afternoon.'

'Why don't I drive you to him, and then go and sort the dress out myself? We know more or less what needs to be done. I don't think you need to be there.'

Sophie smiled. 'I would like that.'

'And you'll let us know what happens?'

'Of course.'

I stood and sighed. 'So how are we going to hide this fiasco from my mother?'

Over the next ten minutes, we composed ourselves, squeezed Sophie carefully back into her dress and applied concealer to her puffy eyes, then instructed her to keep her arm covering the split seam the whole time.

Taking a deep breath, I went outside to fetch my mother, her eyes shining with anticipation at finally seeing my motley crew of bridesmaids in some semblance of coordinated finery.

Her initial reaction was to clap her hands together, pleased with the result. 'Oh, you all look lovely! I *never* dreamed this colour range thing would work, but it does. How about a twirl?'

The girls obliged, Sophie's movements stiff and unnatural with her arm clamped to her side.

I thought we'd got away with it, until Mum spotted Sophie's necklace on the dressing table and picked it up. 'Isn't this yours, Sophie? Put it on, will you? Then we can see the full ensemble.'

An instinctive reaction, Sophie reached out to take it, exposing the gaping seam.

'Oh!' Mum's hand flew to her mouth. 'Your dress!'

Sophie's face fell at her faux pas.

I rushed into defence mode. 'It's only a little tear, Mum. Nothing to worry about.'

'Nothing to worry about? Hardly! What on earth are we going to do?'

Mindful of Sophie's delicate state of mind, Ellie stepped in, her voice calm. 'It's all in hand, Flo. I'm sure the shop will be able to repair it in time.'

'And what if they can't?' Mum expertly eyed Sophie, and the result came up short. 'I don't remember that dress being so tight before, Sophie. Have you put on weight?'

'Mum …' My tone held a warning that she should have heeded, but of course she didn't.

'It's no good getting that seam repaired if the whole dress is still too tight, is it?'

A tear ran silently down Sophie's cheek, and that was it for me. I took my mother firmly by the arm and steered her to the door.

'Emmy, what on earth …? I need to sort out what …'

'You don't need to sort anything out. Ellie has it all in hand,' I ground out at her, glancing back at Ellie who already had her arm around Sophie, whose tears were coming faster now. When Mum resisted my tug, I only pulled harder, until I'd propelled her through the door and out into the orchard, where I dragged her a good few yards into the trees, out of earshot.

Mum shook herself free. 'How *dare* you manhandle me like that?'

I faced her square on. 'No. How dare *you* upset my friend like that?

'All I said was that she must have put on some weight. That's only stating facts, Emmy.'

'And how is that going to help, two days before the wedding?'

'Exactly,' Mum declared triumphantly. 'Two days before the wedding! The least she could have done is watched her weight. And I didn't say *that*, did I? We have to think of a way to rescue this. Maybe that lemon and water diet? We have forty-eight hours.'

I gaped at her. 'Er. No. I do *not* want a friend going into starvation mode and fainting on my wedding day.'

'Oh, don't be so melodramatic, Emmy. It was only a suggestion.'

'Well, it sucks.'

'Oh? And what do you suggest?'

'I suggest getting the dress fixed if we can, accepting Sophie is the way she is, and leaving her *alone*. You made her cry.'

Mum tutted. 'You're being over-defensive, Emmy, if you ask me. And Sophie is being over-sensitive. If she didn't want all this fuss, she shouldn't have …' She stopped dead, her eyes narrowed.

A woman's instinct. Shit.

'She's pregnant, isn't she?'

I considered denial, but knew it was hopeless. 'Yes.'

'How long have you known?' Mum accused.

'Twenty minutes.'

Her relief that I hadn't been lying to her for long, at least, soon dissipated. 'You weren't going to tell me, were you? Didn't you think I needed to know as soon as possible?'

'For God's sake, Mum, she only just told *us*. So no, telling you wasn't first on my list of priorities, funnily enough. Actually, I thought it might be nice to let Sophie tell Ryan that he was going to be a father before I spread the net wider.'

'There's no need to be snippy, Emmy.' Mum stood with her hands on her hips, then frowned. 'Why didn't Ryan know before you knew? Why would she tell you first?'

I bristled. 'She wasn't going to tell *anybody*, but she was pushed into it because *you* saw fit to drag her over here without a by-your-leave for a dress trial, and her dress split.'

'It's a good job I did, isn't it? Otherwise it would have split on the day, and then where would we have been?' Her wedding organiser hat firmly glued to her head, her mind raced with further problems. 'How far gone is she? Is she being sick much? Will she be okay on Friday? She's not ducking out, is she?'

Her barrage of questions was too much. My blood, already on a slow boil, began to bubble.

'Have you *heard* yourself? I've just told you the wonderful news that one of my best friends is having a baby, and all you can worry about is the dress. You haven't even asked how she is.'

Mum looked like I'd slapped her face. 'But I did! I asked if she was sick.'

'Only because you're worried she might not be well enough on Friday. And then straight on to the dress.'

'I can't help that,' Mum snapped. 'Those dresses took forever to find, and now?'

I stepped closer and spoke through gritted teeth. 'Ellie is doing her best to get it sorted. But hear this. I couldn't care less if Sophie turns up on Friday in her pyjamas, as long as she's there, *if* she's up to it. I don't want her uncomfortable all day because we have a sodding dress plan.'

'There's no need to use that language with me, Emmy. Of course we have a dress plan. All aspects of this wedding have taken a great deal of planning. I've spent hundreds of hours on it!'

'I *know* you have. And Alain and I are genuinely grateful.' I tried hard to moderate my tone so that it matched my words. 'But you need to back off now. It's all in place, and if things aren't perfect on the day, then they're not. You can only plan so far, and then you have to let things just *be*.'

Mum stared me down. 'What in God's name has got into you, Emmeline Jamieson?'

Oh dear. Red flag.

'That. *That!*'

'What?' Mum looked bewildered and angry.

I was past caring. I wish I could say that Alain's words of advice the other night had permeated through and I was doing as he advised, but that wouldn't be true. The fact was, I was plain old spitting mad.

'Treating me like I'm still ...' I couldn't say 'a child'. Even in my temper, I knew that wasn't fair. 'Like I'm still under your jurisdiction. I'm not. I have a life that's independent from you.'

'I know that, Emmy. I can hardly *not* know, can I, what with you living in a different country and about to get married!'

'But you don't seem to understand. Yesterday, you thought I could take the day off to follow you around. I couldn't. I had work to do.'

Mum took a deep breath. 'I'm aware of that. You made your point, and I didn't insist. I'm not sure why you're making all this fuss over one incident.'

'It's not only one incident, though, is it?' Despair tinged my voice now. The feeling that I needed her to know, needed her to understand, washed over me in a wave. I'd already lost the plot, so I figured I might as well go the whole hog. 'Every step of the wedding, every arrangement, you've pushed and I've had to push back.'

'Oh, for heaven's sake, Emmy. That's called a discussion.'

'No, Mum. You asking me months ago if we wanted a blessing and me saying no was a discussion. Asking me half a dozen times since, including a week before the wedding, is not a discussion – it's you trying to get your own way over something, without trying to see that it's not what I want.'

'What *you* want?' Mum was livid now. 'This whole wedding is about what you want!'

'So why does it feel like I've had to fight you the whole way? I'm *tired*, Mum.' Angry tears were threatening, but I held them back. They were the last thing I needed her to see.

Mum's mouth was tight. 'I'm sure you are tired, Emmy, and overwrought with such a big day coming up.'

'I mean tired of *this*. Of *us*.' I scrabbled for a way to explain, as Alain's words from the other night hovered in my mind. 'You and I need to find a new way of doing things, because I can't do this any more. I do my best to please, to avoid confrontation, but you're too pushy, too bossy, too … too *much*!'

Ah. I don't think that was quite what Alain had suggested. But it was too late.

The impact was devastating. Tears spilled onto my mother's cheeks. I hadn't seen her cry in years.

'Well, thank you, Emmy. All I do is try my best to make things nice for you, and this is the thanks I get.'

'Mum, I *am* grateful for all you've done with the wedding, and I didn't mean—'

She held up a hand. 'There's no smoke without fire, Emmy. I'm sure you *did* mean it.'

She turned on her heel to go, but I grabbed her arm.

'Mum. You can't tell *anyone* about Sophie's pregnancy until Ryan knows. Not Jeanie, not even Dad. *Please.*'

Her face was hard and cold. 'What do you take me for? Do you think I lack any sort of understanding? Nobody will hear it from me. You seem to see me as some kind of monster. I'm not that person, Emmy.'

She stalked away, her back rigid.

Shit, shit, shit.

NINETEEN

I dropped down to sit on the grass, panicking about what I'd done.

Kate came out and sat beside me, her arm around my shoulders. 'You had to tell her about the baby?'

'Yes,' I said, flatly. 'She said she won't say anything.'

'You both said a lot more than that, by the look of it.'

'Yes. Some home truths.'

'Do you want to tell me?'

'I can't, Kate. I don't want to relive it. I just want to blank it out. Do you mind?'

'Not at all. Besides, I can probably guess.' She pulled me close and held me tight.

'Was Sophie upset by my mother?'

'I think she thought it was inevitable. Ellie's taken her to Ryan's, then Ellie will go on to the dress shop.' Kate studied my face. 'You don't look well. How about a lie-down?'

She pulled me to my feet and led me to my room, where I sat on the edge of the bed. 'But my mother ...'

'It was an accident waiting to happen, Emmy. Leave her to think it over. You won't achieve anything now, while you're both so het up. Lie down. Try to rest.'

I nodded, and she left.

But I didn't get the chance to follow her instructions. Two minutes later, Dad came barging in.

'Emmy, what the hell are you playing at? Your mother's in a complete state!'

That did it. The tears I'd held back in front of Mum, even in front of Kate, would not be stopped now. My father had rarely lost his temper with me when I was younger. Never in recent years.

'Oh, for crying out loud, not another one.' He grabbed a box of tissues from the bedside table and shoved them at me, then perched on the chaise longue by the window, his fingers steepled at his knees.

'I said some awful things, Dad.'

'I know. Your mother told me.' He looked me in the eye. 'But they needed saying, if you ask me.'

My eyes opened wide in surprise.

'Emmy, I've been married to your mother for thirty-six years. I'm not blind to the way she is. Most of the time, it suits everyone well enough – or at least, it does no harm. But she's been overstepping the mark for months with this wedding. I tried to rein her in, but I suppose I hoped it wouldn't come to this. Not before the day itself, anyway.'

I dropped my head into my hands. 'What am I going to do?'

He came over and put his arm around me. 'You're going to disappear from *La Cour des Roses*. Go to Alain's. Have some time to yourself – take a nap, whatever you need. When he gets home, he can talk some sense into you while I try to do the same at this end with your mother.' He grunted. 'And I know who's got the easier task. Stay the night. Come back in the morning refreshed and ready for the last lap of the race.'

'I can't abscond, Dad. What about Kate?'

'Mum and I are out with Alain's parents tonight, if your mother can pull herself together. Kate will be fine with Rupert and Nick, I'm sure.'

I battled with what I saw as my duty, but my desperate need to be elsewhere won. I nodded.

'Good girl.'

* * *

At Alain's, I texted to let him know I was there, then lay on the grass in the back garden, my arm flung across my eyes to keep out the bright sun. Despite my upset – or perhaps because my body and brain needed relief from it – the pleasant warmth lulled me into a troubled doze.

When I came round, it was early evening. Dazed, I checked my phone, but Alain hadn't replied to my text. Surely he would be home soon? I poured myself a large glass of wine and began to cobble together something for us to eat.

While I was cooking – in the loosest sense of the word – I got a text from Ellie.

It's only a maybe re. the dress. They're sympathetic, but limited time-wise. Hoping to take out two darts to widen the bodice, let out side seams as far as they dare and fix the tear, but can't guarantee to get it done in time. Shop customers come first.

I texted straight back. *I understand. Thank you. I really appreciate it.*

Five minutes later, she replied. *I'll help Sophie choose something else from her wardrobe, in case it isn't repaired in time. But I don't want to bother her until I know how it went with Ryan. I gather you had a row with your mum. Are you okay?*

I wasn't sure how to reply to that. In the end, all I managed was, *I will be. Need some time to myself. Thank you for asking.*

Of course, when I said I needed time to myself, I didn't mean *totally* to myself. I meant with an understanding man – but he didn't seem interested in making an appearance.

By seven, I began to worry. Where was he? I knew he often had late meetings with clients who couldn't see him during working hours, but I didn't remember him mentioning anything about today.

Underneath my mild anxiety, I felt unreasonably cross. Why hadn't he bothered to reply to my text? The whole idea of coming here was to relax and bask in a little sympathy, not to hang around, wondering where he was.

I jumped when my phone rang and snatched it up, but it wasn't Alain. It was Sophie.

'Hi. Did you tell Ryan?'

'Yes. Oh, Emmy, he is up to the moon!'

'See, we told you he would be.'

'You were right. Thank you for making me face up to it. Now I can be happy about it.'

'Did you hear from Ellie?'

'Yes. She explained about the dress. I will see what I can substitute, if I have to.' She didn't sound confident that she would find anything.

'Can we tell people about the baby yet, or are you keeping it quiet?'

'Ellie already asked me that. Ellie, who likes to keep everything private for herself.'

'Everybody loves baby news.'

'The cat will soon be out of the sack, Emmy. Ryan wants to tell his parents this evening. Once they know, everyone in Pierre-la-Fontaine will soon know, *n'est-ce pas?*'

I breathed a silent sigh of relief that my mother knowing wasn't the end of the world.

As though she could sense the turn my thoughts were taking, Sophie said, 'I am sorry I spoiled your mother's plans, Emmy.'

'Bugger my mother's plans! I couldn't care less about the dress. I'm too happy for you and Ryan.'

'Thank you. See you soon.'

And she was gone.

I smiled at Sophie's pleasure. I hadn't doubted Ryan's reaction for one minute, but it was still a relief to know how supportive he was being.

Talking of supportive men ... Staring into the pan on the hob, I knew that if my pasta concoction was going to be edible at all – already doubtful – it couldn't wait for Alain much longer. And neither could I.

I reached for my phone. When there was no answer on his mobile, I tried his office landline. It rang for a while before he picked up.

'Hi, Emmy. Everything alright?'

No, it is not alright. 'I wondered when you were coming home, that's all. I made supper.' *Kind of.*

A pause at his end. 'Are you at mine?'

I allowed myself to roll my eyes. After all, he couldn't see me. 'Yes. Didn't you get my text?'

'I – er. No. Sorry. I put the phone on silent. Haven't checked it. I've been caught up in something complicated. Needed to concentrate.'

I ground my teeth a little. 'Oh. So when will you be back?'

'I … I was going to work late tonight. I *need* to work late, if I'm going to finish all this by a reasonable time tomorrow. A client dropped in unexpectedly today with a problem, and it set my schedule back.' He waited for me to say something. When I didn't, perhaps sensing hostility in my silence, he added, 'I'm sorry, but I didn't know you'd be there. We didn't have any plans for tonight.'

That was true. But he could at least have checked his phone. 'I know. It's just that I had words with Mum, and I needed to get away from *La Cour des Roses* for a while. I was hoping you'd be here.'

'Oh, no, I …' I heard him stifle a sigh. 'You're okay, though?'

No, I am not okay. But what could I say? 'Yes, this is a dire emergency, drop everything and get back here because I need a shoulder to cry on'? I was a big girl now. I was in one piece physically if not mentally, I was tired, the pasta thing was ruined, and I was going to be upset about my mother all evening whether he rushed home or not. But if he did that now, I would have to add guilt to the mix. If he had stuff to do, he had stuff to do. No point in him wearing himself to a frazzle tomorrow, the day before the wedding.

'I guess.'

'Emmy, I can't leave this right in the middle, but I'll be home as soon as I can. We can have a glass of wine and you can tell me all about it.'

'Okay. See you whenever.'

I clicked off with a pathetic chin wobble and drained my wine glass, then peered into the pan. No way was I eating that. Besides, I wasn't hungry any more.

Refilling my wine glass, I grabbed a large pack of crisps from the cupboard and took them both upstairs to bed.

Halfway down the crisps, the salt and grease had only made me feel sick. That and the horrible knowledge that I'd seriously fallen out with the person who had brought me into this world, whether everybody thought she deserved it or not. I suspected Mum wasn't enjoying her evening much, either, although at least she would have had a better dinner than me.

I flung the crisps to one side and picked up my wine, glaring into it, affronted. This wasn't right, drowning my sorrows in Muscadet instead of pouring them out to my beloved … who was apparently more interested in his spreadsheets than the mental and emotional wellbeing of his bride-to-be.

To top off my fun evening, I indulged in a lengthy and cathartic sobbing spree.

I was asleep before I'd finished the second glass.

When I woke, I felt crap. Not hungover – I hadn't drunk that much – but with a headache and a hollow sensation in my stomach, presumably due to the lack of nourishment yesterday.

Scrubbing blearily at my eyes, I glanced at the time. Six o'clock. Alain wasn't in bed, although his side looked crumpled.

He appeared two minutes later with a mug of tea, waited while I sat up, placed it in my hands and perched next to me on the bed.

'What time did you get home?' I asked.

'Nine. I didn't expect you to be asleep that early.'

'I was tired,' I said grumpily.

'I saw the wine. The crisps. That pan downstairs. Didn't you eat?'

'No. Wasn't hungry.'

'Are you mad with me?'

'If you had to work, you had to work.' My misery broke. 'I wanted you home, Alain. I'd had an *awful* day. I *seriously* fell out with Mum. I texted you but you ignored it, I rang and told you I needed you, but you didn't come!'

He looked taken aback at my outburst. 'I told you I never saw the text, and I'm not a mind-reader, Emmy. You only said you'd had words with your mum. That's nothing new. I asked if you were okay, and you said you were.'

'I could hardly say anything else, could I? Not when you'd made it patently obvious that you had better things to do.' I knew I sounded sulky, but I felt rubbish and I couldn't help myself.

Alain nudged my mug to my lips and took a sip of his own tea. 'Why don't you tell me about it now?'

Sensing his impatience, I almost refused – I wasn't in the mood – but that would have been childish. He needed to know about the situation with my mother before the wedding eve supper at *La Cour des Roses* tonight.

Grudgingly, I began my tale, starting with Mum's presumption and high-handedness in inviting the girls over for a dress inspection, but it soon became a torrent. I hadn't even got to the argument with her when he stopped me, his hand gripping my arm.

'Wait! Sophie's *pregnant*?'

'Yeah. Great news, huh?'

'Wonderful.' The first smile I'd seen from him that morning told me he was thrilled. 'But I interrupted. Go on.'

I managed it without tears, my tone monosyllabic and tired. I was all cried out from last night.

'When you phoned last night, I had no idea how bad it was,' he said when I'd finished. 'I was caught up in my work. Desperate to finish off by the end of today. I guess I wasn't listening properly.'

I thought back to what I'd texted, what I'd said to him on the phone. I'd wanted him to know how upset I was without actually telling him. All I'd said was that I'd expected him to be home. That I'd had words with my mother. He was right – I shouldn't expect him to be a mind-reader.

'I should have been clearer.'

'And I should have read between the lines. I assumed you'd only had a tiff. I had no idea it was so serious.' He sighed. 'If I hadn't said anything to you about her the other night … I didn't mean for you to … you know.'

I thought about telling him the truth – that his words earlier in the week *had* lodged in my subconscious. That if I thought about it, I *could* lay some of the blame on him for what had happened. But we were already on eggshells.

I shook my head. 'I'm not sure I was thinking about that when I let rip. I was so mad, I probably would have said it anyway.' And there was some truth in that, too.

'Your dad's right. It needed saying.'

'Maybe. But not two days before the wedding. Now my mother won't be talking to me on my wedding day.'

Alain tried to lighten the conversation. 'Is that a bad thing?'

But it wasn't funny. 'Alain, I need to go, but there's something else I have to talk to you about first.'

'Oh?'

As I washed my face, brushed my teeth and threw on my clothes, I told him what Gabriel had told me about his parents shouting at each other all the time.

Alain's face fell. 'They do seem to be going through a bad patch. Mum was right – something's going on there.' He followed me downstairs, where I found my sandals in the kitchen and put them on.

I glanced at the sink. 'You washed up? You didn't eat that, did you?'

'Er – no. Dare I ask what it was?'

'A pasta sauce thing. I made it up.'

'So I gathered.'

At the door, I said, 'By the way, you owe me ten euros. Mum finally slipped.'

'Crikey. Things have got bad!' He took a note from the hall table and slipped it into my pocket. But I could tell his jovial tone was forced, and his comment about things getting bad could be taken in all sorts of ways.

As I left, we finally smiled at each other – but it was a smile that said we were both wounded that we were so out of sync.

TWENTY

When I got back to *La Cour des Roses*, Rupert was in the kitchen enjoying a cup of tea with Kate. Gloria had her head in Kate's lap; a sucker for whatever fondling and stroking she was willing to dole out. She wasn't allowed in the kitchen.

'Hi, are you okay?' Kate asked immediately.

'I'm fine,' I lied, and when they both gave me a look that told me they didn't believe a word of it, I qualified, 'As fine as can be expected.' *Considering I've seriously fallen out with my mother and I'm not far from the same with my husband-to-be.* To change the subject, I asked Kate, 'Did you hear from Sophie? Or from Ellie about Sophie?'

'I did.' She inclined her head Rupert's way with a look that said, *Can we tell him?*

I nodded.

'What? What are you plotting?' Rupert asked suspiciously.

'Not plotting. We have some news for you, that's all.' I told him about Sophie's pregnancy.

He stood and did a little jig, right there in the middle of the kitchen, and my heart immediately lifted.

'Is that what the row with your mother was all about?' he asked, peering round the kitchen door to make sure she wasn't lurking in the hall or on the stairs. 'The bridesmaid dress?'

'Not the whole thing, but it's what set it off.'

Rupert shook his head in despair. 'I don't see what all the fuss is about. It's only a dress.'

I gave him a despairing look. 'Rupert, this wedding is like a finely tuned machine, and my mother is the chief mechanic. In her eyes, there can be no loose screws at this stage.'

Rupert snorted with laughter. 'I think you'll find it was a loose screw that caused the problem in the first place!' And off he went to phone Ryan to congratulate him.

When Mum and Dad appeared for breakfast, my mood immediately plummeted again as my worst fears were realised – Mum wasn't speaking to me, other than the necessities.

Determined to remain calm, I filled her in on the progress with the dress and the fact that Sophie's pregnancy would soon be common knowledge.

She merely nodded, then asked curtly, 'Will you still go into town to check on the cake?'

'If you want me to,' I tried to mollify. 'But it's all sorted, and the *pâtisserie* will deliver it to the *château* tomorrow.'

Mum rubbed at her temples. 'All we ever saw was a sketch, Emmy. What if it's not right?'

'Why don't you and I go, Flo?' Dad suggested, perhaps hoping the activity might pull her out of her mood.

But she shook her head, then winced. 'I have a banging headache.'

Great. Ladle on the guilt, why don't you?

Kate looked from one to the other of us. 'I'll go with Emmy, Flo.' When I opened my mouth to protest, Kate gave me a glare. 'I'd love a coffee in town.'

Mum patted Kate's hand. 'Thank you, Kate. You're a good girl.' With the unspoken implication that I wasn't.

As we left, Mum called out, 'Don't accept anything shoddy. If it's not right, tell them.'

In the car, Kate burst out laughing. 'I presume we have no intention of complaining about the cake?'

'No – for two good reasons. Firstly, I can't imagine there'll be anything wrong with it. We used that *pâtisserie* last year for a golden anniversary cake, and it was spectacular. Secondly, what the hell does my mother expect them to do, if it's not right? Start again, with twenty-four hours to go? These things take days to make. Sometimes, I think she's on another planet.'

'You wish.' Kate glanced across at me. 'Your dad told me the details of what happened with your mother yesterday. Are you okay?'

'Yeah.'

'Did you have a good evening at Alain's?'

I wasn't in the mood to lie. 'I needed to be away from the guesthouse, and he needed to know what's going on. Only …' I told her how the evening had really worked out.

'Alain was the one who wanted me to stand up to my mother,' I finished as I negotiated the road into town. 'So I did. But then he wasn't there for me when I needed him.'

'It sounds like a misunderstanding to me,' Kate soothed as I found a small parking spot and squeezed the car into it. 'You're both tired and overwhelmed. Bound to happen. You were feeling bruised after your row with your mother, and Alain didn't realise. But that's not like him, Emmy. Don't be too hard on him. At least you talked it out this morning.'

'I wouldn't say talked it out, exactly. It felt … like we weren't really *us*. When I left, things weren't right between us.'

As we strolled towards the centre, Kate linked her arm through mine.

I sighed. 'And on top of that, this thing with my mother … I don't know if she'll forgive me *ever*, let alone in time for the wedding.'

'You can't be responsible for her actions, only your own. And I agree with Alain and your dad – it needed saying. Has done for a long time. Yes, the timing's unfortunate, but your mother brought that about by going too far yesterday. You would have held your tongue otherwise. Don't blame yourself.'

Kate was saying all the right things, about my mother, about Alain. But what my head told me, and what my sinking heart told me, were two different things.

'Oh, I love this place,' Kate exclaimed when we reached the main square, turning on the spot as she drank in the fountain, shops and cafés.

I smiled. '*Pâtisserie* first, then I'll buy you coffee in the square.'

'Done.'

When we entered the shop, the manageress immediately came around the counter to greet me and tell me my cake was beautiful, then ushered us to a side counter. 'I will be one moment, and you will see.'

She and an assistant carefully brought the cake through on a trolley.

Kate and I gasped. The other customers in the shop came over to see. They gasped, too. It was a work of art.

The manageress gave me a knowing look. 'You got the best of both worlds, after all, Mademoiselle Jamieson, did you not?'

I beamed, a smile that started out genuine but soon had to be forced to hide a sudden wobble as I thought about the wedding, only twenty-four hours away, and the way Alain and I were with each other this morning.

'I see from your face that you like it,' she said, pleased. 'But will your mother?'

I looked at her anxious face and immediately reached out my hand to touch hers. 'How could she not? Thank you so *much*!'

Leaving her to take the cake away – heaven only knew how they would get it to the *château* in one piece tomorrow – Kate and I made a beeline for the nearest café.

'That cake is magnificent,' Kate said as we grabbed a table near the fountain and ordered. When I told her how much it cost, her jaw dropped. 'Ouch! It's worth it, though.' She looked around the square. 'It's a shame the market isn't on today. I loved all those stalls last time. Everyone compliments that handbag I bought. I still can't get over that corset stall, though. Who wears stuff like that nowadays?'

Knowing she was chattering to take my mind off my troubles and loving her for trying, I gave a pointed stare at her upper half. 'Old ladies who once had a figure like yours but need sturdy scaffolding nowadays. Don't mock.'

When her coffee was placed in front of her, Kate indulged in her favourite sport – people-watching.

'That fountain is fantastic. And the flowers. I like the red ones best. Ooh, look at that woman's trousers. Talk about a perfect cut. I wonder where she got those? Have you *seen* that dog? It's no bigger than a rat! It'll be lucky not to get stepped on. I don't know how that bloke dares be seen out with it. It's hardly macho, is it? Mmm, I wonder what kind of cake that woman's got in that big box? Oooh, *he's* a bit of alright, isn't he?'

This stream of verbal consciousness stopped as she took time to admire the man she'd spotted.

'That's the mayor,' I told her.

'Really? I always pictured mayors as short and tubby, with ridiculous chains around their necks.'

'Not ours.'

Patrice Renaud was smart-casual as usual, in chinos and a dark blue shirt with the sleeves rolled up, revealing tanned arms.

'How old is he? Is he married?' Kate gushed.

'Mid-forties, maybe. I believe he's divorced. No doubt his wife got sick of women drooling at him from pavement cafés.' I gently pushed under Kate's chin to close her mouth. 'Stop it. The last thing you need is an affair with a playboy Frenchman.'

'Oh, I don't know. I wonder if he'd like that French maid outfit I bought when my relationship with Jamie was flagging?'

The mind boggled. '*If* you can tear your eyes away from our illustrious mayor …'

But Patrice had spotted us. He came over and bent to kiss me on both cheeks.

'Emmy. How are you? All ready for your wedding tomorrow?' All this in French, in a swoonworthy accent. I could sense Kate melting in her seat.

'Yes, thank you. We're in town to check on the cake. This is Kate, a friend from England. She'll be acting as a witness tomorrow.'

'*Enchanté*, Kate.' He politely shook hands, although I suspected Kate would have been fine with kisses, too.

'*Er – merci*,' Kate stammered.

'I will leave you to discuss your cake,' he said to Kate's cleavage, where her boobs were currently doing their best to fall out of a gypsy blouse. Dragging his eyes away, Patrice turned to me. 'It will be an honour to marry you and Alain tomorrow, Emmy. I look forward to it.'

'Thank you.'

And he was gone, back to the *mairie* and his beloved red tape.

'Mmmm.' Kate sighed. 'Gosh, he's handsome.'

'Yes, he is,' I agreed. 'Now, change the subject before you combust with lust.'

'That little brother of yours is handsome, too, nowadays.'

'I know, but then I'm allowed to say that. He's enjoyed seeing you again.'

'Yeah. It's been good to catch up with him.'

And that was when the realisation hit me. Sure I must be wrong, I thought back to Kate's arrival, when Nick had greeted her with such enthusiasm, then fast-forwarded through the times I'd seen them together since.

I grabbed Kate's arm. 'Oh my God.'

'What is it?' she asked in alarm.

'Nick hasn't stared at your boobs once.'

'*What?*'

'Passing glances at most.'

'Emmy, what *are* you talking about?'

'Remember you were complaining that men always look at your chest when they're talking to you and not your face?'

'Ye … es.'

'Nick doesn't.'

'That's because he's known me for years. They've been there since I was thirteen, after all. It doesn't mean anything.'

'Yes, it does. It means he likes you, Kate. It means he likes *you*. Person-Kate, not boobs-Kate.'

As I let that sink in, I said, 'Better get on. Things to do, cakes to report on, mothers to throttle.' And immediately my brain switched back to worry mode.

When we got back to the guesthouse, Ryan was dragging tools from his car, the dog at his heels.

We rushed over to give him a congratulatory kiss. The dog got excited about the effusive greetings and joined in by slobbering on his bare knees.

Ryan was always a smiley kind of guy, but I'd never seen a smile like the one we got now – one that lit his whole face and shone from his eyes.

'Thanks. I still can't believe it. It's pretty amazing.'

'Yes, it is. You're going to be a great dad, Ryan.'

'I hope so. But I need to find work here over the winter. And I might need to up the ante with the summer work.' He hesitated. 'Emmy, I know you don't officially do websites, but you did a great job improving Rupert's. I don't have one – I've always relied on word of mouth – but I wondered if you'd consider doing something simple for me. I'm no good at that stuff. I'd pay you, but I can't afford a proper person.' He made a face. 'And that came out wrong.'

I laughed. 'I'd be happy to, if it can wait a few weeks. And don't want payment. Count it as a favour to a very good friend.'

He took my hand. 'Thank you. Emmy, will you …' His voice hitched. 'Will you look after Sophie for me, if I do have to go back this winter?'

My heart jolted for him. 'Let's hope it doesn't come to that. Surely if everyone you know asks around for you, something'll come up?'

'I hope so. I spent the morning making a few enquiries, and Mum and Dad are on it, too.' He patted the boot of his estate car. 'This isn't big enough. I *had* been thinking about investing in a van.' He gave us a lopsided grin. With his forthcoming expenses, we all knew that van might be a long way down the line. 'Oh, and I'm sorting the lavender for your bouquets right now. I'll take it straight to the florist before she closes for lunch.'

'Thanks, Ryan.'

He turned to go, then looked back, his dimples flashing. 'Sophie told me about the dress. I'd better stay out of your mother's way, if she's going to hold me responsible!'

I smiled, but with the way things were between me and my mother, and the delicate tightrope Alain and I were walking, my heart wasn't in it.

As we walked to the patio doors, Kate tried to joke me out of my worry. 'You know you were saying how much gardening appealed to you nowadays?' She looked pointedly over to where Ryan was getting started, his shirt off, shorts frayed, muscles rippling. 'Me, too.'

I elbowed her lightly in the ribs. 'He's spoken for.'

I continued to worry all afternoon that things would still be stilted between Alain and me for our wedding eve supper.

But when he arrived and I politely asked if he'd got everything finished at work, his answer was a kiss and a smile, and his tone was bright enough as he said, 'Yep. There's a message on my answering machine and voicemail telling everyone to sod off till I get back from my honeymoon. I'm raring to get married and enjoy the weekend with everyone, then whisk my wife away for a fortnight of unbridled lust.'

I raised an eyebrow.

As did Aunt Jeanie, who was too close to avoid overhearing. Oh dear – and Mum, who leaned towards her sister-in-law and said, 'Twenty years, Jeanie. You'd have to be *twenty* years younger.'

I laughed along with Alain and Jeanie, but my heart sank a little as I wondered if Alain's show of cheerfulness might be just that – a show. Still, if he was making the effort to brush over this morning's awkwardness, that raw uncertainty of feeling between us, then the least I could do was join him in that effort.

Rupert was busy organising a simple but delicious cold spread of charcuterie, salads, olives, breads, fruit and desserts, and I was given no opportunity to talk to Alain about our differences as we were roped into helping ferry food and drink out into the garden.

When Ellie arrived, she answered my question before I could even ask it. 'Sophie's dress *is* a going concern, you'll be pleased to know. It's not a perfect fit, but at least Sophie can breathe now.'

I let out a sigh of relief. 'Thank goodness. And thank you, Ellie, for dealing with it.'

'You're welcome.'

'Is Sophie coming tonight?' Alain asked.

'No. She doesn't want to risk getting too tired. Ryan's insisting on looking after her.'

I smiled as I imagined the two of them curled up in Sophie's tiny flat, adjusting to the idea that they would soon be parents. It would have been nice if Alain and I could have had two minutes to ourselves, too, but that wasn't to be.

I looked round as Gabriel and Chloe piled out of their *gîte*. 'Time to greet the troops.'

Everyone settled in the garden for a drink, while Chloe and Gabriel played with the dog. It was still hot, with no breeze, so they were soon red-faced.

'Aunt Emmy, can we go and see the chickens?' Gabriel called over.

'Only if someone goes with you.' I started to get out of my seat.

Alain stopped me. 'I'll go.'

But Rupert began to bring the food outside, which Chloe and Gabriel decided was more interesting than the chickens – as did Gloria.

'Time for you to go inside,' Rupert told her firmly. With nibbles everywhere, that dog was *not* to be trusted, and those large, doleful eyes fooled nobody except the children.

'Does she *have* to go in?' Chloe's chin wobbled.

Rupert's resolve crumbled, and he ruffled Chloe's curls. 'We can tie her to a bench instead. But no feeding her any titbits, Chloe. We don't want her to be poorly.'

'I promise.' She bestowed him with a smile that would melt the hardest heart.

Jeanie tutted. 'You're such a soft touch, Rupert.'

She and Ellie helped Rupert play host, topping up drinks and plates, while everyone else relaxed. Mostly.

'It's too hot,' Mum complained, fanning her face. 'I hope it won't be this hot tomorrow. We'll all wilt.'

'Can't control the weather, Flo,' Dad chided mildly, his tone suggesting he knew damned well that my mother wished she could control the elements like she controlled everything else.

Nick had stationed himself next to Kate on a bench, where they chatted away like long-lost fr … Well, like long-lost soulmates, actually.

'Do you remember that hamster in Mrs Jones' class?' Nick asked her. 'The one with the gammy leg?'

Kate shook her head. 'You were two years behind me, remember. We had a gerbil called Boris. Until the caretaker accidentally switched the heating off over the coldest weekend of the winter and it froze to death.'

They were so at ease with each other, it was like being back at home in our teens again.

Adrien looked tired and snapped at the children from time to time, gaining him nothing but frowns from Sabine.

'Gabriel, stop aggravating that poor dog!' he called across, when his son was only stroking her. Gloria's tongue was hanging out with the heat, but she didn't seem to mind his attentions.

Ten minutes later, it was Chloe he was cross with. 'Can't you eat anything without spreading half of it down your front?' He tried to make it sound light-hearted, but it fell flat and only made Chloe's eyes brim with tears.

Mireille cast anxious glances their way, only half-listening to Mum regaling her – yet again – with full details of the *château* and the menu, along with hints aimed at me, no doubt, about how much time she'd spent organising it all.

'I still think *you* could have had a blessing, Emmy,' Mum said pointedly after Mireille had tried to make it a two-way conversation by telling Mum about a recent wedding she had attended which had, unfortunately for me, included a church blessing.

I opened my mouth to respond, but frankly, my mind was a blank as to what I could say on the subject that would be new.

Mireille, realising she had put her foot in it, tried to backtrack. 'But you know, Flo, such things do not suit everybody …'

Mum only huffed. It seemed that Chloe and Gabriel weren't the only ones who were going to have a parent on their back all evening.

When I went into the house to fetch more wine, Dad followed me in. 'She'll come round sooner than you think, Emmy.

Trust me, the minute she sees you in your wedding dress, all will be forgotten and she'll be the proud mother-of-the-bride.' He delivered a reassuring kiss to my cheek.

I managed a wobbly smile. 'I hope so. Thanks, Dad.'

Jeanie came bustling in. 'Less of that soppy stuff, Dennis. They're waiting for wine out there. And you need to do something about that wife of yours. Steer her on to another subject. Christopher looks ready to throw himself off the nearest cliff.'

Dad winked at me. 'For better or for worse, remember?'

Back outside, Sabine decided to take the children back to the *gîte* – they were too hot, she said, and they needed showers and an early night before the big day tomorrow. Adrien reluctantly went with her, and everyone else settled, the atmosphere more relaxed without the children running around – and without Adrien and Sabine glaring at each other.

Alain leaned towards me, his gaze intent. 'I presume you won't let me stay over?'

'Certainly not. You're not allowed to see the bride on her wedding day.'

'I'll be glad when we're married and you're moved in and I can see you whenever I want.'

I laughed. He'd sounded rather proprietorial, and I wondered if he was joking around, trying to lighten the stiffness between us. Then I figured he may just have meant what he said in a very literal sense. Then I decided that over-analysing was overrated.

I kept my tone light. 'We have two whole weeks in the Spanish sunshine coming up,' I reminded him, touching my lips to his, while reminding myself that this time tomorrow, we would be married, and there was nothing I had ever wanted more.

And then the shouting impinged.

'What the …?' Alain looked across the courtyard towards the *gîtes*.

Mireille sat forward in her chair as though to hear better, as the noise flowed through an open window – Adrien shouting, Sabine shrieking, the kids crying.

'*Merde*,' Alain murmured. 'That sounds nasty.'

The door opened, and Gabriel appeared in the doorway in his pyjamas.

'You come back here now!' Adrien yelled from inside.

'No! Not until you stop *shouting*!' Gabriel had his hands over his ears.

Mireille jumped up from her chair and stormed over there, Christopher hot on her heels. Alain and I followed. From the corner of my eye, I saw Dad lay a hand on my mum's arm and shoot her a warning look.

Gabriel threw himself into Mireille's arms, sobbing. 'Mummy and Daddy aren't going to live together any more!'

The colour drained from Mireille's face. 'What? *Mais non*, Gabriel.'

'I *heard* them. Mum said she couldn't stand it any longer and Dad said he couldn't stand *her* any longer and …'

'Okay, sport.' Christopher lifted Gabriel into his arms and cradled him against his chest like a baby.

Adrien came to the doorway, his expression thunderous, and reached out his arms. 'I'll take him.'

Christopher shook his head. 'Not a good idea, son. Not if you're going to carry on making that racket. Where's Chloe? What's going on?'

Adrien stood aside. Sabine was in the lounge, her face livid, Chloe clinging to her legs.

'We do not need an audience for this, Adrien,' she snapped. 'It is not going to change anything.'

Alain looked from one to the other. 'Is what Gabriel said true? You're splitting up?'

'Yes,' Sabine said definitively. 'Not that it's anything to do with *you*!'

We stood in our motionless tableau, an awkward silence filling the room as we all realised her statement wasn't quite true.

'We're getting a divorce,' Sabine declared, defiant.

Mireille's lips trembled. 'I knew it.' She turned to Christopher. 'I *told* you things weren't right.'

Adrien cast Alain and me an apologetic look. 'You weren't meant to know. Not before tomorrow. I'm sorry you found out this way. We were hoping to hold it together till after the wedding.'

Sabine seemed to gather herself a little, and her tone softened a fraction. 'I'm sorry, too.' She lifted her chin and glared at Adrien. 'But sometimes there is a limit to how long you can keep on pretending.'

Alain was silent, his fingers shaking lightly against his thigh, and my heart went out to him. Adrien had betrayed his trust, having an affair with Sabine and taking her away from him. They'd had a family, and he'd had to be civil when it was the last thing he felt like. And now, all these years later, Sabine was leaving his brother, too.

Adrien must have been thinking the same thing. 'Alain, this is more awkward for both of us than it should be.'

But Sabine had had enough of this attempt at civility and our intrusion into her private affairs. 'You have to go now,' she announced to the crowd gathered in her doorway, her voice brittle. 'Adrien and I have more to discuss.'

'To discuss? Or to shout at each other?' Mireille asked her, lips tight.

Sabine gaped at her, affronted. 'That is not your business!'

Christopher looked pointedly across at Chloe, still glued to Sabine's legs, then down at Gabriel in his arms. 'Yes, it is. We're their grandparents and we don't feel this is appropriate for them. Mireille and I will take the children over to the guesthouse, well away from the upset. Let us know when you're calm enough to have them back without distressing them any further.'

He looked at his wife and she nodded, moving into the *gîte* to prise Chloe away from her mother.

'Come with Grandpa and me, Chloe, while Mummy and Daddy calm down. Adults argue sometimes, but you mustn't worry about it. Come along. I'll ask Rupert to get you some milk.'

As they led the children away, Chloe wide-eyed, Gabriel red-eyed and pale, I glanced back to the patio.

Kate, Nick and Jeanie had gone inside. Dad was ushering my mother to do the same, while Rupert and Ellie quickly gathered the supper things.

'I'm sorry, Alain,' Adrien said. 'We've been keeping this from you for weeks. But what with the wedding and everything, we couldn't …'

'Will you *stop* apologising to other *people*?' Sabine shouted at him, her body rigid, her fists at her side; the thin veneer of civility that had briefly shone through while Mireille and Christopher were there now falling away. 'This is nothing to do with anyone but *us*!'

Adrien rounded on her. 'Oh? You think so, do you? It's nothing to do with the children's uncle and grandparents that you're going to uproot them and take them away from their own father and move them to your blasted parents' in Rouen?'

'*What?*' Alain looked from one to the other of them. 'Sabine, you can't do that.'

'Alain, we should go,' I said under my breath. 'This isn't our business.'

'Emmy is right,' Sabine snapped. 'Why are you still here?'

Nodding, Alain took my hand and we began to walk away.

Adrien had turned back to Sabine. 'You can't take my own children away from me, Sabine.'

'I can do what I like,' she shrieked. 'What makes you so sure they are yours, anyway, Adrien? Gabriel could just as easily be Alain's!'

TWENTY-ONE

A slow-motion bubble enveloped my world.

The colour draining from Alain's face. His Adam's apple bobbing in his throat as he tried to swallow. The whoosh of breath from his body.

My heartbeat stuttering in my chest, trying to catch its rhythm.

Alain turning back to the doorway of the *gîte*.

Adrien standing stock-still, staring at his wife.

The rush of colour to Sabine's face as she realised what she had said. Her eyes darting from Adrien to Alain and back again.

My pulse hammering as an image of Gabriel sprang to mind – tall for his age, brown hair, brown eyes. But Adrien had brown eyes, too, and brown hair, a little darker, perhaps. He wasn't as tall as Alain, but Sabine was tall. Maybe it wasn't true ...

Alain stepped back through the doorway, and somehow I dredged up the presence of mind to close the door behind us.

The slow-motion bubble burst.

'What the hell are you saying?' Adrien rounded on Sabine. 'You're saying my brother is the father of my son now? After all these years?'

Sabine looked desperately between them. 'I didn't mean it. I shouldn't have said anything.' Her voice held pure panic.

'But you did,' Alain said quietly, his eyes fixed on her. 'And I want to know. Am I Gabriel's father?' When she didn't answer, he repeated it, grinding it out through his teeth. '*Am I?*'

I could only stand there, my hands trembling with an adrenaline rush, watching as Sabine's mind raced for a way to backpedal out of it.

There was none. Defeated, she wailed, 'I don't know. I don't *know!*'

Alain stared at her in disbelief. 'For God's sake! How can you not know?'

A little defiance crept back in. 'I was sleeping with you both, remember? How *could* I know?'

Alain jerked back, as though she'd slapped his face.

'Then why didn't you *say?*' Adrien yelled at her. 'Instead of letting me believe, all that time …' He jerked a thumb at Alain. 'You left him for me, Sabine. I assumed that meant the baby was mine. Why did you let me believe that?'

Sabine's defiance broke. 'I was scared,' she whispered. 'When I found out I was pregnant, I had already told Alain that I was leaving him for you. I convinced myself the baby must be yours. I hoped it was.' She looked from one to the other of them. 'But I cannot be sure.'

A long, painful silence stretched between us.

Alain looked across at Adrien. 'We could get a paternity test done.'

At this, it appeared that Sabine still had a little fight left. 'But what about Gabriel? What about Chloe? What would you tell them? Why would you *do* that?'

Adrien looked at her in astonishment. 'Why the hell do you think? I've spent the past six years believing Gabriel is mine! You're the one who brought this up. Didn't you think I'd want to know? That Alain would want to know?'

Sabine's face was streaming with tears now. 'And I have kept that secret to myself for six years. How do you think *I* have felt all that time?'

'Doesn't make any difference now,' Alain said, his voice shaking with emotion. 'We have to decide how we're going to deal with this.'

Adrien turned on him. 'This isn't one of your small-town accountancy meetings, Alain. This is my life. My son. Or the boy I *thought* was my son. This is still between me and Sabine, for now. I want you out of here.'

Alain stepped closer, and I worried they might come to blows. A movement caught my eye, and I glanced through the window. Mireille was crossing the courtyard.

I spoke for the first time. 'Your mother's coming.'

'*Merde.*' Alain looked at Adrien and Sabine. 'They can't know about *any* of this,' he hissed. 'Not until or unless they need to. Understood?' He swallowed hard, then shook his head. 'You have bloody awful timing, Sabine. I'm supposed to be getting married tomorrow, and now I could be a father?'

Her voice was barely above a whisper as she murmured, 'I know. I'm sorry.'

I could have put my two penn'orth in at this point and said that sorry wasn't nearly enough. That this wasn't how I'd planned to spend the night before my wedding, wondering if my fiancé, the man I planned to have children with in the near future, might already have a child.

But it was too late. Mireille opened the door. 'What is going on?'

Alain simply brushed past her and stalked across the courtyard with long strides I had no hope of keeping up with.

I broke into a run, catching his arm. 'Alain.'

He looked at me as though he'd only just realised I'd been there the whole time. That hurt, but I understood.

'Alain, we need to talk.'

'What, with a house full of sodding guests?'

A rush of anger flooded my veins. 'The guests can fend for themselves. They're friends and family. They already know something's up. Mireille will fill them in. You and I need to …'

'The only thing I need is to go.'

I stared at him, disbelieving. 'How *dare* you? How dare you assume this hasn't upset me too? You don't think I feel sick over what Sabine said? You don't think I need to discuss with the man I'm marrying *tomorrow* that he might have a child?'

He seemed to focus on what I was saying. 'Emmy …'

But Christopher had appeared, storming over to the *gîte* to deal with his family.

'Not here,' Alain growled.

Steering him around the house to my room, I practically pushed him through the doorway. Ignoring him for a moment, I rummaged in my dressing table for the miniature whiskies that had sat there, an unwanted Christmas present, for months.

I handed one to him. He screwed off the top and downed it in one.

I did the same. I hate whisky.

With the liquid still burning my throat, I asked him, 'What did you mean, "supposed to be"?'

'What?'

'You told Sabine you're *supposed* to be getting married tomorrow. What the hell did that mean?'

He shook his head dismissively. 'It didn't mean anything. It was a figure of speech. I'm not interested in semantics, Emmy. There are bigger things to worry about here.'

I let it lie as I tried to get my swirling thoughts into some sort of order. 'How could you not know, Alain? How could you not suspect? When Sabine left you and had a baby however many months later, did you not think that Gabriel could be yours?'

Alain's hands flew into the air in exasperation. 'Of course I did! I'm no fool.' Realising he was shouting, he took a deep breath and spoke more calmly. 'They announced the pregnancy a couple of months after she left me, and naturally I was worried. I phoned her and asked outright whether there was any chance the baby was mine.' His chest heaved as he fought the painful memories.

'She laughed and told me not to be so bloody stupid. To press her point home, she reminded me that she'd been having an affair with Adrien for weeks before she left me. She also pointed out that during that time, she'd had sex with him many more times than with me.' The lamp highlighted the shadows on his face. 'I can't account for my brother's activities. But as for my own? Sabine and I had indeed … slowed in frequency.'

I'd never wanted to delve into this painful chapter of Alain's past so deeply. He'd got over it and he was marrying me – there was no need to pry open old wounds. Until now.

'So at the time, she made it clear that Gabriel had nothing to do with you?' I pressed him.

'Yes. And I took her word for it. Everything she said made sense. I knew she wanted children, so once she'd decided who she wanted to be with, I wasn't surprised they started a family so soon. They went on to have Chloe, and I let it go. I loved the kids as an uncle. I couldn't let lingering doubts plague me and affect my relationship with them – treating Gabriel as a favourite over Chloe or some such nonsense. I thought I was doing the right thing.'

'And now? How do you feel about the fact that Gabriel might be your son?'

He looked at me, the impact of the notion written across his face. 'Gabriel is a lovely child. I love him very much. I'm proud of him as a nephew, and I would be proud if he was my son. But for now, I don't have the luxury of knowing.'

'So you do want a test?'

'Yes. I … I have to know.'

I nodded understanding, but I felt sick. This could change our about-to-be-married life in a very big way.

'It'll take time,' I pointed out. 'Finding out about the test, getting it done, waiting for the results.'

Alain's brown eyes were earnest. 'Yes. But it's been six years. I can wait a little longer.'

I blurted out my thoughts before I could stop myself. 'If you're Gabriel's father, will you still want to have a family with me?'

Alain looked at me in shock, then drew in a shaky breath. 'Why would you say that? I love you. I said I want children with you. The outcome of this test won't change that.'

'Won't it?' My voice came out small.

He paced the room. 'Well, it would change our situation, I guess.'

Trepidation made me ask, 'In what way?'

He ran a frustrated hand through his hair. 'I have no idea! I … I suppose I'd want to see Gabriel more. Sabine's talking about bringing them to France. If she moves to Rouen, that's maybe three or four hours away. I'd have to consider moving nearer, if I want more of an input.'

I couldn't believe my ears. '*You'd* have to consider moving nearer? You mean *we'd* have to consider moving nearer. Alain, I've built my new life here. I work here. My business is based here. All my friends are here. And you're asking me to move with you?'

'If Gabriel is my son, then yes. Maybe. Oh, God, I don't know. There's so much to consider.'

My heart was heavy. 'Yes. There is.'

Alain stared at me, his eyes filled with turmoil. 'Don't look at me like that. This is a lot to come to terms with.'

'Yes. It is.'

He walked to the door.

'Where the hell are you going?'

'Home. I need time to process this. So do you. Standing here shouting at each other won't achieve anything, will it?'

'I guess not.'

''Night.' And he was gone.

I stood there in the middle of my room, staring at the half-open door, wondering if he'd walked out on our argument or whether he might even be walking out of my life.

In the bathroom, I splashed my face with cold water and stared in the mirror. Hardly the image a bride-to-be wanted to see, with strain on every part of her face.

Don't be an idiot, Emmy. It was a hell of a shock, that's all. He needs time. You need time. You're getting married. That means sticking by each other. Married couples hit hitches all the time.

I barked out a bitter laugh and glared at my reflection. 'Yeah, but they don't usually find out that their husband's nephew might be his son the night before their wedding, do they, smart arse?'

Walking back into the bedroom, I lay on the bed for a few moments, the acid in my stomach roiling around with the wine and food I'd had earlier, wondering what I'd – we'd – done to deserve everything going so spectacularly wrong on the eve of our wedding.

I thought about all the fuss tomorrow – hair, make-up, dresses, cars. Trying to look radiant, chatting chirpily to all our guests, with the spectre of Sabine's revelation hanging around us like a shroud.

My brain simply couldn't compute it. All it wanted to do was shut down for the night.

But with a jolt, I remembered the rest of the household. I could hardly just close my door and go to bed. People would expect me to say goodnight, even if Mireille or Christopher had already filled them in. And I had no idea what was happening with the children.

With a pang, I thought of the fun Alain and I had with Gabriel and Chloe when they came to stay. The happy chatter, the good-natured bickering. Their excitement over a simple thing like walking a dog. They were so young, oblivious to the fact that their world was about to be turned upside-down. I wished I could save them from it, but it was out of my hands.

I sat up and tried to decide whether my body would see me through ten minutes of pretending everything was okay, or as okay as it could be under the circumstances.

Well, it would have to be.

Almost everyone was gathered in the kitchen with mugs of tea. Good. The opposite end of the house from my room. Nobody could have overheard.

Ellie and Kate were washing up, sorting out leftover food, loading the dishwasher.

'Emmy. Sit down.' Rupert pushed me into a chair. 'Tea?'

The idea of swallowing a mugful of tea was beyond me. And I didn't want to prolong this. I needed my own sanctuary. 'No, thanks.'

'Are you alright?' Nick asked, concerned. 'Christopher told us what happened.'

I jumped a little, but realised he only meant the divorce. I couldn't believe that my brother- and sister-in-law were getting divorced, and I was referring to it as 'only'.

'Where's Alain?' Dad asked.

'He went home. He needs an early night. And he's upset, obviously.' *To say the least.* 'Where are the children?'

'Mireille and Christopher have taken them to their *gîte* for a while. They'll take them to Sabine when she's calm enough to have them back.'

'And Mum?'

'She and Jeanie are in the lounge. Your mum still has a headache.'

I nodded and forced a smile. 'Thanks, everyone.'

Kate came over and put her arm around me. 'I'm so sorry, Emmy. For them – and for you and Alain. What a thing to happen, the night before your wedding.'

You don't know the half of it.

'It'll be okay, Emmy,' Ellie said from the sink, her tone practical. 'All the high drama is over and done with now. You know – like a volcano or a steam kettle. Now it's blown, things might be calmer. Mireille and Christopher have a little time to get over the shock. The wedding will take the children's minds off it for a short while. As for Adrien and Sabine, they'll manage to be civil for such a special day, surely?'

Nick grimaced. 'As long as they don't start throwing punches at each other in the town hall or pouring champagne over each other's heads at the reception.'

He was only trying to lighten the atmosphere, bless him. I rolled my eyes at him, then stopped as I realised I was subconsciously thinking along the same lines myself. Except I knew there was so much more to throw punches about.

My nerves were at breaking point. I couldn't do this. I stood. 'Would you all mind if I have an early night?'

'Of course not,' Dad said kindly. 'You have a big day tomorrow.'

'Yeah. I'll say goodnight to Mum.'

In the lounge, Mum and Jeanie were seated on the sofa, and Jeanie was trying to rub the tension out of Mum's shoulders.

'I'm going to bed now,' I announced.

Jeanie smiled sympathetically.

Mum scrutinised my face, and hers softened a fraction. 'You need your beauty sleep. I hope you get some, Emmy.' The concern in her voice was genuine. A tiny glimmer of hope between us.

When I got back to the kitchen, Christopher came through the patio doors. 'Sabine's calmer now. She has the children.' He sighed. 'It must have been such a strain for them, pretending, knowing their own marriage has ended while someone else is building up to theirs. Seeing Alain and Emmy so happy together.'

I looked at his grey face. I couldn't imagine what he and Mireille must be going through – both their sons with broken marriages involving the same woman.

He pulled himself together. 'Any chance of the keys to the spare *gîte*, Rupert? Adrien needs somewhere to sleep tonight.'

Rupert stood. 'No problem. They're in the hall.'

Christopher followed him through.

Kate took me firmly by the arm. 'I'll walk you back to your room.'

I waved goodnight to the others and allowed her to steer me away.

When we got there, we stood in the doorway for a moment.

'I don't know what's going on, Emmy, but …'

'I'm bound to be upset,' I said defensively, in a desperate attempt to deflect her from probing. Nobody could know about this. 'Close family have announced their divorce on the eve of my wedding!'

'There's more to it than that. I don't want to leave you like this. Don't you want to talk about it?'

When I shook my head, she wrapped me in a hug, transmitting a world of love for me. And that was my undoing.

Out poured the tale in all its complexity and ugliness, while Kate patiently listened and tried to piece together my incoherent ramblings, gradually edging me into my room, closing the door and mopping my face with tissues until I was done.

'Oh, Emmy. I knew something was up, but I never imagined …'

'Me either.'

'The timing's *awful*. Bloody Sabine.'

'She was as shaken up as the rest of us, Kate. You could see that it was one of those things that had to come out eventually. She'd held onto it for too long.'

'And you say Alain walked out?'

'Yes. Our conversation – if you can call it that – was going nowhere. Maybe he was right to leave. We might have said things we couldn't take back.'

'But he's left you in all kinds of limbo.'

'Yes.' My hands twisted in my lap. 'I don't know how he feels, Kate, or what will happen. Will he expect us to up sticks and move our entire lives north, so he can be near Gabriel? I'm not sure I could do that. I moved here to be at *La Cour des Roses*. To be with my friends.'

'Don't jump ahead too far, Emmy. Until the paternity test's done, it's only fifty–fifty that it's even a possibility. You'll have time to discuss it. You'll be married, after all.'

My chest tightened painfully, making it hard to speak. 'But I don't even know if he still wants to.'

'Emmy, that's ridiculous!'

'Is it? If he wants to move to Rouen and I don't … He might think differently about marrying me now.'

'He's had a huge shock, that's all. When you see him at the town hall tomorrow …'

'What if he doesn't turn up?' I asked her, my voice small.

She took my face in her hands and gave me her best friend glare-stare. 'He will. I've never seen a man so in love. There's no question he'll be there. And if he isn't, he'll have me and half the Loire valley to answer to!'

I managed a wobbly smile. 'Kate, you can't tell anyone about this. Not until we know. If Gabriel is Alain's son, it'll probably come out eventually. But if he isn't, if Adrien is the father, nobody can know there was ever any doubt. For Adrien's sake. For the children's. Please.'

'I won't say anything, Emmy. I promise.'

'Thanks.'

'Time for you to try to get some sleep.'

I only grunted.

'I didn't say you *would* get any. I only said you should try to.' Another hug, a kiss, a wave, and she left.

And finally, I was alone. How alone, I wasn't sure.

I undressed and brushed my teeth on automatic pilot, climbing into bed with no hope of sleep.

Gabriel could be Alain's son.

He was a lovely boy, but I still couldn't comprehend that he might be my husband's son … and therefore my stepson. What if Alain really wanted to move? Being with Alain was the most important thing to me, but the idea of leaving *La Cour des Roses* behind was heartbreaking. As for having our own family, Alain had said he still wanted that – but he'd said a lot of other things, too.

What he hadn't said was, 'See you tomorrow' or 'See you at the *mairie*' or 'I can't wait to spend the rest of my life married to you.'

TWENTY-TWO

My wedding day, and I was awake far too early. Nerves and worry must prevent most brides from getting a good night's sleep – totally unfair, for someone expected to look their best – but with everything that had happened yesterday, it was hardly surprising I'd lain awake most of the night.

I hauled myself out of bed and went over to the window to gaze at my favourite view – the sunlight dappling through the trees in the orchard and making the dew on the grass sparkle like crystals. It was going to be a beautiful day, weather-wise. As for the rest, who knew?

All I knew for certain was that I needed a large mug of tea.

Showered and in a thin robe, I went around the side of the house to the kitchen. Nick was already at the table, a mug in front of him, blond hair flopping across his forehead.

'Hi, sis. You know it's strange, coming around the outside of the house like that?'

'Yeah, I know. It's just the way the house is configured.'

I made my tea – must rehydrate the complexion before Sophie arrived with her magic make-up – and joined him at the table.

'Are you okay?' he asked, his eyes full of concern.

'I'm fine.' When he gave me a disbelieving look, I viciously held back a confession of my wider troubles, only saying, 'We could have done without it. But it's only a question of bad timing.'

'Do you reckon they'll both come? Adrien and Sabine? Together?'

'I'd like to think so, if only because the children need them both today. They had enough trauma last night.' I sighed. 'Gabriel and Chloe were already nervous about the wedding, Nick. I don't think we can expect them to play out their roles now. Especially if Sabine doesn't come. And I won't be surprised if it's only Adrien.'

Nick cocked his head to one side. 'You're taking it well, considering.'

You have no idea.

He reached for my hand across the table. 'I'm so proud of you, Emmy.'

I looked at him quizzically. 'What for?'

'For being brave enough to come out here and start a new life for yourself in a place you love. And for being too sensible to get around to marrying a dick called Nathan, and getting married to a great guy called Alain instead. You're gutsy and fun and kind, and Alain's a lucky man.'

My stomach lurched as I thought about the events of last night and how things had been left between me and Alain. But that couldn't detract from my little brother's words.

'Awww, Nick. What a sweet thing to say.'

'If I can't be mushy on your wedding day, when would I ever get around to it?'

We grinned inanely at each other.

And then I heard Mum's voice at the top of the stairs, bossing Dad around before the poor man had even set foot out of his bedroom door.

'For heaven's sake, Dennis, stop faffing with it and come along. I need a cup of tea.'

'That's your morning peace over,' Nick observed. 'All three minutes of it. Prepare to be bossed, bullied and primped.' A knock at the door. 'I'll go. You're not decent.'

He was back thirty seconds later. 'Did you order flowers, by any chance?'

'Duh.'

'The florist wants you to check them over, and she doesn't trust me to do it. Can't think why.' He grinned. 'She's at her van.'

I went out in my robe – they must see hundreds of brides in robes on their wedding morning, surely? – and took a look.

Perfect. Simple and effective, not too showy. The white and lilac roses with the one deep purple in each bouquet were elegant, and the slim sprigs of lavender inserted in between wafted a light scent that would last all day.

I startled Madame Pascal by thanking her with a kiss, then sighed as I looked at Chloe's sweet little basket of roses. I could only hope that she might want to go ahead with being our flower girl, but I had a sinking feeling she wouldn't feel able to.

Mum's attitude was *slightly* less icy towards me this morning – even she couldn't ignore the trauma I'd been put through the night before my wedding – but there was still a fair covering of frost as I gave her the heads-up as I saw it.

'We could be one page boy and one flower girl down today, Mum.'

She nodded curtly. 'I'm not surprised. Those poor children.' Her voice softened a little. 'Let's hope they feel able to attend at all, shall we, and be grateful for that?'

'If they do, I suspect it will be just with their dad. I can't see Sabine wanting to come now.'

Mum pursed her lips. 'I *told* you she should never have been invited.'

'And I told *you* it was impossible not to invite her if we were inviting Adrien and the kids.'

'Well, that's all gone to pot now, anyway, hasn't it?'

Talk about stating the obvious. 'Yes, it has.'

Yup. Plenty of frost. I could only hope the wedding today would melt it a little, as Dad had suggested.

A knock at the door brought welcome relief in the form of Mireille. She accepted the cup of tea Mum offered her and sat at the table with us.

'I came to tell you that I've spoken to Sabine this morning, God help me.'

Mum nodded in sympathetic solidarity.

'She's talked to the children, and they still want to come to the wedding, but Sabine told them she couldn't join them. That they would have to come with their father. They were so upset.' She sighed. 'Chloe is in no state to be your flower girl, Emmy. I doubt Gabriel could perform his role, either.'

I reached across to take her hand. 'It doesn't matter. I'd love it if they could be there, but they mustn't feel they have to come.'

She nodded. 'Sabine will do her best to encourage them to come, even if they're in their ordinary clothes.'

'Thank you.'

Mireille left, and Mum cleared away the cups.

'Will you call Alain and tell him about the children?' she called over her shoulder.

My heart sank. 'No need. He'll have guessed.'

I'd reached for my mobile a dozen times already, since I got up. And each time, I'd bottled out with every excuse under the sun. It was too early – if he'd lain awake all night like me, but managed to doze off, let him sleep. If he … if he'd changed his mind about today, surely he would call me. He was a good man. He wouldn't leave me hanging. I could call him later, when I was sure he'd be up. When he'd had time to come to terms with the sudden upheaval in his life.

The next time I reached for my phone, alone in my room, determined that this time I *would* dial, the girls arrived and took my chance away.

Or gave me yet another excuse, depending on how you looked at it.

'How do you feel?' I asked Sophie, who'd been driven over by Ellie. I was concerned that it would be too long a day for her. 'No sickness?'

'No. Sometimes I feel blurgh, but not today.' She wouldn't tell me, even if she felt dreadful. 'But how are *you*? Ellie told me what happened last night. I am *so* sorry.'

Kate, who had joined us in her robe, shot me a worried glance.

I shrugged. 'It's not perfect, but you can't have everything, can you?'

'I suppose not. Well, I have some good news for you all, at least.' Sophie pulled make-up and hair tools and heaven knew what from her copious holdall, while Kate cooed with undisguised delight.

'We had enough excitement with the last news you gave us,' Ellie commented drily, pointing at Sophie's middle. 'Don't tell us there are twins in there!'

'I don't think so.' Sophie smiled. 'Ryan has found work here for the winter. He won't have to go home.'

'Oh, Sophie, that's brilliant.' I gave her a hug. 'What kind of work?'

'The decorator in town. They have taken on a lot of jobs and they would like someone to help temporarily. And we're going to look for somewhere to rent together before spring. We want to be settled before the baby is born.'

'No wedding plans?' Kate asked curiously.

Sophie laughed. 'No. I think I have caused enough change for Ryan by getting pregnant. And if he *had* proposed, I would have said no.'

Ellie frowned. 'Why?'

'Because I would always worry that he only asked because of the baby. I think we will be good together without being married.' She looked worriedly at me. 'No offence, Emmy.'

'None taken. I'm so pleased for you, Sophie. You two are made for each other.'

'Talking of which.' Ellie turned to Kate. 'You and Nick were getting along famously last night.'

Kate's cheeks went a little pink, but she managed a nonchalant shrug. 'We've known each other for years, that's all. We're old friends.'

'No possibilities between you two?'

Kate fidgeted with a blusher brush. 'Nick's the flighty sort. That's not what I need right now, even if I *was* interested – which I'm not.'

Sophie, Ellie and I exchanged glances.

'Oh, I wouldn't say that,' I said carefully. 'Nick said something the other day that made me think he might be ready to settle down. He just needs to find the right person.'

But Kate shrugged again, feigning disinterest, and Sophie let her off the hook by getting going with our beautification.

I was conscious that Kate was watching me like a hawk, and shot her a look that said *I'm going to pretend my head isn't in turmoil and I don't feel sick.* She gave me the slightest nod of acknowledgement back, but I knew that wouldn't stop her worrying.

Hair was tied back while potions and primers and foundations were applied. Then hair. Ellie's short and darker red crop was tweaked till it looked choppy and fun, Kate's was straightened into perfection, and mine was loosely waved as planned. Sophie had little to do with her own pert, wavy bob. Then back to the make-up – blushers matched to each skin tone, eyes, eyelashes, with lips to be left till the last minute.

'I want to take you back to England with me,' Kate said to Sophie as she gawped at her reflection. 'I need you every morning before I go to work.'

Sophie tutted as she inspected her handiwork on my face. 'You need more concealer, Emmy. You didn't sleep well?'

'No. Sorry.' I spied Madame Dupont's little leather box on the dressing table in front of me and decided a change of subject was in order. Reaching out, I opened the box to show them the antique earrings, and explained all about my unexpected gift.

'Oh, Emmy. They are absolutely gorgeous!' Sophie held them up to the light. 'They will glint in the sunshine, and they will go perfectly with your dress.'

Ellie nodded, taking them from her and holding one against my ear. 'How beautiful! And how thoughtful of her.'

Kate took up her camera and snapped a shot of the moment. She'd been doing the same all morning.

I knew I'd argued for informal, personal shots from Bob – but there's personal and there's personal, and I wasn't sure about these photos of our transformations. But Sophie and Kate insisted that everybody took them nowadays, Kate had promised not to take any of us in our underwear and plaster them on social media, and she'd agreed we could veto any we weren't comfortable with.

Ellie laughed as Kate lowered her camera. 'This is the part of the day where Bob should be grateful he isn't a professional wedding photographer, or he'd be in here with us, taking pictures whilst trying not to look!'

'I wonder if he'll come to the wedding in jeans,' I mused.

'Maybe he'll iron them in honour of the occasion.'

'Maybe he will even iron his beard!' Sophie moved past the bed, knocking off the hair straighteners. She and Kate bent at the same time to retrieve them and banged heads.

'This room's too small,' Ellie complained. 'Who said it was a good idea for you to get married from here?'

'*I* did,' I reminded her. 'Heaven knows, we discussed it often enough. Surely you remember?'

Ellie curled her lip. 'My brain may have shut down when it got bored.'

Sophie laughed. 'Ellie, you *know* why. Emmy and Kate are already here, and my flat is too small for playing with kittens.'

Kate's eyes opened wide.

'She means too small to swing a cat,' I translated.

'I recall making you a generous offer to use *my* house,' Ellie said, hands on hips as she surveyed the chaos in the room, every surface covered in make-up and tools, every doorframe bearing a dress, the floor littered with shoe boxes and accessory boxes.

'Your house is too far out,' Sophie told her. 'And Emmy's mother wants to help with the dresses.'

I inwardly sighed. My mother *had* wanted to help with the dresses, but that was before I told her she'd been helping too much. That I was sick of her help.

Ah, well. I could only play that one by ear.

'Do we get a glass of something bubbly soon?' Ellie asked hopefully. 'Isn't that tradition? A bit of Dutch courage?'

Sophie laughed. 'What do you need Dutch courage for? It is Emmy here who needs it. She is the one committing herself to a lifetime of domestic harmony.'

My heart stopped for a moment before kick-starting again. *I'm willing. But I don't know if Alain is.* I glanced at the bedside clock and told myself he would have phoned by now, if he had any doubts.

Kate sent me a sympathetic look – whether at the idea of trying to include my mother after all that had passed between us or the doubt about my impending marital harmony, I wasn't sure. What I was sure about was that I needed a break from all this *bonhomie*.

Kate knew it. 'Will bubbly make you less grumpy?' she asked Ellie.

Ellie thought about it. 'Possibly.'

'Rupert put some in the fridge for us. Emmy and I can go and get it.'

'If we open champagne, won't Emmy's mother expect to join us?' Sophie asked.

Ellie thought about that, too. 'I can live with that.'

Playing her part, Kate laughed. 'You want to squeeze her mum in here, too? Heaven help us!' She tightened her robe. 'Emmy and I will fetch the bubbly. *Then* we'll rouse the wedding beast that is her mother.'

She led me around the side of the house. 'This is a stupid system, having to come outside in our dressing gowns.'

'Either that, or we walk in on Rupert in his boxers or something equally disturbing.'

'Have you phoned Alain this morning?'

'I thought about it. All morning. But there was always a reason not to.'

'You mean you bottled out.'

'Yes. But they were good reasons. Besides, how would it look to him, if he intends to come and I phone because I'm doubting him?' I stopped her at the door, not wanting to be overheard. 'Surely *he* would phone *me* if he didn't plan to go through with it?'

'Emmy, Alain's not the kind of man to leave you standing at the equivalent of the altar, is he?'

An awful thought struck me. 'Oh, God, Kate. You're right – he *isn't* that kind of man. And because he isn't, he *would* go through with it. He'd feel obliged. What kind of start is that to married life?'

Kate tutted in annoyance. 'I told you yesterday that I've never seen a man so in love. You can't tell me that what happened last night has altered the way Alain feels about you or about marrying you. All this speculation is only making you poorly. Look, I have my phone in my pocket. I'll take the bubbly back and tell Sophie and Ellie that you got caught up with your mother. You find a quiet corner of the garden and phone Alain. Put your mind at rest.'

Sabine came out of her *gîte*, making for Adrien's, and Kate hustled me into the kitchen. I was about to open the fridge when we heard a loud banging noise.

Kate got to the window first. 'It's Sabine on the warpath after Adrien. Lord knows, we could do without any further unpleasantness from them.'

I joined her at the window. Sabine was at Adrien's door, speaking urgently to him and waving at her own *gîte*. Voices were raised, although it sounded more like panic than anger.

As we watched, they both rapped on Mireille and Christopher's door. Mireille opened it, listened a moment, looked behind her into the *gîte*, and her hand flew to her mouth.

The feeling in my gut was not to be ignored. 'I need to see what's going on,' I said to Kate, and before she could answer, I shot across the courtyard in my robe.

'Is something the matter?' I asked as I got there.

Mireille had disappeared into her gîte, and she and Christopher were calling to each other, one upstairs, one down.

Sabine turned to me, her face pale. 'It's Gabriel. I can't find him. He is not in the *gîte*. Or in Adrien's.'

Mireille reappeared at her door. 'He isn't in here, either.'

I looked from one to the other. 'I don't understand.'

'He and Chloe were watching a DVD,' Sabine explained, her hands flapping in agitation as she talked. 'I thought it would keep them quiet and calm before the wedding. I went upstairs to get their things ready. Their ordinary clothes – and the wedding outfits, in case they changed their minds. When I came back down, only Chloe was there. She said that Gabriel had told her he was going for a nap. So I went upstairs, but his door was closed. I would have checked on him, but he'd looked so tired this morning, and the door creaks. I didn't want to wake him.' Her voice caught on a sob. 'I left him to sleep. When it was time to wake him up, I went in, but he wasn't there. He isn't *anywhere*.'

'Where's Chloe now?' Christopher asked her.

'In the lounge.'

He turned to his wife. 'Mireille, you should go to her. Keep her occupied while we look for Gabriel.'

Mireille nodded and dashed off.

Sabine was shaking, and Adrien put a tentative arm around her shoulders. 'We'll find him, Sabine. He must be somewhere.'

Christopher and I exchanged looks. He might as well have said, 'He could be anywhere.' Suddenly, a five-year-old boy seemed very small and *La Cour des Roses* unbearably large.

'You two start on the grounds,' I said to Adrien and Christopher as calmly as I could, although the rate of my heartbeat was anything but. 'I'll do the guesthouse.'

I ran back to the house, colliding with Rupert in the doorway.

'Heading over to Alain's now,' he said jovially. 'Moral support from the best man and all that.' He took in my expression. 'What's up?'

'Gabriel's missing.'

Kate had already fetched Sophie and Ellie, so I only had to explain Sabine's story once.

'Well, he's not in my rooms unless he climbed into a cupboard while I wasn't looking, but I'll double-check.' Rupert hurried back to his quarters.

'He can't be in your room, Emmy. We've been in there all along,' Sophie said.

'I'll go upstairs. You three help Adrien and Christopher in the gardens.'

Ellie glanced at Sophie and Kate, all in their robes. 'Two ticks to throw some clothes on, Emmy. We can't scramble through bushes in these.'

Ignoring my own state of undress, I ran upstairs, knocking on my parents' door first. My mother opened it, already dressed for the wedding in a pale mint trouser suit, her auburn hair piled loosely on top of her head.

'I was about to *ask* if you and the girls need help getting into your dresses,' she said, her tone suggesting she wasn't sure how welcome she would be, but then she took in my panic. 'Is something wrong?'

'Gabriel's missing. He's not in any of the *gîtes*. He couldn't be in your room, could he?'

We both knew the question was ridiculous but had to be asked.

'No. Your dad and I have been in here for ages. But I'll check with everyone else. What about the cupboards? The lounge? The hall?'

'I'm on it.' I threw open the doors of the huge wooden *armoire* on the landing where we kept bedlinen and towels, ruffling hopelessly through them, but no small child came to light.

With the sound of my parents banging on the other doors ringing in my ears, I hurried downstairs to check the broom cupboard in the hall, the wooden bench chest, and then into the guest lounge to look behind all the chairs. If that child thought he was playing a fun game of hide-and-seek on my wedding day, he was in serious trouble.

But I instinctively knew that wasn't the case. And then I refused to listen to my instinct any further, for fear it might come up with something I didn't want to think about.

'I already checked in here,' Rupert said from the doorway, his breathing rapid. 'No sign of him anywhere. What about upstairs?'

'Mum and Dad are on it.'

'Go and get dressed, Emmy. Two minutes won't make any difference, and then you can help outside.' He pulled out his mobile. 'I'll phone Alain.'

'Thanks.'

Back in my room, I threw on a tee and shorts, then shot outside. People were fanning out across the gardens and orchard, hunting through trees and bushes. All those quiet corners and hidey places that our guests loved so much.

At that moment, I hated the size and variety of the grounds at *La Cour des Roses*.

We gathered in the courtyard, a bundle of nerves. It was forty-five minutes since Gabriel had been found to be missing, but because of his nap ploy, we had no way of knowing how long he'd really been gone. The sense of panic was palpable.

Everyone on the premises had joined in the hunt. We'd searched every corner of the guesthouse. Every corner of the *gîtes*. The shed. The generator outhouse. Every nook and cranny of the gardens and orchard. At least three times.

Alain had arrived in his car, panicked and out of breath, within ten minutes of Rupert's call. We'd shared a quick, troubled look that I couldn't interpret beyond knowing there were things to be said, but now was not the time.

Sophie had phoned Ryan, and he'd rushed over, too. He and Alain had paired up to search the thick hedgerows and trees surrounding *La Cour des Roses* from the outside of the premises.

Mireille was still in Sabine's *gîte* with Chloe, watching TV and pretending everything was okay, the door firmly closed. It occurred to me how hard that must be for her, to shut herself away from what was going on and pretend that everything was normal, when she must be worried sick.

Mum looked around at everyone as they tried to make conjectures and formulate plans, and in her best seasoned committee chairwoman voice – often irritating but now much needed – she brought us to order.

'I know none of us have dared imagine that Gabriel might have ventured along the lanes,' she said loudly, waiting as everyone hushed, 'but we need to consider that now. He can't have got far on foot.' She turned to Alain's father. 'Christopher, take your car. Drive a couple of miles in each direction from *La Cour des Roses*.'

Christopher dragged a shaking hand through his thinning hair. He looked ten years older than he had yesterday.

Mum clicked her fingers at Nick. 'Nick, you take half. We need to cover ground quickly.'

They went off to their cars, heads together, planning their routes.

Mum turned to me, her voice barely above a whisper. 'You're going to miss the *mairie*.'

'I know.'

She called Ellie and Sophie over. 'Ladies, I need to borrow you. My French is rubbish, and I don't want Emmy to have to do this.'

Ellie glanced at her watch. They knew what was coming.

'One of you should phone the *mairie*,' Mum said. 'That's dead in the water now. And one of you needs to phone the *château*. Get them to stop the guests from leaving for town and explain what's happening. *If* Gabriel's found soon, there's a chance we could go ahead with the reception, but the guests will have to wait for an update.'

Ellie and Sophie pulled out their mobiles and made for the guesthouse, where they could perform their allotted tasks in quiet.

Mum addressed the rest of the group. 'If Gabriel has left the grounds, he may not be somewhere as obvious as the roadside. We should divide out the area and go off road on foot – beyond the verges, checking the ditches, and onto any tracks. Rupert, you know the area. You should coordinate. Is that okay with everyone?'

Not a murmur of dissent.

Her next statement blew through the ensuing silence like a cold wind. 'And it's time to phone the authorities. That child has been missing for too long.'

TWENTY-THREE

My mother had voiced our worst fears. The possibilities were too numerous and unbearable to contemplate.

I'd never seen a person go as white as Sabine did then. Adrien reached for her hand, a gesture of comfort, but she shook him off, hugging her arms tightly around her as though she were cold. It was nearly thirty degrees out here.

'Yes. Please. Call them.' Sabine forced the words out.

'Sabine, you come into the kitchen with me while Rupert calls,' Mum ordered. 'You're in shock. You need hot, sweet tea. Adrien, you too. The police will need to speak to you both when they arrive.'

She turned to everyone else. 'Please get yourselves into pairs, preferably where someone who knows the area is with someone who doesn't. Rupert will be back out in a moment to give you directions.' She forced a reassuring smile. 'Don't worry. We'll find Gabriel. I can feel it.'

Sometimes, my mother's strength came across as hardness or bossiness. Right now, it was what was needed, and it held warmth and concern. Anything else – anxiety, panic, despair – had been viciously damped down for the common good. Others were too close to what was going on. Mum had seen that and knew that someone on the outside needed to jump in and do what had to be done. I loved her for that.

She turned to me. 'Emmy, you need to make some phone calls. Get Ellie and Sophie to help you. Phone all the guests who aren't based here or at the *château* – people like Jonathan, Madame Dupont, Bob. Stop them from setting off, or at least turn them back.'

Mum patted my cheek and crossed to Sabine, taking her by the hand to lead her across the courtyard. When it looked like Sabine's legs would buckle, my mother put an arm firmly around her shoulders for support. Adrien followed, head down, shoulders stooped. A lost soul.

Glancing at the kitchen window, I saw Rupert with the phone at his ear, speaking urgently into it as he gazed across his courtyard.

Kate, standing with my father, caught my eye and shot me a sad wave.

As I walked over to the house, Alain and Ryan came back from their perimeter search with a shake of their heads and joined Rupert, his phone call made, to get everyone off on their searches.

In the kitchen, Mum placed mugs of sugary tea in front of Sabine and Adrien and urged them to drink.

Sophie and Ellie were in the lounge on their phones. I found a piece of paper, scribbled down the names of people to call and placed it on the coffee table, ticking Jonathan to show that I was starting with him. They held thumbs up to indicate they understood.

It took time, but we got there between us.

'Patrice is so sorry,' Sophie told me. 'He'll talk to you about fitting you in at the *mairie* some other time, when the crisis is over.'

'Bob was already at the *mairie*,' Ellie said. 'He'll stay there to head anybody off at the pass who's already set off. Then he'll join in the search. The manager of the *château* phoned me back to say that some of the guests have offered to help, too, but I asked him to put them off for now. We have a lot of people, and it would only be helpful if they know the area.'

'Good girl, Ellie.' Rupert came in and sat next to her. 'The *gendarmes* are on the way.' He held out a hand to me, and I took it. 'Emmy, love. Not the big day you anticipated, eh?'

I glanced at the clock on the wall. Alain and I should be at the *mairie* now, committing ourselves to a lifetime together. 'All that matters is finding Gabriel.'

Mum bustled in with a tray of tea for us all. Grateful, we helped ourselves, and she shot off back to the kitchen to minister to her charges like a bustling matron from an old-fashioned comedy. Except none of this was remotely funny.

I couldn't stop thinking about Gabriel. Who knew what went through a child's mind? What was happening with his parents must have been too much for him. Maybe he wouldn't go far. Maybe he wasn't running *to* anywhere, but just needed to be alone for a while.

Something glimmered in my brain for a split second, but it was gone before I could grasp it.

There was a loud knock at the door.

'That'll be the authorities. I'll go.' Rupert hoisted himself out of his chair.

We heard voices in the hall, moving through to the kitchen.

A couple of minutes later, Mum came in. 'They're nice,' she said chirpily, as if niceness alone meant that Gabriel could be found.

'We're not needed now,' I said. 'We should be out searching for Gabriel.'

'Wait until Rupert's finished talking to the *gendarmes*, Emmy. They might need you to make more calls; relay information to the volunteers.' She hesitated. 'And there'll be decisions about the reception. The guests at the *château*.'

Ellie pulled Sophie to her feet. 'We can give *La Cour des Roses* another once-over while we're waiting. Gabriel might have snuck back by now and be hiding somewhere. It's worth a try.'

I stood, too. 'That's a good idea. Mum, could you do upstairs again? I'll do the *gîtes*.'

I went across the courtyard, first tapping on the door to Sabine's *gîte* and letting myself in. Mireille looked up from the sofa. French cartoons were playing on the TV, the sound low, and Chloe was curled up in Mireille's lap, fast asleep.

'That's good,' I said. 'That she's asleep.'

'Only just,' Mireille whispered. 'So many questions about why everybody was out there and where they all went and where Gabriel is and when it will be time to put her dress on.' Her face was drawn and tired. 'Emmy, I'm sorry about your wedding.'

'Thank you. Has anyone updated you?'

'I had to put my phone on silent, but Alain and Christopher have texted. I saw the *gendarmes* arrive.'

'Yes. They're talking to Adrien and Sabine now. Some of us are having another trawl of *La Cour Des Roses*. We'll let you know as soon as we hear anything.'

Half an hour later, Ellie, Kate, Sophie and I had achieved nothing, other than taking phone calls from searchers to confirm they'd not had any luck either.

By the time the officers left, Sabine was sobbing, her head on her arms on the kitchen table, while Adrien looked on, helpless.

'Adrien, why don't you phone Alain?' Mum said kindly. 'Join the search. We'll take care of Sabine.'

He nodded, anxious to do something physical to help find his son, and disappeared.

'What did they say?' I asked Rupert.

'They're organising a search team. They know we already have people out on the roadsides and paths, so they're asking us to stay off private property – they'll go door-to-door at the local farms and search the land, to save any confusion.'

'Sounds sensible.'

'Could you get back on the phone and let all the volunteers know that?'

'Of course.'

Rupert glanced down at Sabine and hesitated. 'They … they can't rule out abduction. They're getting the word out for any sightings.'

Sabine let out a long wail – an animal cry.

Ice ran up my spine.

We went back into the lounge to make our calls, while Mum and Rupert stayed with Sabine, murmuring useless words of comfort.

With the calls done, we looked at each other in one accord. We'd had enough of being telephone operators.

In the kitchen, Sabine was being plied with a small brandy, and Mum and Rupert were self-medicating a little. I couldn't blame them.

'We're going out to search for Gabriel,' I informed them in a voice that brooked no nonsense. 'We've done everything we can here.'

'I'll act as Switchboard Central,' Rupert confirmed. 'Text me with any messages you get, so I can keep track of everyone.'

'You and Sophie go and search,' Mum said to me. She looked pointedly at the clock, and we followed her gaze. We should be at the *château*, sipping bubbles and dodging Bob's camera. 'But Ellie, could you come to the *château* with me? I need your French, and I need that practical nature of yours. We have to update the guests and speak to the management. Looks like the meal isn't happening, either.'

Ellie put her arm around my mother, the first one to offer support and comfort to a woman who, on the surface, didn't appear to need it. If those two redheads got to know each other too well, they could become fearsome partners in crime.

'And Rupert. I could do with a quick word before we go.' Mum crooked her finger at him and led him off to his quarters.

I phoned Alain to ask where he wanted us.

'Nobody's done that path between the farms where you turn right onto the main road and go right again.'

'I know which you mean. I've walked the dog there. We're on it.'

We piled into my car and set off, Sophie keeping her eyes skinned all the way.

'I don't know how Alain's doing it,' I said as we began to trek on foot, Sophie looking left, me right, so we couldn't miss anything. 'He has a handle on every pair and where they are.'

'He's an accountant. He has a logical brain.'

'Thank God for it today.'

We walked until the path petered out into nowhere, then carried on, picking our way through long grass and shrubbery.

'This is no good,' I said eventually. 'I can't imagine Gabriel got this far, or even wanted to. There's nowhere for him to hide. Let's go back.'

Despondently, we retraced our steps, jumping at every rustle in the hedges lining the path, but it was invariably rabbits.

'How are you?' Sophie asked.

'Worried. Trying to block the word "abduction" from my mind.'

Sophie linked her arm in mine. 'I know. Me too. But I meant about the wedding.'

'Ah. Well. "What will be, will be", as my mother is fond of saying.'

'Your mother has been brilliant today, Emmy. I was scared of her before, but now I have seen the other side of her. She is bossy, but she has a good heart.'

I remembered all that had been said between us the other day. So many accusations. So many hard words. 'Yes. She does.'

When we reached the car, I was about to call Alain to ask where next, but Sophie stopped me. 'Could we go back to the guesthouse? I feel sick.'

'Sophie, you should have said.'

'It might be because I haven't eaten.' She gave me a sheepish look. 'I know I shouldn't be thinking about food.'

'That baby doesn't know any better, does it? I don't want you to dehydrate, either. And I ought to drop in on Mireille.'

I texted Alain, then drove the short way back.

While Sophie went into the house to find something to settle her stomach, I went across to see Mireille. She put her fingers to her lips, but this time it wasn't for Chloe. Chloe was wide awake, watching television.

It was Sabine who was lying on the sofa, her head in Mireille's lap, while Mireille stroked her hair to soothe and Chloe held her hand.

I looked at Mireille in admiration. Here was a woman, worried sick about her grandchild, comforting the daughter-in-law she disliked so intensely, the woman who had broken both her sons' hearts. I would never have more respect for my future mother-in-law than I had at that moment.

I crept into the kitchen, poured Chloe some juice, made Mireille and Sabine some tea, and placed them carefully on the table near Mireille.

'Thank you,' she whispered. 'No luck?'

I shook my head. 'I'm sorry.'

'What is happening with your reception?'

'Mum and Ellie went to the *château*, but nothing can be done now. We need to find Gabriel before it gets dark.'

'I am proud to have you in our family, Emmy.'

She held out a hand and I took it. We squeezed tight before I let go, let myself out and crossed to the guesthouse.

'Are Mum and Ellie back yet?' I asked Rupert.

'No.' He'd made tea and toast for Sophie, who was looking green around the gills as she forced it down, and he pushed a mug across to me. 'I expect they'll chat to all the guests, as well as speak to the management. They may be a while.'

I chewed my lip. 'I should have gone. All those people came for my wedding. They must think it's awful that I'm not there.'

'Emmy, nobody will think like that. A little boy is missing, and that little boy is your very-nearly-husband's nephew.'

He could be his son.

'I'll go there now.' I stood, but Rupert applied gentle pressure on my shoulders until I was forced back into my chair.

'You're not going anywhere until you've drunk that tea.'

'Rupert, there are goodness knows how many people out there searching, without so much as a cup of tea.'

'But you're here, so you have access to one. I don't want a pregnant, fainting woman on my hands, so you can stay for five minutes till Madam here perks up. Then you can phone your mum and gauge the lie of the land at the *château*. How's that?'

'Okay.' It was deathly quiet, and it occurred to me that I hadn't seen the dog for hours. 'Where's Gloria?'

'In my lounge. I didn't want her getting in everyone's way. She'll need a walk later, but she's fast asleep for now.'

I squawked in frustration. 'Haven't we heard from *anybody*?'

'People check in from time to time, to let us know where they are, or to say they haven't found him yet, or to ask if anyone else has.'

'And the *gendarmes*?'

'They're coordinating with Alain and Adrien, since Alain knows where everyone's looked. No point in going over the same ground twice.'

My chest felt tight. I couldn't bear the thought of Gabriel, lost and alone. Or worse – not alone. For a moment, my breath stopped as my mind ran with the possibilities.

I willed them away. We had no evidence for that, yet. And we knew he hadn't been taken from the *gîte* but had left of his own accord.

Where did he go? Did he have somewhere in mind, or had he set off with no destination in his head? And *why* did he go? To be alone with his misery and confusion over his parents? To think things through? To get away from everyone?

There it was again. That glimmer of something. *Damn!* What had I just been thinking?

I rewound, concentrating hard, my hands clutched in my hair, raking through my thoughts for what they were trying to tell me.

'Emmy? Are you alright?' I heard the alarm in Sophie's voice but ignored it as I grasped after whatever it was.

Alone. Privacy. The children had asked about privacy, and I'd explained that it was when you wanted to be on your own for a while, away from other people. What had I said? Something along the lines of when you needed to think, or if you were upset.

Well, *that* didn't help. We'd already established that Gabriel wanted to be alone; that he must be upset.

But the memory of the afternoon I'd shown the children around the garden was lodged in my head now. The orchard. Gloria running through the trees. The kids nosing about in my room. The chickens. '*Their little house makes them feel cosy and safe from anything bad that could happen to them.*'

The chicken house. Had anyone checked it?

I shot outside and raced down the garden at a speed I hadn't known I was capable of, crashing through the gate and startling my feathered friends into a frenzied panic. But when I fell to my knees and peered into the coop, there was no Gabriel.

Rupert appeared, out of breath. 'Emmy. Are you okay?'

'Yes. Sorry. I had a sudden thought, and ...'

'It was a good idea. But I already checked in there. Twice. It looked Gabriel-sized to me, too.' Helping me to my feet, he bent to ineffectually brush the dried mess off my knees. 'Come on, love.'

He led me indoors, where I dutifully sat down again and sipped at the tea he plied me with.

'I was so sure about that chicken house,' I explained. 'I … Shit, shit, *shit*!'

TWENTY-FOUR

I jumped up from the table, sending my mug of hot tea flying across it, grabbed my keys from the window sill and was across the courtyard and in my car before Rupert and Sophie could do anything other than leap up to avoid being scalded.

As I shoved the car in gear, they reached the door.

'Emmy! Wait!' Rupert shouted.

'Be careful, at least!' Sophie's panicked shout faded as the tyres fought gravel and I set off.

The lane was too narrow for speed, but I covered the half mile in record time, braking jerkily outside Madame Dupont's wreck of a house.

Please, God. Please, please, please.

I pushed my way through the gate, snapping the rusting bolt, through the side gate and into the yard. Running across it, I tripped and fell, scraping my hands and knees, but it barely slowed me down.

'Gabriel! Gabriel!'

No answer.

Please, please, please.

The chicken house was closed up. Had we left it open or shut? I couldn't remember. I tugged, and the ramp came clattering down, showering splinters of old, dried wood across the concrete.

Adjusting my eyes to the gloom, I saw a lumpy shape up on the ledge.

Gabriel.

He was huddled under his hoodie, fast asleep, but the clattering must have woken him because he startled with a shout.

'Gabriel, it's only me, Emmy,' I soothed, my voice calm while my body shook with adrenaline and relief.

He struggled to sit up, but I couldn't wait for that. I scooped him up and hugged him tight against me.

'Oh, Gabriel, we looked for you everywhere! You had everyone so worried.'

'I'm sorry,' he mumbled against my shoulder, still half-asleep.

'It's okay, sweetheart.' I sat on the floor of the coop in the entrance, where he blinked against the evening light. 'But you mustn't ever do it again. Anything could have happened to you.'

'But you said the chickens were safe if they were shut up in their house.' His chin wobbled.

'I did. But you're not a chicken, are you?' I smiled at him to reassure and got a weak one back. 'This chicken house is old. It might have broken and hurt you. Or you could have been hurt on the way here. You do know you're not supposed to go anywhere without someone you know, don't you?'

He nodded, then began to cry. 'Will Mum and Dad be cross with me? Am I in trouble?'

'They're not cross, sweetie, only worried. Why did you come here? You told Chloe you were going for a nap in your room.'

'I did,' he mumbled. 'I was tired and I wanted to sleep, but I couldn't. Then I remembered the chicken house. Rupert's was too small, so I came here.'

He said it as though it was the most logical thing in the world, to bunk down in a chicken house, then he yawned, long and loud. He must have been exhausted to sleep on that rickety old wooden shelf for so long.

'Why were you so tired? Were you upset about Mummy and Daddy arguing?'

'Yeah. I don't want them to … I can't remember the word. The one that means they won't live together any more.'

'Divorce?'

He nodded glumly.

My phone buzzed in my pocket, but I ignored it. If Gabriel felt able to talk, two more minutes wouldn't matter. Once we were back, there would be chaos, and then he might clam up altogether.

Gabriel's chest heaved. 'Mum told Dad that she's going to bring me and Chloe to France. To live. To *school*!' The last word was wailed.

'You wouldn't like that?'

He shook his head. 'She said we have to live in France and Dad shouted at her and said that would be bad for me and Chloe because we wouldn't know anybody and I'd have to start at a new school and people might make fun of me because I've come from England and term starts soon so it couldn't be sorted out in time and we'd be squished in Granny and Grandpa's house in Rouen and he wouldn't see us because he won't come to live in France, so now I *know* he doesn't *love* us any more!'

It all came out in such a rush, I had trouble registering everything he said. But it was the last part I was most concerned with.

I took his face in my hands. 'Gabriel, your dad loves you very much.' My heart twanged as I realised I could be referring to either Adrien or Alain.

'No, he *doesn't*! If he loved us, he'd come to France.'

'Oh, Gabriel, you know your dad and mum don't want to live together any more.'

'I know *that*. I mean somewhere *near* us. Not hundreds and hundreds of miles away.'

'That doesn't mean your dad doesn't love you. The grown-up world is complicated. Your dad needs to work to make money to look after you all. His job is in England, so he has to stay there.'

'Why can't he get a job in France?'

'Maybe he won't be able to. He's lived in England for a long time.' I sighed. This was out of my jurisdiction. I couldn't answer his questions. 'But I do know, cross my heart, that your dad loves you very much.'

My phone vibrated angrily in my pocket. I couldn't delay any longer. The way I'd stormed off, everyone must be having kittens by now.

'Gabriel, I need to tell someone I've found you.'

He sobbed against my T-shirt as I answered the phone to Rupert, then phoned Alain.

'Come on. Let's get you back where you belong.'

Gabriel stood. 'I need a wee. And I'm hungry.'

'I'm not surprised. How about that tree over there?'

He went over to pee, while I willed my legs into a consistency beyond jelly.

The idea that Gabriel thought Adrien didn't love him broke my heart. I thought about the impending paternity test and felt sick. What would the poor boy think then, if it went the 'wrong' way?

With no child car seat, I strapped him carefully into the back and gave him a mint. 'Best I can do for food,' I said cheerily.

'You're not in your dress,' Gabriel piped up as I put the car in gear.

I glanced at his enquiring face in the driver's mirror. 'My dress?'

'Your wedding dress. I'm sorry I slept so long and missed the wedding, Aunt Emmy.'

Oh, the innocence of children.

I took a long, shaky breath. Gabriel already had the weight of the world on his shoulders. I didn't want him to take the blame for this. But I couldn't see any way around telling him the truth – in as light a way as I could.

'We didn't have the wedding today, Gabriel. We were looking for you, so we didn't feel like it.'

'Oh. I'm sorry.'

'It's more important that you're okay. We can do the wedding another time.'

'But when?'

'I don't know, sweetie.' And *that* was the truth. 'Sometime soon.'

Yeah. With the mairie *fully booked up on a Saturday morning and the* château *holding another event tomorrow, and most of my guests leaving by Sunday, and a flight to Mallorca booked for Monday?*

But that wasn't Gabriel's problem. He had enough of his own.

Sabine was waiting in the courtyard with Mireille and Chloe. Sabine hugged Gabriel so tight, I thought she would crush him. Chloe touchingly did the same, as did Mireille. All the while, Sabine murmured endearments to her son. Not one hint of anger or accusation as to all the trouble he'd inadvertently caused. Relief was the overpowering emotion.

Rupert and Sophie rushed out of the house.

'Alain's phoning the authorities,' Rupert told me. 'I phoned some of the volunteers, and they'll ring others. Sophie phoned Ellie at the *château*.'

Alain's car roared into the courtyard, Adrien in the passenger seat. Adrien stumbled getting out, then ran across to join in with testing out the strength of Gabriel's ribcage, while Gabriel cried and muttered about being sorry that he'd fallen asleep.

Alain went across for a long hug, too, then came to me and wrapped his arms around me, burying his face in my hair.

'Thank you so much,' he murmured. 'You'll never know how grateful I am to you.'

I held him tight until I sensed him calm, then pulled away. 'I *do* know, and you don't have to be grateful. It was luck, really. A sudden thought.'

'He was in Madame Dupont's chicken house?'

'Yes.' I explained the whys and wherefores, such as they were.

'Thank God you thought of it. Imagine if he'd woken in the dark? Tried to get home on his own along the lanes? I can't believe nobody checked there already.'

'That chicken house is right around the back of the house, Alain,' Rupert explained. 'You can't see it from the roadside. And with the house boarded up like that, everyone would know that nobody could be in the property itself.'

'Nobody could guess a small boy would choose to hide in an abandoned chicken house,' Sophie added, her hand splayed across her stomach.

'Except Emmy,' Alain said proudly, squeezing my hand.

'If I'd never let him explore it a few days ago, he'd never have thought of it, would he?'

'You weren't to know he'd use it as a bunkhouse,' Alain said sternly. 'And he could have ended up somewhere far worse.'

We fell quiet as we absorbed that – and the fact that Gabriel was now safe, with no harm done.

Gabriel approached, a parent holding each hand. 'Aunt Emmy. Uncle Alain.' His voice was small. 'I'm sorry about your wedding. I know it was my fault.'

'We haven't asked him to apologise,' Sabine said proudly. 'He worked it out for himself.'

I crouched down so I was on his level. 'Gabriel, listen to me. *Nothing* is more important to grown-ups than their children. The wedding can happen another time. All that matters is that you're safe. I don't want you to worry about it any more. Promise me?'

'I'll try.'

Sabine and Adrien both gave me grateful smiles, then exchanged a rare tender look between them.

Adrien hoisted Gabriel into his arms. 'We're giving Gabriel and Chloe supper and putting them to bed.'

As they walked away, Alain said, 'That was good of you, Emmy, trying to set Gabriel's mind at rest like that.' He managed a wobbly smile. 'If I hadn't already been about to marry you, I'd have proposed all over again.'

That brought a chuckle from Mireille, who had come over to hug me and thank me for my intrepid discovery of her grandson.

And it lifted any last lingering doubt I had that Alain truly did want to marry me. That he would have turned up today, and gone into it with all his heart.

'Alain …'

Sensing we needed our privacy, Rupert, Sophie and Mireille melted away, while Alain gently pulled me to the corner of the house, away from everyone.

He stroked my cheek with his thumb. 'I'm so sorry. About the wedding. About everything.'

'It doesn't matter now.'

'I thought, after the way I behaved last night …'

'I understood, Alain. You were stressed.'

'Yes. But I'm sorry for what I put you through. For the way I spoke to you. I can't tell you how sorry.' He gently traced the shadows under my eyes with his thumbs. Sophie's concealer was impressive, but it wasn't a miracle worker. 'You got no sleep?'

I shook my head.

'Me either.' He bent his head to touch his lips lightly to mine. 'Emmy, Adrien and I aren't going to take a paternity test.'

My heart skipped a beat. 'How come? You were so sure you needed to know before.'

'Yes, well, "before" is the word, isn't it? This thing with Gabriel today turned everything on its head. We were all beside ourselves, but Adrien and Sabine …'

'I know. I've never seen anyone look so ill. So terrified.'

'Exactly. That feeling of terror. The possible loss of his child. It brought home to Adrien that it's not a question of *thinking* he's been Gabriel's father all these years, but that he *has been* Gabriel's father. Gabriel is his son. Only a piece of paper can tell him otherwise. We talked a lot while we were searching together, and the fact is …'

'He doesn't want to know?'

'It would make no *difference* for him to know. It wouldn't change his feelings about Gabriel one iota – his love for him, or his responsibilities towards him.'

'I can understand that. But where does it leave you? Have you only agreed because it's what Adrien wants? Because it's what's best for everybody else?'

'It *is* what's best for everybody. But it's also what I want. What happened today was like a nightmare. I love that boy so much. But after seeing the state that Adrien was in, and Sabine …' He sighed. 'Adrien says their split is final, and today won't change that. They've been struggling for a long while. That week away together was supposed to be a chance to work things out, but it only brought home to them that they were finished.' He took a deep breath. 'Sabine will bring the children to France, but they'll still be a family. Adrien will visit the children as their dad. In the light of that, what use would that test be to any of us?'

'If Adrien is Gabriel's father, at least you'd all have peace of mind.'

'True. But that's quite a gamble. If it fell the other way, where would we be, then? What would we tell the children? How would you tell Gabriel that his father isn't his father, but his uncle is? How would you tell Chloe that Gabriel's her half-brother? There's no way I could do any of that. Those children will be hurt enough by their parents' divorce, without me making it worse.'

I smoothed the lines at the corner of his mouth. 'You're saying that if things are going to stay the same, there's no point in knowing?'

'Yes.'

I nodded. I would support him through this, however it turned out. Whatever could be done to move the situation forward as smoothly as it could for those little children must be done. But that didn't mean that, in a brief, selfish, petulant moment, I couldn't wish it wasn't happening.

'You're a brave man, Alain.'

'I can go on loving Gabriel and Chloe the way I always have.'

'What happens if you can't live with that decision? If you change your mind later?'

'We'll cross that bridge if we come to it. But I hope it doesn't work out that way.'

'What will Sabine say?'

'Adrien will talk to her when they've got the children to bed.' He rested a hand on my cheek, and touched his forehead to mine. 'Thank you, Emmy. For being so understanding.'

I laid my hand over his. 'We're getting married. That means we're in this together.'

I sensed a kind of relief wash over him. 'You're sure? About getting married? I didn't know, with all this going on …' His voice hitched.

'I'm sure. I was sure when you proposed, and I'm sure now. I love you, Alain.'

'I love you, too. More than you'll ever know.' He pulled back to look at me. 'And what you said last night? Please don't doubt that I want to start a family with you. This doesn't change that, I promise.'

He pulled me tight to him, and I rested my head against his shoulder.

The clamour in the courtyard became louder as it filled with weary expeditioners who'd heard the news, and we could no longer ignore the people who wanted to come over to congratulate me for my discovery of Gabriel. I was hugged by all, the longest from Christopher.

Rupert set to organising large vats of tea, and everyone flopped on the patio, grateful for a seat and the outcome of the day. When Dad got back, he gave me a silent cuddle. Somehow he transmitted thanks, sympathy and reassurance with no words whatsoever. That was my dad for you.

Kate, who had been searching with him, took her turn to wrap her arms around me and whisper in my ear, 'Is everything okay with Alain?'

I nodded, and in this public arena, she accepted that for now. Explanations could wait for another time.

The *gendarmes* arrived and were directed to Sabine's *gîte*, presumably for details so they could wrap up this case and move on to the next.

'Thank God we don't need them any more,' Dad voiced everyone's thoughts.

Ellie and Mum returned just as Alain had moved onto the patio and held up his hands to get everyone's attention.

'Two minutes of your time, everyone, please! I'll keep this short, because we're all tired. As you'd expect, my brother and his wife are with the children, so I'd like to thank you all on their behalf for helping us today. I know it wasn't the kind of day you were looking forward to, and this wasn't the speech I expected to make.' Polite chuckles all round. 'But there'll be time for that.' He held up his mug in a toast. 'A heartfelt thank you.'

A cheer, and everyone went back to their tea. It was beginning to get dark, and I couldn't be more relieved that Gabriel had been found before night fell.

Ryan came over to us, his arm around Sophie. 'I'm taking her home. She's not well.'

I reached out to take her hand. 'I'm sorry, Sophie.'

'I am fine,' she asserted. 'He is only fussing.' But she didn't look it. 'Can I leave my stuff in your room? The make-up and hair tools? My dress? I can't face dealing with it now.' She glanced across at Ellie, who gave her a surreptitious nod.

'We'll worry about it tomorrow,' I agreed, although my heart sank at the idea of spending the night surrounded by reminders of today's non-wedding.

I smiled as I watched Ryan play the solicitous dad-to-be, helping Sophie into the car.

Alain quietly stepped away as Mum approached and gave me a voluminous hug.

'You did well, Emmy. Not just in finding Gabriel. For bearing up so well, too.'

'Thanks. I …' I choked, suddenly in such a rush to say all the things I needed to say to her. 'Thank you for all you did today, Mum. You did just what was needed, when it was needed. You're truly amazing. I'm so sorry for everything I said to you the other day.'

'No, Emmy.' Mum cut me off, her tone firm, making me look up at her in surprise. 'Don't you *dare* apologise for that, just because I happened to do the right things today.' She took my face in her hands. 'I know how hard it was for you to say what you said before. I might not have liked it.' She managed a wan smile. 'What am I saying? We both know I *didn't* like it. But that doesn't mean you should take it all back now. If it needed saying, then it did. Your dad had a go at me, too. I'm sorry I put you both in that position, so near to your special day.' She paused. 'You're still my little girl, Emmy. I just … I wanted to make today perfect for you.'

'I know. And it would have been.'

She leaned in to whisper, 'Alain's family has a lot to answer for, don't they?'

We laughed together, looking round at our guests slurping mugs of tea instead of sipping at flutes of champagne.

Mum took my hand. 'I'll try harder, Emmy. I might make mistakes. It's not easy, changing the way you do things at my age. But I will try, I promise.'

I squeezed her fingers. 'I don't want you to change who you are, Mum. But I do need you to see me as who *I* am now – an independent woman in her thirties who's getting married and thinking about starting a family.' My mother's eyes lit up. 'I know I'll always be your daughter and that you'll always worry about me, but we need to . . . reassess the dynamic between us. I don't mind us discussing things and disagreeing about things. That's only natural. But I'd like you to respect the decisions I make and understand that I'm old enough and capable enough to make them.'

'And a little less interference in general wouldn't go amiss?'

I shrugged sheepishly. 'That would be nice. This life of mine, here in France, is a new start for me. I'd like you and me to have a new start, too. Would that . . . would that be okay?'

Mum nodded, tears in her eyes. 'That's fine by me.'

I tucked a strand of loose auburn hair behind her ear. 'You looked so lovely today, Mum, in that outfit.'

Stroking my cheek, she said, 'And you will, too, Emmy. When the time is right.'

I became aware that my head was banging – so loud that I was amazed I hadn't been aware of it till now – and there was a gnawing hunger in my stomach. I'd been running on adrenaline all day, and the aftermath felt like crap.

I kneaded at my temples, and Alain was magically at my side again, as though he'd sensed it.

'What happened at the *château*?' he asked Mum.

'It's all sorted. Don't worry about it.'

'But what about the guests?' I chipped in.

Mum cast a glance at Ellie, who came over to join us. 'Everybody understood. Once we knew that nothing was going ahead, they went off to restaurants, and they were happy to do so.'

'I should have come with you.'

'No, Emmy. Your place was here.' Seeing my expression, she said cautiously, 'You can go round there tomorrow to see people, if you like.' A look at Ellie that I was too tired to decipher.

'But what about the *château*? The food? The reception? The band?'

'Emmy. You're exhausted and overwrought. Ellie, tell Emmy that she looks shocking, will you?'

'Your mother's right, Emmy. Why don't you have something to eat and call it a night?'

'I can't go to bed now. What kind of a wuss would that make me? Everyone else here is in the same boat.' I waved a hand at people flopped in chairs, gratefully grabbing at the sandwiches that Rupert had hastily put together.

At this, Aunt Jeanie butted in. 'Hardly, Emmy. Nobody else, other than Alain here, has missed their own wedding, have they? You're both entitled to a little TLC and self-pity, if you ask me. Now, come along with me to your room. I'll run you a nice, hot bath. You can have a sandwich while it's running.' She grabbed two from Rupert's tray as he passed by, shoving one at each of us. 'And then you're going to bed to console each other in whatever way you see fit. Come along.'

With a surprisingly strong grip, she took me by the elbow and led me, clutching my sandwich to my chest, around to my room, Alain following bemusedly behind. Jeanie took in the girly disarray and tutted, then shoved me unceremoniously into a chair while she messed about in the bathroom.

When she came back through, I glared at her. 'You're not going to undress us as well, are you?'

Alain burst out laughing.

A withering look from Jeanie. 'Hardly.' I stood, and she came over to kiss my cheek and Alain's. 'You need to sleep, both of you. Tomorrow is another day.'

And with that blatantly obvious and pointless saying – one she'd no doubt got from my mother – off she went, leaving us to undress in peace.

I sighed as I sank into the fragrant lavender bubbles and allowed my poor tense muscles to release a little.

Alain kissed my forehead and climbed in with me. He was so tall, there was no room, but we shifted so he sat with his back against the bath and I sat with my back against his chest, our legs entwined in front of us. I leaned my head back, enjoying being close to him, aware that today could have ended so differently, and we stayed silently like that, nibbling at our sandwiches and dropping crumbs into the bath, until the water cooled and we disentangled ourselves to get out and get dry.

In bed, Alain leaned over for a gentle kiss. 'I can't believe this should have been our wedding night.'

'Me either.'

'We'll talk about that in the morning,' he murmured. 'Don't worry. We'll get married somehow, soon.'

'I'm not worried. I'm marrying you whether you like it or not.'

'I like it.' His voice was quiet, sleepy. 'I'll phone Patrice. Figure out what to do.'

My bones felt so tired. 'Mmm. In the morning …'

We lay quietly for a while, half-asleep, my back against his chest, his arm curled around my stomach, until it drifted slowly upwards to cup my breast. I turned to him.

We made love slowly and in silence, only intent on chasing away the shadows and confirming that we loved each other.

TWENTY-FIVE

The next morning, I woke early. I use the word 'woke' loosely, since I'd been semi-awake half the night, despite my exhaustion.

Alain had been restless, too, although now I could hear his steady breathing beside me and was thankful that he was getting some sleep.

I glanced at the clock. Not long after five. And yet I felt good. Relief over finding Gabriel, happiness that Alain and I were still together, still in love, and the knowledge that Mum and I had made up, and Mum understood my viewpoint ... All those things overrode any underlying tiredness.

Slipping out of bed and into a robe and flip-flops, I pottered around the side of the house to let myself in quietly through the main door, my only thought a steaming mug of tea.

And came face-to-face with Ellie, silently slipping her shoes on in the hall.

We stared at each other, mute.

'Er. Emmy. Morning,' Ellie whispered eventually. 'You're up early.'

My brain tried to compute what was happening. It wasn't even five thirty yet. Ellie had no reason to be here other than if she'd ... *Oh. My. God ...* spent the night.

'Yes. I. Er.' I glanced at Rupert's closed door. I knew those two had become closer over recent months, but I'd assumed it was closer, as in firm friends. Not closer, as in ...

Ellie gave me an *Oh, for heaven's sake* look. 'Come into the kitchen, and I'll make us some tea. You look like you need one.'

She shut the kitchen door behind us to minimise noise and filled the kettle, while I tried to get my head around the fact that she and Rupert must be sleeping together.

When the tea was ready, Ellie picked up both mugs, jerked her head in the direction of the patio doors and led me down the garden, where she patted a bench and I sat down beside her.

'This is awkward, isn't it?' Ellie said brightly, thrusting a mug into my hands. 'I thought getting up at five was mad but safe.' She narrowed her eyes at me. 'Apparently not.'

'Sorry,' I mumbled, taking a gulp of tea. God, that was good. 'And I'm sorry if I've made you feel awkward. I didn't expect it, that's all.'

'So I gathered.' Ellie grinned. 'Looks like we've done a better job of keeping it quiet than we thought.'

'Guess I haven't been on top form. Things have been a bit manic lately.' I smiled. 'But I'm pleased for you both, really I am.'

'Yes, well. That's why we need to talk.'

'What do you mean?'

'Emmy, I don't want you getting any ideas about Rupert and me having some grand romance. It's not like that at all. I won't debase it by saying it's merely a fulfilling of mutual needs …'

I hastily took another sip of tea.

'Because it's more than that.' Ellie stared into the distance. 'You know, I think Rupert and I would have been closer friends sooner, but Gloria complicated things. After she'd gone – for good – Rupert and I learned that we had a lot more in common than we'd been allowed to discover before. We get annoyed by the same things. We laugh at the same things. We like the same people. Eventually, we realised we'd been ignoring a spark. Both of us had been scared to mention it because we valued our friendship. Maybe we didn't want to muck it up. But then one night at my house, we had a glass of wine too many, and I forbade Rupert from driving home and said he'd have to stay in the spare room. It brought us a kind of freedom we hadn't had before, and one thing led to another.'

My eyes were as wide as they would go. 'How long has this been going on?'

'Three months.'

'Three *months*? But why not tell anyone?'

'Rupert and I are hardly the kind to go shouting from the rooftops. And it's not a romance or an engagement or the kind of thing people do shout about. We can hardly announce, "By the way, we're having regular sex now" to the world, can we? And the last thing we want is the kind of reaction you're doing your best not to have, but can't help: "Oh, how lovely, Rupert and Ellie found each other after all Rupert's been through and after all Ellie's said about not wanting a long-term relationship."' She stuck a finger in her mouth and made a puking noise.

I laughed. 'Okay, I take your point. So … no plans?'

'Absolutely none, Emmy,' she confirmed sternly. 'Neither of us wants anything more from this.'

'I get it. And you want me to keep it a secret?'

'I suppose you'll have to tell Rupert that you know. We're all adults here. And it might be better, not having to creep around *La Cour des Roses* all the time.'

'But what about other people? What about Sophie?'

'You must be joking. Mademoiselle Romance? No thanks.' She sighed. 'You're going to tell me that we're a trio and you'll feel guilty knowing something she doesn't, aren't you?'

'Yes.'

'Grrr. You two drive me mad.' She puffed out her cheeks. 'I'll discuss it with Rupert. It's his sex life as well as mine, after all.'

'I only meant for you to tell Sophie that you're … you know. Not to discuss the finer *details*.' I drained my mug. 'Having said that, is it …? I mean, you two, I presume it's …?'

'Yes, Emmy, we are sexually compatible. That's all I'm prepared to say on the subject – and all you want to know, I'm sure.'

I grinned. 'I wasn't being nosy. Honest. I was only thinking that it's quite a risk you two took, after being friends for so long. If it hadn't gone well …'

'I agree. And there's nobody more relieved than me that it's working out.' She stood. 'Right, I need to go home and get changed and …' She stopped suddenly. 'See ya.' A quick wave, and she was off.

I watched her walk up the garden, her narrow, jean-clad hips sashaying. This was … Well, it really was quite excellent.

When Gloria ran off with Nathan, it had been hard for both Rupert and me. But I'd got together with Alain, and although Rupert swore blind that he never wanted another relationship, I felt guilty that I was moving on and he wasn't. He said he wouldn't contemplate marriage again – that he wasn't cut out for it – but I hadn't liked to think that should preclude *some* kind of relationship. Companionship. A release valve. Rupert was too lively to settle into his dotage on his own.

I couldn't be more pleased that he and Ellie had got together. But I also knew I had to avoid 'doing a Sophie' by thinking roses and confetti. Ellie didn't believe in that stuff, and Rupert had had his fill of it. For once, I had no intention of meddling.

Heading back up the garden, I doubted I could sleep, not after this, but maybe if I lay down a while, that would count as rest.

Alain was still fast asleep. I would've loved to wake him and tell him the news, but I didn't have the heart. I climbed in and lay there, trying not to disturb him, but he murmured something and his arm came around my waist. And somehow, with that familiar warmth and weight against my skin, I managed to drift off into sleep.

* * *

'Emmy. Get up!'

I groaned and rolled over.

'Emmy.' Rupert rapped on the internal door.

A distant part of my brain told me there could be another emergency. The rest decided that someone else could deal with it.

But I was not to be left in peace. I heard rattling, and a minute later, Rupert was in the room.

'I have my eyes closed if you're not decent. Now will you *please* pay attention!'

Startled, I sat up, then looked down to check I was decent – or as decent as you can be in a five-year-old three-quid T-shirt. Glancing at the bedside clock, I was amazed to see that I'd slept in, after all.

'I'm decent,' I snapped. 'What do you want?'

'It's more a question of what *you* want.'

'Huh?' I scraped yesterday's wedding waves out of my eyes. Rupert was looking rough himself, but he was dressed, at least.

'Do you want to get married to that accountant of yours or not?'

My lip curled. 'I believe you have the date wrong. That was yesterday.'

'No, I believe that I and numerous others have waved our magic wands, and that date is now today, if you want it to be.'

'What?' I looked at the empty space beside me. 'Where's Alain?'

'He came round to the kitchen for coffee, and I sent him home. A groom's not supposed to see his bride on their wedding day.'

'Huh?'

'Try to focus, Emmy. As you know, the *mairie* is booked all morning, it being Saturday, but I phoned Patrice to see how much heart he has. Quite a lot, it turns out. He and his staff will stay behind to fit you in at the end of the session.'

'Oh! That's good of them.' My mind raced. 'It would be nice to have that part of the wedding, at least.' I sighed. 'A lot of people have come a long way for not *much* of a wedding, though.'

Rupert held out his hand. 'Come with me, lovely Emmy.'

I swung my legs out of bed, checked I was wearing the other half of my nightwear before flinging off the sheet, and allowed him to lead me barefoot through the house to the patio doors.

The garden was a hive of activity. Ryan was up a stepladder, his parents feeding him the strings of fairy lights we'd used for last year's anniversary party for Julia Cooper's parents. A van was parked in the courtyard, and two men were unloading trestle tables, directed by my mother. My dad was blowing up white balloons with a helium machine, tying them in clumps and handing them to Nick and Kate to dot amongst the trees. Kate gave me a wave from her precarious spot at the top of her stepladder.

I turned back to Rupert. 'What's going on?'

'A wedding's going on. I suggest a shower and breakfast. Sophie and Ellie will be here by eleven for hair and make-up. We need to be at the *mairie* for one. Then back here for the reception.'

I looked helplessly around me. 'Rupert, we *can't* have a reception here. We discussed this months ago. That's why we booked the *château*.'

'We did, and it is,' Rupert agreed. 'But that was before yesterday happened. The *château* can't accommodate you today, but I can.' He stretched an arm towards the blue sky, small white clouds scudding across it on a light breeze. 'No rain forecast. The garden will be as pretty as we can make it. Patrice lent us the trestle tables from the town hall – the ones they use for town festivals. They're wobbly, but they'll do. The *château* still has the wine and champagne, obviously, and the table flowers. They'd already started cooking the food by the time we knew we couldn't go ahead, but your mum and Ellie caught them in time to adjust, so they went ahead with as much as they could, for us to serve cold today. They need it out of their way by eleven, so I'll take my estate car and Ryan can take his – we'll manage in a couple of runs. The *pâtisserie* will collect the cake from the *château* and bring it here in their van. Daren't put *that* in my car. The *château* will spare us two wait staff. Juliette's coming to help, too. Oh, and the hotel are loaning us glasses and crockery.'

'Why on earth would they go to all that trouble, after we cancelled?'

'They know the circumstances, Emmy. They're not heartless. Besides, your dad forked out a fortune to that place. They want you to have a wedding as much as everyone else. And your mother and Ellie were in charge, remember. That manager would need a spine of steel to stand up to them! Your mum spoke to the guests last night, and most of them aren't leaving till tomorrow anyway. A few who were going today have managed to extend their stay. Ryan and Sophie got hold of everyone else. The band's available, too.'

I gaped at him. 'I can't believe you're all doing this. When on earth …?'

'We had a conference after you went to bed. I'm sorry we couldn't say anything, but we didn't want to get your hopes up until we were sure we could pull it off.'

Now it made sense. All those glances between Ellie and Mum, Sophie and Rupert.

'I *thought* Aunt Jeanie was trying to get rid of us.'

'Are you saying you didn't need a bath and bed?' When he saw tears in my eyes, his face fell. 'Please don't cry, Emmy. Any wedding's better than none, right? Everyone will do their best, I promise, even though it's not what you wanted.'

I looked around the busy garden at the mayhem and goodwill. As I saw Ryan teeter on his ladder with strings of fairy lights dangling, I remembered how enchanting the garden had looked for the anniversary party last summer, guests dancing on the lawn to the music from the band.

I shook my head. 'That's not why I'm crying. Quite the opposite, in fact. Rupert, this is so *perfect*. Thank you!' I rested my cheek on his shoulder and he wrapped his arms tightly around me.

'Now, Emmy, we can't have tears, or your eyes will get puffy.' My mother approached in her usual whirlwind manner, Aunt Jeanie in tow, and prised us apart – but I only switched my hug to her. A quick pat on the back, and she pushed me away. 'I said stop it, or Sophie won't be able to do *anything* with your face.'

Dad waved at me from his balloon machine as Adrien hurried over to stop the dog popping the balloons.

'Come into the kitchen,' Mum ordered. 'Tea, breakfast, plan of action. Then I need to wipe those tables down with some disinfectant.'

Allowing myself to be led away, I couldn't stop smiling. I was getting married, after all.

After I'd allowed Mum to feed me, I told her I needed a word with Rupert and went outside to find him.

He was on the patio, on the phone – to the limo company, I gathered.

When he clicked off, he said, 'They still have the limo available, surprisingly, but the two smaller cars aren't.'

'The limo was the most important. Thank you.' I hesitated. 'Rupert, I'd like a word.'

He inclined his head towards the orchard, where we went to stand in the shade. He already knew what I wanted to talk about.

'Ellie told me about this morning,' he admitted, then waited a moment, perhaps for some quip or jibe from me. When none was forthcoming, he said, 'I'm sorry you found out like that.'

'You're entitled to a private life.'

'I thought you'd be cross with me for not telling you.'

'No. But I'm glad I know now. Less chance of putting my foot in it. Or maybe more chance, if I'm supposed to be hiding it from everyone else.'

'It wasn't meant to be this huge a secret,' Rupert said. 'At first, we wanted to be sure we weren't making a mistake that would embarrass us and everybody else. Then we kept it quiet because we didn't want everybody making a fuss. It snowballed from there – the longer it went on, the odder it would seem that we *hadn't* said anything.'

'Well, it's up to you, but I think you'd be safe letting the cat out of the bag. You must be fairly sure where you both stand by now, and it'd be less stressful for you to not have to watch yourselves all the time. I'm sure everyone'll be pleased about it.' When he made a face, I said sternly, 'You won't avoid that. People know what you've been through, and they want to see you happy.'

Rupert rolled his eyes. 'I know for a fact that you won't be able to stop yourself from telling Alain. But *if* we come out into the open with this, I don't want people having overly romantic *expectations.*'

I couldn't help myself. Just one little play at being devil's advocate. Tongue in cheek, I asked, 'No wedding bells in the air, then?'

Rupert spluttered. 'Not even in jest, Emmy, please.'

'Maybe you could have one of those binding ceremonies instead.'

He gave me a look. 'I don't think Ellie's into that kind of thing.'

I laughed. 'I mean like New Agers and pagans do.'

'Don't fancy dancing naked in the orchard under a full moon, either. Leave it out, will you?'

'I'm only teasing.' I placed a hand on his. 'I'm glad you've got someone.'

'Thanks, love. Now, you'd better get off and make yourself beautiful – and by that, I mean more beautiful than you already are, of course – before your mother lynches me for waylaying you.'

But on the way back into the house, I was waylaid by Adrien.

'Emmy, I want you to know that the children will be at the wedding.'

'I'm so pleased. I didn't think Gabriel would be up to attending.'

'Not just attending,' Adrien said. 'They want to be your page boy and flower girl, after all.'

My eyes lit up. 'Really? I thought after yesterday …'

Adrien smiled. 'Gabriel feels terrible about that. He wants to make amends.'

'Then I shan't stop him.'

'The only thing is, Emmy, they want their mum to come. They won't feel able to do it otherwise, and they so want to, for you and Alain. I know, after all the upset she's caused …'

'If the children need her, Adrien, they do.' I laid my hand over his. 'Please tell her she's welcome.'

He nodded gratefully and strolled off across the courtyard, leaving me to greet Sophie and Ellie.

Our bride and bridesmaid preparations were like a surreal rerun of the day before.

'See? I told you we needn't have bothered with all those stupid dress and make-up trials,' Ellie grumbled. 'We could practically do this in our sleep now.'

Kate laughed as Sophie began on her make-up. 'I don't know about you, Ellie, but I couldn't do what Sophie does to my face while I was wide awake, never mind in my sleep.'

A knock on the door. 'Are you decent?'

I opened it to find Rupert bearing a tray with four steaming, frothy cappuccinos.

'Thought you might need something to keep you going.' He sent a pointed look Sophie's way. 'Except you, Mama Bear. Yours is decaff, in the red cup.' He indicated an envelope on the tray. 'This got mixed up with my post, Emmy. I might have had it a couple of days. Sorry.' He cast his eye around the room to find a flat surface, tutting at the clutter. 'Women never cease to puzzle me.'

'That's patently obvious,' Ellie said wryly. 'Here.' She pushed make-up to one side, so he could put the tray down.

I sniffed appreciatively at the coffee, then kissed his cheek. 'You're a star. Thank you.'

'I agree.' Ellie didn't stand on ceremony. She took his face in her hands and kissed him full on the lips, causing us to whoop in delight.

Kate and Sophie both gaped at Ellie, while Rupert's cheeks flushed red, and he scurried off before anything else could befall him.

Sophie was the first to recover her poise. 'What was that?'

Ellie looked across at me over the rim of her cappuccino. 'You tell them. I know you're practically bursting.'

'No. It's for you to tell.'

Ellie huffed. 'Rupert and I are seeing each other. More than friends. In a relationship.'

Sophie squealed. 'Since *when*?'

'Three months.'

'Why didn't you *tell* us?'

'She wouldn't be telling you now if I hadn't caught her sneaking away from *La Cour des Roses* at dawn, like a teenager,' I said mildly.

Sophie gasped. 'You knew?'

'I only found out this morning.'

Sophie threw her arms around Ellie's neck. 'I think it is wonderful!'

'And that's precisely why I didn't tell you,' Ellie said drily.

'Oh.' Sophie's face fell. 'Is it a secret?'

Ellie sighed. 'It won't be for long, if you have anything to do with it. But don't make a big deal out of it. Please? We don't want a lot of fuss.'

Kate grinned. 'I love it, but I'm not sure I can get my head around it.'

'A good reason to be more out in the open, then,' Ellie said firmly. 'People might as well get used to the idea.' She fixed us with a glare. 'What are you all staring at?'

To rescue her, I reached for the envelope on the tray. Another wedding card. But when I opened it and saw who it was from, my eyes nearly popped out of my head.

'From someone who can't come?' Ellie asked.

'No. From someone who wasn't invited.'

'Who?'

'From Nathan. Listen to this: "Dear Emmy, I want to wish you all the best for your wedding. I hope you and Alain will be happy together. I didn't behave well, Emmy – not in France and not since. That's my loss. I didn't see what I had and I didn't appreciate you. I apologise for that. And I sincerely wish you a happy future. Love, Nathan".'

Kate gaped. 'Crikey.' She put her arm around me, rereading the card over my shoulder. 'Are you alright?'

'Just surprised. He knew I was getting married, but I never mentioned a date. He must have asked around on the grapevine.'

'It's nice, that he sent a card. And that he said what he said,' Sophie said quietly.

'Yes. It takes away some of the nasty taste of our relations over the past year. I wonder if he's with anyone new, now?'

'Ha!' Ellie shook her head. 'A few weeks with Gloria probably put him off for life.'

I laughed. 'I hope not. He's been a total brat and an idiot, but maybe that would improve if he found the right person.'

Kate kissed my cheek. 'And that's exactly why you're too good for him.'

'Never mind Nathan,' Ellie said. 'We need to get this show on the road, otherwise we'll have Flo breathing fire – and I think my dress might be flammable.'

TWENTY-SIX

Dressed, primped and made up, my bridesmaids and I indulged in a group hug, then went out to the limo in the courtyard. Everyone else had already set off.

At least we wouldn't have to pile into Rupert's estate car, which probably smelled of the mountains of poached salmon he'd ferried from the *château* earlier. Luckily, our limo smelled only of the roses and lavender in our bouquets.

'How on earth did these survive overnight?' I fingered the petals.

'Your mother emptied the *gîtes'* fridges and put them in there,' Ellie explained. 'You're not meant to, but needs must, and as long as there are no fruit and vegetables nearby to emit decomposing something-or-others, you can get away with it.'

I laughed. 'Internet?'

'Internet,' Ellie confirmed.

'You learn something new every day.'

We were driven out of the courtyard and down the lane to join the main road, where I stared in surprise at a long line of cars – guests from *La Cour des Roses* and the *château* – patiently waiting to join our procession.

As we made our way into town, a long snake of shining metal, the traditional tooting of horns had people on the streets stopping and smiling, knowing a wedding was in the offing.

The main square bustled with smartly dressed people from the previous ceremony, taking photos and heading back to their cars.

By the time we added to the throng, there was plenty of illegal parking going on, but nobody seemed to worry.

Alain was waiting on the steps of the *mairie*, handsome in a dark grey suit tailored to his tall, lean frame. The sight of him still made my stomach flip after all these months. I was certain it would do the same for many years to come.

Rupert stood by his side, also handsome, his silver hair combed and waving over the collar of his suit. By his side, Gloria sat patiently, her black coat glossy, a new, smart red collar around her neck with three white helium balloons tied to it, floating high above her head. How they'd managed that without her popping any, I had no idea.

Bob stood to one side, camera at the ready. He was in jeans but wearing a shirt and jacket – although he'd drawn the line at a tie and had plumped for one of those shoelace things instead. He'd trimmed his beard, too. I felt ridiculously honoured. I suspected my mother merely felt relieved.

'Emmy. You look so beautiful,' Alain said with something like awe in his voice.

I allowed myself a moment of smugness for choosing the right dress, and we entered the building. I doubted dogs were allowed in, but Gloria looked such a treat, you'd have to be a total misery to make a fuss. Nobody did.

Alain, Rupert and the dog went ahead, while my bridesmaids got Gabriel and Chloe organised. The children were a picture, Gabriel solemn in his shirt and tie, and Chloe scrumptious in her frilly dress, holding her basket of white and purple flowers as though they were the crown jewels.

She carefully fingered my dress. 'You look like a princess, Aunt Emmy.'

'I feel like one.' I kissed her cheek, and Gabriel laughed at the lipstick mark I left there, scrubbing it off for his sister with spit on his fingers. Sweet.

Once everyone had gone in ahead of us, with my bridesmaids in position, we entered the *salle de mariage*.

Nerves took me by surprise. Since ceremonies were open to the public, I'd attended a couple earlier in the year for the express purpose of *avoiding* nerves. I wasn't fazed by my surroundings, or by Patrice looking so official in a dark suit with his red, white and blue striped sash across his chest. It was more the realisation that this was actually happening. After the last couple of days, I was beginning to think it never would.

I looked around. Sophie held her bouquet self-consciously in front of her belly. Gabriel was subdued, but Ellie bent and whispered something to him, making him giggle. Sabine couldn't take her eyes off her children, as though they might vanish at any moment. Adrien looked pale and ill. My heart went out to him. Sitting next to Jonathan, Madame Dupont already had her handkerchief out. When she caught my eye, she gave me a wave and a smile. Mum and Dad were tightly holding hands, Nick beside them.

The short ceremony passed in a blur. I don't remember what was said. Patrice had once asked if we wanted an interpreter, but since I was – in theory – capable of understanding, and the ceremony consisted mainly of reading out marriage-related parts of the civil code (yawn), Alain and I had decided against it, thinking it would hold up proceedings and not be of any real interest to our guests.

I let it wash over me. All I cared about was that these lovely people at the *mairie* had fit us in at all.

I remember signing the register with our witnesses. And when the official part was over, Patrice read a French poem about love, then invited Alain to kiss his bride. I remembered *that*, along with the claps and cheers from our spectators, Patrice included, as Alain put every feeling he had for me into it.

Presented with our *Livret de Famille* (family record book), we filed out of the town hall, where Bob took a few group photos to pacify my mother, then we piled into cars and went back to *La Cour des Roses*, where the orchard and garden that I knew and loved served as a backdrop to what would be my wedding album.

Alain and me holding hands under the apple tree where he proposed last year, the sunlight dappling through the leaves. Alain shaking hands with Rupert. The bridesmaids comparing dresses on the patio. Chloe and Gabriel looking cute. Jonathan and Madame Dupont in a regal pose under an arbour of late-blooming roses. Sophie by a weeping pear, Ryan standing behind her, his sleeves already rolled up, tanned arms curling possessively around her waist, his hands resting lightly on her belly. Gloria proudly sporting her balloons, ridiculously appealing.

The young man and woman that the *château* had spared us as wait staff arrived to join Juliette – who was actually smiling – and they set to, ensuring everyone had a drink while we milled around, and Bob weaved his way casually around the garden, catching the photos I'd *really* hoped for.

Aunt Jeanie reaching up to straighten Nick's tie. My parents gazing into each other's eyes while nobody – except Bob's camera – was watching, my father's hand resting on my mother's cheek, still so much in love. Ellie lifting Chloe high above her head – and that was a long way for a small child to go – and making her giggle, her curls flopping forwards. Ellie and Rupert in an off-guard moment, sharing a kiss amongst the trees, with Gloria nudging at their legs in jealousy. And Bob himself, taken by Rupert, determined to capture his friend in formal(ish) wear.

As Alain and I watched the moment, I whispered the news that I'd been bursting with all day – about Rupert and Ellie.

His eyes lit up. 'I *thought* there was something there last year at Rupert's party, but like you said, it all seemed to fizzle out.'

'They were trying to ignore it themselves, but it got the better of them.'

He smiled. 'I'm glad. For both of them.'

'Me, too. But you'd better play it down, because ... Shhh. Here he comes.'

'I assume you're talking about my sex life?' Rupert said with comic exasperation.

'Oh. Er. Ah,' Alain managed.

'You *said* I could tell Alain,' I reminded him.

'I said I knew you wouldn't be able to help yourself. There's a difference.'

Alain laughed. 'I'm happy for you, my friend, and I promise not to blab.'

'Thank you. Although I think you'll find there's no need for any such promise. Ellie told Sophie and Kate, so ...' He spread his hands wide.

Jonathan came shuffling up to us, one hand on his stick. 'Emmy and Alain. Can I borrow you for a moment?'

He led us over to a table set at the side of the house, laden with beautifully wrapped gifts to be opened at leisure later.

'I know you can't start opening all these now,' he said hesitantly. 'But I wondered if you wouldn't mind opening mine. It's delicate, and I couldn't wrap it very well. I'm worried the sun will damage it if it's out here too long.'

I smiled. 'We'd love to. Which one?'

He reached for a large, flat parcel, wrapped in brown paper, with a silver bow on the front.

Together, Alain and I tore off the paper to reveal a painting of the market square in Pierre-la-Fontaine, the stone fountain instantly recognisable with its base smothered in flowers, the façade of the *mairie* with its flags fluttering, and indistinct figures sitting outside the café opposite.

I recognised this picture. Painted by his much-missed late partner, it usually hung in Jonathan's lounge.

'But this is one of Matthew's!' I said, drinking in the colours and detail.

'I know how much you love it, Emmy. I thought you and Alain might like to have it.'

'Oh, Jonathan, you know we would,' Alain reassured. He glanced at me. 'But I'm not sure we feel we can take it.'

Jonathan placed a knobbly hand over Alain's, his knuckles swollen, blue veins straining against thin, mottled skin, then transferred it to mine. 'I have Matthew's art all over my house. He would have been proud for you to have it.'

Fighting fiercely to hold back tears, I said, 'Then thank you. With all my heart. We'll treasure it. Alain, could you take it inside straight away, so it won't get damaged?'

'Treasure what?' Rupert ambled over, curious. Alain showed him, and Rupert patted Jonathan's shoulder. 'That's a wonderful wedding present, old friend. Well chosen.'

Jonathan nodded, pleased, as Alain carefully carried the painting indoors. 'I don't want to dominate your time, Emmy, but since Rupert's here too, there's something else.' He looked around, located Madame Dupont and gestured for her to come over.

'I want you all to know that I've asked Renee to stay,' he announced as Alain rejoined us.

Renee, now? If Jonathan wasn't gay, I'd think they were becoming quite the couple.

Rupert smiled. 'I'm glad you managed to persuade her.'

Knowing she wouldn't understand our English, I added, 'It'll be such a weight off her mind to know she's welcome until her house is fixed.'

'No, you don't understand,' Jonathan said. 'I asked her to stay indefinitely. And she's agreed. She doesn't want to go back to her house. She wants to live out her old age in town. And I would like her to do that with me at my house, so we're suited.'

'Oh, Jonathan. That's lovely!' I threw my arms around his neck and hugged him tight.

'That is enough of that, Emie,' Madame Dupont tutted at me. 'He is an old man. If you squeeze too tight, he cannot breathe.' But she smiled at my delight.

I switched to French. 'I'm so happy for you.' And I threw my arms round her neck and squeezed her tight, too.

'There is no need to be so emotional,' Madame Dupont scolded. 'We are just two old people who happen to need what the other can help with. I need a place to live, a house to clean and be proud of, someone to cook for. Jonathan needs someone to do those things.'

'But what will happen when your own house is fixed? Will you sell it?'

'Yes. My nephew is getting married next year and he needs a house. A cheap one.' She cackled. 'Mine will be cheap, alright.' She spotted Jonathan's empty wine glass. 'If you are determined to drink, Jonathan, you should not dehydrate. I will fetch you some water.' And off she went.

Jonathan waited until she was out of earshot. 'You should all know that I'm going to change my will,' he said hurriedly. 'I'm older than her, and that pneumonia last year taught me that you can never count your chickens. I want her to be able to stay in my house after I'm gone. For as long as she needs or wants to. Then, what I have – such as it is – will go to a cancer charity. What do you think?'

Jonathan had been with Matthew for only ten years before he died of cancer, and even though Matthew had been gone for over a decade now, Jonathan still missed him. Such a charity would be important to him. But knowing that he would have Madame Dupont's company, that she would care for him, and in return he could offer her a home in town for as long as she needed it, was an outcome beyond what any of us could have hoped for.

'I think that's a brilliant idea,' Alain told him. 'If you're sure.'

'I'm sure.'

Madame Dupont came back and placed a glass of water in his hand. 'Drink that before you have anything else.'

Rupert laughed. 'Better do as you're told, old chum. Madame Dupont is not a woman to mess with.'

Even though Rupert had said it in English, she shook her head. 'You are all good friends, and it is time you called me Renee. Times change. No need for such formalities any more.'

Well. That was most certainly an honour.

'That couldn't have worked out any better, could it?' Rupert rubbed his hands together in old-fashioned glee as they both tottered off. 'I can't blame him for leaving his house to charity. Not after his family disowned him the way they did. But if it *is* going to charity, it doesn't matter when they get it, does it? By doing this, he knows he's paying Madame Dupont back in advance for the way she might have to care for him if he becomes frailer.' He shook his head. 'Renee, eh? I can't believe you earned that honour after only a year, Emmy, and it's taken me seven!'

The wait staff began to transfer food and wine to the trestle tables. Rickety they might be, but with the flower arrangements and the wedding favours Mum and Jeanie had spent so long over, they looked cheery enough.

Now that food was on the scene, Gloria was firmly shut away in Rupert's lounge with the sulkiest expression I have ever seen on a dog.

That meant the cake could be transferred carefully to an *unrickety* side table set with a white cloth. Everyone oohed and aahed at the *pâtisserie*'s masterful fusion of two nations' customs as they passed by to settle themselves at the tables.

There was some hilarity as guests tried to be elegant about clambering onto the bench seats. The gents kindly helped the ladies and the elderly, and everyone got there in the end – with the occasional flash of underwear unavoidable.

The 'top table' – two trestles pushed together, with throws spread over the benches in deference to our delicate dresses – caused momentary confusion. The order we were *supposed* to sit in had been planned along with everything else, but it didn't seem important any more. Mireille smiled at Mum, gave a Gallic shrug, and breaking with tradition, they sat in couples on either side of Alain and me. Rupert sat with Ellie at one end, sliding a hand down the soft satin of her dress as he 'helped' her (she had to hitch it rather high, causing a few raised eyebrows) and Kate and Sophie settled in a giggling pair at the other end.

Alain took my hand and kissed it. 'Happy?'

I nodded. 'Happy. You?'

A long gaze from sugar-brown eyes that made my heart giddy-up. 'You know I am. I'm also hungry. Let's eat.'

Country pâté was perfect to start, with fresh bread that Rupert had got the local *boulangerie* to deliver.

The garden was filled with the sound of happy chatter and the clatter of cutlery. I heard Gabriel ask whether he could have some champagne later. Alain smiled at his audacity and caught his eye across the tables, holding up a thumb and forefinger in a gesture indicating that he would be allowed no more than a quarter inch. Adrien smiled back.

As the starters were cleared away, Dad leaned behind me to hold a hurried discussion with Alain, then went over to speak to the wait staff, who nodded their agreement to whatever he was plotting. He went to Mireille and had words with her, too.

When the tables were free of debris, Dad tapped a spoon against his glass until everyone quietened and looked his way.

'Thank you, ladies and gentlemen.'

Gabriel and Chloe giggled at the grown-up address.

'The groom and I have decided that since the order of the day has already veered so far from our original plans, we can do what the heck we like now, so we've decided to limit the boredom – or stretch it out, depending how you look at it – with a speech between each course. Since so many of us don't speak French – typical Brits – and a few of you don't speak English, I'd like to introduce your interpreter – Alain's mother, Mireille Granger.'

I glanced at Alain, and he shrugged. It seemed so obvious now, but it had never occurred to either of us to worry about the speeches.

There was polite applause as Mireille stood and repeated in French what my father had said.

Dad cleared his throat and began, stopping after each sentence for Mireille to relay.

'I'll keep this short and sweet, since everyone is still hungry. Besides, those of you who know me will know that I'm not used to getting much of a word in edgeways.'

He looked fondly down at my mother, making everyone laugh.

'I confess that when Emmy said she was jacking in her job and everything she'd ever known to start a new life here in France, I was worried she was making a mistake.'

That was the first I'd known about it. All he'd ever shown was wholehearted support.

'But Emmy's mother is made of sterner stuff than I am. Flo told me to stop worrying and admire my daughter for the brave thing she was doing. Well, I already secretly did. More than that – I was jealous that she had such guts.' He smiled. 'But whether she was brave or foolish doesn't matter now, does it? We're all here today because she made the right choice' – he swept his arm around the grounds and across the array of smiling faces – 'in location, in job, in friends. And, of course, in her choice of husband.'

He turned to Alain and me. Alain linked his fingers in mine.

'Alain and Emmy. If you achieve one iota of the happiness and love that Flo and I have enjoyed over the years, you'll have a wonderful life together.'

Mireille relayed his words with a choke in her voice.

Dad had promised 'short and sweet'. He lifted his glass. 'To Emmy and Alain.'

Glasses lifted and the echo came back, 'To Emmy and Alain.'

Alain used the toast as an excuse to kiss me again. I wasn't complaining.

There were murmurs of approval as the next course was brought – platters of cold poached salmon, dishes of green beans cleverly transformed into a salad with slices of orange in a vinaigrette dressing, asparagus with cold hollandaise sauce (surprisingly good) and new potatoes with sliced shallots in a reduced white wine stock that tasted as good cold as it would have warm. The *château* had done a fabulous job for us, converting everything like this.

I looked out across my friends and family, the beautiful gardens, delicious food – and said a silent thank you. The months of planning and preparation had not been lost. Far from it. I was in the dress of my dreams, married to the man I loved, sharing a celebration with the people I loved. Only the menu and venue had changed. And that venue was the place I loved and where I belonged. I couldn't have been happier.

'What are you smiling about?' Mum asked.

I almost answered without thinking, but stopped myself. Mum had invested such time and energy in the reception at the *château* – and Dad had invested deep recesses of his wallet.

'I'm pleased that we could do this, after all – you know, before everyone goes home.'

Mum nodded knowingly, her X-ray specs boring into the furthest corners of my thoughts. 'This is lovely, Emmy. It all worked out very well.'

As the main course was cleared away, Alain became fidgety. Guessing he was nervous about making his speech, I squeezed his hand for support and he squeezed back before standing.

'Ladies and gentlemen.' He waited for quiet, and when his mother hesitated – perhaps thinking that as her son was bilingual, he could do her job himself – he indicated that she should stand. I suspected he wanted to concentrate on what to say, rather than how to say it.

'First, I'd like to thank Dennis for his words earlier. For a man who doesn't often get a word in edgeways, that was quite a speech.'

Mum proudly kissed Dad on the cheek.

'Naturally, I would like to thank everyone for coming today,' Alain went on. 'For taking in your stride the change of date and venue, and for all your help and understanding with yesterday's … excitement.'

I smiled, knowing he'd worded it carefully so as not to make Gabriel feel uncomfortable.

'It's at times like these when you realise how important your friends and family are, and I couldn't wish to have a nicer bunch of people in my life.'

Alain hesitated, as though he was deciding whether to go ahead. A slight nod told me he'd made up his mind.

'As for Emmy and me? I've never been down a road that felt so right from the start. From almost the first moment I met her, I knew there could be something special between us.'

I glanced over at Sabine, thinking she might be upset – no doubt why Alain had hesitated – but she was smiling, a little sadly perhaps, Chloe cuddled on her lap and Gabriel at her side.

'Of course, I owe my best man Rupert an enormous debt of gratitude for his tenacity in ensuring that we got together, whether we liked it or not.'

Laughter from our guests, and a modest smile from Rupert.

'And to Emmy's family, for being so supportive of her move to France. Now, it's tradition for the bridegroom to thank the bridesmaids. So thank you to Kate, Ellie and Sophie – you all look *très belle* today. Thank you also for taking care of Emmy over these past weeks and months. I'm sure your influence has kept her sane – or as sane as she's ever going to be.'

A snort of laughter from Kate.

'And last but not least, thank you to Chloe and Gabriel, our delightful flower girl and page boy, for behaving so well and putting up with all this grown-up stuff.'

Giggles from the children.

'After dessert, and with some trepidation on my part, you will hear from my best man.'

Rupert grinned wolfishly.

'But for now, a toast – and if you can get this in the same order as me, you haven't had enough to drink – to Kate, Sophie, Ellie, Chloe and Gabriel.'

His toast echoed back in varying formats, accompanied by laughter.

When the desserts were brought out, Dad admired his. 'We made the right choice here, ladies,' he said to Mum and me, making us both smile.

During lengthy discussions over the menu at the *château*, we couldn't choose, and the catering manager had suggested plates of tiny samples – half a dozen bites of heaven in the form of slivers of tarts and pastries. Our indecision had been a good decision, after all.

Our guests felt the same way, from the comments I overheard. When I looked across at Adrien's table, Chloe and Gabriel were busy bargaining with their parents, swapping the mouthfuls they didn't like the look of for the ones that appealed more.

The wait staff swooped in to clear away again, and I wondered what on earth they were doing with all the dirty crockery. Rupert's dishwasher wasn't up to this volume.

Rupert stood and 'Ahem'ed until everyone looked his way, while Juliette, the waiter and waitress began to do the rounds with the bubbly – and Gabriel got his quarter inch. Well, it was nearer an inch, but don't tell anyone. Chloe took one sniff of her mother's, turned her nose up and demanded lemonade.

'This is a turn-up for the books, isn't it?' Rupert began. 'I've never been described as a best man in any shape or form, so this is a new one for me.'

Laughter rippled around the tables, accompanied by an unlady-like snort from Ellie that made everyone laugh more.

'It's a time-honoured tradition at weddings for the best man to reveal embarrassing details about the groom's youthful – and not so youthful – indiscretions. But I'm pleased to say that as I've only known Alain for seven years, I'm woefully unsupplied with such anecdotes and can therefore abrogate all responsibility for passing them on.'

An exaggerated sigh of relief from Alain and more laughter from the audience.

'As for the seven years I *have* known him?' Rupert glanced down at Alain. 'I'm afraid I've rarely known Alain to be anything other than an upright citizen. He is the town accountant, after all. But that doesn't make him boring. He's warm and funny and kind and generous and loyal. And I'm reliably informed that he's breathtakingly handsome, although I suspect my source was biased.'

He winked at me, and everyone laughed – including Mireille, as she relayed what he'd said.

'For those of you who require at least *some* lesser-known details: Alain plays saxophone but doesn't like anyone to know about it, so don't tell him I told you. His omelettes always come out better than mine, for some reason. And he holds his drink pretty well – which is, let's face it, a prerequisite of any close friend of mine.'

A cheer from Jonathan, Bob and Ellie.

'But in all seriousness, I couldn't ask for a better friend, and I couldn't be raising my glass to a lovelier couple. And I get to be the one who toasts with champagne. So, once more, to the bride and groom!'

It echoed through the garden, and Rupert sat down, patted on the back by my dad.

A small cheese selection made its way to the tables – after all, we were in France, where it's unofficially against the law not to include cheese somewhere in a meal.

But before everyone could get stuck in, I made my decision and shakily stood, causing a murmur of interest amongst the guests and a puzzled look from Alain and my parents.

TWENTY-SEVEN

I hadn't known until now that I was going to do this. But as everyone kept telling me, this was my big day.

I chinked my knife tentatively against my plate. 'I – er. Sorry, everyone, if you thought that was end of the speeches, but I've heard that some brides say a little something. Why let the men have all the fun? And, after all, I am my mother's daughter.'

Everyone laughed, my mum loudest of all, and Mireille smoothly stood to perform her linguistic duty once again.

'To be honest, I think most of it's been said already.' I took a deep breath. 'But I want this to come from *me*. It's not often you get the chance to tell people how much they mean to you. We Brits are so dreadful at that.'

Mireille smiled.

'So, here goes. I'd like to thank my parents for their unwavering love and support. People say you never stop being a parent, even when your children are grown-up, and with what mine have had to put up with over the past year or so, I can see that now. Thank you to Nick for … Well, for being Nick. He's the best little brother, when he's not pulling the legs off your favourite dolls.'

Nick grinned, and Aunt Jeanie tutted at him.

'Thank you to Aunt Jeanie and the rest of my family, simply for being a part of my life.'

I moved my glance over to Alain's family. 'And thank you to Alain's family for accepting me into their fold. I hope we can become closer as the years go by.'

I stared out across the sea of faces, at a loss as to where to start. 'I have friends old and new here, and it would be impossible to pick you out individually or we'll be here all day, so I shall simply say this. To old friends: your friendship over the years has meant more to me than I could ever tell you. To new friends: you are the warmest and most welcoming set of people I could have the privilege to know.'

I looked down the table at the wavy silver head next to Ellie. 'I know I said I wouldn't pick out individuals, but I do need to make one exception, because without Rupert, none of this – my life here in France, this wedding – would be happening at all.'

A cheer amongst those who knew him, and a blush from the man himself.

'And most of all, thank you to my new husband. For taking a chance on me.'

Alain took my hand.

'But since he's already been toasted – twice – I would like to propose my toast to *all of you* here today. To the people who mean the world to me.'

Glasses were raised, chatter began again, and I plopped down in my seat with relief that it was over and that I'd had the courage to do it.

My speech earned me another kiss from Alain and a pat on the hand from my mother as our wait staff brought plates for the cake.

Mum ushered Alain and me over to it and everyone gathered round with their cameras. When Mum handed me a knife, and I stared at the frankly un-cuttable structure, the entire crowd burst out laughing. But my mother was insistent on the traditional shot, so we posed, pointing the knife threateningly at the pyramid of confectionery, then left the wait staff to expertly do whatever they had to do to deconstruct it and serve it with coffee.

Sitting back down, I frowned down the table at Rupert. 'How the hell will they produce coffee? That machine of yours will take hours to make sixty-odd!'

'They brought a dozen large cafetières with them,' he said smoothly.

My eyes widened. 'They thought of everything, didn't they? But what about the dirty dishes?'

Rupert rolled his eyes. 'Emmy, this is your wedding day. Dirty dishes shouldn't be bothering that pretty head of yours. But as I can see that they are? They're boxing it up. Ryan and I will take it back tomorrow, where their industrial dishwashers can work their magic.'

'Wow!'

'Yeah. Wow. Now, concentrate on that handsome husband of yours. I doubt he's interested in dirty dishes today.'

'Damn right,' Alain agreed. 'You should be more worried about packing for Mallorca.' He laughed at my expression. 'You'd forgotten all about that, hadn't you?'

'Er. Kind of.' I felt ridiculous. How could you forget about your own honeymoon?

Alain smiled. 'It's not like you haven't had anything else to worry about, the last couple of days.'

'True.' I leaned in for a kiss. 'Have *you* packed already?'

'Yes.'

'Ugh. You're so *organised*.'

'Don't worry, it won't take long. You don't need much. Something for the beach. Nothing for bed.'

I sighed at the idea of relaxing, just the two of us. Nobody to answer to for two whole weeks. 'Mmm. Sounds good.'

'Certainly does. You look incredible in that dress, Emmy.' He dropped his voice. 'I presume you'll need help getting out of it, later?'

'There's hours to go before that. I want to get my money's worth first. Or Dad's money's worth.'

'I can wait.' There was a world of promise in those three words. I had a feeling my wedding night was going to be one to remember.

When coffee was finished, guests began to mingle and table-hop, and I told Alain we should do the same.

He helped me out of my seat – not an easy task in a floor-length dress. 'Over here first, Emmy. There's someone I want you to meet.'

He led me to a table where a dapper couple in their late sixties were chatting to their neighbours.

Alain lapsed into French. 'Emmy, I'd like you to meet Paul, my old boss – the man I came to work for when I first moved to Pierre-la-Fontaine. And this is his wife Charlotte.'

We exchanged kisses.

'Pleased to meet you.'

'Likewise,' Paul said. 'Alain told me what a gem of a girl he found, and now I believe him.'

I smiled. These Frenchmen with their compliments.

'But I must correct him,' Paul went on. 'I was never his boss. He is too modest. He joined me as my partner.'

'Maybe,' Alain conceded. 'But you taught me how to become an accountant in a small town which I came to love, and for that, I'm eternally grateful.'

Paul beamed. 'Then I did a good job.'

We continued to circulate, making sure we spoke to everyone. When Alain got caught up with an old college friend, I excused myself and approached our mayor, who as usual was chatting casually while being ogled by every woman in the vicinity between the ages of twenty-five and seventy. His official sash had been removed along with his jacket, making him instantly more approachable.

'Monsieur Renaud, I want to thank you for the poem you read out at our ceremony today,' I said in my very best French, not bothering to add that I hadn't quite understood all of it.

'You're welcome, Emmy. Nobody knows better than I do that our marriage ceremony is a little … dry, shall we say? It needs *something* to sweeten it.'

I smiled. 'We're so grateful that you allowed us to get married today.'

'My staff and I were happy to oblige, after what happened yesterday. We're relieved that you found Alain's nephew.'

I glanced over at Gabriel, who was trying to take off his tie and almost strangling himself in the process. Adrien caught him before he could make it any worse and relieved him of the burden.

My heart stuttered. The knowledge that Gabriel could be Alain's son, but we might never know, would take me quite a while to come to terms with. But come to terms with it, I must.

'Thank you, yes. It was a difficult day.'

'Then you must enjoy today all the more. Am I permitted to tell you how beautiful you look?'

I smiled. 'Just for today, I'm taking as many compliments as people are willing to give me.'

Bob came over with Renee. 'Madame Dupont has asked me to take a picture of you both for her room, Emmy.'

That choked me up a little. 'How lovely!'

As we stood by side, the old lady in her best summer dress (but still in support stockings – no rest for them, even at a wedding), barely reaching my shoulder, Renee told me how pleased she was that I was wearing her grandmother's earrings, and that she was thrilled to hear Ryan and Sophie's news.

'That baby will be a good-looking baby, Emie. Such a handsome father and pretty mother.'

'It certainly will.'

We posed for Bob with beaming smiles. Afterwards, as she lifted a hand to my cheek and told me how beautiful I looked and how happy she was for me, I heard Bob's camera click. And I knew *that* was the shot that I would love, of me and this indomitable old lady who had been my no-nonsense mentor and friend for over a year now.

'Emmy.'

I turned to find Sabine at my shoulder. 'Oh. Er. Hi.'

Bob and Renee exchanged a glance and scarpered while the going was good.

Sabine managed a tentative smile. 'You look lovely.'

'Thank you. So do you.' And it was true. Her plain navy shift dress, cut above the knee, teamed with high navy and white heels, emphasised her tall, slim figure. For a brief moment, I wondered how she'd looked on the day she married Alain. He'd never spoken about it or shown me photos.

I banished the thought.

Sabine pursed her lips in a knowing expression. 'This is awkward.'

'Yes, a little.'

'I thought it would be better for me not to come today – for you, for Alain, for everybody. But the children …'

'I know. They need you here. You're welcome, Sabine.'

'Thank you.' She laid a hand on my arm. 'Emmy, I want to thank you again for finding Gabriel. I don't know what would have happened if you hadn't.' A tear escaped down her rouged cheek. 'I'm so sorry for the trouble we've all caused.'

'It couldn't be helped.' I waved an arm at the garden. 'And it worked out well, in the end.'

'Yes.' She lowered her voice to a whisper. 'This thing with Adrien and Alain. The paternity test? I am so grateful to you and Alain. It will be hard for everybody, but together, we will make it right for the children, *n'est-ce pas?*'

'Sabine, I'll go along with what you and Adrien and Alain have decided. I have no intention of rocking the boat. I'm happy to be a part of the children's lives in whatever capacity I'm required.'

'Thank you. I am so sorry that I said what I did. That I set all this off. All this time, I carried the uncertainty by myself. It was hard, but that is the way it should have stayed.' She hesitated. 'I am sorry for the extra hurt I have caused Alain, when he has got his life back together. I wish you all the best.' She pressed a kiss to my cheek. 'Alain is a lucky man.' She backed away.

Kate immediately sidled up. She'd been hovering at a distance, ready to defend if the need arose. Kate had had my back ever since primary school.

'*That* looked intense.'

'She was thanking me again for finding Gabriel,' I told her truthfully. Now wasn't the time to discuss it further. Changing the subject, I inclined my head towards Patrice. 'Are you planning on collaring our delectable mayor for a dance later?'

Kate followed my gaze. 'He *is* moreish. But I bet he's a heart-breaker. Besides, I have a different target in mind.'

'And who might that be?' *Although I could hazard a guess.*

Kate looked over to where Nick was chatting with Christopher. 'Your little brother. You don't mind, do you? We've been getting on so well the last few days, and we have so much in common.'

'I don't mind. Far from it.'

We heard a shout and looked round to see Rupert standing on one of the trestle tables. It didn't look too stable to me.

'Sorry to interrupt, folks. If you could steer away from the tables, me and some of the lads will fold them away so we have room to mingle and make space for the band. There are plenty of seats dotted around the garden, and we can bring more from the house. Thanks.'

Rupert, Ryan, Nick, Adrien and a couple of Alain's mates set to, while Kate and I looked on and hoped they wouldn't ruin their suits.

The wait staff, presumably having magicked all the dishes into boxes and stashed them somewhere out of sight, were mingling with drinks again.

A van squeezed its way into the courtyard and the band began to unload. Alain went over to greet them and received handshakes and hearty pats on the back.

'Did you say they'd played here before?' Kate asked.

'Yes, for that anniversary party last year.'

'And didn't you say Alain played with them?'

'Yes, but only because one of them was sick and he had to stand in. As Rupert said, he's not one for playing in front of people he knows.'

'Shame. Bet that man of yours looks sexy, playing the sax.'

'You betcha.'

The band set up on the patio and began to play mellow jazz. As the light faded, fairy lights twinkled in the bushes and trees. A light breeze was welcome to those of us with cheeks flushed from excitement and too much bubbly.

I was whisked around the flowerbeds by Ryan, Bob, Adrien – another one effusive with his gratitude for my rescue of his son, and mine and my husband's understanding – and by my little brother … The whole world wanted to dance with me, and for someone who avoided attention whenever possible, I couldn't get enough of it.

As my dad waltzed with me, his back straight in the classical ballroom pose his own father had drilled into him, I spotted Ryan and Sophie dancing close, cheek to cheek, lost in their own world of two-and-a-bit. Sophie had said there would be no wedding bells, but I had a feeling they were one of those couples who would stay together for ever.

'Emmy,' Dad whispered at my ear. 'Is it my imagination, or are Nick and Kate getting on rather well?'

I shot a furtive glance in the direction he'd inclined his head. Sure enough, Nick and Kate were dancing together. He was looking into her eyes, and as we passed them, I heard snatches of 'You didn't! You told me it was Jez who put that frog in Emmy's bed' (I would have to punch Nick for that later) and 'I always thought your mum's hot chocolate was the *best*.' Childhood reminiscences that gave them a starting point for something more – I hoped. Kate deserved someone who appreciated her for her bubbly personality and generous spirit, and Nick needed to find someone who could stop him endlessly flitting from one girl to another. Perhaps Kate might be the one.

'As for Aunt Jeanie …' Dad murmured.

'What? Where?' I craned my neck. Aunt Jeanie was dancing with Bob. Not closely, not smoochily, but they were laughing a lot. Kindred spirits? Hmm.

Dad grinned. 'If my little sister starts coming out to stay a lot once we find a house out here, I'll be suspicious as to why.'

'If Aunt Jeanie starts coming out to stay a lot, she and Mum will probably kill each other!'

'May I cut in?' Jonathan tapped my dad on the shoulder.

'Of course.' Dad bowed out gracefully.

Jonathan put an arm around my waist, and with the other holding his stick, we tottered around on the spot, content in each other's company.

'Happy, Emmy?'

I smiled and brushed a wave of white hair from his forehead. 'Deliriously. And you?'

'I can hardly complain. I have a good Frenchwoman looking after my every need, *and* I've managed not to croak before your wedding. Dancing with a beautiful bride on a balmy summer's night takes some beating. Matthew must be smiling down from wherever he is, I'm sure.'

'I'm sure, too. I wish I could have met him.'

Jonathan smiled acknowledgement, then inclined his head to one side. 'They make a handsome pair, don't they?'

I followed his gaze to where Rupert and Ellie were dancing, Rupert's hand on Ellie somewhat lower than the traditional small-of-the-back position. 'They do, indeed.'

Jonathan chuckled. 'I'd never have thought to pair those two up in a month of Sundays. But now they're together – or as together as they'll allow anyone to call them – it's so obvious, isn't it?'

'Yes. Unlikely, but perfect. As long as neither of them wants more than the other. But I don't think that'll happen, do you?'

'No. They've got to a point in life where they know what they need and want – and what they don't need and want. I suspect they'll amble side by side through the years and into old age without even thinking about it.'

We finished our dance in contented silence, and then there was a lull in the music as the band took a well-deserved break, accepting champagne in deference to the occasion.

When the band took up their instruments again, their sax player called out to the crowd.

'Attention, everyone!' He spoke in English, his accent strong, then repeated in French. 'We have a guest performer for you tonight. It will only be one song because, you see, it is his wedding. But he would like to play this one song for his beautiful wife. And so she can know why he has chosen it, and he cannot sing while he is playing – although if you ever heard Alain sing, you will be grateful for that …' There was laughter in the audience. '… I will sing the words for him. The song is an old one, and it is called "All the Things You Are".'

My mum gave a little gasp of approval, and Dad took her hand.

Alain appeared on the patio with his sax to rapturous applause. He smiled shyly, then brought the instrument to his lips.

The song was slow and beautiful, and the audience stood quite still. I would never tire of watching and listening to my husband play, no matter how rare the occasion: his long fingers on the keys, his shoulders swaying. But to know he'd chosen this song for me, and that he would play it at our wedding, melted my heart into a hopeless puddle of love.

As he played the final notes, Nick put his arm around me. 'That's quite a guy you've got yourself there, little sis. Makes me feel a bit mushy.'

'Good. It's about time.'

When Alain lowered his sax, I rushed onto the patio and glued myself to him, kissing him long and deep, oblivious to the cat calls from those watching.

'I love you so much,' I told him – not for the first time, and most definitely not for the last.

'I love you so much, too, Emmy.'

Happiness is an elusive thing. You can spend a long time searching for it. But when you find it, hang onto it and never let it go. That was what I intended to do. I had my family, old friends and new, a gorgeous place to live and work … and I had Alain.

I was never letting him go.

LETTER FROM HELEN

Thank you for choosing *Summer at the Little French Guesthouse*. I hope you enjoyed reading it as much as I enjoyed writing it!

So many readers have said that they felt like they were a part of Emmy's world – that visiting *La Cour des Roses* was like visiting old friends – and I can only say that it has been the same for me. Emmy, Rupert, Alain, Jonathan, Madame Dupont, Sophie, Ellie, Ryan, Bob … they are all like real people to me now, and it has been a joy to bring them to life and to share them with you. Knowing that I've given readers a respite from their hectic lives, a brief escape to the sunshine and beauty of the Loire valley, is just wonderful.

For me, there is both a sense of satisfaction and, of course, a tinge of sadness in coming to the end of Emmy's story. But I will continue to imagine her living happily ever after in her French idyll, as I hope you will, too.

If you enjoyed the read, I would love it if you could take the time to leave a review. It makes so much difference to know that readers enjoyed my book and what they liked about it … and it might encourage others to buy it and share that enjoyment!

You can find me on Facebook, Twitter and Goodreads, and at my website and blog. If you did enjoy *Summer at the Little French Guesthouse* and want to keep up-to-date with all my latest releases, just sign up at the following link. Your email address will never be shared and you can unsubscribe at any time.

www.bookouture.com/helen-pollard

Thank you!
Helen x

 HelenPollardWrites

@helenpollard147

www.helenpollardwrites.wordpress.com

ACKNOWLEDGEMENTS

I will be eternally grateful to my publisher Bookouture for allowing me to share life at *La Cour des Roses* with the world, in particular to my editor Natalie Butlin who has shared the ups and downs that has entailed with me …

… As have my family and friends. I couldn't do it without your support. It is very much appreciated.

The romance author community that I have become a part of on social media and in a small way in 'real life' is an incredibly supportive one. Writing can be a lonely job, and I value the interaction I have with online friends. Thank you all.

Thank you to author Marie Laval for her patience in answering my occasional panicked e-mails about France and the French!

I must use this opportunity to give another huge shout-out to the bloggers who have taken the time to read and review and spread the word. Your devotion to books and sharing your love of them with the wider world is admirable.

And of course, a heartfelt thank you to all my readers. Knowing you have enjoyed reading my books makes all the hard work worth it!

Printed in Great Britain
by Amazon

25934800R00198